Penetrate

Penetrate

Kathleen Kelly

P.D. Publishing, Inc.
Clayton, North Carolina

SECOND EDITION

ISBN-13: 978-1-933720-26-5
ISBN-10: 1-933720-26-3

First Edition: 2006 (ISBN: 0-9765664-3-5)

9 8 7 6 5 4 3 2

Cover design by Kathleen Kelly

Published by:

P.D. Publishing, Inc.
P.O. Box 70
Clayton, NC 27528

http://www.pdpublishing.com

Dedication:

For T — Being there for me has meant more than I can ever say.

pen·e·trate

1: to pass into or through 2: to enter by overcoming resistance 3: to discover the inner contents or meaning of 4: to pierce something with the eye or mind 5: to affect deeply the senses or feelings

Chapter One

The setting sun warmed Kali's back as she stood on the open-air flybridge and scanned the horizon. By her calculations, the dark outline of the freighter *Caballo* should appear at any moment now. She knew her course plot was perfect, but in the expanse of the ocean, she could never quite get over the possibility of missing her prey completely.

As the bow of the *Avatara* plowed through the water, she could feel her tension rising. The timing of her operation was critical. She had to overtake the *Caballo* before they entered the more risky international waters. At that point, any nearby ship, including foreign naval vessels, could respond to a distress call.

"There!" her pilot, Philippe yelled, pointing ahead. "Is that her?"

Kali looked in the direction of his finger, a grin splitting her tanned face. Rising from the waves was the tall bridge tower and dark hull of the *Caballo*. It was like a lumbering brontosaurus moving across open land. There was no escape now.

"Sharp to starboard," she ordered. "More power!"

The bow of the sixty-foot *Avatara* angled in the water on the turn, and Kali could feel the twin diesel engines surging to life two decks below. It was a superb feeling that almost made her laugh with delight.

"Are you sure it's the *Caballo*?"

The smile fell from her face and Kali felt her eye twitch.

Philippe glanced at her. "It just took longer to find her than you promised," he said, nervously. "I want to be sure."

Philippe wasn't the first man who dared question her, but she'd long ago learned how to deal with such defiance. His time would come, sooner than he thought, but right now, the task at hand required her total concentration.

To many she was just a pirate, but when compared to others, Kali took the profession to a whole new level. Equipped with the latest technology, she could track, board and subdue any vessel under way. Sometimes she would seize the entire ship, but more often, like with the *Caballo*, she would merely help herself to predetermined, and very lucrative, cargo items.

The target ships were identified long before they left port, and shadowing them into the vast emptiness of the ocean wasn't difficult. It was the approach and boarding of a moving ship that required skill, precision and stealth.

There were barely an hour outside the port of Macapa, Brazil, but by now the small crew of the *Caballo* would already be slipping into familiar routines of life at sea. The setting of the sun would mean dinners would be cooking, card games would be starting and tall tales about port adventures would be in full swing. No one would be thinking of a pirate attack.

As a whiff of oil and diesel fumes passed by her on the wind, Kali grinned. "This is going to be good!"

"Should I activate the jammer?" Philippe asked pointing at the military issue satellite dish perched off the port side. It was a handy piece of equipment that successfully blocked any radio or satellite signals within a one-mile radius. The jammer had cost Kali a pretty sum on the black market, but with the tenfold increase in anti-theft maritime devices, she had little choice.

Instead of answering, Kali leaned forward and flipped the switch.

Philippe's knuckles were white as he gripped the wheel. "How long are you going to be on board, and where should I wait?"

Pulling a black sweatshirt from around her waist, Kali shrugged herself into it. "Like I told you earlier, we'll be twenty minutes." She lifted her long dark hair from under the collar and dropped it. "And since you obviously haven't recovered from your bar romp last night, I'll remind you again to wait in the wake until we're done."

"That's quick for a ship this size. You sure?"

Kali's hand stopped as she was tying her hair into a tight ponytail. "You're getting dumber with each fucking beer. In less than forty minutes we'll be in international waters, and I'd like to be back on our way to Macapa without encountering any do-good ships. So just do what I fucking tell you. Got it?" She finished her hair.

"Oui, mon capitaine."

Shaking her head, she turned and descended the stairs to the *Avatara*'s aft deck, stopping on the last step to wait until her crew gathered at her feet. As the cold, hard faces looked up at her with hungry expectation, Kali gave a feral smile. These were her boys. Killers. Thieves. Soldiers. Mercenaries. The only loyalty they shared was to money, and that suited Kali just fine. Her current crew consisted of five men of various nationalities. It mattered little what made up a man so long as he knew his job and followed her orders without question.

"Target is just ahead," she announced, letting her smile grow bigger. "The cargo is good, but the safe is much better. This is a quick snatch and grab."

Jack, the only American, stuffed a piece of gum in his mouth. "What's the take this time?" he asked between noisy chews.

"You get what you get," she said, looking away from him in disgust. "Assignments are as follows. Tajo and Renny will keep the deck clear. Sergio and Jack will secure the crew and clean them out."

"We're not killing them?" Renny asked.

"Did I say kill them?" Kali pinned him with a hard stare.

"Kali, does the freighter have a fence?" Tajo asked, the lilt of his West African intonation made his words sound more formal.

"Probably."

The question annoyed her. Most large vessels were equipped with anti-piracy devices. The nine thousand volt invisible security fence was one of the latest developments to deter unauthorized boarding. When combined with satellite tracking systems, vessels were supposed to be theft proof.

"The captain is no dummy," Sergio said, his Nordic blue eyes shinning with devotion. "She's using a Trojan."

Kali smiled at the big blond. Technology was an amazing thing that required constant vigilance and understanding. Overcoming a security device could sometimes be beat with counter technology, but in cases like this, Kali liked to rely on an old-fashioned approach.

"Who is it this time?" Renny asked.

"Raphael," she said, twisting her wrist to check her watch. "And he should be just about ready for our arrival."

"Then he's disabling the emergency systems, too?" Paco asked, shifting his Ukrainian Vepr assault rifle in his hands.

Kali looked at him icily. "You never learn, do you? The emergency systems are on a bypass that can't be disabled."

"Then we'll be jamming their signals?" Renny scratched nervously at his two-day beard.

"Not that it fucking matters," she said, with a shrug. "Even if a transmission gets out, we'll be long gone before anyone responds."

"We know you have everything planned," Tajo said, calmly. Of all her crew, he was the most diplomatic. "We trust you."

She acknowledged the comment with a nod of her head. "Then are there any more dumbass questions?" she asked, staring at Jack.

"I still don't understand why we're not killing the crew," he said, popping his gum. "Killing them is safer. They'll know our faces."

She shook her head as Tajo chuckled. "Just how long have you been doing this, Jack? It doesn't matter if they see us." Dismissing him with a wave, she looked around. "Anything else?"

"Si. You did not say what I'm doing?"

"Oh you, Paco?" Kali smiled, grimly. "You're with me." His face went white. "Everyone knows what an honor it is to accompany your captain to the bridge." No one missed the sarcasm in her voice. If they knew what it meant, they wisely held their tongues.

"But Kali—"

"No buts." Kali cut him off before turning to look up at the flybridge. "Where are we?"

"On approach," Philippe yelled back.

Needing to see for herself, Kali grabbed onto the railing and swung her upper body over the side. The massive black hull of the *Caballo* nearly dwarfed them.

"I see the platform," Tajo said, from next to her. "It's down."

Of course it would be down. Kali swung back to the deck. "Get ready to jump."

Under her feet, she could feel the engines being adjusted to match the speed of the freighter. Jumping onto a moving ship required a delicate touch at the wheel, and Philippe was one of the best.

As Philippe pulled them closer, the starboard hull of the *Caballo* slowly inched past. It felt as though the ships were so close that Kali only had to put her hand out to touch the wet metal of the freighter. Instead, she climbed up on the *Avatara*'s low bulk wall and waited.

Every muscle in her body was tight with anticipation as the platform drew closer. It looked so small with the dark water churning under it. When it was within reach, Kali pressed her rifle to her chest and jumped. The sea surged as her boots hit the platform, and she scrambled to keep her balance. As soon as she got her legs under her, she moved up the stairs and waited for the others.

Dr. Madeline Cross stood in the fading daylight and counted the boxes again. "There are supposed to be sixteen crates of food. Why are there only thirteen?" She turned to face her colleague, who did not look at all fazed by the suffocating humidity and heat.

"Quit worrying," Dr. Robert Fisher replied, his tone patronizing. Reaching over he gave her butt a quick pat. "I'm sure they're here somewhere."

Maddie pulled away from him. "If I'm worried, Rob, it's because this is our food. It's the only real food we're going to have for six months."

"Trust me. We'll have plenty."

"We brought the food because we need it," she said, following him up the gangway to the deck of the research vessel *Luna Nueva*. "And although they claim to be worldwide, I highly doubt that we'll find a McDonald's on the Amazon River."

"You hate McDonalds."

"But I like to eat. What's more, I like knowing I can do it everyday."

Rob rolled his eyes. "Sweetie, I've been doing this for awhile, and there's always enough food on an expedition."

The condescension in his tone dissolved the last of her patience, and she tossed the manifest to the deck. "Fine," she said, glaring at him. "But if we run out, we're eating you first."

"Jesus, Maddie!"

She covered her mouth. "I'm sorry. I didn't mean that."

"I should hope not." He frowned. "We're supposed to be getting along here."

"I know."

"Otherwise, it's going to be a long six months for us all."

"I know!" Frustrated, Maddie pushed at a damp clump of streaked blonde hair clinging to her forehead and sighed. "All I want to do is find these crates and go inside to cool off. I'm hot, tired and anxious to forget this whole miserable day." She slumped against one of the boxes and shook her head. "I didn't know it was going to be this hot."

Despite her apology, Rob still looked irritated. "C'mon, Maddie. You study climates for a living. How could you not know it was going to be hot. It's Brazil. The rainforest. The jungle."

"For your information, I may have been academically prepared for the climate, but I wasn't physically prepared for this," she wiped at her gritty neck and showed it to him. "The air is so heavy with moisture, I can hardly breathe. Even the simplest task leaves me exhausted, and I feel like I'm trapped in a wet sauna. So while my books told me it was hot, being here is quite a different experience."

Rob looked at her for a moment before his face softened. "You're right," he said, with a smile. "I forgot that you're not used to it. Maybe I pushed you too hard on your first day."

That was an understatement, but Maddie bit her tongue. "It doesn't matter. I'm only here to advance my theories on hydrocarbons."

"And we shall."

Maddie didn't like the way he was increasingly taking ownership of her theories. Rationally, she knew that if their small expedition succeeded, Rob Fisher would get joint credit, but they were *her theories.* She was the one who had spent five years tweaking her climatic data models. It had been her published papers that had slowly gained her the respect of the scientific community. She was the one her peers called brilliant and insightful. She was the one with a future.

And Rob Fisher? As far as Maddie was concerned, or most of the academic world for that matter, Rob was more of a TV scientist than a real one. He was lightheartedly known as the "King of Field Research", because it seemed that Rob and his trusty DigiCam were always off on one shallow story after another. He had traveled from Antarctica to the North Pole spouting on about global warming, shrinking glacier fields and decimated rain forests. He waxed and waned about the planet's climatic history, but in the end, he really came off as nothing more than a glorified narrator.

When he'd shown up at MIT, Maddie wasn't sure what to make of his proposal to do joint research in the Amazon basin. He had secured a private grant that would fund a six month bare bone expedition, and he shrewdly pointed out that just such a mission was what both their careers needed. He could use the legitimacy of working with her, and Maddie would finally get some much needed field research. It was a win-win situation as Rob described it.

At first Maddie hadn't been interested, but Rob knew her trigger. For months she'd struggled to discover a true data format for her computer models, but had come to the ultimate conclusion that they were flawed. There were just too many varied environmental factors to account for them all in her database, and because of that, any conclusions she drew were going to be unreliable.

The Amazon rainforest, Rob had told her, was the perfect place to put her theories into practice. The environment was teeming with every possible variable, and because it was a live ecosystem, her findings would only bolster her computer models. Rob had also pointed out that without field research, she would never be offered the tenured position she'd always coveted. It was a low blow directed totally at her ego, but it worked all the same.

In the end, his arguments were so persuasive that Maddie hadn't bothered questioning the details. Besides trusting in his expertise, she had been too focused on the rewards of her research to suspect the process. She now found herself sadly disappointed in the end results.

For starters, Maddie had expected a larger contingent of scientists. True, Rob had said the expedition was limited on funding, but she thought that, at the very least, they should have some graduate students along to assist with collections, data input and modeling. Apparently Rob had made arrangements to host some post doctoral students from the local university, but since Maddie didn't speak Portuguese, she didn't know how that would help her.

So it appeared that it was just her and Rob for six months, and Maddie cringed at the thought. With any luck they would have enough work to keep them both too busy to engage on any other level. Her one affair with Rob had been more than enough.

"C'mon," Rob said, holding out his hand. "I think it's time to quit for the day. Let's go cool off."

The innuendo was obvious and Maddie shuddered inwardly. There had been a time when she had found Rob charming and attractive, but that was long ago. This trip was only about her research, and Rob needed to understand that. "Thanks, but I'd rather look for the food and then go to my cabin."

"Absolutely not. I can't let you be alone on your first night in Brazil." Rob waved his hand at the shore. "Macapa is one of the busiest river ports on the coast, Maddie. There's so much to see, and I promise that after dark, the heat gets a bit more bearable." He held his hand out again. "The boxes will turn up before we leave. I imagine they're merely delayed at customs."

"But I'm tired."

"No, you're not." He smiled, the corners of his brown eyes crinkling. "You're just looking for an excuse to go hide in your cabin and start working."

It wasn't true, but Maddie didn't bother correcting him. "I do have some ideas I want to get down."

"Well, I won't allow it. Tonight we're going to go out and celebrate. We'll get some beer and food." He grinned. "Ice cold beer, Maddie. Think about it."

She licked her lips involuntarily. "Ice cold?"

"Frost on the glass cold. And food so good you'll orgasm."

"Oh!" She looked away.

"Don't waste this opportunity. In a month you'll be begging for civilization." He stepped closer. "And we always did have fun together. Remember the conference in Vienna?"

How could she forget? For almost four days she'd felt alive in ways she'd never dreamed possible. Later, she realized that it had very little to do with Rob Fisher and more to do with herself. For the first time in her life, Maddie had let go of all the conformities and obligations controlling her life and just lived for the moment. It was as exhilarating as it was terrifying.

"There's plenty of time for work, Maddie."

She looked at him, knowing he didn't really comprehend her conflict. This wasn't Vienna, and Rob Fisher wasn't a convenient distraction during an otherwise dull conference. What had happened there would never happen here.

And yet, as she shifted her gaze to the nearly endless line of docks clinging to the shore, would it be so wrong to experience something of this exotic place? There would be plenty of time for work later. Six months of confinement on the ship with nothing to do but work As long as Rob understood she wasn't going to fall for his shallow charm again, she saw no problem with enjoying herself tonight.

Looking back at Rob, she nodded. "All right. Let's go celebrate."

"Excellent!" Rob cried, encircling her with an arm and pulling her tight against his side. "We're going to have so much fun!"

Maddie froze in his touch. "I'm sticky and hot, Rob." She stepped out of his embrace and smiled cordially. "So where are we going?"

"To the market. There." Rob waved his arm at the rambling assembly of buildings and shacks that swarmed the banks of the Amazon River. "Every strange thing you'd ever want to buy." He slipped casually into what she was beginning to see was his jungle expert mode. It was a role he relished.

"Like what?" she asked, as Rob led them off the ship and into the crowds. A squat Indian woman waddled with a basket on her head, but Rob deftly maneuvered them around her.

"Alligator parts, medicinal herbs, fresh fish, wildlife, fruits, pottery."

"Alligator parts?" She wrinkled up her nose in disgust. "Why on earth would anyone want that?"

"I haven't asked, but like I said, everything you could ever want."

"Well, all I want is that cold beer." She rubbed her stomach. "And maybe something to eat."

"Admit it," Rob said, reaching for her. "You're enjoying yourself."

It would have been safer to deny it, but looking around at everything, Maddie suddenly felt quite a part of it all. The sights, sounds and smells swirled around her in an exotic dance that she wanted to join. This wasn't her sterile lab and nothing here reminded her of her empty life in Boston. It was all so alive that she could feel its pulse with every humid breath she inhaled.

"Admit it," Rob repeated, more forcefully. "This is what makes life exciting. Your damn sterile lab is never going to make you famous. It's never going to be your destiny. This, Maddie, this is where *we* make history."

The last part was sanguine thinking. In six months her theories could prove worthless, and she would limp home a failure. Yet, as she let Rob lead her deeper into Macapa, the more she realized that she did want this trip to be her destiny. There had to be more to life than just her lab.

"I'm ready," she said, grinning wildly.

Rob leaned over and kissed her cheek. "I know you are."

Boarding a moving freighter was always dangerous. Successfully navigating the distance between two moving ships required a tremendous amount of skill and courage. In the past, Kali had lost two crew members. One made a bad jump, and was sucked under by the ship's giant screws. His death had been quick. The other one wasn't so lucky. He had succumbed to fear, and had been ruthlessly punished.

Tonight though, her men all navigated the jump with ease. They were, by far, the best crew she'd hired.

When everyone was across, the bow of the *Avatara* rose in the water as Philippe reversed the engines and the ship fell back. Turning, Kali motioned Renny and Tajo up the stairs to sweep the deck. Anyone unfortunate enough to encounter them would be eliminated. Since this was the last chance of escape, Kali and the others waited below in case her men failed and an alarm was raised.

As their dark forms disappeared on deck, Kali slipped a hand inside her pocket and activated a transmitter to notify Raphael, her inside man, that they were now on board. If everything had gone as planned, in two minutes she would see him at the door of the bridge tower.

Two quick flashes from a flashlight at the top of the stairs drew her attention, and she smiled. The deck was clear.

"Let's go," she said, motioned the rest of her crew forward.

As Paco passed, she pinned him with a lethal look. She could smell the fear on him. That was good. He should be afraid.

On the deck, Kali let her eyes run over the rows of forty foot containers stacked three high. She knew from the manifest that the containers were filled with computer components and consumer goods. If fenced on the black market, the items would bring a nice sum. But it was the nearly half a million dollars worth of currency that had drawn Kali's interest.

Taking the lead, she moved her group along the deck towards the bridge tower. This was the control center for the entire freighter. Inside were crew quarters, computer rooms and the main bridge, perched three stories up over the deck. This was her ultimate destination.

As they approached the tower, Kali was relieved to see Raphael waiting for them by the door. He gave Kali a quick nod as a greeting.

"It's a crew of eight," he said, getting to the point. "The captain and one are on the bridge."

"And the rest of the crew?"

Raphael grinned lecherously. "They're busy."

Next to her, Paco dropped his hands to his hips and rocked his pelvis back and forth. "Porno, si?"

Grabbing Paco by the shirt, she pushed him at the door. "Get inside."

The interior of the bridge tower smelled of dust, oil and diesel fumes just like any other large ocean vessel Kali had boarded. She wrinkled her nose at the odor as she followed Raphael towards the main elevator.

When the doors opened, she blocked Raphael from stepping into the box. "Go help with the crew. Meet us back here in ten." She pushed Paco into the elevator.

Selecting the bridge, Kali reached down, pulled out a Beretta PX4 9mm from her thigh holster and checked the magazine. She held it casually in her hand as the elevator rose to the top.

"I thought you said no killing," Paco commented, dryly.

Blinking slowly, she shifted her eyes to his face and just stared at him. "And I thought I warned you to keep your fucking mouth shut when you drink."

"What?" He looked confused. "What did you hear?"

It wasn't a denial. There was nothing to deny. A sheen of sweat was breaking out on his forehead, and Kali smiled. It unsettled him, just as she expected.

"Why are you smiling?" he demanded, nervously licking his lips.

She didn't respond. Let him worry about what she was planning. He'd know soon enough why she was smiling. "Get ready," she said, as the elevator began to slow. "You know the drill."

"I don't know what you heard, Kali, but I'd never betray you. You know me."

She glanced at him with revulsion. "We'll talk later."

The doors of the elevator began sliding back, and Kali tightened her hold on her pistol. The second she walked onto the bridge, she needed to dominate. It was imperative for her to establish fear and submission before any thought of resistance surfaced in her captives.

Stepping onto the bridge, Kali looked around at the various navigation and communication stations. She cared nothing for these things. Instead, her attention went directly to the two men near the helm.

So unaware they were of her presence that neither even looked up as she walked across the floor. Sitting in the pilot's seat was an older man with a well-established bald spot. A younger man with muscular arms and a strong back was busy with some electronic chart.

Not one to jump to conclusions, Kali looked between them with a smile. "Captain?"

It was the younger man who turned to her voice.

Kali tilted her head to watch his expression. It was always the same. First, his eyes began to widen. Then his mouth fell open in shock. Finally, the real threat of the situation hit him and he began to calculate a response. If he was going to react, it would be at that moment.

Unfortunately, Kali never gave him the opportunity. Raising her gun, she shot him in the middle of his thigh. Like so many others, he went down with a cry.

She turned her gun on the old man, holding him in place until Paco pulled him viciously from his chair. Of all her crew, Paco was the most brutal.

Once the old man was subdued, her attention returned to the captain. Blood was flooding from his wound, and Kali assessed it quickly. Her shot must have hit an artery, and now she had even less time to get what she needed.

Stepping up to him, she tapped him with the tip of her boot. "Look at me," she said, her voice edgy. When he complied, she touched a spot near her groin where the femoral artery passed over the pelvis bone. "Press here. Hard. It will slow the bleeding."

The captain stared at her for a long moment, uncertainty in his eyes.

"Do it or I'll have him," she pointed at Paco, "put a tourniquet on you. I can't have you bleeding to death before I get the safe open." She looked around. "Now, where is it?"

In an act of defiance, the captain looked away from her as he applied pressure to his femoral artery.

Infuriated, Kali kicked his hand away and pressed her gun to his head. "Answer me or I'll take your ship and kill your crew."

"Aren't you going to do that anyway?" He replaced his hand on his wound. "That is how this works, correct?"

"That depends completely on you, Captain. All I want is the safe."

He hesitated, but then gestured towards the back of the room. "It's there. Behind the paneling."

With a jerk of her head, Kali sent Paco to check. She grinned broadly when he pulled back the teak faced paneling to reveal a tall, steel safe. The first step was done.

Squatting down, she looked directly into the captain's eyes. "You know what I want now, don't you?"

"Kill me if you want, but I won't tell you."

"Again, Captain, your sacrifice will only doom your crew." She tapped her gun against his forehead. "But that's your decision."

His eyes betrayed his fear.

"My time is limited, so let me help you decide," she said, glancing at the old man cowering nearby. Swinging her gun around, she looked back at the captain.

"No, wait," he yelled, as she fired.

"Too late." She frowned. "One down, seven to go."

"I don't know the combination!" he cried, but Kali just waited. "Really, I don't. I just do what I'm told. I follow orders." He was nearly hysterical.

Twisting her wrist, Kali looked down at her watch. "You have a minute."

"My crew. If I tell you, what will happen to them?"

"Forty-eight seconds."

"Swear that they'll live."

Kali looked up, surprised. "You'd believe me?"

"Do I have a choice?"

She chuckled and dropped her eyes. "Thirty-one seconds."

"I have a family."

"Twenty three seconds." She rocked her head back and forth. "Tick tock, tick tock."

"Alright! Alright!" He shook his head. "I can't get there, but I'll tell you the combination."

"I know it's a biometric safe, but if you prefer, I'll cut off your hand for verification." She looked back at her watch. "Nine seconds."

"Then help me get there. Please!"

She glanced at Paco. "Get him."

Setting his rifle on a nearby chair, Paco leaned down and roughly dragged the captain to the safe. It took effort, but Paco got the captain to his feet, where he entered a string of numbers into the electronic keypad and pressed his thumb to the biometric scanner. The safe beeped its acceptance and the latch slid back.

Kali sighed in relief. It was done. There were just a few more loose ends to tie up. "Face me," she said, her voice hard and resolved.

The captain hesitated. "I did what you asked," he begged. "I'm not a threat to you."

"You never were." Kali took a small step towards him. "Now it's your choice how you die. I like to see the eyes, but I can do it this way, too."

His head fell forward in acceptance, and he allowed Paco to turn him around. Kali felt a modicum of respect for him. It took courage to accept and face death, and she waited for him to lift his head one last time. When she could see his eyes, she fired a bullet into his head.

"Get him out of the way," she said, after the captain had slumped to the ground.

As Paco was moving the body, Kali bent over and grabbed Paco's rifle. Slipping it over her shoulder, she knew he wouldn't miss it until it was too late.

"*Mio Dios*!" Paco cried, pulling open the safe to reveal row after row of neatly stacked bundles of money. "All U.S. dollars?"

"For what they're worth." Kali reached for a bundle of hundred dollar bills and flipped through it. Digging in her cargo pants, she withdrew a black plastic bag and handed it to Paco. "Fill it up."

"It may not all fit," he said, laughing casually.

Her contempt for him grew. She knew he had laughed like that last night.

"We can retire if we want."

"Not likely," she said, moving away from him.

"I forget," he said, casting a glance over his shoulder. "You enjoy this life." He kept dropping the money into the bag. "Killing pleases you the way sex doesn't."

The comment rolled off her. He'd said so much worse, so why would that one matter now? Paco didn't know when to quit. He had become a liability to her operations. It was business, she'd told herself, but she knew deep down that it was so much more.

"Is that what you and Philippe told everyone in the bar last night? I heard you said I was a dry bitch who killed because I couldn't come." She tightened her hand on her pistol. "You said I needed to be fucked so badly you could smell it on me." Her finger played with the trigger.

"Kali...I didn't..." Paco kept his back to her. "I was joking...I was drunk...I didn't—"

"Drop the bag and turn around!"

Why did it have to come to this? She asked for nothing but respect and obedience. She made them rich. She gave them a purpose. Why did they have to ruin it?

"I don't know who has been lying to you, but—"

"Turn around!"

"No."

"I'll shoot you in the back, Paco. You never were much of a man, so dying like a coward shouldn't bother you."

"You bitch! I was right, you are a dry cunt. You feel nothing for anyone. You never have."

He looked over his shoulder, and even without seeing his eyes, Kali knew what he was thinking. He was wondering where he had left his gun and if he could beat her to it.

"You were always going to end up here," she said, forcing a laugh. "I knew it the first day you stepped on my boat."

"You wanted this," he said, taking a step backwards. "Killing men is what you love most."

"I'm only giving you what you deserve," she said, aiming for the back of his neck. "Remember that." She pulled the trigger. It took a moment for his body to fold forward and then spasm back as the 9mm bullet blew a hole through his face.

Lunging forward, she grabbed the plastic bag and flipped it over her shoulder. She was glad that she'd waited until he'd finished with the money. Blood was so hard to get out.

Stepping into the elevator, she stared straight ahead as the doors closed. The ride to the main deck seemed shorter than the ride up, and Kali was relieved to find Sergio, Raphael and Jack waiting for her. The large Russian looked behind her for Paco, and she shook her head. "He's dead. Let's go."

"But—"

Lunging forward, Kali pinned him to the wall. "No fucking buts! He's dead, and I'm leaving. Are you staying?" She didn't wait for a response. Holding the moneybag tightly, she hurried to the exit.

Tajo met her by the door. "A success?" His teeth glowed as he smiled in the darkness.

"Signal Philippe," was all she said, as she headed for the stairs.

The night grew brighter as the African slapped a glow flare to life and waved it over the side. Below, Philippe flipped on the *Avatara*'s running lights and pulled out of the freighter's wake.

Descending to the platform, Kali didn't wait to see if anyone was behind her. She had the money. They would follow. As Philippe pulled the *Avatara* alongside, she quickly judged the distance and jumped.

She climbed halfway to the flybridge. "Back to Macapa," she yelled to Philippe, before turning for the salon.

The air inside was warm, but Kali didn't notice. Crossing the salon, she dumped the money onto the small dining table and stared down at it with satisfaction. The sight of it was her way of affirming the success of another mission. Tomorrow, her share would be deposited into one of her many bloated accounts and promptly forgotten, but for tonight, it represented her leadership and rigid determination to always come out on top.

Behind her, she heard the salon door open and close as her crew came into the room. They knew better than to speak to her at such a moment, and so she gave them little notice as she took her seat and began the tedious task of dividing up the spoils.

It took nearly an hour to count and recount the amount. By the time she had divided it all up, the lights of Macapa were twinkling in the distance.

Sitting back, she looked up at her crew, their greed hanging on their faces. At that moment, she hated them all. Her only consolation was that she'd soon be rid of them – at least for the night. Jack was the first one brave enough to speak. "How much?" he demanded, almost drooling at the money.

She gave him a cold look before answering. "Including what we took from the crew, $479,000 and some change. Shares are divided as follows." She lifted her notes. "As usual, the top twenty percent goes to the cartel equaling $95,800." She pushed that pile aside. "That leaves $383,200. My cut is thirty percent, leaving $268,240."

"And how much is that?" Renny asked, leaning forward expectantly.

"Divided by six, it's $44,700 each" She waved at a pile of jewelry and other things. "And whatever you want from the crew's crap."

"I'm taking the Krieger." Jack grabbed the chunky platinum watch from the pile. It was a fake, but Kali would let him figure that out. "And what of Paco's share?" he asked, his tone accusatory.

"What about it?"

"Shouldn't it go to his family?"

Kali shrugged. "Does he have one?"

"He has a mother in Guadalajara," Sergio said, bowing his head. "Very poor. Like my mama in Kiev."

"And?" she snapped. "Do you have her fucking address?"

"No," Sergio confessed.

"Then that's that."

"Yes. That's that." Renny nodded his approval.

Standing, she dropped the cartel's share of the money into a paper bag. Her own, she stuffed back into the plastic bag. She pushed one pile at Renny. "Take that to Philippe. Tell him he can come to me if he wants to question the amount."

"He won't," Renny said, pulling the money towards him. "It's more than fair."

Kali rolled her eyes as she turned away. They were all six thousand dollars richer without Paco's share. Even someone as dense as Philippe would understand that type of math. Dropping the money on a countertop in the ship's small galley, she pulled open the refrigerator.

One look inside and she slammed the doors. "Which one of you fuckers drank my last Xingu?" She didn't bother waiting for the non-existent confession. Yanking open the door again, she grabbed a bottle of some piss-poor American beer. "There will be a new six pack in here by morning."

Or what?

The unspoken question hung in the air. It was always there.

Tearing the top off the beer, she tossed it into the sink with a clink. "When we reach Macapa, I want you all off my boat," she said, grabbing the money. "You got that?" Not waiting for a response, she turned and descended the stairs to the stateroom level.

At sixty feet, the *Avatara* was comprised of three decks. It was, perhaps, an eccentric choice of vessel for Kali's profession, but it was also her home. Her own cabin occupied nearly a third of the lower deck. The rest of the space was used by the engine room, a full head, two smaller staterooms and the electronics room.

Opening the door to her cabin, she swept her hand along the wall to turn on the lights. The room was spotless. Everything from the neatly made queen size bed to the polished teak nightstands and desk gleamed. Even her laptop, sitting open on her built-in desk, was a clean line. She stepped into her cabin, closing the door behind her. Immediately, she felt more at peace with herself. This place was her sanctuary, and she shared it with no one.

The beer in her hand was cold, and she looked down at it with contempt. There was nothing worse than cheap American beer.

Angry again, she stalked across the room and dropped the money on the desk. Setting down her beer, she pulled out the chair and sat. By placing her hands on the keyboard, she activated her computer. The aquarium screensaver disappeared immediately, and she was presented with the first of many password screens.

Once logged on, she initiated a satellite Internet link. Her boss would be waiting for a report...and an accounting of her take.

Criminal cartels dominated most of Brazil. The one which controlled Macapa was the *Rato de Agua* cartel. Nothing came in or out of the port that they didn't know about or authorize. Someone like Kali had little choice but to align herself with the cartel or risk certain elimination.

While the computer established the satellite connection, Kali stood and opened a false cabinet in the wall over her head. Behind it was her private safe. After keying in her ten-digit code and holding her eye to the retinal biometric scanner, she pulled it open.

Sticking her share of the money into the safe, she closed the door and resumed her seat in front of her laptop. While her safe was very secure, Kali never left any sizable amount of money in it for too long. She and her crew were thieves, and stealing was a way of life. Therefore, she knew better than to tempt them.

When the Internet connection was made, she opened a new email and addressed it to Duarte de Tueste, the leader of the *Rato de Agua* cartel. Her reputation for ruthlessness and competency had earned her his special attention, and it was to him that she always delivered the cartel's share of her jobs. With any luck, Duarte would already have another plump pigeon lined up for her.

Chapter Two

Holding a *garrafa* in one hand and a large piece of crabmeat in the other, Maddie grinned as she tried to decide which to consume first. She stuck the crab in her mouth and washed it down with the beer. "Delicious!" she cried, pounding the bottle on the rough wood table.

Across from her, Rob shook his head. "God, Maddie. I've rarely seen such carnage." He pushed at a broken piece of crab shell. "You really enjoyed it, didn't you?"

"It was good." Setting her plate aside, she reclaimed her big bottle of beer. "But this," she held it up, "is really, really good." The dark Bohemia Escura beer was starting to go to her head. She felt relaxed and happy. Even the possessiveness in Rob's eyes didn't bother her.

Holding his glass in the air, Rob singled for another round. "*Mais um, por favor.*"

"Trying to get me drunk?" She giggled. "I'm not going to sleep with you again."

He gave her a lopsided grin. "Maybe I won't ask."

"Oh, you'll ask." She took her fresh beer, tipping some into her mouth. "What was this again?"

"It's called a *garrafa*. Most Brazilians share them, but you're doing fine all by yourself."

"How many have I had?"

"That's your second."

After considering the amount of liquid, Maddie nodded, seriously. "No wonder I feel so drunk."

"It's the heat, too."

She didn't know why the heat should matter, but didn't care enough to ask. "I like this place," she announced, looking around at the weathered plank floor boards, the tables made from old doors sitting on wooden barrels, and mix matched chairs. The air smelled of the river, fish, alcohol, sweat and smoke. "It's rather charming in a third-world sort of way."

Rob shook his head. "How kind of you to join us down here in the dirt, princess."

"Are you mocking me?"

"You do sound rather portentous."

"Is that so?" She set her beer down. "I'll have you know—"

Rob cut her off by smiling broadly. "You are so beautiful when you're indignant. Do you know that?"

The mood shifted, and Maddie was suddenly uncomfortable. "Rob, please."

"What? It's just an observation."

It wasn't that and they both knew it. However, she was saved from trying to respond by the sound of a guitar strumming behind her. Turning in her seat, she located the instrument which was nearly dwarfed by a corpulent man.

"I didn't know there was music, too!" she said, looking back at Rob with excitement.

Reaching across the table, Rob took her hand. "You didn't think I'd let you spend your first night on the cusp of the rainforest without experiencing real Brazilian music, did you?"

With a weak smile, Maddie pulled her hand away and turned in her seat to watch as a small group of musicians gathered around the guitar player. First a flute, then a mandolin and finally a saxophone appeared in the hands of patrons. It was amazing to listen as each musician expertly wove their song around the guitar.

When the waiter came by to collect their plates, Maddie looked up. "What type of music do they play?"

"Choro."

He left without further explanation, and Maddie frowned in confusion.

"Choro is a little like jazz," Rob explained, his eyes a little glossy from the beer. "You really are beautiful."

Nervously, Maddie gestured at the musicians. "Let me listen."

The guitar began first, a complex rhythm that moved up and down the scale before restricting its range to the lower notes. To Maddie, it almost sounded as if the guitar was weeping, and just when she thought it was going to wrench her heart, the flute entered with a higher, almost comical tune that contrasted and danced around the guitar. Each of the remaining instruments joined the dance until Maddie wasn't sure what to feel because the song made her feel everything.

"So what do you think?"

"It's wonderful," Maddie said, turning to Rob. She was about to smile at him when the door to the bar opened and a tall woman strode into the room.

As she strained to see her through the haze of smoke, Maddie became aware that with the exception of the gentle strumming of the guitar, all sound had ceased. For a few seconds, time seemed to stand still. Then, slowly, like a rusty squeak box being cranked, the musicians once again picked up the song, but it was too late to recapture Maddie's attention. She was too interested in what type of woman could cause such an interruption.

"Maddie," Rob said, and she jumped at her name. "Please stop staring. Look away from her. Look at me."

As the woman's gaze swept around the room, Rob reached out and grabbed her hand. Maddie winced when he squeezed too hard, and she looked up just in time to see the woman's eyes narrowing with a dark intensity.

"Maddie," Rob said, his voice strained. "Get up. We're going." The grip on her hand tightened, and Maddie felt herself being pulled to her feet. "Come on. Get up."

The sudden movement coupled with too much beer made the room spin and her legs wobbled. Trying to sit back down before she fell, Maddie felt her arm being wrenched upwards again.

"No!" Rob said, digging in his pocket for some money. "We're leaving." He dropped the bills on the table.

Over his shoulder, Maddie saw the woman moving towards them, her strides long and powerful. "Is there a problem?" she asked, her accent, surprisingly, American.

"No, no problem," Rob said, not looking up at her. "We're just leaving. You may continue your business."

"My business?" the woman demanded, her voice cold and hard. "Just what do you mean by that?"

Maddie had never seen anything like it before. Although the woman was about an inch shorter than Rob, her presence totally dwarfed him. She was larger than life and Maddie felt the air around her crackling with something unknown yet alluring.

"I don't mean anything." Rob almost seemed to shrink as he spoke. "I'm sorry if I offended you."

"You offend me by not looking at me." Reaching out, the woman used the tip of her finger to slowly lift Rob's chin. "Is that it, *bundão*, are you too good to look at me when I'm speaking to you?"

The Portuguese slipped from her tongue like a native, although by now Maddie had picked up a distant southern drawl in her English.

"No I'm not too good," Rob was muttering. "I'm sorry. My wife and I were just leaving."

The woman's green eyes jumped to her and Maddie shook her head. "I'm not your wife," she heard herself saying. "Sleeping with you once was too much."

She thought she saw the woman's lips twitch with a smile, but the icy coldness that etched her features quickly froze it out. "Is that so?" the woman asked, locking eyes with Maddie.

Never had Maddie felt so captivated by a stare. It consumed her like oxygen in a fire.

"*Meu querida*," the fat guitar player called out, and the woman blinked, releasing Maddie from her gaze. "Leave the *Americanos* alone."

"*Num minuto*," the woman said, glancing at him.

It was then that Maddie realized how tense the room had become. Glancing around, she saw that with the exception of the guitar player, who was watching them with a mixture of amusement and anger, no one else dared to look in their direction.

"Kali, why do you bother them?" the guitar player asked. "Let the little doves go and come sing with me, si?"

"Kali?" Maddie asked, swinging her eyes back to the woman. "Like the Hindu goddess?"

For the briefest of moments, the woman's eyes softened. "You know?" It was whispered so quietly that Maddie nearly missed it.

Before she could respond, Rob interrupted her. "Maddie," he pleaded, his head still bowed in submission. "Just leave her alone."

It was as if the sound of his voice transformed Kali's face back into ice. "And why's that?" she asked, her attention once again focusing on Rob. "Why should she leave me alone?"

"I meant no disrespect—"

"The hell you didn't!" She grabbed him by the shirt and nearly lifted him off the ground.

"Kali!" the guitar player said, his tone harsh and commanding. "I really must insist. Leave this and come join me." There was something in the man's voice that left little doubt that he expected to be obeyed.

Acknowledging him with a hitch of her head, she kept her gaze intent on Rob. "You," she said, releasing her hold and pushing him backwards. "Get out and don't let me see you again." Looking away, her eyes touched ever so briefly on Maddie before she turned. "*Eduardo, onde está my cerveja?*"

It was over, and Maddie felt abruptly dismissed. Although not sure why, she didn't want it to end so quickly, and reaching out, she laid her hand on Kali's arm. Before she could speak, Kali had spun around and seized her hand. The strength of her grip surprised Maddie almost more than the speed, and she heard herself cry out in pain.

"Don't touch me," Kali spat, her face so close Maddie could feel her breath.

Looking up, Maddie was startled to see that the green eyes she'd so recently found enthralling were now dark and angry. Until then, she really hadn't comprehended the danger the woman represented.

Kali released her arm, but didn't look away. It was almost as if she was waiting for something more.

"I'm sorry," Maddie whispered, contritely. "I only wanted to thank you."

This seemed to amuse Kali and she laughed coldly. "Save it," she said, holding her eyes for a second longer before turning for the bar and grabbing a big *garrafa*. Standing there, she lifted it to her lips and drank deeply. When she finished, she dragged the back of her hand over her lips.

"*Gratidão, Eduardo. Muito bem.*"

"Kali," the guitar player said, gesturing to a chair. "Come. Sit with me and we'll talk."

Maddie was barely aware of Rob taking her hand. "Let's go."

Nodding, Maddie let him meekly lead her from the bar.

Kali didn't notice the pair leave. Her attention was on the fat man who was trying so hard to figure her out. For such a powerful man, Duarte de Tueste's flabby face was an open book. "So, my pet," Duarte said, smiling. "What was that all about?"

"What's it matter to you?"

"I think you were trying to save her."

She sipped her beer. "I didn't know you gave me any thought at all."

He laughed. "You intrigue me and you know it. Now, tell me why you decided to get involved in that little spat."

"My friend," Kali said, the endearment merely words to her. "If I intrigue you, it must be because you know I never explain myself."

"Yes. But this time I insist." He strummed at his guitar. "Was it the man or woman who caught your eye?"

She shrugged. "Neither was particularly interesting to me."

"Or so you would have me believe." He smiled a reptilian smile. "I find it interesting how concealed you think yourself to be. That those high walls and clever indifference keep the world from seeing your true nature."

"You have a point?"

"I always have a point, but this time I won't presume to tell you what I saw."

"You can tell me anything you want. You make me rich, and that's all that matters to me."

"Is it?" Duarte asked, the tune turning into a familiar song. "I've often wondered what was important to you." He nodded at the flute player, who easily wound his notes around the guitar.

"*Triste*?" Kali said, swirling her beer. "Are you in a romantic mood tonight?"

"I play it for you," he said, his fingers tickling the strings. "Sing for us."

"I don't feel like singing."

"But your voice gives me so much pleasure. It contrasts you, Kali."

Which was exactly why she did not want to sing. She'd already shown too much of herself that night.

"Come, *quierda*. Sing *Triste* for me."

Staring at her beer, Kali knew she had little choice but to comply. She'd learned early on that Duarte de Tueste was not a man she wanted to upset. With a nod, she closed her eyes, letting the song inside. It had to touch her before she could sing. As she inhaled, she could feel the somber notes tickling her throat before delving into her chest to constrict her heart. *Triste* was a song of loneliness, and Kali had to choose to acknowledge and release that emotion.

"Sing, Kali," Duarte said, nodding his flabby chin.

"*Triste é viver na solidao*," Kali began, letting her voice slide into the song. "*Na dor cruel de uma paixao.*" Without realizing it, she slipped into English. "Sad is to live in solitude, to know that no one can ever live on a dream. My heart stops when you pass by, only to cause me pain."

She dropped her voice, gently humming with the rhythm, her body swaying slightly and her eyes closed. Duarte concluded the song, and she opened her eyes to find him smiling gently at her.

"I wonder who's the romantic."

"I'm not a romantic."

"Then you sing like you know sadness and loss."

"And you play like shit," Kali countered, sitting her beer on his table and pulling a chair out. "Now, are we going to talk business or gossip like old women all night?"

Duarte laughed, his belly rocking the guitar in his lap. "Go," he said, to his fellow musicians. "Maybe we play again later."

"You got my email?" Kali asked, propping her foot up on a chair and leaning back.

"Yes," Duarte replied, setting his guitar aside. "You've got my money?"

Leaning her body forward, Kali pulled a small backpack from her shoulders and dropped it on the table. "The safe was just like you said, but," she shrugged, "unfortunately, one of my crew was shot."

"Does this make you angry?"

Kali laughed. "Not anymore."

There was understanding in his eyes as he nodded. "Then I will send you a replacement. Perhaps this one will please you more."

She was about to object, but stopped herself. A warm body was a warm body. "Fine."

"I've never known you to give in so easily." He studied her. "Is anything wrong?"

"No," she started, but sighed. "I think I want to take some time off."

"A pirate taking a vacation!" He laughed. "And just where will you go?"

"What do you care what I do?"

"I have a special place in my heart for you, *quierda*."

She almost laughed, but swallowed it. Duarte had no love for anyone save his family and his money.

"But before you take your vacation, I have a small job for you."

"Another ship?"

"No. This job is more," he gestured, "delicate. It would require all your discretion."

"Don't they all?"

"*Si*, except this would be a contract between just us."

Kali understood immediately. "It's something you want to keep from your partners." She narrowed her eyes. "But why me?"

"You're the only one I know who won't screw it up."

"And if I do, I'm expendable."

Duarte smiled coldly. "Yes, there's that."

"So what's the job?"

"There's a group from Columbia moving a large quantity of product down the Amazon and through Macapa without paying us their share. I need to deal with them swiftly before others realize the depth of their betrayal."

Although she kept her face emotionless, what she was hearing worried her.

"My partners," he gestured dismissively with his hands. "I'm afraid they have begun to suspect me."

"And this group from Columbia. Who are they?"

"Pasqual de Tueste," he sighed, heavily. "My brother."

Kali struggled to keep her eyes on Duarte when she really wanted to look away. Getting in the middle of a family duel was not her thing. Especially when she knew what was coming next.

"I want him dead," Duarte said, his voice icy in its finality.

Refusing him outright would serve no purpose, so Kali could only think of one thing to say. "If it's drugs, I'll have no part of it. You know that."

"Yes, and I know why. You served time in American jails for drugs."

Kali's eyes flashed. "You're information is wrong. It wasn't drugs."

"But you were in prison," he said, blithely.

"And just what else do you know about me?"

"Only what I need to be able to trust you."

"Too bad you didn't check your brother out first." Kali lifted her beer and drained it. "Thanks for the offer, but I think I'll be going." Placing the empty bottle on the table, she stood.

"Before you do, tell me if you know how much three thousand kilos of cocaine is worth?"

"I said I'm not interested in drugs. It's not worth the risk."

"Is sixty to seventy million dollars worth the risk?" He leaned forward, his massive stomach pressing against the small table. "I'll split it with you."

Slowly, she resumed her seat.

"You only have to deliver the shipment to me and I'll split half the profits with you," Duarte continued. "It's probably more than you've made in your entire murderous career."

"And what of your cartel partners?"

"They need never know." He leaned back and laced his fingers over his gut. "Pasqual has been cheating us for many months. What's one more shipment?"

She considered it quickly. "I'll do it for thirty million."

"I said half the profits."

"And I say flat fee." She shrugged. "That way if you sell it for more, all the better for you."

"What if I get less?"

She smiled. "The cost of doing business. Isn't that what you always say?" Raising her finger, she shook it between them. "And only we know of this arrangement?"

"I'm not stupid, Kali." His voice took an edge. "I would hardly tell others of my brother's treachery."

"Then we have a deal?"

As he studied her, she could almost see him weighing the decision. Finally, he nodded. "Yes, we have a deal."

He wanted this badly, and that scared her. Thirty million dollars was an unbelievable sum to seize a cocaine shipment and kill someone. It made her wonder what Duarte wasn't telling her. Did it even matter? This wouldn't be the first job she'd ever worked on bad or manipulated information.

"Now, I'll show you where you can find Pasqual." Duarte snapped his fingers, and the bartender delivered a manila folder to the table. Withdrawing a map of the Amazon River, he pointed at a spot where the Negro River flowed into the Amazon. "Today, my assistant, Luis, confirmed that Pasqual reached this location," he said, indicating Santarem, one of the few sizable cities in the interior. Duarte let his fingers trail down the twisting river. "There is a spot, which I'm sure you know, here." He stabbed at a small tributary that jutted off the Amazon a few days west of Macapa.

"I know it." She looked up from the map. "This is where you want me to attack?"

"If Pasqual's barge maintains the same rate of speed, he'll be there in four days. It's isolated. No one will see you intercept him."

Studying the spot, she nodded her agreement. "And after I have done this for you, how do I know you'll pay?"

His hand splayed across the map. "Same way I know you'll always deliver your percentages. Trust, Kali. It's all we have."

"Yes, there's that," Kali said, unwavering. "However, thirty million dollars is quite a bit more than my usual sum."

Duarte waved her off. "Money is money, *meu querido*, but trust...trust cannot be replaced."

"I want half up front."

"No. It's not possible." Kali just waited silently. "You know I cannot transfer such sums without raising suspicion."

"You're going to raise suspicion the second you sell that much cocaine. Which is why I need half up front or you can get someone else to murder your brother."

"Are you saying you don't trust me?" He twisted his thick head back and forth like a bull. "Do you so easily forget that it was I who gave you your first job in Macapa? I trusted you, Kali."

"It's not trust, it's business."

"It's disrespect." His eyes narrowed. "If we don't have trust, then what's stopping me from having you killed upon your return? That would only be business. Good business."

"I've already considered that possibility. And quite simply, your transfer will live beyond me. It will be our tangible promise to each other. Kill me and your partners will know everything."

"Very clever." He smiled thinly.

"Do we have a deal?"

It took a moment, but finally he nodded. "I can transfer five tomorrow morning."

She knew what he was doing, but was content to allow it. "Like you said, it will take your brother four days to reach this spot." She touched the map. "Transfer five million for three days. If it's all in my account by the time I intercept your brother, I will proceed."

"And if it's not?"

"Then I'll follow him until it is." She dragged her finger down the line of the river. "Maybe we'll make it all the way back to Macapa."

"I warn you, Kali. Do not play with me."

"I do what I promise."

"Which is why I came to you."

"But once this is done, I'm afraid I'll become a liability, as you just indicated. Perhaps my head will sit next to your brother's?"

Duarte leaned forward, meeting her eyes. "You know me too well. I do not betray those who faithfully serve me."

Despite the force of his words, Kali doubted the sincerity. This, she realized, would most likely be her last job for Duarte de Tueste.

"Very good. That's all I needed to hear," she said, pleasantly. "Then we have terms?"

"Nearly." He gave her a crooked smile. "One final point. To guarantee my stake, I'll be sending my son along with you."

"Amado?" Kali shook her head. "No."

"That is non negotiable. The boy will be no trouble. He will only make sure that you do as you've promised and return to Macapa."

Kali clenched her jaw, but knew her options were limited. With a nod, she gave in.

"Treat him no differently than the rest of your crew." Duarte reached for his guitar. "Only please don't kill him like you did your chatty Paco."

"It was your information I acted on."

"Yes. See how I protect those loyal to me?" He studied her. "Do I have your word that you will, in turn, protect my son?"

It was the last thing Kali wanted to promise. Bringing Amado on board would be like dancing with a cobra, but it appeared she had little choice. "You have my word."

With a nod, Duarte called out to the musicians who sat waiting for him. "*Amigos*, come join me." His fingers strummed the guitar. "Will you sing again?"

All Kali wanted was to be away from there. "No. I have preparations to make."

"Very well." He had been expecting such a response. "Email me your bank information and I'll confirm the first transfer tomorrow."

She stood. "I'll keep in touch."

"Yes, do that. I'm most anxious to have this matter settled." He tuned his guitar. "We will sing when you return."

She met Duarte's eye. "I'll see you then."

"Be warned, Kali, if you fail, not even the great rainforest will be able to hide you."

"Trust," she said, seriously. "It's all we have."

Duarte laughed. "I like you, Kali. Don't force me to kill you." He looked at the flute player. "Pick a song, my friend."

The high pitched notes of the flute followed her out the door. She had much to do before tomorrow.

Chapter Three

The air outside was still hot and muggy, and Maddie struggled to keep up with Rob's long steps as he led them along the complex network of docks. So far he hadn't said anything about what had happened in the bar, but she knew it was only a matter of time.

"This way," Rob said, pointing her down another line of docks.

She considered saying something to pre-empt what would probably be an angry outbreak, but everything that came to mind seemed feeble. Her thoughts kept turning to the final cold look in that woman's eyes. It was almost unnatural and definitely like nothing she'd ever seen before.

"If it's possible," Rob said, his voice strained. "I'd like you to explain what the hell you thought you were trying to do in there?"

"I wasn't doing anything."

"Don't play stupid, Maddie. That was a dangerous situation. At least tell me you saw that?"

No, she wanted to say. *Not until the end.*

"I was trying to protect you," Rob continued. "But I can't do that unless you let me."

"I didn't ask for your protection."

"No, because you're too dense to know what was happening. That woman could have killed us both, and I swear no one would have done a thing to stop her."

"She wasn't a killer," Maddie said, but found she doubted her own words.

"No? You think maybe she was there to collect for the poor?" He laughed derisively. "If you're going to survive down here, you'd better learn to keep your head down and avoid notice."

Maddie stopped to face him. "That's interesting considering it was you, Rob, who got us noticed. You!"

"Only because you were staring at her!"

Maddie frowned as a thought came to her. "Is that why you're upset? Because I stared at her?"

"You don't look at people like that. Who knows what that woman—"

"Kali," she interjected, but Rob held up his hand.

"No! I don't want to know her name." He jabbed a finger at her. "And you should forget it."

How could she? It was burned into her mind.

Rob was staring at her. "You can't let it go, can you?" He shook his head in disgust and walked off.

Following, Maddie once again struggled to keep up with him. The lingering heat and exhaustion made her body ache. "Can you slow down?" she finally asked.

Rob stopped. "Why did you do it?" he demanded. "Why did you stare at her for so long? What did you see?"

Relieved to rest, Maddie caught her breath.

"Answer me. Tell me why your eyes lit up when you saw that woman? What was it about her?"

Maddie shrugged him off. "I don't know what you're talking about. The way she came into the bar was dynamic. Besides, I was in a good mood. And drunk to boot."

"Dynamic?" Rob snorted.

Behind him, Maddie could see the white hull of the *Luna Nueva*. She'd made it home. The realization hit her abruptly. That ship was going to be the only home she knew for the next six months and Rob the only friendly face she'd see. The idea of spending half a year in the rainforest had seemed like an exotic fantasy, but that had been back in Boston. The reality was far more bleak.

"I don't belong here," she whispered, staring at the white ship.

Rob stared at her blankly. "What? What did you say? You don't belong here?"

"I'm sorry. This wasn't what I thought it would be. I want to go home."

"Oh no!" His head shook almost violently. "It's out of the question."

"This is a mistake. Surely you can see it, too? We can't work together."

"I only see that it's a little late for second thoughts, Dr. Cross," he said, reverting to her professional title. "You're committed to this venture now. Completely."

"No," she argued. "We'll say I'm sick. Someone else from the department can take my place. Dr. Merchant has experience in this area. It's not like—"

"You selfish bitch," Rob cut her off. "Have you thought what your quitting would do to my career?"

Maddie blinked in astonishment. *His career?* "This isn't about careers."

"Cut the bullshit. It is about careers. And I won't have mine ruined because you didn't weigh the consequences beforehand. That's life. Learn to deal."

"It won't ruin your career. I'll just remove my name from the grant, and you can go forward with the research."

"Doing what?" He laughed. "It's *your* theories. *Your* data. *Your* brilliance that will make it work. I'm just along for the ride."

"And the credit," she added, grimly.

Rob shrugged. "If you're unconcerned about my career, then what about your own? What will happen to that tenured position you want so desperately? Abandoning your research like this will reflect badly on MIT. You think they'll reward you for such behavior?"

"MIT isn't the only university doing climate research."

Again, Rob laughed. "Do you seriously think any other institution will touch you once I let everyone know how unreliable you are?"

"You'd ruin me?"

Reaching out, he ran a finger down her cheek. "Please don't make me do that."

Maddie pushed his hand away. "Don't touch me."

"This is my expedition, and I'll do what I want." He stepped closer, his body nearly pressing against her. "If you'd relax and let me take the lead, you might actually enjoy yourself."

She backed up, relieved when he didn't follow. "Stop it."

"As you wish," he said, with a sick smile.

Staring at him, Maddie fought the urge to hit him. "I want to leave."

"And will you?" Rob shook his head. "Not likely. Your job is your life, Dr. Cross. It's all you really have."

It was malicious, but true.

"I hate you," she said, with as much force as she could muster. "I really do."

"I can live with that." Turning, he gestured at the boat. "Unless you want to invite me in, I think you can find your cabin from here."

As he disappeared down the dock, Maddie felt her body begin to shake and she felt slightly sick to her stomach. From the look in Rob's eye, she had little doubt that he would ruin her if given the opportunity. In fact, she thought he might just enjoy it. Her body twisted in a powerful surge of nausea that made her grab her stomach and double over in pain. When she didn't wretch, she slowly lifted her head and stared at the *Luna Nueva*.

The questions before her were exactly how much did she value her career and could she live without it? Sadly, Maddie knew the answer. Her whole life had been leading to this moment, and just walking away because of someone like Rob Fisher was not an option she wanted to entertain. If she returned to Boston a failure, she'd not be able to live with herself.

Six months would go by quickly. The rainforest would just be her extended lab and she'd take from this experience a wisdom that she'd lacked before. She'd let Rob Fisher ride her coat tails to legitimacy, but she wouldn't throw her life's work away for anyone — not even herself.

A loud, low horn penetrated Maddie's sleep and she slowly opened her eyes. A slit of sunlight was passing under the shades of her small windows, but she had no idea what time it might actually be. Turning over, she pulled a pillow against her chest and snuggled down. The sound of the horn was repeated, but Maddie just blended the noises into the sounds of the docks. In a moment she was working them all into a nice rhythm that lulled her back to sleep.

A banging at her stateroom door made her eyes snap open. "Up and at 'em," Rob yelled, through the wood. "We've got work to do."

Maddie turned her head to stare at the door. "Bastard." The handle of the door was turned and quickly released. Seeing it, Maddie rolled instantly out of bed.

"Come on, Maddie." Rob knocked again. "Are you up?"

Grabbing her watch, she stared at it in disbelief. "It's five thirty," she yelled at the door.

"Yes it is, and it's not getting any cooler outside. I'll meet you on the deck."

"Sadist," she whispered, going into her small *en suite* bathroom.

A few minutes later, she emerged from her stateroom and crossed the lounge to the starboard side door. Opening it, she stepped onto the deck and looked out at the river and dense vegetation that lined the opposite bank. Soon, she knew, the jungle would be all she would see.

"Okay," she said, smiling. "This is pretty cool. Even if I have to live with that jerk, I will make this good."

"What jerk?" Rob said, coming up behind her. "You didn't mean me, did you?" He feigned a hurt look.

Maddie chose to ignore him. "Where can I find coffee?"

"Galley." He pointed at the stairs. "Below deck."

"Is there breakfast?"

"Not today. Meals start after we leave port."

She moved past him and towards the stairs.

"Then I take it you're staying?"

Maddie stopped on the top step. "Our relationship will be strictly professional. You will benefit from my brilliance, as you put it, and I, in turn, will benefit from your absence whenever possible."

Rob stared at her for a moment, his tanned face frozen in thought. Finally, he nodded. "I left your computers and equipment in the lab, so you can set it up your way."

"Thank you." Turning, Maddie continued down the stairs.

"I'll be off the ship for a while," he called after her. "I'm going to check on those missing food crates."

Rounding a corner, Maddie entered the belly of the research ship. When Rob gave her a tour yesterday, she had been surprised by the sheer space. Besides the lab and galley, there was a dining room, entertainment center and crew quarters. Not including their tiny research staff, the *Luna Nueva* carried a crew of twenty.

She found the galley with no problem. There were two women chattering away as they stowed food supplies. Maddie smiled. "*Buenos dias*. Is there coffee?"

"*Si*." The woman pointed at a large carafe.

"*Gracias*." Maddie took a mug and filled it. "This I could get used to," she said, inhaling the rich, nutty scent.

Grabbing a banana, she walked down the hall to the lab. The room was large, but with Rob's desk already a cluttered mess, she thought that perhaps the space might prove too small. She peeled her banana as she sat on the edge of her desk. Being in this room, with Rob's things everywhere, Maddie realized just how difficult six months was going to be.

After making her decision to stay last night, she rationalized it by focusing solely on achieving a tenured position. Her reputation was solid and her classes popular, but without adding successful field research to her C.V. Maddie knew her position would never be secure.

It had been her work in developing a computationally efficient global climate model that had garnered the interest of Rob Fisher. He was an opportunist who had come to her after reading her latest article entitled "Plants,

Nitrogen and Global Change" that she'd published in *Science Magazine*. In it, she'd put forth her counter-theory on global warming by outlining the effects of green house gasses in sub-tropical trees.

It was a bold premise that had shown some merits in computational computer modeling, but Rob had driven home the fact that proving something through computers would never fly with the wider scientific community, let alone the competitive field of global change biology. Her only chance of carving her name into the annals of history, so he said, lay with him. In that, Rob had played on her vanity and she'd fallen for it, hook, line and sinker.

Well, what was done was done. Now, Maddie just wanted to make the best of a bad situation, and hopefully she'd come out of this with something she could use. It was with a sigh of resignation that she set her coffee on the desk and began unpacking her three main computers. Each one held a different climate module that she would use to run their findings.

"At least you all got here safely," Maddie said, putting the computers on a table at the far end of the room. Since they would both be inputting data, Maddie wanted to designate the area a safe zone.

Although it only took her about thirty minutes to set everything up, she wasn't privy to the ship's computer network. Access to that came from Rob, a fact Maddie abhorred. She knew the ship had a wireless satellite link, and as soon as she could, she planned on sending her findings back to her graduate assistants at MIT. If Rob questioned her, she'd claim it was backup purposes, but in reality, she wanted to keep her data as pure as possible.

Staring at the computers, she reached out to adjust the spacing until they were balanced on the table. She backed up to check the gaps, moving forward again to push the middle computer a little to the right. "Perfect."

"A little anal, aren't we?" Rob said, from the doorway.

"You weren't gone long." Maddie didn't try to hide her disappointment.

"I don't waste time."

Maddie regarded him. "Well good for you." She moved to her desk. "So, did you locate our missing crates?"

"They were delayed at customs but will be delivered this afternoon." He dropped a stack of papers on her desk. "Be a good girl and wait for them."

"Excuse me?" She looked up at him. "And where will you be?"

"I have some friends in Macapa I'd like to see."

She folded her arms over her chest. "Well, I'd like to visit the natural history museum. I hear it's very good."

"Hey, it's the food you were so adamant about. If you've changed your mind," Rob lifted his hands, "*c'est la vie*."

The gesture infuriated her, so Maddie turned and pointed at the computers. "And who sets up the network?"

"I do." He smiled smugly. "It can be quite complicated if you don't know what you're doing."

Maddie smiled back. "Well, while you're doing that, I'm going into town. I'll be back in time for the delivery." She looked at her watch. "Say noon?"

"No, wait—"

Maddie grabbed her coffee on the way to the door. "See you in a bit."

She felt quite proud of herself as she gathered her money and found her way off the ship. That should teach Rob Fisher that she wasn't going to be pushed around.

Kali stood on the bow of the *Avatara* as the first rays of light split the dark sky. Holding on to the railing, she stared off into the west, trying to envision what lay ahead.

It had been two years since she'd been up the Amazon. If she remembered correctly, her last trip to Santarem was to pick up a shipment of guns from Peru. Where they went after she delivered them to Macapa wasn't her business. It had been her lack of curiosity that had helped keep her relationship with Duarte honest and secure.

However, this job was far different than anything she'd done before. It would be foolish for her to think that simply looking the other way would save her from a potential double-cross. He had every reason to dispose of her once she'd completed her job, and Kali knew that avoiding such a dark fate would require her to be at her best.

Last night, when Duarte had insisted on sending his son to join her on the job, she'd been reluctant. She'd only been able to see the liabilities of having Amado on the ship, and she'd seriously considered stashing the boy in some remote location. It had been during her sleepless night that she'd started seeing Amado as an asset. He was Duarte's only living son and sole heir. Holding onto him would assure her safety.

If she knew Duarte at all, she guessed that Amado would be given orders to kill her before they returned to Macapa. It was an angle that she'd have to be prepared to counter, and if worse came to worse, she'd kill the boy and disappear with her fifteen million. Duarte may think he could find her, but the world was a big place.

She'd been forced to run before. It was part of the life she'd chosen — or that had chosen her. Kali couldn't remember making a decision to do the things she'd done. It was action and reaction. To stay ahead of the game, to stay alive, she had learned to react faster than others. That was what she'd do now.

The clanking of a bell pulled her from her thoughts and Kali looked around. Even at the break of dawn, activity on the docks was heavy. From tiny dugout canoes to massive commercial barges, the Amazon accepted them all. Turning from the river, Kali studied the *Avatara*.

It's length and the newness would make the white motor yacht gleam on the river like a pearl among pebbles. This meant that not only would the *Avatara* stand out, but she would be remembered. To succeed, Kali needed to camouflage her ship. It may never look like a dingy river craft, but there were ways to make it fit in better. She'd have her crew start on it immediately.

Her crew. Kali dropped her head forward. She felt weighed down with the problem of what exactly to tell them about this job. It was quite a departure from their normal operations, and Kali questioned not only their skills but also their loyalty. If things went wrong, she could find herself friendless. If things went *really* wrong, she could find herself dead.

Straightening up, Kali looked down at her watch and realized her crew would start arriving soon. Since she wanted to leave as soon as possible, she needed to finalize her plans and give her crew orders. While they prepared the ship and gathered supplies, Kali knew she would need to go into the city in search of some special weapons to attack what she assumed would be an alert and armed barge. No one would move three thousand kilos of cocaine without some guns to back it up and Kali would need some different tools to guarantee her success.

"Kali!" Tajo called, his dark face appearing on the dock under her. "I received your page and I am here."

"The others?" she asked, leaning over the edge.

"They will arrive, I am sure." He smiled. "My family thanks you for the excellent money I sent home last night."

His family? Kali nodded although she'd had no idea that Tajo had a family. "Come aboard."

They waited on the aft deck until the rest of her crew stumbled down the dock. From their bloodshot eyes, Kali knew where their spoils had gone.

Philippe was the last to arrive, his inebriated state only increasing his normally bad attitude. "This is too fucking early," he said and yawned. "It better be worth it."

"Not this time," she said, making a quick decision. "You're not needed."

He blinked in shock. "What? I'm the pilot."

"Not any more. I have no use for you. Get off my boat."

Philippe was not loyal to her. He never had been, and on this job, she couldn't risk surrounding herself with such a pit viper. She'd likely end up bitten. The rest of her crew had gathered to witness the commotion, and Kali turned to them. Better to weed out any others who might prove too dangerous to handle. "Philippe is off my crew," she said, tonelessly. "Anyone who thinks this is unfair is free to join him on the dock. Decide now."

Renny actually laughed. "I'm staying. A bird in the hand is better than nothing."

"And you, Tajo?"

"I stay."

Kali polled the rest of her crew, finally turning back to Philippe. "I guess that's it."

His face colored with rage. "I won't forget this!" he yelled, sweeping his arm across the back deck. "All of you are warned."

Turning her back on him, she gestured towards the salon. "Go inside and I'll brief you on the job."

"I'll kill you, Kali," Philippe hissed, as everyone filed inside. "If I see you again, I'll kill you."

She glanced at him. "Don't let me see you first," she said, before turning for the door.

"I know what you did to Paco," he called after her.

Kali closed the door on him. So what if he did know? Philippe should count himself lucky that she hadn't done the same to him.

"So what's this job?" Jack asked, glaring at her as she walked across the salon.

"We're heading up the Amazon. There's a barge we're going to take."

"It has to be drugs," Renny said, chewing on the end of a cigarette. "I don't know much else worth our time on the river."

Kali shrugged. "If any of you have a problem with that, you can stay behind for this job. There will be a place for you on my crew when I return, and I won't think any less of you for your decision."

"What's it pay?"

Carefully, Kali met each of their eyes before speaking. "A two million dollar split."

Renny was the first to divide it out. "So $500,000 each?" He squinted. "And what are you getting?"

"More," Kali said, simply.

"Naturally," Jack said, with a smirk.

"I don't really need a full crew, so if any of you want out," her voice trailed off. When no one spoke up, Kali nodded. "Good. Here's what I need done."

For the next ten minutes she outlined her plan for disguising the boat and buying supplies. With Philippe gone, she needed someone to handle the secondary details, and her eyes fell easily on Tajo. Of them all, he was the most capable and trustworthy.

"So that's it." She checked her watch. "I'll be back around noon. Work fast because we'll be leaving then." She motioned to Tajo. "I'll give you the money to purchase supplies."

"And where will you be?" Jack asked.

The preparations she had to make had nothing to do with her crew, and she didn't respond to Jack's question. All they needed to do was follow her orders.

"Tajo, wait for me on the dock." Her eyes slipped around the room. "The rest of you should get to work."

After retrieving her money and laptop from her cabin, Kali joined Tajo on the dock and held out a thick roll of bills. "Do you want Philippe's job?"

"Do I receive more pay?"

Philippe hadn't, but Kali always thought that was because he was too stupid to ask. Apparently, Tajo wasn't.

"Five percent more on normal jobs. An extra fifty thousand for this one."

"Ten percent."

"Eight." She grinned. "It doesn't come off my share, so it's your crew you're taking money from."

He held out his black hand. "Fine."

Kali pressed the roll of money in it. "Then congratulations. You're now responsible for making sure my orders are carried out." She pointed at the *Avatara*. "Make her look like she belongs on the river."

"Not very likely, but I will do my best."

"Do better," Kali said, leaving Tajo on the dock.

Chapter Four

The morning proved to be exhausting for Madeline Cross. Since the local tongue was Portuguese, her college Spanish left her incapable of even rudimentary communication, and by the time she returned to the *Luna Nueva*, she barely had the energy to face Rob Fisher.

"You look beat," Rob said, as she climbed the gangway to the main deck of the ship. He was leaning against the railing sipping a bottle of water. "Macapa not what you expected?"

"Is the network set up?"

"Absolutely. The satellites are at our beck and call."

"The Internet and email, too?"

"Configured. I left your password on your desk." He smiled. "I have the administrator's."

"Planning on spying on me?"

"Just keeping things running smoothly, Dr. Cross."

"Of course." She pulled at her damp ponytail. "I'm going inside."

He slapped a nearby wooden crate. "By the way, these were delivered about an hour ago. I took care of it for you. So feel free to take the rest of the afternoon off." The condescending look on his face made Maddie want to slap him. "Our post-doc assistants have also arrived. They're in the lab getting acquainted with our plans and charts."

"Do they speak English?"

"I didn't think to ask," Rob said, with a fake concern. "I forget how sheltered you are."

"Because I don't speak Portuguese?"

"Because you only speak English." He smiled contemptuously. "Well, I'm going to go see my friends before we leave. Why don't you go say hi to our guests?" He descended to the dock and was quickly lost among the crowd.

"Pompous ass," she said, turning on her heel and marching into the salon.

Her initial urge was to go to the lab until she remembered the mocking tone in Rob's voice. It was exactly what he wanted her to do. He'd have a good laugh if she was unable to communicate with their assistants. Well, she'd show him. She'd just wait until he was there to do the introductions.

She hated that she was already thinking of undermining her success just to beat him. It was unlike her, and she knew that before they left, she had to come to some sort of agreement with herself. This trip wasn't about Rob Fisher. She had to remember that.

With nowhere else to go, she made her way to her cabin and closed the door. The air conditioning was blowing cold, and she stood in its icy path for a moment before lying down on her berth. It didn't take long for her to fall into a fitful sleep.

When she awoke, the ship was moving and Maddie sat up to look out the window. Gone were any signs of human habitation. The Amazon was wide and dark, and the bank showed nothing but green. Smiling, she watched as their course took them directly into the setting sun, and deeper into the jungle. A knock at her door forced her to look away, and she scowled when she heard Rob's voice.

"Maddie, are you awake?"

"What do you want?"

"I've been plotting our course and wanted to know if you had anything to add."

"I thought we were going to start taking readings in Boca do Jari."

"We are." He rapped on the door. "Will you open this so I don't have to shout at you?"

Although childish, Maddie chose to remain where she was. "How long before we reach Boca do Jari?"

"We'll be there by morning."

"Then after we get some initial reading, I'll look at the map and decide if any changes to our plan are necessary."

"You'll do what?" He banged on the door once. "I'm in charge of this expedition."

"Then go ahead and stick to your course, but don't blame me if everything fails." Maddie stared at the door, wondering what was going through Rob's head.

"Fine," he finally said, his voice tight with frustration. "We'll talk about it tomorrow."

"Fine," she echoed.

"Are you going to join us all for dinner? The post-docs have been asking about you."

"No, I don't think so."

"You can't spend the whole six months in your cabin, Maddie."

Maybe not, she thought, turning to look back out the window. *But I don't have to spend my free time with you.*

"Maddie?"

She just stared out the window. The sunset was going to spectacular.

Kali sat alone on the flybridge as darkness descended around her. This close to the equator, it didn't take long for the sun to disappear, but as it did, the sky came alive with colors.

They had stopped for the night about an hour east of Boca do Jari. It was possible to travel the river at night, but Kali didn't think the benefits outweighed the risks. Besides, there was ample time to intercept the barge, so she didn't want to push her crew too fast too soon.

Below her, she heard the faint beat of music and laughter as her crew relaxed. It was good for them to fall into an easier routine. As the days wore on, the heat and humidity of the jungle would make tempers short.

The slap of shoes on the stairs drew her attention, and Kali turned to see the dark head of Amado de Tueste step onto the flybridge. Born the second of two sons, Amado had been thrust into his father's favor after the accidental death of his older brother during a skiing holiday. Although she didn't know much of Duarte's first born, she had heard rumors that Amado had a cruel streak.

"Are you avoiding everyone, Kali, or just me?" Amado asked, his voice softly accented.

"I prefer my own company," she replied, not inviting him any closer.

"Well, after spending time with your crew, I understand." Even in the growing darkness, she could see the eternal boredom in his eyes. "But I'm not like them, so perhaps you will make an exception?"

"I don't make exceptions."

"Even if I tell you how beautiful you are?" Kali didn't respond. "My father told me you were a beauty, but happily this time he spoke the truth."

"You don't usually believe what your father says?" Kali tilted her head to the side. "Interesting."

"My father is archaic." He took a step towards her. "But we, Kali, we are young."

"Yes, you are."

He took the jab in stride. "But I'm also old enough to know what I want."

"Congratulations." She looked away. "Now if you don't mind, I'd rather be alone."

"If you're up here because you enjoy the heat and humidity, we could go to your cabin and make our own."

"Would that impress your father?"

Amado laughed. "Of course it would."

"Would that finally make you a man in his eyes?"

The gleam in Amado's eyes froze. "I'm already a man. Conquering you would—"

"Prove that I have no taste," Kali interjected.

"Don't mock me."

"Don't try my patience. When I desire your company, I'll ask for you. Until then, you will remain with the rest of the crew."

"I am not one of them!"

"You are when you're on my ship." She kicked her feet up on the seat opposite her. "Get used to it."

"I could kill you."

"Yes, I'm sure you could. But you won't."

"At least not until you've murdered my uncle." That he said it surprised Kali, but she managed to keep her face impassive. "Did you know my father is doing this in secret?"

"I've learned to not question your father. You should do the same."

Amado leaned forward. "There are things at work here that you do not understand, Kali."

"I'm listening."

He laughed. "I'd hardly tell you when you've so clearly chosen to dishonor me."

"I should fuck you to honor you?"

Amado shook his head slowly. "How vulgar. I would prefer to make love to you." He shrugged. "But then again you are my father's whore, so perhaps fucking is a more appropriate."

"At least we got that out of your system." Climbing to her feet, she towered over him. "If you'll excuse me, I have some things to attend to."

"I'm not your friend, Kali," he called after her. "If you were as smart as my father claims, you'd find a way to change that."

Kali didn't bother responding. The boy had just told her a great deal about himself, and she only had to formulate that information into her plan. Most importantly, he'd confirmed that Duarte's plans for her were not as honest as he'd indicated. Which meant that she needed to do her best to set up a trail incriminating enough to hang him if she failed to escape alive.

Crossing through the salon, she descended to her cabin and went immediately to her computer. Once a satellite connection was established, she opened an email to Duarte.

Papa,
My brothers and I have left. We hope to return in less than a week. Your favorite son is fitting in well and we all have great hopes for success provided all terms are met. Thank you for your financial assistance this day. I hope that our transaction tomorrow keeps our status on track. We have stopped for the night. All is well. Please let me know about any details important to our enjoyment.
– Sua Filha

Closing her laptop, she lay down on her bed to contemplate her next steps. In her head it all played out like a chess game. She just had to pick the right piece to move at the right time. For the next few days, her moves were going to be almost textbook. She had to get to the rendezvous point and successfully take Pasqual's barge. After that, it would be a dangerous game to checkmate.

Shouts outside her port window woke Maddie early the next morning, and sitting up quickly, she pulled back the shade to reveal her first river village. Excitedly, she threw off the covers and rushed to dress. If possible, she wanted to be the first one ashore.

The engines surged back and forth as the ship edged closer to the dock, and Maddie felt like a giddy tourist as she grabbed her camera and rushed out of her room. In the salon, she could see the village better from the large windows, and she watched as the gangway was lowered into place. Opening the door, she hurried to the railing, nearly colliding with Rob as he rounded a corner.

"Whoa! Where's the fire?"

Maddie backed up to widen the distance between them. "Where are we?"

"Vida Nova," he replied, his eyes running over her body. "You look sporty."

Ignoring him, she peered over his shoulder. "And where is Vida Nova? I don't recall the name being among our stops."

"It's a bit more remote than Boca do Jari. I thought it would be a good place to establish a baseline soil reading."

"You did, did you?"

Beyond Rob, she could see a group of children playing near the bank of the river. It made her smile. Turning, Rob followed her sight line.

"I'll take you ashore after breakfast," he said, looking back at her. "Since you missed dinner last night, I'm sure you're starved."

"I'll eat later," Maddie said, not wanting to confess that she'd feasted on a secret store of cookies and peanut butter crackers she'd brought with her. "I'd like to go see the village first."

"That's not a good idea."

"You mean without you to protect me, it's not a good idea?"

"Yes," Rob said, complacently. "You don't know the jungle, Maddie. And if that's not enough to make you think twice, the *Cabocolos* inhabit this area. They don't take kindly to visitors. Especially Americans."

"I'm sure the natives won't bother me."

"You're so conceited and ignorant," he said, with a sneer. "The *Cabocolos* are not what you'd think. Descended from Portuguese explorers and Amerindian tribes, they are civilized enough to use this village as a restocking point, but that's about it. I must, therefore, insist that you don't go into the jungle without me or one of the native guides. Understand?"

"You make it sound like I'm going to be kidnapped or killed."

"Or bitten by a snake or insect or just get lost. Ten feet into the jungle and you're not sure which direction you came from."

She gave him a sour look. "I wasn't planning on going into the jungle. I only wanted to see the village. May I go there or do you think I'm going to fall prey to something horrible a mere fifty feet from the boat?"

"You don't have to get caustic, Dr. Cross. I'm only trying to keep you safe."

"I'm sure I'll be just fine without you," she said, scowling as she passed him.

Walking down the gangway, she stepped onto a rather dilapidated dock. It was a few more steps until she was standing on the impacted earth of the village common.

"Don't go far," Rob called down from the deck of the ship.

She didn't even glance back up at him as she let her gaze wander around the small village. It consisted of about a half dozen stone or wood buildings in various states of decay. Rusted tin roofs, and other rusted metal spoke to the village's constant humidity and rain. It was early enough that Maddie barely felt the heat as she walked towards the buildings.

For its scant number of structures, the village was actually quite busy. Dark skinned people moved with an urgent sense of purpose that she wouldn't have expected. If any of them noticed her, it was to dismiss her with a glance. It was obvious that she didn't exist in their world.

In front of the general store, Maddie saw a woman casually nursing an infant on her large breast. Approaching her, she smiled. "*Buenos dias. Café, por favor?*"

The woman barely looked up before dropping her eyes back to her baby.

An old man, as weathered and wrinkled as leather, exited the store with a box, and she held up her hand to stop him. His ancient eyes were uninterested in her.

"*Café?*" she repeated, pantomiming a cup in her hand.

"*Me deixe em paz!*" the man yelled at her, waving her off with his free hand. "*Me deixe em paz!*"

Bewildered, Maddie had no choice but to step out of his way. As she stood in the middle of the village, she felt acutely out of place. It was an epiphany when she realized this wasn't Disneyland and she wasn't a tourist. Holding onto her camera, Maddie returned to the *Luna Nueva*.

Rob was leaning arrogantly against the railing as she climbed the gangway. "Well, that didn't take long," he said, with an arrogant smile.

"You have fun watching me?"

"Yes, I did. Thanks for asking."

"Bastard," she muttered, as she walked by him.

"Hey, don't get mad at me because these people didn't welcome you with open arms. Did you really think they'd gather around you like some novelty? If you'd listened to me, I could have made your visit more enjoyable."

"I'm glad you got to be right, Rob."

"I tried to warn you, but," he shrugged, "you were determined."

"Why did they ignore me?"

"Because you acted superior. From the way you're dressed to the way you walk, you thought yourself their better."

"I only wanted to be a part of it."

"No. You wanted to experience them." Rob shook his head. "They live hard lives out here, but you only saw some *National Geographic* special issue."

"That's not true."

Rob chuckled. "Don't lie, Dr. Cross. You do it so poorly."

Bristling, Maddie stared at him with hatred. It didn't seem to phase him.

"Well, if we're done with assessing your experience in the village, I'm going to go get the Zodiacs ready. There's a small tributary around the bend where we can get our first soil and particle readings." He smiled thinly. "If you approve, of course."

"I'm sure it's fine," she said, ignoring the sarcasm in his voice. "But I'll decide what our baseline will be once I see the first particle readings."

"Naturally." Rob slapped the polished wooden railing. "Then we'll leave in an hour. And if I were you, I'd douse yourself in mosquito repellant and wear pants and long sleeves. It's going to be thick."

"What would I do without you?" Maddie asked, acidly. "You're more help than the Internet."

Rob laughed. "If you hurry, you might have time for breakfast."

With the morning sun hot on her back, Kali activated the Global Positioning Satellite system attached to her navigation equipment. The GPS intercepted data from stationary orbiting satellites before triangulating her position and displaying it on a localized map.

"Where are we?" Tajo asked, looking over from the pilot's seat.

"About an hour west of Boca do Jari. We're making good time." She nodded at him. "You're doing well at the helm."

Tajo laughed, a deep satisfying sound. "You act surprised. My father taught me how to pilot a boat when I was a boy."

Kali frowned. "I thought Philippe and Renny were the only ones who knew. Why didn't you tell me?"

"You never asked."

"That's not an answer."

Tajo looked at her. "You are a woman who thinks she knows it all, and what she doesn't know, she wants to discover on her own."

"Is that so?" She didn't like people telling her things about herself.

"Did I offend you?" He dipped his head. "I apologize if I did."

Kali climbed to her feet. "Since you're so skilled at piloting, I'm going below." She pointed at the horizon. "Keep us at this speed and we should near Porto Franco by dark."

"As you command," Tajo said, as she descended from the flybridge.

Standing on the aft deck, she stared at her surroundings. The river was wide here, but it still felt wrong to be traveling between the two banks. She missed the open expanse of the ocean, and she looked at the thick jungle with loathing.

On the ocean, Kali had options. If the situation grew dire, she could always run. But here, she felt trapped. If she needed to escape, her plans would be limited and potentially disastrous.

To rationalize her apprehension, Kali had decided to focus on the money. It was almost mid-morning, and her second confirmation of Duarte's transfer should be waiting for her. Another five million dollars should be sitting in her Belize account ready for a second and untraceable transfer to the Seychelles. If Duarte thought he could double-cross her, he'd be surprised to find his money long gone. The irony was that should she fail, neither of them would see the money again. She just had to make sure that didn't happen.

Pushing off the railing, she entered the salon. Jack and Renny were asleep with the DVD blaring away. Shaking her head, she crossed the salon and descended the stairs to the cabin level. The doors to the smaller staterooms were closed, and Kali assumed that Amado and Sergio must also be sleeping. It wasn't as if there was much else to do.

Pushing open her cabin door, she was shocked to find Amado on her computer. "What the hell are you doing in here?"

He glanced at her. "What the fuck is up with these stupid passwords? Don't you trust me?"

"No one is allowed in my cabin."

"Then you should lock the door."

"I don't need to lock my door. My crew follows my orders, and you'd better learn to do the same." She stalked across the room. "Now, did you try to enter any guesses?"

"And destroy your pretty computer?" Amado stood. "Hardly. But I could have figured it out."

Kali looked down at her laptop, the cursor blinking on her password box. "If you've done anything, you're dead."

He shrugged. "I only wanted to check my stocks."

Not buying a single word, Kali pointed at the door. "Get out of my cabin. Come in here again and I'll kill you."

"No you won't," he said, brushing past her. "We will make Porto Franco by night, correct?"

"Am I supposed to be impressed with your map reading skills?"

Stopping by the door, Amado laughed lightly. "If you were impressed with that, I would be disappointed in you." His black eyes gleamed. "Why don't you let me really impress you? I know you'll like it."

"Get out," Kali repeated.

Grinning, Amado backed out of the room, and Kali slammed the door in his face. Returning to her desk, she sat at her laptop. She took a deep breath and entered her password carefully. The password screen disappeared and she was presented with her desktop. At least Amado wasn't stupid enough to mess with her secured system.

It still bothered her that he'd come in her cabin. This was her sanctuary, and she shared it with no one. Although she knew it was just a power play, seeing him in her cabin was enough to make her skin crawl. Suppressing her anger, she checked her email, relieved to see that Duarte had responded.

It was one more crumb in the trail of their dealings.

Hija,

Second delivery has been made. Are you still on schedule to meet Uncle? If so, look for a thirty-foot coffee barge. His ship is secure for river travel. I anticipate your safe return next week. — Papa

Kali read the email again before nodding her approval. The job was becoming more familiar. If there was anything she knew how to do, it was seizing another ship.

It was time to start planning her attack. If Pasqual's barge was moving as quickly as Duarte had indicated, she figured she might encounter him tomorrow.

Attacking the barge head-on would be suicidal. In an all out gun battle, Kali could not control the outcome. Surprise was the key.

Tracing the tributaries near Porto Franco, she thought two places on the map looked the most promising. She could hide behind Camandai Island, or — her fingers traced a little farther southwest of the village.

"Yes," she said, staring an area where the Amazon and Xingu rivers connected with thick tendons.

Here the river split and fractured around the Ururicaia islands. The water would be deep enough to navigate the *Avatara* into the thick overgrowth, and her view of the Amazon would be much better. It would also put her far enough off the main water routes that she would go unnoticed.

All she would have to do was lie there, like a river crocodile, and wait for Pasqual's coffee barge to pass. If the river was quiet enough, the barge captain might not sense the danger they had floated into until after Kali had snapped, devouring her prize with power and precision.

"These readings are skewed," Maddie complained, swatting at a screen of mosquitoes hanging in front of her face. "The carbon dioxide numbers are all over the charts."

Rob barely looked up from his water samples. "I've noticed that before."

"So what causes it?"

"Dunno," he said, bending over the bow of the rubber Zodiac and dropping his sample collector back into the water. "Just keep taking them. Everything could make sense when we input them into the computer."

Maddie rolled her eyes and lifted the analyzer to grab another chemical particle reading. The carbon numbers jumped from six parts per million to over fifteen. The spread was too wide to draw any conclusions, and every notation she wrote in her field notebook felt like a wasted effort.

The jungle growth around them was dense. It looked untouched, but Maddie realized it was impacted by a variety of invisible environmental factors. Anything from the boat traffic on the Amazon to shifting air patterns could cause these tainted readings.

"I think I've got enough water," Rob said, dropping a test tube into a protected pack and zipping it. "Do you think we should get some tree diameter numbers or core samples?"

Maddie looked up from her notebook. "I don't see the point."

"What about going further up?" He pointed deeper into the forest.

"Besides the fact that I don't have enough blood left to go on," she said, swatting at a fat mosquito on her arm, "the area is obviously tainted." She waved her pen at his pack. "I imagine you're going to find highly elevated carbon levels in your water to prove that."

"I told you to use repellant."

Maddie clenched her jaw. "I think the area is useless, and unless we encounter similar readings as we go on, these numbers aren't good enough to establish any baseline readings. As such, I'm going to classify these readings as anomalies." She replaced her CO2 monitor in its bag.

"I suppose you're right," Rob conceded. "We're heading for Porto Franco tonight, so maybe tomorrow will be better. We'll be able to locate areas around there which are more remote."

Nodding, Maddie pointed to a tree. "Take me there," she said, looking back at the weathered Brazilian guide who piloted their raft. "I want to leave a particle catcher."

She dug in her bag and removed a small metal pod. Pulling open the mesh screen she checked to make sure the specially treated filter was inside before closing the lid again. The filter would grab particles in the air for the next six months. When they collected it on their way back to Macapa, Maddie thought she might be able to make more sense of the area over the long term.

"You have to hang it high," Rob said, indicating the water line against the tree trunk. "The rainy season starts in a few months."

Annoyed with his authoritative tone, Maddie tossed the pod to him. "Then hang it high." She swatted at more mosquitoes. "I'll be amazed if I don't catch malaria before this is over."

"Are you taking your primaquine?"

"Of course I am." She glared at him.

With a shake of his head, Rob stood and hung the pod in the tree. "There," he said, taking his seat. "Are you ready to hook up with Azevedo and Becker before we go back to the ship?"

Instead of responding, Maddie began repacking her field kit. She wasn't impressed with the two post-doctoral students Rob had brought along. While they both spoke fluent English, neither seemed to really grasp the research, instead focusing too much on outdated climate theories. So she was more than happy to let Rob manage them while she pursued her own research.

As the guide turned the raft around, Rob radioed the other Zodiac, but Maddie paid little attention. She leaned back against the pontoon and waited for the raft to pick up speed. The air that blew across her face wasn't cool, but it felt wonderfully refreshing.

"Why don't you have a shower when we get back?" Rob called out, over the noise of the outboard motor. "And I'll start putting the data into the computer."

Maddie's eyes snapped open. "Thanks, but I think I'll do that myself."

"You don't trust me."

She didn't dispute it.

"Jesus Christ, Maddie. We're going to be working together for six months. You can't possibly do everything."

"I can try."

"And what if I don't trust you? What if I think you're planning on sabotaging me?"

Maddie forced a laugh. "And ruin myself in the process? No, Rob. If anyone's facing risks here, it's me."

"I'm a liability?"

"You said it, not me."

His eyes became angry. "And just where would you be without me? You know nothing of the jungle. It's my knowledge that you need." He slapped his chest. "Me, Maddie. You need me."

"To what? Film me doing my job?"

"You know I'm not documenting this trip. I'm here to work."

"Well, that would be a first." She laughed. "Just do me a favor and stay away from my computers, okay?"

"I have the right to see what you're doing. It's my name on this research, too."

"I can't help that now, but you enter nothing into my climate models without my knowledge. Got that?"

"Fine, but don't think you're going to secretly send your data back to MIT. I control all outgoing communications, Maddie, and I'll know. Don't forget that."

Maddie shifted in her seat as the raft took a river swell. "Let's get something straight. If it were up to me, I'd have returned to Boston two days ago."

"If you hate it so much," he shrugged, "leave."

"And let you ruin me? No thanks."

"Then I suggest you improve your attitude."

"In order to get along with you?" She laughed contemptuously.

For a moment, Rob looked almost sad. "It wasn't supposed to be like this."

Unwilling to let what she'd seen sway her, Maddie glared at him. "No, I know exactly what you thought it would be like."

"No, that was just a bonus," he said, as the white hull of the *Luna Nueva* came into view. "Believe it or not, I wanted us to work together. We could both use the win."

"Listen," she said, softly. "If that's what you want, I'll agree. But we both need to act professionally."

"I'm trying."

She shook her head. "You're baiting me every chance you get. We both have roles to play, Rob. Let's just accept that and move on. With luck, we'll get through this with as little pain as possible."

"Our roles? Meaning, you're the brains and I'm just the goddamned tour guide?"

The Zodiac slid up to the open rear hatch of the ship. "Let's just try to get along," Maddie said, as the guide tossed a rope to a waiting crewman.

"That's what I've been trying to do." He stood up and then jumped out of the raft. "You're the one who's intent on being a class A bitch."

"If that's what you want to believe," she said, reaching for one of the field kits and holding it out to him. "But this isn't what I wanted either."

"Why the hell do I care what you once wanted?" Rob turned and walked away.

Maddie lowered the kit to her lap and just sat there. Behind her she heard the second Zodiac coming in, and she looked at it with chagrin.

"It's all right, Dr. Cross," the guide said, standing and offering his hand. "We'll take care of the equipment."

Maddie took his hand and stepped out of the Zodiac. "Thank you," she smiled shyly, "I forgot your name."

"Cruz."

"Of course. Thank you, Cruz."

The guide gestured in Rob's direction. "It's none of my business, but it's better that you spoke your mind. Dr. Rob will get over it."

Or get even, Maddie thought, watching as the guide began passing her equipment to the crewman.

Chapter Five

At dawn, Kali climbed to the flybridge to survey their position. The previous evening, she had anchored the ship on one of the tendons that connected the colossal Amazon River with the Xingu River.

With so much of Brazil covered by virgin rainforest, the rivers were the commerce highways of the country. The Xingu River was one of the largest tributaries that ran north and south. It gave life to many villages and its routes were busy with barges and boats. Most of the Xingu's traffic used the wide river route to the southeast of the Ururicaia Island, leaving the many canals that crisscrossed the island in solitude.

It was on one of the narrow canals that Kali had anchored the *Avatara*. The thick growth on the nearby banks virtually camouflaged her from sight, and if the river stayed quiet, she would slip out behind Pasqual's barge as it passed by north of Ururicaia Island.

Sitting, with her coffee, Kali looked up as a family of macaws squawked. It was barely six in the morning, but already the air was thick with humidity. She knew that as the day wore on it would only get worse. Since there was no way she would risk draining the generators to power the air conditioning while they waited, everyone was going to have to suffer. With that thought in mind, she tossed her warm coffee over the side.

Leaning forward, she activated the GPS and waited for her position to be drawn on the map. Staring at the village names, she located Paranaquara. If Pasqual was keeping the same pace, he would have passed by there yesterday. That put him right on track to pass her today. The exact timing was the only unknown.

Kali glanced at her watch. In two hours she could confirm Duarte's third and final transfer. Ten million dollars was already sitting in her African bank. If the final five million arrived before Pasqual's barge passed by, she would attack as planned. If it didn't, Kali intended to shadow the barge until she received confirmation.

Returning her gaze to the GPS map, she knew that striking the barge here would provide the best chance of seizing it quickly. With the narrowing of the river and the location of the islands, Kali planned to run the barge aground. Once it was immobilized, she could confiscate the cargo and eliminate the crew at her convenience.

The only pesky mystery in her plans was how to handle Amado. He wasn't as simple to read as his father, and Kali had a sneaking suspicion that he was working on his own agenda. To her thinking, he could just as easily be working for Pasqual as Duarte. Maybe he even planned on seizing the cocaine for his own. No matter how she looked at it, the boy was a liability.

Her instinct was to kill him, but doing so would break her word to Duarte. Yet, she couldn't be foolish enough to let Amado remain in a position to harm her or her crew during the attack. Although she didn't know how, she was going to have to find a way to control him.

Tilting her head back, she stared up at the macaws. With luck the answer would come to her before the barge passed.

The bow of the rubber Zodiac bounced as it hit a small wave, and Maddie grabbed onto a nylon strap to keep from being thrown into the river. Despite the fear, she felt a sudden rush of adrenaline and turned to beam an excited smile at her guide, Cruz. It was exhilarating to be out without Rob's stifling presence at her back.

She had seen Rob at breakfast, but hadn't sat with him. They had tacitly agreed to keep their distance from each other. He hadn't even bothered trying to coerce her into conversation at dinner last night, preferring to regale their assistants with stories of his other expeditions. It was still with a sense of relief that she'd escaped to her cabin immediately after the meal.

With the *Luna Nueva* traveling through the night, she awoke to discover that they had docked slightly south of the village of Porto Franco. According to their schedule, they were going to get readings near a densely forested island isolated by the Amazon. Maddie only hoped the remote northern tributary of the river would provide purer samples than those they had collected yesterday.

As soon as she saw Rob going into the lab after breakfast, Maddie had grabbed her maps and field kit and headed to the Zodiac. Although they were supposed to leave together, she had no intention of spending another day with him. Let him entertain his PhD buddies all by himself.

She found her guide, Cruz, waiting by the raft. The equipment had already been loaded and she smiled kindly before stepping into the boat.

"Where is Dr. Rob?" Cruz asked, his brown face a map of wrinkles.

"He can go in the other Zodiac." She gestured at some of the equipment. "We'll leave these for him."

"But Dr. Rob has our route already planned."

"Which was?"

"We are to go to the island near the Xingu River. The island is more untouched than our sites yesterday."

"Well, that's not where I want to go. That island may not be inhabited, but it is certainly not untouched. With all the diesel fumes and carbon emissions from passing boats, we might as well get samples near the docks of Belem."

"Then where do you want to go?"

Feeling slightly victorious, Maddie had opened her map and scanned the area around Porto Franco. It appeared that the river not only cut a tributary around another island, but there were several smaller rivers nearby.

"What is up near Saracuru and Sao Paulo?"

Cruz smiled. "I had suggested that area to Dr. Rob, but he disagreed with me. In my opinion, your readings will be superior. The area is rarely used and far enough from the main ribbon of the Amazon to limit contamination."

"Then take me there," she said, grabbing for one of the field kits and handing it to one of the crewmen.

Within minutes, Maddie was sitting in the bow of the Zodiac feeling freer than she had in days. Suddenly, everything was interesting. A flock of brilliant scarlet macaws flew over her head and she watched mesmerized by their easy flight. *The jungle,* she decided, *was much better without Rob Fisher*.

"We're turning here," Cruz said, adjusting the speed of the raft to edge them into a much smaller river.

Everything was quieter here. Off to the left side of the boat she caught sight of a small colony of white whiskered spider monkeys at play. Their screeching cackles were very similar to the high pitched laughter of children.

"Look!" Cruz slowed the raft and pointed towards the shoreline. "Do you see it?"

"What?" Maddie asked, scanning the shore for anything moving.

"There," Cruz said, pointing again. "It's a sloth."

Maddie practically threw herself into the water. "Where?"

The three-toed sloth was one of Maddie's favorites. She found them fascinating not only because of their complex biological make-up, but also because they looked like giant stuffed animals. Since the sloth spent nearly its entire life in the tree canopy, Maddie hadn't counted on seeing one.

"He's lifting his head. See?"

"Oh yes." She caught sight of the round face lifting above the grass line. "He's magnificent."

"There should be more around here," Cruz said, looking up the trees.

Maddie didn't want to take her eyes off the animal. She swore it was looking right at her.

"He's got a green back," Cruz said, taking out an oar to slow their progress.

"That's because algae grows there," Maddie said, slowly lifting her camera from her bag and focusing it on the sloth's face. "They move so slowly that it grows in a symbiotic relationship that helps camouflage it in the tree tops." She snapped a few pictures. "He's beautiful."

"I haven't seen too many," Cruz said, giving up on the oar and letting them float slowly past.

Maddie replaced her camera in its bag. "Thank you for spotting him. It made my day."

Cruz smiled, his eyes shining. "Thank you for appreciating my country."

She did not know how to respond. "Where to now?"

"There is a crick in the river ahead. Very dense growth."

"Good," Maddie said, looking over her shoulder one last time.

When they reached the spot, Cruz jumped out and held the raft close to shore while Maddie exited. After securing the small craft, Cruz lifted Maddie's field kit and started walking into the jungle.

"Watch your step," he said. "There are many things which can bite you if you're not careful."

Maddie looked down at the thick growth swirling around her legs, and hesitated. "Okay," she said, laying a hand on his shoulder and stepping behind him.

Cruz held a tree branch back for Maddie to pass. "You tell me when you want to take a reading."

"I want to get some soil from in here," Maddie said. "It looks very organic and undisturbed."

"Yes. Few humans have been here despite it being near a village."

"Was that Saracuru we passed?" Maddie took Cruz's hand to jump over a small brook.

The guide nodded. "It is mostly a trading post for the people who live in the forest."

Maddie looked around. "This is a good place to start." She stopped and reached for her kit. Dropping to one knee, she opened it and extracted a tightly coiled metal band that she handed to Cruz. "Look for the biggest tree around here and wrap that around it."

"Are we going to get a core sample?"

Maddie shook her head. "I gave Dr. Fisher the drill. We'll have to content ourselves with trunk measurements, soil data and some air samples."

As Cruz moved off, Maddie pulled out a small shovel and a dozen tiny Ziploc bags. With her eyes moving before her feet, she slowly moved into the forest, kicking aside the undergrowth and searching for a good spot to start getting samples. The area needed to be free of any recent activity. When she located a likely area, she bent over and stuck the shovel into the moist earth, tapping some dirt into the plastic bag.

"How's this tree?" Cruz called out.

"Looks good," she said, taking a few steps to the left to gather more dirt samples. "Course without the drill core, it's just a guess on the age."

Some of the larger trees in the rainforest could be nearly fourteen hundred years old, but without taking a core sample, it was impossible to dissect the growth patterns. The diameter readings Cruz was taking would only serve to add cohesiveness to the overall study.

Maddie was moving to her sixth collection site when the two-way radio Cruz carried crackled to life. She watched as he lifted it and acknowledged their position and activity.

"Hold on." He looked at her. "Dr. Rob wants to know where you are and when we're coming back. He wants to get moving."

"Tell him we'll be back shortly," she replied, squatting down and stabbing the spade into the earth. She half listened as Cruz relayed her message, and she smiled into her chest when she heard Rob's elevated voice.

"Dr. Rob wants us back now."

She didn't lift her head. "I'll be done when I'm done." She shook dirt into another plastic bag.

Whatever Rob said back made the old guide stand taller and he shook his head vehemently. His voice dropped when he replied, so Maddie missed most of the conversation, but she knew it wasn't pleasant.

"Dr. Rob says he's going to move the *Luna Nueva* farther up river. We have to return immediately or find him later."

"Why's he doing that?" Maddie asked, standing up.

"He says the samples here are degraded and he wants to go to Almeirim."

"What do you think?"

Cruz frowned, the creases on his face deep canyons. "His reasons don't make much sense."

"Should we head back?"

"No." Cruz shook his head. "If you go back, Dr. Rob will only make it harder for you. He's doing this to see how far you can be pushed."

Maddie smiled. "My thoughts exactly."

"But I will take you back, if you want."

"Will it be hard to find the ship?"

"No, Dr. Cross. The *Luna Nueva* is very large and will move slowly towards Almeirim. But we shouldn't be too long."

Looking around, Maddie nodded decisively. "Very good." She picked up her spade and walked past Cruz. "Continue with the tree measurements."

Sitting with her feet up on the console, Kali rubbed at the back of her neck where a tension headache was digging into the remains of her patience. Ever since she had confirmed Duarte's third and final payment, the wait for Pasqual's barge had dragged by with infinite slowness. It was almost one thirty and still there was no sign of her target. Pulling off her baseball hat, she shook her dark hair loose. Immediately, it felt hot and heavy against her neck.

"You should get out of the heat," Tajo said, climbing to the flybridge. "I'll watch for a while."

"No. I'm fine." She pointed at the co-pilot's seat. "Join me."

"Do you think they know we're coming?"

It was a fear Kali didn't know she had, and she sighed. "I'm not sure, but I doubt it."

"What about Amado?" Tajo dragged his hand across his forehead where a glossy sweat clung to his dark skin. "Where do his loyalties lie?"

It was a question that Kali hadn't been able to answer, and she knew her time was running out. "What do you think of him?"

"I wouldn't want him at my back." The African's dark eyes held her. "No one trusts him."

She nodded her understanding. "Do we have any blanks?"

Tajo chuckled. "You're going to give him a gun with blanks? What if he gets shot?"

"As long as it's not one of us who shoots him, it's not my problem. So do we?"

"I don't know."

"Find out. Or..." she hesitated, trying to come to a decision.

"Or what?"

"Send him up to me during the attack."

"He won't like that. He's the type that will want to be in the action."

Kali shook her head. "That's not his call. I'll tell him it was my promise to his father."

"You think he'll—"

"Quiet," Kali cut him off by holding up her hand. "Listen."

Off in the distance, a faint but discernable rumble tumbled over the trees. It was an engine. Old by the sound of it.

"Is it coming from the west?"

"I can't tell with the trees." Leaning forward, Kali switched on her AIS receiver. The Automatic Identification System was a requirement for most ocean ships, and Kali relied on it when tracking one of her freighters. It gave her valuable information about a ship's heading, speed and differential GPS position.

Today, it did her no good as only her own position blinked on the screen. "Damn," she said, flipping the AIS system off.

"If it's our barge, it wouldn't have a transponder tag anyway."

"That's obvious now, isn't it?" Kali growled.

The sound of the old engine grew louder, a rhythmic chug, chug, chug that danced over the trees. Suddenly, like an elephant bursting from the brush, the boat entered her horizon and Kali reached for her binoculars.

Sitting on the bow was an old man, his skinny legs hanging over the side, right over the barge's Colombian registry. Stacked on the deck were large crates and burlap bags. It could be coffee. It had to be coffee.

"That's got to be it," she whispered, lowering the glasses.

"I'll get everyone ready."

As she heard him calling everyone awake below, Kali assessed her options now that she'd seen the barge. It helped that it was piloted from a small wheelhouse that sat smack in the middle of the deck. The wheelhouse was the only structure on the deck, which meant that when she approached, the number of men on deck would be easier to assess and attack.

It also helped that the two ships were almost level in height. If she could get close enough to the barge, it wouldn't be difficult to send a few of her men across. Whether she did this before or after she ran the barge aground was the only question.

"I brought you your weapons." Tajo laid her SIG 552 Commando rifle and Beretta PX4 9mm pistol on the console. "I checked. We don't have any blanks."

She hadn't thought that they would. Blanks didn't do much good. Shrugging, she powered up the *Avatara*'s engines and raised the anchor. "Fine. Give him the grenade launcher and send him to me."

"Is that safe?"

Kali grabbed her Beretta and tucked it into the back of her waistband. "If necessary, I'll take care of him myself."

"And the rest of us?"

"I anticipate one pilot and a few men on deck. I don't know if there are more below."

"Are they armed?"

"I'd count on it."

"And what are our plans?"

She shrugged. "Depends on how they react. I want Renny and Sergio on the bow, with their guns out of sight, looking relaxed." She knew they didn't stand much of a chance of passing as some sort of pleasure cruise, but it was her best option. "We're going to approach as innocently as possible."

"What if they're expecting us?"

It was highly probable, but Kali couldn't change her plan on an unknown possibility. "Doesn't matter. If we play it right, they won't know what hit them."

Kali check her watch, trying to calculate how far up river the barge had gone in the last few minutes. If it continued at its present speed, she guessed maybe a half mile.

"The river turns about a mile east. If we can board before then, fine. If we can't, I'm going to run them into the bank."

Tajo pointed at the bow. "Renny and Sergio would be in the best position to cross."

She nodded. "Tell them to wait for my signal."

"And once we take the barge?"

Kali knew what he was asking. "No one survives," she said, pushing the twin throttles forward and kicking the engines into gear. "Get ready and send Amado to me."

As the *Avatara* moved towards the Amazon, Kali felt her body tingling in anticipation. The hunt was on and she could feel it pulsing in her veins. A smile split her face as the wind began to lift her hair.

Below her, on the bow, Renny and Sergio positioned themselves in the sun lounge, their rifles pressed tightly to their sides. Sergio had stripped off his shirt, his pale chest shinning in the sunlight. When compared to the swarthy Frenchman, they were night and day, but no one would look close enough. Appearance was all Kali needed.

"This is where the *Luna Nueva* was," Cruz said, his voice carrying over the hum of the raft's outboard motor.

Maddie stared at the spot in disbelief. It didn't seem possible that in order to prove some ridiculous point, Rob would actually leave her.

"Don't look so worried, Dr. Cross. We'll find them." Cruz gave her a kind smile. "They won't go far up river without you."

Too angry to respond, Maddie distracted herself by digging out a bottle of water from the small ice chest at her feet. The water was cold, and she passed another bottle to Cruz.

The guide, despite his bolstering words, looked upset. "Thank you." He took the water, but set it aside as he concentrated on the river.

With nothing to say, Maddie turned towards the bow and watched the jungle rush by. It was obvious that Rob was going to make things as difficult as possible for her, and in sight of a deteriorating relationship, six months might be more than she could bear. Especially if Rob was going to endanger her life by irrationally moving the ship whenever she displeased him. That went above and beyond ruining her career.

Taking a sip of her water, Maddie stared at the rainforest, trying to imagine what it would be like to be stranded here. There were villages along the river, but would anyone help her? Her one experience ashore had proved discouraging. The people she'd seen had no interest in anything but survival. Would any of them help her? Maddie didn't want to find out.

"Cruz," she said, turning on the pontoon to look at him. "Are there any sizable villages nearby?"

"What do you mean sizable?"

She shrugged. "I don't know. What's the next large city on the river?"

"Santarem. It's a few days west of here."

"Do they have an airport?" The question surprised her, but she waited for his answer.

"Yes, I believe they do. If not, Manaus has an international airport."

"How far is that?"

Cruz waved his hand at the horizon. "Many days, Dr. Cross. Where the Amazon meets the Negro River." He frowned. "Why do you ask, if you don't mind?"

Maddie sighed. "I don't know. Curiosity."

The old guide stared right through her. "According to Dr. Rob's plans, we're not going to Santarem for at least a month. He is planning on taking us up a tributary for deep research."

"I see." Maddie turned forward in the raft to hide her disappointment.

"There you are, you bastard," Kali whispered, her green eyes alight with anticipation as she finally caught up with the barge.

Now that they were in sight, she pulled back on the throttles to slow the *Avatara*. Even at this distance, she could see her presence had caught the attention of two men on the deck of the barge. It was imperative that she kept her speed steady and unthreatening. Alternating her glance between the GPS map and the river, she grinned when confirming the turn ahead. It was now or never.

Next to her, Amado studied the vista before them. "You're going to beach them."

"You have a problem with that?"

"That's your job, right? It'll be easier to get the cocaine off."

Satisfied, Kali pointed to the grenade launcher. "Do you know how to use this?"

He seized the weapon and broke open the barrel. "Of course. It's a U.S. made M79 grenade launcher. Crude but effective." Amado looked around. "Where are the shells?"

"I'll give you one when I'm ready."

Amado laughed. "How predictable. I wondered why I wasn't given a gun." He licked his lips. "You don't know what I'm going to do."

"Just be ready to do what I tell you."

They were gaining on the barge. Her hand was tightening around the wheel when the two men at the rear of the barge suddenly revealed rifles. The guns were an overt warning that Kali saw perfectly. She needed to get the *Avatara* closer. Renny and Sergio looked relaxed on the bow, but she decided on one more part of the picture.

"Come here and put your arm around me," she said, to Amado. "Look like we're having fun."

As his body pressed against her, Amado leaned in and whispered, "I knew you would want me eventually."

Resisting the urge to take out his knee cap, Kali turned the wheel sharply to give the illusion that they were only going to pass. "Not so tight," she hissed, as Amado pulled her closer.

"Tell me your plan," he whispered, into her ear.

Her plan, at this moment, should have been obvious to him. "Put a grenade on the deck," she said, pulling away from him slightly. "Aim for the wheelhouse."

"I'll need a shell."

It was now or never. She either trusted him or she didn't. Reaching under the console, she passed the box of grenades to Amado. "You get one shot. If you intentionally miss, I'll kill you."

Amado moved away from her, and Kali breathed easier. Taking a shell from the box, he cracked open the barrel and slipped it inside. "Just keep us straight," he said, snapping it closed.

The weapon looked natural in his hands. Almost too natural.

"I need to be closer. This piece of shit only shoots one hundred fifty meters."

"Aim it higher and you'll get three hundred."

She slowed the *Avatara* so it kept parallel with the barge. The men on the barge were watching her every move, and feeling daring, she lifted her hand in a wave.

"Now!" she yelled, as Amado lifted the grenade launcher and jammed it into his shoulder. "Now! Fire now!"

He squeezed the trigger and the small grenade flew from the barrel. It whistled its way towards the barge, where there was a sudden flurry of activity. The men raised their guns, and she motioned for Renny and Sergio to fire back.

The water at the rear of the barge exploded in a great column, and she turned on Amado. "You missed!"

"We were too far away." He cracked open the gun and reached for another shell.

"Do better this time!"

His second shot hit the back of the barge, where a stream of black smoke began pouring into the air. It took Kali only a second to assess the damage.

"The engine. You hit the engine."

"That'll stop them!"

"Not soon enough." Ahead, the bank of the river was rushing towards them.

The barge pilot saw the same thing, and Kali felt him turning into them. "Oh no you don't!" She grabbed the wheel and turned it sharply to the right. "Hold on!"

"What are you doing?" Amado demanded, as the rear of the *Avatara* spun around, pointing the boat directly at the barge.

On the barge, the men were firing furiously at them, the muzzles of their guns flashing with each controlled burst. A spray of bullets ricocheted off the metal of the windshield, and Kali ducked.

"Turn the boat!" Amado cried. "We're going to be killed."

Leaning over the windshield, Kali yelled to Renny and Sergio, "Keep firing!"

The distance between the boats was disappearing rapidly. If she didn't turn soon, the *Avatara* would crash into the center of the barge. She waited, needing every second of thrust, before spinning the wheel away from the barge and reversing both engines. The *Avatara* leaned sharply to the left as the rear slipped around, putting the ship parallel to the barge.

"C'mon," she yelled, fighting for control.

The sound of gunfire surrounded her as her crew exchanged rounds with the barge. Out of the corner of her eye, she saw Renny grab a hold of the railing and wait. She knew she only had to get him close enough and he would jump.

As the *Avatara* spun in the water, Kali powered up the port engine, hoping to thrust them sideways just enough to kiss the side of the barge. Even as she was trying to narrow the distance, the barge pilot was trying to widen it. She was bumping the wheel a little towards the barge when the barge suddenly swerved into her.

Shifting her eyes from the gap, Kali saw how close they were to the turn in the river. If she kept her course for a little longer, the barge would have no choice but to run aground.

"That's right," she yelled, to the barge. "That's where you're going!" In response, the barge pilot turned sharply towards them, and Kali had no choice but to back off. She couldn't let the boats collide.

A bullet smashed into the fiberglass near her, and she glared at the barge. "Hold the wheel!" she yelled to Amado. She grabbed the grenade launcher and pushed the gun into her shoulder.

With the boats so close, she would have to aim directly at the barge. Pointing the weapon right at the wheelhouse, she squeezed the trigger.

"He's turning into us again. What do I do?"

Kali didn't have to answer when the grenade impacted with the wheelhouse. The explosion nearly threw her to the floor.

"Jesus!" Amado cried. "You hit it. They can't steer now!"

She could smell victory, and Kali laughed a loud, wicked laugh. The pilot's last corrections may have cleared the shore Kali had intended, but with no steering, the barge was going to hit something.

The explosion had caused confusion on the deck of the barge, and Kali realized that she either had to take advantage of that disorder and get her men on board now, or wait for the barge to hit ground. Both had risks.

"What are you waiting for?" Tajo yelled up the stairs. "Get us on board!"

Kali felt her hand tighten on the wheel as she swallowed her indecision. Powering up the engines, she nudged the boat to the right. When the side of the *Avatara* skimmed alongside the other boat, Renny and Sergio jumped onto the bow of the barge and disappeared into the smoke. It was then that Kali realized

Amado had left, and looking over the side, she saw him follow Tajo across the gap. "Amado!"

He glanced up at her before holding up her Commando rifle. With a grin, he moved across the deck.

"Jack!" Kali yelled out, stopping him before he crossed. "Get up here."

With all the smoke, she couldn't see what was going on. Amado could be picking them off one by one and she was responsible.

"What do you want?" Jack demanded, coming up behind her.

"Take the wheel."

"What?" He looked struck.

"I have to get over there. You just have to keep us straight."

"And then what? I can't. I've never done this before."

She grabbed his shirt and pulled him closer. "Take the fucking wheel and point the bow straight. When I cross, I'll try to send Tajo back. If not, pull these back to the neutral position. The ship will slow and stop." She put his hand on the throttles. "Then just wait."

"But why?" Jack called after her, but Kali was already down the stairs.

Climbing up on the bulkhead wall, she judged the distance. It was a long way, but she had no choice. Kali took a deep breath and jumped.

"What was that?" Maddie asked, as a loud rumble moved across the treetops like a wave.

"Sounded like an explosion," Cruz answered, his body instantly alert.

"An explosion," Maddie repeated. "From where?"

"Shhh," Cruz said, holding up a hand. "Listen. Gunfire."

Maddie fell silent as a popping sound reached her ears. It was like firecrackers, and she was about to tell Cruz that when another explosion rocked the jungle. Overhead a flock of birds catapulted themselves into the air. Maddie felt her heart beating faster.

"What's going on?" Staring up at the sky, Cruz slowed the Zodiac and Maddie stared hard at him. "What are you doing?"

"It's best to go slow." He reached for an old metal toolbox that sat near the engine. "We must be cautious."

"Cautious? Why?"

"The jungle can be dangerous, Dr. Cross." Cruz opened the box, and withdrew a heavy, black pistol. "Just pray it's not the *Luna Nueva* under attack."

"Attack?" Maddie was shocked. "Why would they be under attack?"

Cruz only tucked the pistol under his leg and took control of the raft engine again.

"Answer me." Her breath was catching in her throat. "Why would they be under attack?"

In the distance, the popping sounds of gunfire seemed to be traveling faster and faster. They were moving into it. Cruz wasn't stopping. He had a gun. He was planning to take them into whatever was happening.

"Stop! Please. We don't need to do this. I'm a scientist, for Christ's sake. I'm not here for this!"

"Don't worry, Dr. Cross. We will be fine," Cruz said, solemnly.

"Worry?" Maddie repeated, her voice rising.

"We'll be fine."

She shook her head. "If you want to protect me, then turn this raft around. We don't need to go into that..." She gestured lamely towards the popping gunfire.

"If we can help, we have to go." Maddie dropped her head into her hands. "If you weren't with me," Cruz said simply, "we would both be on the *Luna Nueva* and the Lord only knows what we'd be facing."

Lifting her head, Maddie stared at him. She hadn't thought of it that way. If the research ship was under attack, she could die. People were being killed. That was what the gunfire meant.

As another explosion sounded, Maddie's body jerked. "That's it," she said getting to her feet. "I have to get out of here." The boat rocked under her feet.

"Sit down!" Cruz said, his voice hard and commanding. The speed of the boat decreased.

"I want to go back to Macapa," she said anxiously. "Take me back to Macapa."

She saw Cruz's mouth open, but she never heard his words as the bow of the Zodiac rose on a wave and she lost her balance. With a strangled cry, she tumbled from the raft.

The warm water embraced her and the swift current swirled around her body. She was torn between a sudden desire to sink and the overwhelming need to breathe. Throwing her head out of the water, she gasped for air.

"Here," Cruz called, holding out an oar.

Giving into her survival instinct, she reached for the oar. Her fingers brushed it twice before a strong kick with her legs brought it into her grasp. Cruz began pulling her in like a big fish until she could grab onto one of the of the rubber pontoons.

"I want to go home," she whispered into the rubber, as Cruz grabbed her shoulders and hefted her into the boat.

"Sit here," the guide said, depositing her on the floor of the raft.

"I don't want to—"

"We go forward, Dr. Cross, because there is nothing to be found behind."

Maddie stared at him as he took his spot by the outboard motor and kicked the engine to life again. Blinking, she turned her head as a plume of dark smoke rose into the air above them.

"It will likely be all over when we get there."

Maddie couldn't bring herself to ask what they might find, so she only stared silently ahead.

The barge seemed to lurch as Kali's feet hit the deck, and she threw her arms out to keep her balance. Smoke engulfed the surface, and she could see that not only was the wheelhouse gone, but the engines were ablaze, too.

"Tajo!" she yelled into the smoke. "Renny? Anyone? Answer me." Two gunshots sounded near her, and Kali instinctively ducked. "Tajo?"

"What about me?" Amado said, materializing out of the smoke. "You have not called for me."

Kali looked at him and felt herself go cold. "Where's Tajo?"

Amado shrugged. "Dying, I'd say. Perhaps dead already."

"Then where's your uncle?" she asked, shifting her eyes around, hoping to catch sight of Renny or Sergio. She had to get someone back on the *Avatara*.

Amado looked behind her. "Jack can't drive, you know." He said it so nonchalantly that he might have been commenting on the weather.

"Where's your uncle?" She sucked in a mouthful of smoky air that burned its way down to her lungs.

"Don't you care about your boat? It's going to crash."

"Then help me stop the barge."

"No point in that, is there?"

Lifting her pistol, she pointed it at him. "Then I have no use for you."

"Look, there's Renny." Amado pointed to where the smoke briefly cleared.

As soon as she turned her head, Kali knew her mistake. By the time she looked back, Amado had disappeared into the smoke.

"Kali!" Renny yelled, trotting towards her.

She shook her head. "Get on the *Avatara*," Kali ordered. "Jack can't pilot."

Renny only paused long enough to gauge the distance between the boats before launching himself onto the *Avatara*. Kali watched him land before turning back to the smoke filled deck. She could almost feel Amado watching her.

Holding her gun tighter, she moved into the haze, her senses alert for any movement around her. She wanted to call out for Sergio or Tajo, but she couldn't give her position away. Not until she had Amado.

A draft caused the smoke to shift on her right, and she spun towards it with her pistol held out. There was nothing there. A gun fired to her left and she turned in that direction. Somewhere a man was moaning. Was it Tajo?

She inched her way across the deck. Her heart was pounding in her chest and her lungs burned from the smoke. In her head one command echoed again and again: *Get off this barge. Get off now.*

"Kali!" Renny's voice from the *Avatara* spilt the smoke, and she turned towards it as a horn blasted.

It was as if the hand of God pushed the smoke out of the way and Kali found herself staring up at the white hull of a large ship. The name *Luna Nueva* towered over her.

"Oh shit," she rasped, turning to see Renny pulling the *Avatara* away.

The horn on the ship blasted, but Kali could see there was no way to avoid a collision. The *Luna Nueva* had taken the river turn too wide, and the barge was out of control. They were going to hit.

Briefly, Kali considered jumping overboard, but didn't think she'd survive in the water. As soon as they hit, the collision could push both ships over her. She'd never be able to swim fast enough.

"Kali!" Amado cried, from nearby. "Come. We have to jump." Even at this distance, she could see his young face was white with fear.

"Hold onto something," she said, running past him.

As the *Luna Nueva's* horn sounded again, she picked up her speed. She had to get away from the impact site. That was the only way she would survive.

Chapter Six

It had been almost a minute since Maddie had heard the rapid sound of gunfire, but slower cracks still cut through the jungle. The dark plumes of smoke rising high above the treetops were like fingers that beckoned them closer. They were hypnotic and as much as Maddie wanted to look away, she couldn't.

"It's gotten quiet," Cruz said, the hum of the outboard motor an octave higher than his voice.

Maddie nodded, her eyes still held by the smoke.

"I think we shall be there soon."

Just the thought of going there was enough to make Maddie's heart pound in her chest. She didn't want to see what had happened. It had nothing to do with her.

"It will be all right, Dr. Cross," Cruz said, reassuringly. "You will see that—"

His words were cut off by a long, loud blare of horn. The horn was repeated in shorter, more insistent blasts.

"That's the *Luna Nueva's* horn," Cruz said, turning the throttle up on the Zodiac.

With the engine at full throttle, the Zodiac flew down the river. Maddie could do nothing but stare forward and wait. She'd never been so afraid in her life.

Running towards the center of the barge, Kali searched for shelter. She didn't dare look behind her. The impact was inevitable at this point. Smoke still covered the deck of the barge and she coughed as her lungs sucked it up. There were others scrambling for safety now. She didn't know what had happened to Amado and she didn't care, either. It was all about saving herself now.

There was precious little to hold on to and with the impact only seconds away, she climbed into the stairwell and wrapped her arms around the steel railing. When the horn blew one long blast, Kali closed her eyes and waited.

She heard the crash before she felt it. The sound of metals grinding together was like the earth shattering, and she winced at the sound. The impact began pushing through the barge and Kali felt the pressure increasing on her arms as her body started to twist and slide. She tried to hold on, but finally was ripped loose.

Her body fell into the darkness of the stairwell, and she gave a strangled cry as her forehead slammed into a step and her shoulder wrenched under her. Everything seemed to move in slow motion, and reacting was a conscious decision. She thrust her legs out in the narrow stairwell to pin herself between the walls. It was painful, but she knew the hold of the barge might already be filling with water, and if she fell into it, she could be trapped.

The brief glimpse she'd had of the prow of the *Luna Nueva* had been enough to realize it was going to shred the hull of the barge. Just how far it would push into the barge would depend on its speed on impact, but she knew it couldn't go on forever.

With a death shudder the boats stopped moving and an eerie silence descended. She held her position for a minute longer before unfolding and climbing out of the stairwell.

The barge was keeled to the starboard side, and Kali had to compensate to keep herself upright. One look at how far the *Luna Nueva* had pushed into the center of the barge and Kali knew the barge was going to sink.

With her head throbbing, she staggered towards a pile of tumbled crates to try and see better. Shells cracked under her feet, and Kali bent to scoop up a handful of small, hard green pieces. Coffee. Unroasted, green coffee. The cocaine, she knew, would be hidden inside the crates of coffee. She would need time to go through all the bags and crates to extricate the cocaine, but would she have time before the barge sank?

Looking around, Kali knew she needed to get back on the *Avatara* as soon as possible. Once there, she would regroup and decide how to best approach the situation. Her first thoughts were to use the chaos of the collision to board the *Luna Nueva* and take over. Killing a boatload of otherwise innocent people didn't please her, but she had no other choice. The cocaine was her only priority now.

"Hello down there," someone yelled from the bow of the *Luna Nueva*. "Is everyone all right?" His accent was very American.

On instinct, Kali dropped behind a toppled crate. She didn't want to be seen. At least not yet.

"*Hola*!" the person yelled. "Someone please answer."

She wasn't expecting the sound of gunfire, and she peered over the edge of her crate to see one of Pasqual's men firing at the ship. The American was hit first and she watched as he toppled over the edge and landed on the deck.

A torrent of bullets tore across the ship, striking more people. It was obvious that she wasn't the only one thinking of getting the cocaine off the sinking barge. As the brightly flashing muzzle moved back and forth, Kali didn't know if she should intervene or let him keep going. He was, in effect, doing her job.

She felt movement near her, and she spun around to find Amado crawling towards her. Blood dripped down his face from a deep cut near his eye. Wounded or not, he was still a threat and Kali reached behind her only to find that her gun had been knocked out of her waistband.

"We have to stop him," Amado whispered, wiping at the blood. "We have to get the cocaine off the boat."

"And your uncle," Kali said, remembering the second part of her contract. "Where is Pasqual?"

"I can't let you kill him."

"I don't have a choice." Kali didn't have time to argue with Amado. Behind her, she heard the gunfire stop and she knew the man was reloading.

"He's going to come find us eventually."

It was true, and as she stared at Amado, she tried to figure things out. If Amado wouldn't let her kill Pasqual, that meant he must be alive. Was he on the barge or had Amado done something?

"We must work together," Amado continued. "All I want is my uncle's life."

"Then he's still alive?"

Amado hesitated. "I made him jump overboard earlier. Hopefully, he's on the shore or has been picked up by the *Avatara*."

The air above her once again crackled with gunfire and she looked up to locate the shooter's position. He had shifted to the starboard side of the *Luna Nueva* and was firing up and down the hull. Kali's mouth opened in shock as one of his bullet's hit the large propane tank.

"Oh God," she breathed, as more bullets pounded into the tank.

"What?" Amado lifted his head to see.

"Run!" She barely looked at him as she started for the rear of the barge.

She didn't stop to see if Amado was following. There wasn't enough time to care about anything but her own life, and casting one last look at the *Avatara*, she dove head first into the Amazon. The last thing she saw was a flash of light as the propane tank exploded.

Closing her eyes, she used all her strength to pull herself deeper into the water. The collision had almost certainly spilled fuel into the river, so she couldn't risk surfacing too soon. Her arms were straining against the current when another explosion boomed above her.

The surface was glowing red with dancing flames. Her lungs were aching, but she had to keep swimming. She had to get to the *Avatara*. Every stroke was harder than the last, and she fought for every yard of progress. She had to get as far from the barge as possible. If the ship sank quickly, it would pull a tremendous force of water and if she wasn't far enough away, she'd be dragged to the bottom.

When the pain became more than she could bear, she thrust herself to the surface. Gasping for air, she stared in horror at the burning debris littering the water around her.

"Kali!" Renny yelled, and she turned towards his voice, relieved to see the *Avatara* in one piece. "There, Kali! Behind you, look!"

Spinning around in the water, Kali searched the surface for whatever Renny was seeing. There was so much debris around her that it was hard to identify anything. She was about to give up when she saw him. "Amado!"

It looked as though he turned towards her voice, but then he disappeared from the surface. Not stopping to think, Kali swam towards him, pushing at pieces of burning debris as she went. If it hadn't been for the shimmer of sunlight off his wristwatch, Kali wouldn't have seen his hand snagged on a piece of wreckage. Swimming over, she reached under the surface and pulled his head up.

The crackle of nearby flames tickled her ears as she turned Amado on his back. She cast a glance at the hollow hull of the *Luna Nueva*. It had completely exploded. She couldn't tell if it had taken the barge or if she still had a chance of recovering the cocaine. Not able to think about that now, she started swimming for the *Avatara*.

"Kali!" Renny yelled, as she pulled them closer. "Swim to the stern, and we'll get you on board."

She was so close. *Just a bit farther*.

"You're almost there," Jack said, leaning over the edge of the platform and extending his arm towards her.

"Take him." She passed Amado off.

"Here," Renny said. "Let me help you."

"I'm fine," Kali said, hanging off the platform, exhausted.

"Let's pull him up," the small Frenchman said, grabbing for one of Amado's elbows. "Now." With Jack's help, they hefted Amado from the water.

Kali paid little attention to them. Her head was throbbing where she had struck it, and she was feeling a little sick.

"Now you," Renny unfolded the swim ladder and held out his hand.

"I'm fine," she repeated. Proving this, she grabbed the ladder and climbed out of the water.

"I didn't think you were going to make it," Renny said, matter-of-factly.

"Did you see what happened?"

"Not really. I saw you dive into the water. The boy was behind you, but then something exploded. I think he was thrown."

Closing her eyes stopped the spinning in her head. She felt quite dizzy. "And the second explosion?" she asked, leaning against the stern of the ship.

"It was awesome," Jack said, his voice excited. "The whole top of the white ship went up."

"And the barge?" She opened her eyes and looked at Renny.

"Almost gone."

Kali nodded, turning to look back at the site. Renny was right. Great bubbles of water were rising around the barge as the river slowly dragged it to the bottom. "Damn," she mumbled, leaning her shoulder against the stern and staring at the water. "Did Tajo make it?"

"No," Renny said.

"And Sergio?"

"I don't know. I never saw him."

"What about him?" She pointed at Amado. "Is he alive?"

Kneeling, Jack felt for a pulse. "I think so, but he doesn't look so good."

Half of Amado's face was blistered with burns and the cut across his forehead bled freely. His shirt was torn and blackened, and what skin Kali could see on his arms and torso was also red with angry, deep burns.

"What do we do for him?"

Kali paused. "I don't know. Let's get him into the salon and we'll clean him up."

"Kali," Renny said, hesitantly. "There's an old man on board who says his name is Pasqual de Tueste. Amado pushed him overboard a few minutes before the collision and we circled back to pick him up." He exhaled slowly. "What should we do with him?"

She shrugged, not wanting to face that question just yet.

"Where is the old man?" she asked, suddenly overcome with exhaustion.

"Jack took him inside. He was wet and sick from the smoke."

"He looks really old," Jack added, as Kali stared at the burning wreckage.

She could feel their eyes on her. They were projecting fear and uncertainty, and she could hear their questions silently screamed at her back. *What do we do next? Tell us what you want? Tell us we did good!* The pressure was overwhelming.

"Kali?" Renny said. "Are you all right?"

She almost smiled at the absurd question. Turning from the wreckage, she looked down at Amado. "Let's get him upstairs. I need to see the old man."

"And what do we do?" Renny asked.

"You," she said, meeting his eyes, "look for survivors."

He tilted his head to the side, but Kali could see that he understood. "You don't want any witnesses."

For the first time in her life it was hard to give the order, but she had little choice. With a nod, she committed them to murder.

Maddie stared straight ahead as the Zodiac bounced its way towards the black smoke. The closer they drew, the more removed she became to her fate. It was as if she was somehow outside her body, watching everything. Behind her, Cruz looked determined. The big black pistol lay in his lap, a reminder of the danger ahead. Maddie chose not to look at it.

"It's not much further," Cruz said, pointing at the smoke. "Less than a kilometer."

Maddie closed her eyes and willed herself to stay calm. That feeling shattered with the sounds of more gunfire. She didn't know why she thought it was all over.

"Dr. Cross," Cruz said, calmly. "For your safety, please get on the floor."

"My safety?" Maddie could hardly breathe. "I don't want to be safe. I want to get out of here."

Cruz stared past her. "It is the *Luna Nueva*. We have no choice."

"No. We do have a choice, we can—" her words were cut off by a deafening explosion that rocked the river.

"Please, Dr. Cross!" Cruz said, roughly. "Just get down."

Before his words faded from her ears, there was a second, louder explosion. A massive black cloud mushroomed into the sky and Maddie lowered herself to the floor of the raft. Curling up with her head on her arm, she tried to remember everything important to her. It was surprising that all the images that ran through her head were of her family. Her father's smile, her grandmother's embrace, the gleeful laughter of her nephews, the peace of the beach near her home. She'd never realized how much it all meant to her.

"No matter what happens, stay down," Cruz was saying, and Maddie had to force herself to concentrate on his words. "And pull that tarp over you." He pointed at the dark plastic tarp they used to protect the sensitive equipment from weather.

Too scared to resist, she pulled it towards her, exposing thousands of dollars worth of scientific equipment to the water sprays. It meant nothing when compared to her life.

"Try to stay still," Cruz said, as Maddie settled the plastic over her body.

It didn't take long for the air to get warm under the tarp. It was hard to breathe, and she lowered the tarp a little to get some fresh air. The scent of something bitter and acidic assaulted her nose, and she covered it with her hand. "What is that smell?"

"Burning flesh," Cruz said, simply.

It took a moment for Maddie to comprehend, and then all she could see was the image of people burning. It was horrific, and she shut her eyes to block it out. As she did so, she connected the explosion and the burning with the *Luna Nueva*. Had it been her ship that exploded? Was Rob dead? Were they all dead? What was going to happen to her?

As Cruz slowed the Zodiac, water rushed past her ears. "*Cara Deus*!" she heard him whisper.

Lifting her head over the rubber pontoon walls, she viewed the burning hull of the *Luna Nueva*. The entire top half of the ship was gone. It was like something ripped it apart. Nothing could have survived that.

"Get down," Cruz hissed. "We're not alone."

Out of the corner of her eye, she saw a grimy looking ship. It was large enough to overshadow them, and terrified, Maddie dropped her head to the floor.

Through the wood of the floorboard, Maddie could hear the deep rumble of the ship's engines. They were so much more powerful than the pitiful little outboard on the Zodiac. Closing her eyes, Maddie waited as the rumble got closer.

"*Alô*!" Cruz yelled, and through a fold in the tarp, Maddie saw him holding the pistol flat against his leg.

"Hello, my friend," a man with a French accent replied. "You seem to have missed everything."

"What happened here?" Cruz's finger dropped to the trigger.

"I'll show you," the man replied, and Maddie flinched as a gunshot cracked the air.

Cruz's body seemed to jump and his gun fell from his hand. Maddie watched in shock as blood began oozing from his chest. She wanted to move. To go and help him. To do anything but lie frozen in fear at the bottom of the raft.

A second shot snapped Cruz's head backwards. Time moved in slow motion as his body slowly sagged against the pontoon. He twitched once before going still.

Thrusting her fist into her mouth, Maddie swallowed a scream. If she could, she would have pulled the tarp lower to block him out.

"Damn gun," the Frenchman said, from almost directly over her. "I think the sight is off on this."

"Looked good to me," a deeper male voice replied. "Try again."

Another shot rang out and Cruz's body jumped. It was quickly followed by another shot.

"See," the Frenchman said. "It goes to the left."

"Give me the gun."

Maddie watched as three more shots blasted into Cruz's dead body. When the sound of the last one died away, she heard the hissing of air.

"*Merveilleux*! You hit the raft, Jack."

"So what? We're not keeping it."

His words caused a panic to spread in Maddie. What did that mean?

"You're right," the Frenchman said. "But what of the gun? Is the sight off?"

"Nope. You just suck." He laughed mockingly.

"Give it back to me!" the Frenchman said, with indignation. "You're a real asshole sometimes, you know?"

The gun was fired again, and air rushed out from just over her head. More shots landed at the floor near her feet and the dirty river water started bubbling through. As she watched it, Maddie knew it was only a matter of time before her position was exposed.

"That should do it," the one named Jack said. "Let's move on."

"No. I want to wait."

"Why? The Indian's dead, Renny. We should check the shoreline. If we let someone escape into the jungle, we'll be as dead as that poor bastard."

Maddie listened with hope. That was what she'd do.

Shifting the tarp, she dared to look out, relieved to see that the trees were closer than she'd thought. They looked dense enough that if she could just reach them, she'd be able to hide long enough for these monsters to go away.

The water levels were rising in the raft. Already it lapped near the top of her leg. With the air rushing out of the pontoons, she knew she didn't have much time left before her position was discovered.

The trees. She just had to find a way to get to the trees.

"There he goes," the Frenchman said, and Maddie heard a small splash as Cruz's body tumbled into the water. The men laughed.

"The river crocs will eat good today," Jack said, laughing again. "Here comes another one."

"Where?"

Maddie's heart stopped. *Were they talking about crocodiles?* That was more than she could handle.

"See him? There? Damn, he's a big one."

Panicking, Maddie knew she had to get out of the water. With her heart pounding and her body shaking, she tried to slowly roll onto her knees. The movement caused more water to rush into the raft and it tilted precariously. Adjusting her position, she held herself very still and listened for any sound.

It was impossible for her to try and look to see if the big ship was gone. She was just going to have to take her chances. If she stayed here she was surely going to die.

Pushing the tarp back slightly, she stared at the bank. It couldn't be more than five feet away. If she could get a good jump off the raft, she might make it. The key was surprise. She had to be on the bank and running for the cover of the trees before the men saw her.

Keeping herself hunched over, she carefully got her feet under her. Then, bracing a foot against a ridge in the floor, she took a deep breath. The seconds ticked by and she couldn't make her body move. In her head, she began to count. *One. Two. Three.*

"Now," she hissed, throwing the tarp off and pushing herself towards the shore.

At the end of the raft, the outboard motor was still high enough to force her into jumping sooner than she wanted. For a short lived second, Maddie thought she might just make it, but then she was in the water and gasping for air.

Immediately, she began pulling for the shore. A few more feet. That was it. Then she'd be on the bank and running for the safety of the trees.

"*Halte*!" the Frenchman yelled, but Maddie kept going.

Her foot touched ground and she began scrambling up the bank. It should have been easier, but the bank was slick with thick, sticky mud. It pulled at her ankles, slowing her progress. She felt like a snail and she knew her time was running out.

A bullet grazed her arm and she cried out in pain. Throwing her hands up into the air, she screamed at the top of her lungs, "Don't shoot! I'm an American!"

It was a ridiculous thing to say, she realized.

"Turn around," the Frenchman ordered.

With no option, she complied. "Please," she said, looking up and realizing his was the last face she was ever going to see.

The man raised the gun and Maddie felt her legs begin to wobble. As darkness descended around her, Maddie was sure she'd just died. Falling forward, the water slapped at her face. It rushed into her ears until there was only silence. In it, Maddie felt at peace.

Sitting across from the still wet and bedraggled old man, Kali contemplated him. He appeared to be about sixty, but with his sun-conditioned skin, he could have been any age. He was definitely older than Duarte, but both had the same fearless grey eyes.

"You are the woman he sent to kill me, correct?" he asked, his voice soft and educated. "My brother's favorite. His special assassin."

It surprised Kali that he knew, and she struggled to hide her reaction. "Then you are Pasqual de Tueste?"

His cold eyes pierced her in such a way that Kali felt defenseless. "Will you tell me if my nephew is badly hurt?"

"Do I look like a nurse?"

"Hardly. You're a killer if I've ever seen one."

"Well, I imagine you've seen many."

He dipped his head. "May I assume that since you admit to having no formal medical training that you will be taking Amado to hospital?"

"I'm in control here," she said, wanting to wipe that arrogant look off his wrinkled face.

"Of what?" he asked, with a condescending smile. He tilted his head towards the open salon door. "A boat is approaching."

It was a small outboard motor. Probably someone coming to offer assistance. The smoke was likely visible for miles.

Renny called out a deceptive greeting and Kali felt Pasqual's eyes on her. One look told her that they both knew what was going to happen.

"Witnesses aren't an option," he said, with a slight nod of his head. "Unfortunate for whomever is out there." His body jerked slightly at the first gunshot. "Is that what you will do to me?"

Kali didn't answer because she didn't know. In silence they listened to the repeated shots followed by a juvenile argument between Renny and Jack. It was all somehow surreal. When a scream rang out, Kali felt it echo through her. Its tone was desperate. Scared. Why it affected her, Kali didn't stop to wonder.

Bursting onto the aft deck, the first thing she saw was Renny lowering the pistol with a scowl. Then her eyes shifted to movement on the riverbank. A woman seemed to waver and then fall face first into the water.

"Give me another clip," Renny said to Jack, holding his hand out.

"No," Jack said, pointing near the bank. "Let's watch."

Stepping to the railing, Kali had no trouble finding the big crocodile moving towards the woman.

"Let me shoot her first," Renny said, his voice distant to Kali. "The croc doesn't care one way or the other."

"Going soft, Renny?" Jack asked, with a laugh.

Angry, Kali glared at Jack. Reaching out, she grabbed him by the back of his shirt and dragged him aside. "Get out of my way," she said, yanking open the gate to the swim platform.

She heard Jack say something, but she didn't stop. Jumping down to the platform, she dove head first into the water. As she swam the short distance to the woman, she silenced the nagging questions forming in her head.

A gunshot rang out as she reached the woman. Looking back she was relieved that it was the crocodile Renny was aiming at and not her. She flipped the woman onto her back. Blood was oozing steadily from a wound on her arm, telling Kali she was still alive. Hooking an arm around her, she began the swim back to her ship.

Grabbing onto the ladder, she looked up at Jack. "Help me." He shook his head and took a step backwards. Looking to Renny, she repeated her demand.

"No, Kali. Let her go. She'll drown."

"I won't fucking let her drown. Not now." She stared at him until it was obvious that he wasn't going to help. "Fine. I'll fucking do it myself."

She let go of the woman long enough to climb partway out of the water. Grabbing the woman's arms, she tried to haul her onto the platform, but the woman's unconscious weight was too much for Kali. Exhausted and defeated, she just held onto her, not sure what to do next. The water around the platform was turning red, and the sight of it enraged her.

"Which one of you assholes shot her?" She shook her head. What did it matter? They were only doing what she'd ordered. "Never mind." She felt so tired.

"Here," Renny said, dropping down to the platform. "I'll get her feet."

Climbing onto the platform, she never relinquished her hold as Renny grabbed the woman's feet. Boots, she noticed, as they were lifted from the water. New hiking boots.

"All right," Renny said, nodding at her. "Now."

With his help, they pulled her out of the water and laid her flat on the platform. Bending over, Kali pushed a clump of wet hair off her face before checking for a pulse. "She's not breathing," she said, looking up at Renny with fear.

"She probably took in a lot of water."

"Do I do CPR?" Kali demanded.

"Why do you care?" Jack called down.

Glaring at him for only a moment, she looked back to Renny. "Tell me!"

He hesitated and then waved her off. "Back up," he said, straddling the woman.

"What are you doing?" she questioned, as Renny turned the woman's head to the side and then placed his hands on her abdomen. Using his body weight, he thrust his hands into the woman's stomach several times.

"I have to get the water from her lungs."

Although she'd heard about the procedure, she'd never seen it performed. She watched with interest as water began draining from the woman's mouth, and Renny continued his thrusts until there was no more.

"Now CPR," he said, climbing off the woman and adjusting her neck. As Renny alternated between chest compressions and breathing, Kali felt her tension increasing until finally the woman coughed. Her eyes opened briefly before closing again. Seeing that was like having a weight lifted from her shoulders, and Kali exhaled in relief.

"Well she's alive," Renny said, flatly. "Now what?"

"I don't know," she said, without thinking.

"You don't know?" Jack demanded. "Why don't you know?"

"Don't question me!" she barked, staring up at him. "I'm still in charge here. Don't forget that."

"No one's forgetting that or questioning you, Kali," Renny said, climbing to his feet. "We just need to know what to do."

"Bullshit!" Jack cried. "I want to know what the hell we're doing bringing this goddamn tourist on board! Look at her! You said no witnesses. Look at her, Kali! She's going to ruin us!"

Kali's eyes slipped to Renny, and he nodded. "She saw us kill the Indian."

She knew what they were saying, but she didn't care. "So what?"

"We don't need to spell it out. Especially to you." Renny scowled. "I don't like killing women, but she needs to die here." He pointed towards the still burning wreckage. "There's no other option."

"No. I won't do that."

"Maybe you've lost your touch," Jack said, sarcastically. "Or your mind."

Kali was about to charge up the stairs when Renny held up his hand to stop her. "If you don't want to kill her," he said, calmly. "Then we'll put her in a raft and set her adrift. Someone will find her."

"Someone like us?" Kali asked, callously.

"Or a villager."

"I've already made my decision," Kali said, looking down at the woman. "She's staying on the *Avatara*."

"And this makes sense to you?" Renny asked, without accusation.

It didn't, but Kali wasn't going to admit that to them. Killing her was the only safe option, but it felt wrong. And she'd made enough mistakes for one day.

"What will you do with her once she regains consciousness?" Renny asked, staring at her. "You will have to kill her eventually. Surely you know that? Would it not be kinder to do it now?"

Shaking her head, she looked back at the burning wreckage of the two ships. "We need to get out of here before others come. After that, we'll decide what to do next."

"We'll decide?" Jack said, derisively. "If *we're* making decisions, then I say kill the woman now. Roll her into the river and let her drown. Or even better, let's watch the crocs get her."

Kali looked up at him. "This is my decision. Mine! Question me again and it will be your carcass feeding the crocs."

"But it affects us, Kali," Renny said. "Surely you see that?"

"The only thing I see is disloyalty. I've never put you at risk, Renny. Or you either, Jack."

"You're doing it now. The woman is a threat and I'm not going down because you've developed a soft heart."

"Going down?" Kali forced a laugh. "What the fuck do you think is going to happen? Are the river police going to come arrest us?" She laughed again. "You're so fucking stupid sometimes."

"Enough of this," Renny said, looking between them. "Let's get our priorities straight. Kali is right. We need to get out of this area. That white ship probably sent a distress call, and if we're here when rescuers show up, it won't matter if we have the girl or not."

For a moment, Jack stared off into the distance. "Whatever," he finally said, looking back at Kali. "But if I get the chance, I'm going to kill her myself."

"Do that and you're dead," Kali said, surprised at the surge of anger she felt. "Remember, I don't need you now, Jack."

"Like you didn't need Paco?"

"Paco got what he deserved."

"According to you. It's always according to what you need."

"Enough!" Renny yelled. "Let's do what we need to do."

Kali took a deep breath. "Alright. This is what we're going to do," she said, beginning to prioritize tasks. "First, we'll take the girl to my cabin." Overhead, Jack blew out a disgusted laugh, and Kali glared at him. "We'll secure her for the time being."

"And then what?" Renny asked.

"I want you to take us west of here. If that ship got a distress signal off, any rescue mission will most likely come from Porto Franco to the east."

"But Macapa is east," Renny said. "Shouldn't we be going home?"

"West is safer for now." This wasn't the time to tell them that going home wasn't an option.

Renny motioned at Jack. "Help me get her up."

He hesitated, but then dropped down to the swim platform. "Get out of my way," he growled at Kali. Bending over, he easily lifted the woman and flipped her over his shoulder like a sack of flour.

Positioning herself between him and the river, Kali watched as Jack climbed to the aft deck. This was all wrong. She knew it. This woman was a liability that she would eventually have to face. For a second, she almost stopped Jack from carrying her inside, but then she silently followed Renny up the stairs.

"I'm going to get us underway," Renny said, turning for the flybridge.

"No." She grabbed his arm. "You go help Jack, and I'll move us." Her hand tightened. "And for your sake, make sure she's safe."

"My sake?" He pulled his arm away. "I'm about the only friend you've got right now."

"I don't need friends."

"That's where you're wrong." He shook his head. "I may not understand why you're doing this, but I'll support you for the time being. Because that, Kali, is what friends do."

Kali clenched her jaw and looked away. "I just need time to figure this all out."

"*Oui*. For all our sakes." He sighed. "I'll do as you wish and watch Jack."

She didn't move until she heard the salon door slide close. Turning, she climbed to the flybridge and lowered herself into the pilot's seat.

Starting the engines, she engaged them and pointed the bow west. She had no idea where to go. Her only need was to find a place deep enough to conceal them for the night. If the *Luna Nueva* had sent a distress call, the remoteness of the rainforest wouldn't stop a rescue operation.

Looking down at the GPS map screen, Kali noted the spot they had anchored last night. If it had been good enough to hide them before, it would hide them again. She needed time to figure this all out.

Chapter Seven

Kali stood in the galley, a can of Coke hanging forgotten in her hand, and her eyes staring blankly at the floor. The air conditioning blew cool air against her face, but she barely noticed it.

Renny and Jack were on the flybridge, camouflaging the *Avatara* before nightfall. She had moored them on the same small tributary of the Xingu River, and unless someone was using geothermal imaging, they weren't likely to be found.

Not one to feel secure with probabilities, she planned on everyone sitting a watch shift that night. At this point, it wasn't Duarte she feared as much as Pasqual's men. Since the old man refused to answer any questions about his organization, Kali didn't discount the possibility of a second ship trailing the barge. For all she knew, that boat could be closing on them.

How had everything gone so wrong? The question haunted her. She replayed it all in her head, looking for some point where she could have changed the outcome. Maybe her attack plan was flawed? Maybe shooting at the wheelhouse was a mistake? Maybe letting Amado off the *Avatara* had been her undoing?

Her eyes drifted to Amado. He had yet to regain consciousness, but considering the ugly red burns on his face and torso, that was a good thing. Renny had done his best to clean him up, but their medical supplies were limited. He needed a hospital. Or a grave.

She should have let him drown. He had betrayed her by aligning with his uncle, and Kali felt confused over why she had saved him. Of course, a lot of what she'd done that day confused her.

The woman was another big question mark, but Kali wouldn't let herself think of that just yet. Instead, she thought about the old man confined with her. It didn't escape her notice that she hadn't been able to kill him either. That would have been, at least, one part of her mission she did complete successfully.

For a moment, Kali wondered what would happen if she delivered the old man's head to Duarte along with his fifteen million dollars. Would he let her live? Would Duarte understand that the collision wasn't her fault?

Kali almost laughed at her foolishness. It was her fault. And because of her inability to handle the situation, she was now going to have to pay the ultimate price. If she returned to Macapa, she died.

Since that wasn't an option Kali wanted to face, she set her Coke on the counter and picked up a nautical chart of the Amazon. If she was going to survive, she had to disappear.

The Amazon was one of the longest rivers in the world. She knew it was possible to navigate a ship the size of the *Avatara* as far as Iquitos, Peru — maybe even farther. The trip would be long and dangerous, but at this point it was probably her best chance.

At Iquitos, she would abandon the ship and make her way to the Pacific. With the money Duarte had paid her, she could buy a new boat and head east. She still had some old contacts in Jakarta who might have a job or two for her. Business would go on as usual.

The plan seemed simple enough. All she had to do was convince Renny and Jack to come with her. It was possible to handle the *Avatara* by herself, but not realistic, especially that far up river.

If they refused, Kali only saw one other option. She let her finger trace the waterways towards Belem. One of the larger port cities south of Macapa, it might give her the chance of escaping into the Atlantic. What the route made up for in speed, it compounded in risks. Kali doubted that she could get through Belem without Duarte knowing. Then, even if she did make it to open water, she might find herself under attack, and depending on what Duarte sent after her, she might not survive.

Of course, if she wanted to get out of Brazil quickly, she could head west to Santarem, the next sizable city on the Amazon. There was an international airport there, and with her computer connections, she could book several flights. Duarte might be able to track her to Santarem, but she doubted if he knew her well enough to decipher all her various passports and identities she'd set up over the years.

Her decision, she realized, hinged on how Renny and Jack voted. They were still part of her crew and she owed them a say in their future. They just had to recognize that staying in Brazil was not a viable option for them, either. Her failure was their failure. Duarte would not differentiate between them.

After dealing with Renny and Jack, she knew she also had to consider Amado and Pasqual. While their lives had little meaning for her, she realized that keeping them alive might prove valuable depending on the path she took. At the very least, Pasqual might be a bargaining chip.

Her mind turned to the woman. Did she have to consider her, too? She shook her head. Maybe it would have been easier if she'd let the crocodiles have her. Now she was a factor that Kali couldn't ignore. It angered her that she'd been so shortsighted. She'd seen the name *Luna Nueva* stenciled on the sinking Zodiac. The woman had belonged on that ship. If only she'd been on there earlier, Kali wouldn't have had to deal with her now. The woman would have been just one more casualty among so many that day. A death with no face.

Kali stared off into the distance. Why did it matter that she'd seen her face?

When the air conditioning switched off, Kali caught a whiff of herself, and her nose wrinkled in disgust. Her clothes had dried, but the stench of the river still clung to her. She needed a shower.

The door to the salon slid open and Renny preceded Jack into the room. "We're done," he said, wiping at the thick sheen of perspiration clinging to his pale skin. "I don't think anyone will see us."

Kali nodded and looked away.

"That's it?" Jack said, letting the door slid close behind him. "We're surrounded by the fucking jungle, with mosquitoes so thick I can cut them with my hand, and all we get is some half-assed nod."

"Jack," Renny began, but Kali cut him off.

"Let him talk."

Jack glared at her. "We want to know what you're planning on doing."

"I'm considering our options."

"What options?" Renny demanded, stepping up to the counter. "We go back to Macapa. We go home."

"Home." Kali laughed. "None of us ever have a home."

"I do. And I want to go back." Despite the hard years clinging to his face, Renny sounded like a frightened child.

"We can't go back. If we do, we'll all be killed."

"Why?" Jack asked, snidely. "We're not the one who fucked up."

"Blame me if you like, but everyone knew what failure would mean. You knew the risks."

"And does that make it right?" Renny asked.

"It makes it what it is." She reached for the chart. "I've got two plans in mind. Both have drawbacks, but hopefully we'll make it."

"You think we'll follow you again?" Jack demanded, leaning over the counter and slapping the chart. "You are out of your fucking mind."

It took a second to overcome the urge to grab his scrawny neck. When she did, Kali exhaled slowly. "If either of you want off the *Avatara*, I'll take you to the nearest village."

"And then what do we do? Where do we go?"

"That's not my problem," Kali said, plainly. "If you chose to stay with me, I'll expect your loyalty."

Jack laughed.

"What are your plans?" Renny asked, calmly.

"Like I said, I have two plans." For the time being, Kali decided to not tell them about Santarem. "One is to head for Belem and the Atlantic. The other is to take the Amazon for the Pacific."

"The Pacific? Shit, you really have lost it."

"If we can't return to Macapa, why do you think Belem will be better?" Renny asked, staring down at the chart.

"I don't."

"What about the girl?" Jack gestured towards the cabins.

"I don't know."

"You don't know?" Jack laughed again. "And the old man?"

"I say we use him to negotiate with the cartel." Renny pointed at Amado. "And he's got to be worth something, too."

"Negotiate with the cartel?" Kali shook her head. "They don't negotiate."

Jack stepped closer to Renny. "I think we should try. The collision wasn't our fault. We couldn't stop that."

"That won't matter."

"We have the cartel leader's son, Kali," Renny said, resolutely. "We will make it matter."

"If it doesn't, then what?" She looked between them. "Should we merrily march to our deaths proud that we tried?"

"Amado can tell his father what happened."

"If he survives, which given his wounds and this climate isn't likely."

"Then we take him to a hospital."

"And wait for him to recover?" Kali laughed. "Listen to what you're saying. It's idiocy."

"It's an option," Renny defended. "One we should consider."

"It's a dead end."

"They all are," Jack said.

Across from her, Renny's eyes jumped back and forth as he tried to find another angle. Usually, she found him predictable, but she wasn't prepared for what he said next. "The girl," he announced. "She said she was an American. We'll use her as a hostage."

Kali's eyes narrowed. "In what way?"

"We deliver Amado and the old man to the cartel. We explain what happened. The girl is insurance. Even the cartel doesn't want the blood of an American on their hands."

Sighing, Kali shook her head again. "You think that matters? The girl will be as dead as us, and no one will ever care."

"Then we have her explain!" Renny cried. "They have to listen to her."

"What don't you understand? Bottom line is we lost the cocaine. We cost the cartel money. That's all they'll care about." She shrugged. "And we'll be used as an example for others who think they can fail and come back."

For a moment, both men were silent and Kali studied them. Only Jack dared to meet her eyes.

"If we can't use the girl," he said, with a crooked smile. "Then I say we kill her. She's dead weight anyway."

Kali took a threatening step towards him. "I've already told you that's not going to happen."

"Jack's right," Renny cut her off. "If you don't think the cartel will listen to her, then she has no purpose."

"Unless you have some perverted need we don't know about," Jack added, nastily.

"You son of a bitch!" Kali reached for him. "I'll break your fucking neck."

"Kali!" Renny said, grabbing her as Jack stepped back. "Stop."

"I'm going to kill him!" She struggled to get free, but Renny pinned her against the cabinet.

"Over a girl?" he yelled at her. "All this over a girl?"

She stopped, clinging to Renny. This wasn't about a girl. It couldn't be. She wouldn't let it. "It's about my authority," she said, pushing off of Renny. "And if you don't like it, get the hell off my ship."

"No one is questioning your authority," Renny said, keeping himself between them. "And we know this is your ship."

"Then back off," she said, more to Jack than Renny.

"Not until you tell me why you are keeping her alive. It's not like you."

"No," Kali said, with a shake of her head. "You don't need to know."

"The hell I don't!" Jack yelled. "You owe us answers!"

"Enough!" Renny yelled.

For a moment everyone was silent, and then Jack threw his hands up. "Fuck this. I'm going to get some air."

"That's probably a good idea," Renny said, with relief. "There's nothing to be done tonight." He looked at Kali. "We'll discuss it in the morning, all right?"

She hesitated, but then nodded.

"Like that will change anything," Jack said, stalking towards the door.

Renny waited until Jack left the salon to speak again. "I'm not sure why you saved this girl, but—"

"I don't know," she confessed, feeling weak and insecure. "I just couldn't let her die."

Renny absorbed this with a nod of his head. "It's been a rough day. We all lost friends. I can understand why you would want to save her, but you know she's a liability."

"So what if I do?"

"Then kill her." He pointed towards the cabins. "If you can't do it, I will. For us, Kali. It's for us."

The mere thought of it turned her stomach. "I'm going to clean up."

"Very well, but you know I'm right."

"I'm not ready to make that decision."

"Then let me do it."

Kali met his black eyes. "Why don't you just fix dinner first? I need time to think this all through."

"Time won't make it easier." He shrugged. "But like I said, there's nothing to be done tonight."

Turning, Kali walked away. The steps to the lower cabin level loomed before her. It took all of her will power to descend them to her cabin door. Holding her hand out, she grabbed the knob but couldn't make herself turn it.

It was then that she became aware of voices coming from the other side. The woman was awake. That meant Kali had to go into the room and face the woman. Face her fear and confront her reasons for saving her. It was something she suspected that she didn't really want to know.

"I've already tried to explain it, Dr. Cross," the old man said, wearily.

"No," Maddie said, indignantly. "You've told me I'm a prisoner, but you haven't told me why."

"Because I can't answer that."

"Well someone goddamn better start answering!" She tugged on the ropes that bound her arms to her side. She felt like some farm animal trussed up for slaughter, the image doing nothing to alleviate her growing fears.

When she'd awakened, the old man had been there, bound to a desk chair. He had been quite friendly, but the only information Maddie had learned from him had been his name and the state of their imprisonment.

"I just want answers," she said, but with more resignation. It was all so confusing. Nothing made sense. There was no reason she should be someone's prisoner.

"I'm sorry I can't tell you more." Pasqual looked kindly at her. "The people holding us will decide our fate."

"My fate." Maddie closed her eyes on the finality of it all. It didn't seem possible that she could be facing death twice in one day.

By all accounts, she should be dead. The moments on the Zodiac replayed in her head in vivid detail. The last thing she remembered was the man pointing his gun towards her. Why hadn't he fired? And what had happened between then and now?

"My head hurts," she said, closing her eyes against the bright lights.

"It's probably the toil of the day." Pasqual smiled. "Why were you on the other ship?"

"We were doing research. We'd just started out on a six month expedition." Looking up, she met his ancient eyes. "They're all dead, aren't they?"

"I would assume so." He shrugged.

"How can you say that so blithely?" She felt her anger rising again. "They were people."

He laughed softly. "And just how many did you know personally?"

"What do you mean?"

"A ship that size must have carried many people. Other than your immediate colleagues, how many did you know?"

Maddie saw where he was going and shook her head. "They are still dead. I can still mourn their loss."

"I'm sure you can, but nameless, faceless people are much easier to forget. There were seven on my boat. All were close friends. I knew their families. I knew them personally."

Maddie narrowed her eyes. "And does that make your loss worse? It was a horrible accident."

"An accident. Yes." He laughed. "What happened to your boat was an accident, but only because my boat was under attack."

"Attack?"

"The Amazon is not a safe place. There are many dangerous people looking for easy targets. It was this boat that attacked my coffee barge."

"Are you saying you were attacked by pirates?" It was too fantastical to be true. Although Rob had told her Brazil was highly criminalized, she never dreamed it was as archaic as piracy.

"Yes, pirates. That is a good word for them. An evil group."

"And they just attacked you?"

"From behind." He nodded. "They destroyed our steering, which is why we collided with your ship. Such a waste."

"And those are the people holding us? But why?"

"Me, I cannot say. I'm just an old man. But you must be more valuable." He smiled, "Perhaps they plan on selling you."

It took a second to make the connection. "Slavery?!" Maddie exclaimed. "They couldn't... I didn't even... No."

"Calm down, Dr. Cross. I am only guessing because there is no other reason to keep you alive."

"Is that why they didn't kill me?" Maddie closed her eyes, willing away the tears she could feel there. "Dear God."

"Yes, praying would be good, but perhaps I can offer another suggestion."

She opened her eyes.

"There was some confusion when you were brought on board. Some of the crew didn't agree with the captain's decision to save you, so I would imagine your life is still up for debate." He leaned forward, as close as his ropes would allow. "If we work together, maybe we can play on that confusion and discover some way to escape."

"Where?" Maddie looked around at the stateroom. "We're on a boat. In the middle of the jungle. Where do we go?"

"I only need enough time to contact my company. Once they know what has happened, they will be looking for me. If I can send our coordinates, I promise I'll take you with me. *If* you help me."

And if she didn't? There was something in the way Pasqual de Tueste made his offer that didn't leave room for question.

"It's really your only option, Dr. Cross. You must start thinking about doing what you can to save yourself. Otherwise, no one will."

It was with a sense of disbelief that Maddie looked at him and asked, "What do you want me to do?"

He smiled, a cold glint in his eyes. "Sooner or later, the captain of this vessel will come to see you. I want you to learn everything you can. Play on her confusion. Press every opportunity to befriend her. I don't think things are going well with her crew."

"Her? A woman is in charge?"

"For the time being. But if we coordinate our efforts, I hope to have the ship under my control soon."

Maddie nodded, not understanding. "So you just want me to be nice to her to get information?"

"Information is power, Dr. Cross. Never forget that."

"And what if she doesn't like me?"

"Oh, I don't think that will be an issue."

"Why's that?"

"Because she's the one who is confused about saving you. If we agitate that indecision, it will be her Achilles' Heel."

It sounded simple, but Maddie shook her head. "I don't think I can do it."

Using his chin, Pasqual gestured towards her arm. "That's where they shot you, right?" When she nodded, he continued. "Remember the fear you felt at that moment. Remember how you fought for your life. Remember that you survived. I'm just asking you to do it again."

What he said made sense. This was about survival, and she must do everything in her power to survive. No matter what that entailed, she would survive. "Alright. I'll help you."

"Very good, child. I knew you would." He gave her a grandfatherly smile. "Now, while we're waiting for our moment, tell me about yourself. You are an American, yes?"

Standing outside her cabin, Kali listened to the inane conversation between Pasqual and the woman. In that time she learned that the woman was from Boston and that she'd grown up on Martha's Vineyard. Kali had never been there, but could imagine how unique it must have been to grow up on an island. Or maybe Kali envied the love she could hear in the woman's voice. Her home had obviously been safe and warm, which was something very alien to Kali.

When she found herself suddenly thinking of her own childhood, Kali grew angry. Those were memories better left in the dark. And so was her knowledge of the woman. Her point for coming down here had been to clean up. That was all she needed to accomplish right now. Until she felt more in control of the situation, Kali was going to take her actions one at a time.

Putting her hand on the door knob, she vowed to just enter her cabin and go about her business. Since she had to shower, she would untie Pasqual and send him out to help Renny with dinner. He could earn his keep until she decided what to do with him. As for the woman, Kali had no need to speak with her, and if she was as smart as she sounded, she'd know to keep her mouth shut.

Decided, she opened the door and stepped into her cabin. The first thing she saw was how cruelly Jack had bound the woman. Briefly, she felt a pang of sympathy. It wouldn't be comfortable.

Her eyes slipped to Pasqual, who was tied to her desk chair. Jack had been kinder with his knots. As he looked at her, Kali couldn't help thinking how confident and smug he appeared.

"We were wondering when you'd grace us with a visit. I'm rather thirsty."

Standing in the doorway, she felt the weight of the woman's eyes on her, but avoiding even a glance, she made her way to the desk. "I need you to go help with dinner," she said, unfolding her pocket knife, and cutting the ropes around his wrists first.

"I don't cook," he said, rubbing his wrists while Kali quickly freed his legs.

"I don't give a shit. You're in my cabin, and I need to clean up."

"I was wondering what that stench was."

Leaning over, Kali sniffed him. "You think you smell any better?"

Behind her, the woman inhaled quickly. "It's Kali, right?"

Hearing her name spoken made Kali frown. It was a clever trick. "Did he tell you who I was?" she asked, folding her knife up. "Well, pretending you know me won't help you."

"But I do know you. Don't you remember?"

Kali looked down at her, not seeing anything familiar. "I don't have time for games," she said, turning back to Pasqual and pulling him to his feet. "Go help with dinner, and if you try anything, you're dead."

The old man was still staring at the woman with interest and surprise. "Yes, of course," he said, absently, as Kali pushed him towards the door.

"The bar in Macapa. It was the bar in Macapa."

Her mouth fell open as it all came back to her. She only had to look at Pasqual to know that there was no denying it. Her reaction had given it all away.

"How wonderful," he said, gleefully. "You do know her!" There was a new shrewdness in his eyes. He thought he'd just discovered some advantage, and if given the opportunity, Kali knew he would use it against her.

Roughly grabbing his arm, she dragged him to the door. There was no way she could allow him near the woman again. "Get out," she said, pushing him into the hall and trying to close the door.

"Wait," he said, stopping her. "How's my nephew?"

"Go see for yourself." She forced the door closed, and just stood there, staring at the wood. She didn't know if she could turn and face the woman.

"You do remember me," the woman said, as Kali closed her eyes on the memory. Even now, she couldn't explain why she'd broken into that lover's spat in the bar. True, the man had been behaving like an ass, but Kali knew he wasn't the one who had captured her attention.

Maybe it had just been the lighting in the bar, or the way the woman's hair had looked. The color was similar. And her eyes. Kali shook her head. No. Those were memories she wouldn't entertain. They only ended up taking her down a painful road.

"The old man said it was you who saved me today," the woman continued. "Thank you."

The gratitude made Kali turn around, but she found that she couldn't look at her. Or more precisely, she didn't want to look at her. Doing so would force her to confront the past – and the present – and neither option was appealing.

"I remember seeing you now. You were leaning over me and your hair was wet. It was you who brought me on this boat."

Kali finally looked up, ice in her eyes. "I was also the one who ordered you shot," she said, coldly. "And I may still kill you."

A look of fear entered the woman's eyes. That was what Kali wanted to see, and satisfied, she walked to the wardrobe and pulled it open.

"Why would you kill me after saving me?"

Ignoring her question, Kali focused only on gathering clean clothes. A shirt. A pair of shorts. Underwear. All the mundane things that made up life.

"You don't know why you saved me, do you?"

Kali risked a glance at her. "Keep asking stupid questions and I will kill you."

"The old man called you a pirate. He said you attacked his coffee barge without provocation. And the man you saw me with in Macapa, he said you were a criminal. A killer."

Slamming the door on her wardrobe, Kali turned and stared down at the woman. "I'm worse."

The woman's face went white and she sucked her lower lip into her mouth. "I'm in real trouble here, aren't I?" she asked, tears welling in her eyes.

She looked so afraid – so innocent – that Kali hated her. Staring down at her, Kali felt her ever present anger rising to fill her. As it seeped into her every pore, she directed it all at the woman. Helpless or not, she shouldn't be there tormenting her. The urge to strike out at her was almost overwhelming, and yet she couldn't make herself move.

Then the woman surprised her by speaking with a new found strength. "If you're going to kill me, then go ahead and do it," she said, her eyes hard and unyielding. "If not, then I demand to know what's going to happen to me. I deserve to know!"

That was all Kali needed. "You demand? You deserve?" she whispered, her clean clothes falling from her hands. "You deserve nothing!"

Reaching out, she grabbed the woman's bound legs and savagely dragged her from the bed. She must have landed on her wounded shoulder because she shrieked in pain, but the noise just drove Kali forward into the red of her rage. Bending over, she seized a handful of the woman's long hair, her knee pressing into the small of her back. For a brief second it all felt wrong, but shaking the feeling off, she pulled the woman's head roughly back.

She screamed.

Grinning, Kali leaned closer, her knee digging deeper into the woman's back. "This is a warning," she said, twisting the hair in her hands. "Demand something from me again, and I'll cut your fucking throat. Got that?"

In the blink of an eye, her anger deserted her, and Kali was left with a pressing sense of remorse. Releasing her hold, she got to her feet and stared down at the woman as she began to sob. The sound was muffled, but tortured all the same. Kali's eyes narrowed in confusion, and all she wanted was to be away from it.

Bending over, she scooped up her clothes and fled into the bathroom. She shut the door and leaned back against it. What had she just done? She pushed herself forward, opening the shower door, and as she turned on the water, she was surprised to find her hands shaking. Within a few seconds, her whole body seemed to tremble. It took all her concentration to strip off her filthy clothing and step into the warm water.

As she stood in the stream, she had an overwhelming urge to cry. It surged against her chest with a relentless pressure, and she squeezed her eyes tight to keep any tears inside. She hadn't cried in over twenty years. It hadn't helped her when she was ten, and it wouldn't help her today. There was a solution to this whole mess. She just had to find it.

Out of habit, she picked up the soap and began washing herself. Fresh water was limited on a ship, and Kali couldn't afford to waste too much. Especially not now.

When she finished, she reached for her towel and dried herself quickly. After wrapping it around her torso, she stood at the sink and stared at the blank wall. There was no mirror in her bathroom. She preferred to not look at herself.

Grabbing a brush, she stared at the wall as she pulled it through her hair. It felt longer, and was definitely hotter against her neck lately. Taking a strand, she pulled it down to a few inches below her shoulder. *Time for a cut.*

The tediousness of her thoughts caught her off guard and she almost laughed. The emotion triggered a heavier sadness, and she dropped her head forward with it. With a sigh, she turned from the sink and reached for her clothes. When she was dressed, she looked at the door but couldn't make herself open it just yet. It was safe in here, at least for the time being.

Lowering herself down onto the lid of the toilet, she shook her head. Maybe she was ten again. Hiding here wasn't much different from the way she'd hid in that dirty closet.

She closed her eyes as her mother's terrified face came into her mind. The image never aged. If she concentrated hard enough, she could almost recall the way her arm had ached as her mother had pulled her down the hall and pushed her into the closet. A hasty warning to stay there and be quiet were the last words spoken to her.

When the yelling started, Kali had crawled as far back as she could and just waited. The apartment had gotten very quiet and very dark, but still she didn't move. Even now, she couldn't recall what had finally made her open the door and crawl out. She remembered her stomach rumbling, but it couldn't be that simple.

The images she had seen as she stood at the door of her mother's room had long ago turned to fragmented and disjointed memories. Blood. Torn clothes. Smashed lamps. Her mother's pale body bruised and cut. And then there were her mother's hands laying by the door. At first Kali didn't understand until she got closer and saw the stumps of her mother's arms. That was when she'd screamed.

It wasn't until she was older that Kali understood the significance of her mother's severed hands. She had been a prostitute and a thief who had crossed the wrong people, and the removal of her hands was just a warning to others. Kali suspected that the bullet to her brain was almost merciful after that.

But at age ten, Kali only knew that her world had collapsed. Her life, as she had known it, was over. Which was exactly how she felt today. The only difference was that no one was going to come in and save her now. If she wanted to survive this, she'd have to do it herself. She just needed to find that path back to her cold, calculating reason.

Her world was one of action and reaction. Cause and effect. Every move impacted the situation and created another set of moves. She wasn't dead, which meant she always had another move to make. It might be just a small move, like eating dinner or sitting her watch or getting to sleep. Taking the small steps would give her the confidence and strength to make the bigger ones, like convincing Jack and Renny to head for the Pacific. She shook her head.

That wasn't going to be an easy sell. Although she tried to learn as little as possible about her crew, she knew that both Renny and Jack had attachments to Brazil. Renny had even fathered a young child that he seemed to love. Leaving the country would be hard on them.

It would mean nothing to her. Brazil was just a place where she worked. It had no deeper meaning for her than Russia or Indonesia or any other place she'd worked. There was only one place she loved.

Closing her eyes, she thought of Paris. In Paris, she was just one more lost soul looking for a place to belong. The city embraced the lonely, and Kali never felt like a stranger.

She nodded, a small decision made. If she survived this disaster, she'd go to Paris. For as long as it took, she'd lose herself in long walks through the old streets of the Saint Germain.

Having that goal made Kali feel better about facing her current situation. She stood and opened the bathroom door. The first thing she saw was the woman, still lying twisted on the floor. Her heart ached with a sudden pity, but she hardened it as she walked towards the cabin door.

"Please," the woman called out, and Kali stopped on the threshold. "Wait."

"What?"

"I'm sorry I demanded anything of you. But please don't leave me like this. It hurts."

Caught between conflicting emotions, Kali struggled to find the ground. Why should she care if the woman was in pain? She was about to just leave when she sighed. "I'll send someone to help you."

"Thank you." Her voice slipped past the door as Kali slammed it.

After the fear had subsided, Maddie became aware of how slowly time moved. Light had given way to dusk and finally a pervasive darkness. There was no light in the cabin save the bedside clock, and in the green glow of the LCD numbers, Maddie had tried to make herself feel safer.

No one had come into the cabin since the swarthy Frenchman had brought her dinner and helped her clean up. She had expected cruelty from him, too, but strangely he had been almost kind. Or, at least, Maddie wanted to believe he was kind.

She blinked at the clock again. It was midnight and the ship had grown almost deathly quiet. The only noises she heard now came from the jungle outside the oblong porthole window.

To pass the time, Maddie tried to identify the animal sounds. There was a constant chatter of insects, but beyond that she imagined a monkey making the high-pitched howl. The growl might be a jaguar. Splashes near the hull could have been frogs or water snakes.

After awhile the game grew boring, and giving up on the noises, she just stared at the clock. The isolation was a blessing and a curse. Every minute that passed was another she had survived, but it could also be one minute closer to her ultimate death.

Shifting on the bed, she was again grateful that the Frenchman had not tied her up so restrictively. Instead of pinning her arms to her side, she was only restrained by ropes at her wrists and ankles. Maddie suspected that if she wanted, she could probably use her teeth to work the knots free, but she realized the futility of such an effort. Where could she run on a boat?

As she lay there, Maddie found herself thinking about all the people on the *Luna Nueva* who had died. Did they have families? Children? People who would miss them? It was all so senseless.

It dawned on her, that if she'd been on the ship, she'd probably be dead, too. So why had she survived? Why had she been singled out and saved?

If Rob hadn't tried to dominate her into submission, she would have been on the ship with him. The irony was that she didn't know if she should feel grateful to him or not. In reality, Rob was only a small part of the string of events that had lead here.

It was Kali to whom she owed her life. She'd been the one to pull her from the river. She was the one who held her life in her hands, and for that, Maddie felt more fear than anything else.

When she'd recognized Kali, she had felt a wave of relief. The woman had once tried to help her, or at least that was how Maddie wanted to remember their encounter in Macapa.

Now, she realized it would have been wiser if she'd said nothing at all. It was apparent that Kali had made no immediate connection with her, and that might have been better.

During the hours of solitude, Maddie thought hard on the plan the old man had suggested, but after seeing how unstable Kali was, she had little confidence in her ability to help. Kali, she suspected, had no use for friends, and without her cooperation, Maddie didn't know how she was expected to extract any useful information.

Maybe her crew was a weak point that Maddie could exploit. The Frenchman didn't seem too bad. Perhaps she could befriend him. Of course, she had no idea what she should say or do, but if given the opportunity, she'd try.

The numbers on the clock shifted again. Her eyes were heavy, but she refused to sleep. She knew she'd give in eventually, but for now, she wanted to experience every minute of her life.

At five minutes after one, Kali heard footsteps climbing the stairs to the flybridge. Sitting up, she covered a yawn. "It's about damn time," she said, stretching her back.

"Sorry I'm late," Renny almost whispered. "I was checking on Amado."

"And?"

"He's still alive, but..." He shrugged. "I don't know what more to do for him. He needs a hospital." Renny paused to light a cigarette. "Jack agrees with me."

"Does he?" Kali watched the bluish smoke rise into the sky. "Why the sudden compassion?"

"It seems to be contagious." He slid into the co-pilot's seat and put his feet up on the console.

"Are you talking about the woman?"

He stared at the ash tip of his cigarette. "Perhaps."

"Well don't."

"We think Amado is valuable. Maybe not to his father, but definitely to his uncle."

"What has the old man tried to offer you?" Kali asked, feeling her body tensing. The ball was unraveling quicker than she could wind it back up.

"Nothing," he said, inhaling.

"He hasn't been honest, either. Amado is Duarte's only son. It doesn't get more valuable than that."

He exhaled, the smoke rising around his face. "That makes him a viable option we haven't considered."

"No, I've considered it," Kali said, reaching out and grabbing the thermos off the console. "And I've dismissed it. If Amado survives the night, I doubt he'll make the journey back to Macapa. If he does, then once we hand him over to Duarte, we're dead. It might not happen right away, but you, me and Jack are walking dead." She opened the thermos and poured what was left of her coffee into her cup.

"Then what of the old man? He's got connections. He can help."

"In Colombia, for Christ's sake. He's been cheating the cartel for months. That makes him as dead as us in Macapa. Siding with him will only make things worse."

"So you're ready to leave Brazil?" Renny shook his head. "Easy for you."

"I know about your family."

He snorted at her.

"I've got money, Renny. Maybe I can get them out, too."

"Oh, I've got no doubt that you have money, Kali. It's all you have."

Kali took a drink of her coffee and spat it back into the cup. It was cold and she tossed it over the side. "Just what do you want me to do?"

"I just don't think we should run. Not as our first choice."

"I understand."

"But you've made up your mind."

"No."

"Then at least consider what we want."

"We can't go back. I wish I could change it, but I can't."

Renny took another drag on his cigarette. "Jack and I are going back to Macapa." He flicked the long ash onto the ground, but would not look up at her.

"How?"

"On this ship."

Kali leaned back, stunned. "Are you saying what I think you're saying?"

"We think that between Amado, the old man and that woman, we have a good chance of working something out with the cartel."

"You haven't listened to anything I've said, have you? Running isn't my first choice, Renny, but we failed."

"You failed. Jack and I were only following your orders."

"That didn't work for the Nazis and it won't work for you."

"We're willing to try."

"To risk your lives?"

"My life is in Macapa! I only do this with you to give my family all the things they need. I have no love of it like you do."

Kali was silent for a moment to let him calm down. If she thought she'd simply let them take her ship, they had another thing coming. "And what about me? Are you planning on killing me?"

"No," Renny said, flicking his cigarette over the side. "But you have to decide."

"How long do I have to think on it?" She seriously considered lunging for him right then. If she was quick enough she might just break his neck before he cried out.

Renny's eyes narrowed as if he knew what she was thinking, but he kept his face impassive. "Pasqual said there's a hospital in Porto Franco. We are going to take Amado there tomorrow."

"Even if I disagree?"

"The boy is hurt," he said, vehemently. "Would you refuse to take me or Jack to the hospital?"

"No."

"Then why Amado?"

With no easy answer, Kali held her tongue. "Then what happens after Porto Franco tomorrow?"

"You will email the cartel. Tell them what happened and seek terms for our return."

"And if I don't?"

Renny looked away. "Jack wants to kill you, but not me. If I have my way, you'll be left in Porto Franco."

"Just isolated enough that I'll be a sitting duck for the cartel." She laughed in disgust. "Thanks for the charity, but just kill me."

"We don't want to do it this way, but you're leaving us no choice. Come with us."

Uncommitted, Kali nodded. "Tell me, does Pasqual know of this plan?"

"I've only told him that we'll make sure Amado gets to a hospital. He'll be secured on the ship while we're ashore."

"Have you considered that the old man will be less than cooperative once you point the ship towards Macapa? You will be taking him to his death."

"It's not his decision."

"I see." She nodded. "Then you and Jack have probably also concluded that the old man just might be running his own game plan? Perhaps he has someone waiting in Porto Franco? Maybe he just thinks he can escape while we're docked? I'm sure he cares for his nephew, but Pasqual is shrewder than you think."

"He said the same thing about you."

"What's that supposed to mean?"

"Why didn't you tell us you knew the girl? Why hide it from us?"

"I didn't hide anything."

"The old man said you knew her. If that was why you saved her, you should have told us."

"Would it have mattered? Would it have stopped you from insisting on her death?"

"So you're admitting you know her?"

"I met her once. In a bar in Macapa. The man she was with was getting rough with her, so I taught him a lesson."

"And that's it?"

"I didn't even know her name."

Renny shook his head. "But it's still very coincidental."

"You think my great plan was to fuck things up just so I could save her?" Kali sighed in frustration. "I've never lied to you."

"You're right. Everything is always so black and white with you. Something is or it isn't."

"What's your point?"

"If you didn't know her, why did you save her?"

Looking away, Kali stared into the darkness. "Well that's the million dollar question, isn't it?"

"Do you like her?"

Her head spun back around to face him. "Excuse me?"

"We all know about you. It doesn't bother me."

"How generous of you," Kali said, roughly. "But you don't know shit. If anything, you guessed."

"Then it's true?"

She shrugged. "Sex is a weapon, and sometimes it can be more lethal than a gun. I've seduced both sexes to get what I want. But I want nothing from this woman."

"Then kill her." When she didn't respond, Renny shook his head. "You can't do it."

"No. I don't want to do it. There's a difference."

"Why?"

"It doesn't really matter anymore. You and Jack have everything all figured out. You hold all the cards." She stood and ran a hand over her face. "And I'm tired."

Renny looked up at her. "This isn't personal, Kali."

"That's exactly what it is. I'd never risk your life for my own personal gain. So, Renny, this is very personal."

"It's my family. You can't blame me."

"No, I guess I can't. But I expect you to make an objective decision and not an emotional one." She paused. "Let me ask you a question. Do you trust Jack?"

"We both want the same thing."

"That's not trust."

"It's what we've always had with you."

"That's where you're wrong. I've always protected you. The jobs I took were lucrative but safe."

"Except this one."

Kali shrugged. "Regardless of the outcome, I'm doing my best to protect you." She gestured towards the dark forest. "Going back to Macapa is suicide. Jack knows that. Once he's gotten rid of me, I'm fairly certain he has no intention of going there. Then where will you be?"

"What are you saying?"

"I'm telling you to watch your back, and side with the person who has earned your trust."

"You make me money, Kali. How has that earned my trust when I might be one job away from being killed like Paco?"

"Paco couldn't keep his mouth shut when he drank. He may have started out talking about me, but before long he would have been talking about our jobs. You may not want to believe me, but killing him saved everyone." She held out her hands. "It's blunt but it's the truth."

"And what do you want from me?"

"That's up to you. If you want to take Amado to the hospital, I say we do it. I'll even agree to contact Duarte, but I will not go back to Macapa until we hear back. And I'm the only one who knows Duarte well enough to know if he's baiting us or not."

Renny considered this for a moment. "I think that's fair, and I'll talk to Jack."

"I only want us to survive," she said, with as much sincerity as she could muster. In her mind, she was buying time to figure everything out. If worse came to worse, she'd kill Renny and Jack and struggle to pilot the *Avatara* herself. It would be better to have one other person to help, but she'd be damned if she let them take her ship without a fight. "I'm going to get some sleep," she said, checking her wristwatch. "Wake me at half past six."

"Are you sleeping in your cabin?"

She knew what he was fishing for, but she wasn't going to bite. It was her goddamn cabin. That was where she slept.

"Well," he said, reaching for his cigarettes. "Sleep well."

She heard the flick of his lighter as she made her way down the stairs. Once on the aft deck, she stopped and stared out at the dark trees. Swatting at a mosquito that buzzed near her ear, she decided she hated the fucking jungle.

There was water everywhere and Maddie was drowning. It surrounded her, sloshing and dripping until the pressure was so uncomfortable that she just wanted to let go. As she became more awake, the feeling of discomfort grew stronger. Her body felt groggy and the lure of falling back asleep was strong. She was closing her eyes when her bladder convulsed and she was completely awake.

It wasn't until she tried to sit up that she remembered her legs and arms were still tied. Reality rushed back at her, but she didn't have time to dwell on all of that. She needed a bathroom, and if necessary, she'd hop there. With effort, she threw her legs over the edge of the bed and tried to stand. The ground shifted under her feet and she was tossed off balance.

"Jesus Christ," Kali cried out. "What the fuck is going on?"

The bedside lamp was flipped on, and Maddie blinked against the glare. Kali was sitting on the floor, and just one look at her face and Maddie felt her heart go cold with fear. That, however, did not override her most basic needs.

"Bathroom," she said urgently. "Please. Now." Her bladder convulsed again and she struggled to get to her feet. She didn't dare look at Kali.

"Well, go," Kali growled, gesturing at the door.

Getting to her feet, Maddie contemplated the distance. She couldn't believe that she was going to have to hop to the toilet, but with no other option, she took a little jump. The jolt almost caused her to lose control, and she winced in pain.

"Stop," Kali commanded, just as Maddie took another jump.

Not hearing her, she jumped again. She was about to repeat her movements when her arm was roughly grabbed and she almost toppled to the floor.

"I said stop!" Kali gave her arm a hard tug.

The fear overtook her, and Maddie felt her body begin to shake. It took a second to realize that the warm damp feeling spreading across her shorts and running down her legs was urine. Somehow knowing this just made her shake harder. "I'm sorry," she babbled, as Kali circled around her. She felt tears coming to her eyes.

"Tell me you didn't just piss yourself," she said, gesturing at her wet shorts.

"I'm sorry," she repeated, unable to look up at her.

"I don't fucking believe it."

"You scared me," Maddie said, without thinking.

"I what?" Kali said, her body shifting back and forth like a caged tiger. "I scared you?"

Acutely aware of her mistake, Maddie lowered her head and waited. A tense silence dragged out, but with every breath, Maddie could feel Kali's intense presence pushing into her. She sensed, instead of saw, Kali move. That was followed by the sound of metal scraping against metal, and her heart began to thump loudly. She didn't dare move. As Kali stepped closer, her body coming into Maddie's line of sight, she saw the glint of a short knife in her hand. Reflectively, she shut her eyes. This was it. She was going to die.

When she felt a touch on her foot, she almost screamed. The metal from the knife was cold as it was slipped between her ankles, and she opened her eyes as the ropes were cut away. Rising, Kali then quickly cut her hands free.

"Go clean up," she said, closing the blade and turning away.

Nearly stumbling, Maddie made her way into the bathroom. She was shutting the door when Kali's hand stopped it.

"Leave it open." Kali's eyes met and held hers. "And don't try anything."

Maddie swallowed. "I won't."

Staring at her, Kali nodded. "You can shower, but water is scare on a ship, so do it quickly." She gestured at an array of toiletry items. "Use what you need."

Nodding, Maddie dropped her eyes. "Thank you." She felt Kali staring at her, but then, almost abruptly, she turned away, and Maddie was alone in the bathroom. Well, as alone as she could be with the door wide open.

The first thing she did was strip off her soiled shorts and underpants. It had been an unconscious bodily reflex, but it still disgusted her. To add to her embarrassment, she knew that she needed to wash her shorts out or she'd have nothing to wear.

Going to the sink, she turned on the water and stuck her shorts and underwear into the basin. There was a bar of soap in the tray, and grabbing it, she lathered it in her hands before lifting her shorts. She was in the process of washing them when Kali's shadow fell over her.

"Maybe you didn't hear me when I said water is scarce?" She reached out and turned off the faucet.

"But I can't wear them like that," Maddie said, keeping her voice even. She pulled her body closer to the sink to hide as much of her nudity as possible.

Kali stared down at the sink, almost lost in thought for a moment. Finally, she shook her head. "Leave them. I'll get you something else to wear."

"Alright," Maddie said, holding herself very still until Kali turned and left. Then, exhaling a breath she hadn't even known she was holding, she reached for her shirt and started pulling it off.

She had forgotten about the wound in her shoulder, and the movement made her cry out in pain. When she heard footsteps approaching, she froze, terrified that she'd done something wrong.

"What the hell is wrong now?" Kali demanded, framed in the doorway, a bundle of clothes in her arms.

"Nothing. I'm sorry," she said, as a drop of blood fell from her hand and onto the floor.

Kali stared at the floor. "You're bleeding."

Maddie looked down as the spot was joined by another. Not sure how to react, she did nothing.

That apparently wasn't right either, because Kali growled. "For Christ's sake," she said, stepping into the room. "I'm too fucking tired for this." She closed the lid of the toilet and set the clothes on top. "Can you lift your arms over your head?"

Taking a deep breath, she tried to lift her arms, wincing as her shoulder objected.

"Okay. Stop," Kali said, her voice softer. "We'll do this another way." She almost jumped back when Kali dug her knife out of her pocket again. "Relax. I'm not going to hurt you."

No matter what she said, Maddie still held her breath while Kali pulled her t-shirt out and away from her body. Then slipping the knife up, almost to her chin, she stabbed the fabric and cut it straight down.

"Breathe," Kali said, once her shirt had been split. She folded up her knife and stuck it back into her pocket before reaching out and pushing the torn shirt off her good shoulder. Stepping closer, she guided the shirt around her back and then eased it down and off her wounded arm. Unexpectedly, her movements were gentle. "Well, it's not as bad as it looks," she said, dropping the shirt on the floor. "You were lucky."

Lucky? Maddie didn't know why she should feel lucky.

As if reading her face, Kali smiled. "You're alive, aren't you?"

The smile surprised her. It was almost friendly.

"Now turn around," Kali commanded, twirling her finger.

Complying, she inhaled quickly as Kali's fingers brushed against her skin of her back and deftly undid her bra strap.

"I'll let you get that off," she said, removing her hands. "I won't have a bra that will fit you, so you might want to wash that out. Hang it near the air vent and it might be dry by tomorrow."

Staring at the shower, Maddie nodded again. "Thank you."

"Yeah, whatever. I'll bring in some bandages for your arm. It's going to hurt like hell, but wash the wound. Don't let it get infected."

She spoke as if she almost cared, but Maddie knew better than to believe her.

"And if you could hurry the fuck up so I could get back to sleep, I'd appreciate it."

"Okay."

Kali walked to the door, but stopped. "I'll try and not scare you again," she said, before leaving the bathroom.

Not sure how to react to that, Maddie decided to just let it go. If she could just do as she was told, then maybe everything would be okay. Reaching for the shower door, she opened it and turned on the water. It was warm straight out of the tap, but she still turned it hotter.

She eased the bra straps from her shoulders before stepping into the shower. The hot water stung her skin, but she huddled in its warmth. For the first time that night, she felt safe and sane. Nothing could hurt her in here, and she felt her chest shaking with heavy sobs.

Crying, she turned around in the water, almost yelping as the water hit her wound. She forced herself to endure it, watching as the water cleaned the blood away. The gash was ugly, but not deep. Someone had applied butterfly bandages to pull the edges closed, and it was one of these that she'd ripped away.

Staring at it, she realized it wasn't just a wound. It was a gunshot wound. She'd been shot. If someone had told her that would happen, she would never have believed them. How had she gotten so far from everything she knew?

"Why are you just standing there?" Kali demanded from the doorway, a first aid kit in her hand. "Hurry up." She set the kit on top of the clothes and left the room.

Once again afraid, Maddie searched for shampoo. There was a large assortment of products lining the shelf. That confused her. Kali didn't seem like the type of person who would care about such things as shampoos and conditioners. All the bottles had foreign names, and without the luxury of time to explore the fragrances, she just picked a bottle at random. She could only use one hand to rub the shampoo into her hair, but even with that limitation, it was easily the best moment of her day.

Letting the shampoo set on her hair, she picked up a bar of soap and lathered it as best as she could in her hand. The first thing she washed was her wound. It stung and she wanted to cry again, but she knew it needed to be done. When she finished, she washed the rest of her body, staring in shock at the brown dirt running into the drain. Mindful of her time, she gave her bra a quick once over before rinsing herself and shutting off the water.

Keeping her shoulder as still as possible, she gave her bra a good wringing out before opening the shower door and reaching for the only towel in the room. It was still damp, and she hesitated, knowing Kali had used it. She didn't know if using it would backfire on her or not, but with no other choice she dried herself as fast as she could before hanging it back up.

The gap in her shoulder was still bleeding, so she tore off a section of toilet paper and pressed it into the wound. Opening the first aid kit, she took out another butterfly bandage and a tube of antibiotic. She removed the toilet paper and wiped the ointment across the whole wound before attaching another butterfly closure to the gap. There was a large bandage in the kit, and peeling it open, she fixed it in place over her whole wound. She closed the first aid kit and set it on the back of the toilet. The air conditioning had switched on and she felt a chill against her skin.

She was surprised that Kali hadn't found some reason to yell at her for being slow, but content that she hadn't, Maddie looked at the assortment of lotions and skin care products that Kali had tucked into a wall mounted shelf. Just like the shampoos, this added to her confusion.

Appraising her choices, she reached for a glass bottle of lotion that had caught her eye. Lifting it, she twisted off the cap and smelled. Roses. Immediately, Maddie was reminded of her grandmother's garden in spring. The scent made her feel safe, and so she poured some into her hand. Using her good arm, she spread it, as best as she could, across her body. As the lotion dried, she picked up a brush and frowned when she saw there was no mirror over the sink. Its absence perplexed her, but definitely not enough to question Kali over it.

When she finished, she picked up the clothes Kali had given her. It had been a small kindness that Maddie didn't want to contemplate. The woman was dangerous and unpredictable, and that was all Maddie needed to know about her.

The shirt Kali had given her was a short sleeve button down type. It was made from a soft linen and as Maddie worked it onto her shoulder, she realized it was also a size too large. The cotton shorts she'd been given were also too big, but cinching a draw string at least brought them up on her hips. It wasn't an ideal combination, but with nothing else to wear, she was at least grateful that she didn't have to either wear her soiled clothes or go naked.

Before finishing, she tried to straighten up as much as possible. Kali may be feeling charitable towards her tonight, but tomorrow everything could change again. Turning off the light, she stepped back into the bedroom. It was totally quiet, and looking around, she was surprised to see Kali fast asleep on the bed.

Careful to not wake her, Maddie stood at the edge and stared down at her. Asleep, Kali's face wasn't harsh or angry. If anything, she looked much younger than Maddie had first thought. Watching her, Maddie slowly realized that this might be her best chance to escape, but then she dismissed the idea. What was she going to do? Swim back to Macapa?

But then her eyes fell on the laptop sitting on the desk. She might not be able to physically escape from the ship, but if she could get an Internet connection, she could email her parents or MIT or anyone. If only someone knew, they'd come looking for her.

Survival. That was what this came down to. She had to do whatever she could to survive.

Resolved, she opened the laptop and powered it up. She could only hope that the ship had a satellite connection like the *Luna Nueva*. Glancing behind her, she made sure that the softly whirring fan hadn't woken Kali. As the Windows logo displayed, Maddie felt her heart plummet when it was followed by a password box. She closed her eyes in defeat. There was no way that she could guess Kali's password, and she didn't even want to risk the repercussions of trying.

Shutting the screen, she turned and leaned back against the desk. The clock said it was almost four thirty in the morning. It would be light soon. Then what? What would morning bring for her?

She stared down at Kali, realizing she could kill her right now. All she had to do was give her a strong blow to her head with the laptop. She could do it. She just knew she could.

But then she remembered what the old man had told her. It had been Kali who saved her and fought her own crew to keep her alive. Despite all of Kali's cruelties, Maddie realized that she might be her only ally on the ship. Killing her could just make things worse.

With that decided, Maddie sighed. What now? Her eyes fell on the pillow and blanket that lay discarded on the floor. Was this where Kali had been sleeping? She looked back at the woman in question. Why would she take the floor when she had every right to take the bed? This was her cabin, as she had proved when she easily tossed the old man out. Why hadn't she done the same to her?

The only way to answer her questions was to ask Kali, and Maddie knew she'd never do that. So, as she stood there, watching Kali sleep, she began to feel tired herself. She yawned. The bed was big enough for them both, but Maddie didn't dare risk something as stupid as that. Which only left the floor. She stared at it with resignation.

Lowering herself down, she stopped to first tug the comforter over Kali's body. The action made her frown, but she quickly rationalized it as simply returning a kindness.

She flipped off the bed side light and lay down on the floor. It was hard, but she adjusted the pillow under her head. Pulling the blanket up to her chin, she became aware that she could hear Kali's breathing. It was slow, even and deep. There was nothing hurried or anxious about it, and it slowly became an anchoring sound for Maddie. Before long, her own breathing had evened out to match Kali's, and she felt herself slipping into sleep.

Someone was shaking her, and Kali struggled to ignore it. She wanted to sleep longer. The world would wait.

"Kali." The shaking started again. "It's almost six thirty. You wanted me to wake you."

Renny. Six. Tomorrow. Last night. Bathroom. The woman.

Kali sat straight up. "Where is she?" Her eyes traveled around the room, looking for anything that might have changed. How had she let herself fall asleep?

"Who?" Renny whispered.

"The woman. Have you seen her?" Kali's mind raced to the possibilities. Had she jumped off the ship? No, she'd be stupid to do that. Could she have found any of the weapons? She dismissed the thought. The guns had all been secured in the gun safe before her watch last night, and only she had the combination.

"She's right here," Renny said, softly. "Sleeping." He pointed to floor beside the bed. "Where did you think she was?"

Peering over the edge of the bed, Kali's body was flooded with relief. That was one problem she didn't need. "How was your watch?" she asked, rubbing at her eyes.

"Quiet." He gestured at the woman. "You untied her."

It was an obvious observation, so Kali ignored it. "Make some coffee," she ordered. "I'll be out in a minute."

He gave her a curt nod before turning for the door.

"Make it strong," she called after him, throwing off the comforter and climbing out of bed.

Covering a yawn, she looked down at the woman in amazement. Twice now, she had proven that she was one hell of a deep sleeper. Last night, after returning to her cabin, she had every intention of booting the woman to the floor and claiming the bed. Yet as she stood there watching her sleep, she changed her mind. She told herself that waking her would only mean more questions, so taking a pillow she'd gone to sleep on the floor.

Ironically, if Kali had known how the night was going to turn out, she could have just saved herself the trouble by following her instinct. At the very least, waking the woman might have spared them both the whole bathroom incident.

As she thought back on it now, Kali became angry at herself for falling asleep. She didn't know this woman, and letting her guard down like that could have proven a fatal mistake. If the situation had been reversed, Kali would have killed her captor.

At her feet, the woman stirred and slowly opened her eyes. For a moment, she looked confused, but then Kali saw awareness rushing back. Her chest, which had been rising in easy sleep, now began to heave with anxiety.

"It's all right," Kali heard herself saying. "Relax."

The woman's eyes snapped to her and Kali felt captured by them. It was the most bizarre feeling, as if she had no will of her own to look away. Although she rationally knew it was only a few seconds, time seemed to stand still. She knew she should say something, but her mind was a total blank. Deciding that she didn't need to prove anything, she turned for the bathroom.

"Wait. Please."

Stopping, Kali stood with her back to the woman. "What?"

She heard a rustle of fabric as the woman got to her feet. "I wanted to thank you for letting me shower last night. And for the change of clothes."

It was innocuous enough and Kali nodded. "You're welcome." She continued towards the bathroom, but apparently the woman wasn't done.

"You were asleep when I came out."

She stopped with her hand on the door jam. "Why didn't you try to leave?"

"And where would I go?"

Turning, she avoided the woman's eyes. "You thought about it?"

"Of course I did," the woman said, matter-of-factly. "I thought about a lot of things."

"Did you think of killing me?" she asked, finally looking at her. She needed to see the woman's face as she answered.

"What?" The woman's eyes contracted quickly, but in that instant, Kali knew it had crossed her mind.

"Killing me might have saved you. Why did you pass up on the opportunity?"

"Might have?" She paused. "I guess I didn't know I should trade your life for mine."

"That's what life's about. You only think about yourself."

The woman stared at her, and Kali felt as if she was seeing right through her. "I didn't kill you because I thought you might be my only friend. Killing you might have made things worse for me."

Kali considered that for a moment. "It was a good decision." She looked at her with a new regard. "What's your name?" The woman's eyes lifted in question. "I'd like to know," she added, sincerely.

"Maddie." She shrugged. "Madeline Cross."

Maddie. It wasn't even close to what Kali had imagined, but now that she'd heard it again, she remembered the man using it in Macapa. It had seemed so innocent to her. It was innocent.

"Kali's not your real name, is it?"

She frowned. "Don't ask me any questions."

"I'm sorry," Maddie said, her voice breaking slightly.

The fear Kali saw on her face angered her. It reminded her of all the reasons the woman was here, in her cabin, and afraid. Afraid of her. Afraid of what was going to happen to her. Afraid that she was going to die. And that was exactly what she deserved. If Kali had left her where she belonged, she'd be dead already.

Dropping her eyes, she saw the ropes she'd cut off the woman last night. They were a tangible cue to the woman's place. She had no rights and deserved no consideration. On the desk next to her was a length of unused rope, and walking towards it, Kali snatched it up. "Give me your hands."

"No. Please." She backed away. "I swear I won't try anything."

Kali surged towards her. "Give me your hands!" The anger was close to the surface. It only needed a nudge to spill over.

"No," Maddie said, thrusting them behind her back. "Please. Not that. Not again. I can't go anywhere. Why that?"

Her defiance was the push she needed. As her vision went red, she swung her hand upwards, ripping the back of it across Maddie's face. With a cry, Maddie dropped to the ground, and Kali stared at her hand in confusion. Why had she done that, but more importantly, why did it feel wrong? Pushing back against the feelings, she reached out and seized Maddie by the hand. It only took a single tug to bring her to her feet. The woman moved like a rag doll.

Kali spun her around and brutally bent her arm behind her back. It would have been so simple to wrench it upwards and pull the joint out from her shoulder. Instead, she reached for Maddie's other hand and quickly looped the rope around both her wrists. Pulling the knot tight, she dropped Maddie's hands and stood back.

"Turn around," she ordered, smiling proudly as Maddie complied.

The smirk fell from her face when she saw that Maddie's cheek was already red and swollen. Blood was dripping from the left side of her nose, and without her hands, Maddie tried, unsuccessfully to inhale it back up.

Before she could stop herself, Kali reached out and touched the blood with her index finger. Staring at it with an unexpected sense of confusion, she smeared it across her skin with her thumb. She'd had blood on her hands before, but this felt different.

"Why don't you just kill me?" Maddie asked.

Kali looked up at her. "Get on the ground," she said, dispassionately.

"Why not just get it over with? Kill me! You're going to do it, so do it now."

Her surrender only seemed to add to the turmoil in Kali's head, and without really thinking, she snaked her foot out and swept Maddie's legs out from under her. It happened quickly, but still slow enough for Kali to see the look of shock on Maddie's face as she fell with a thud.

Part of her wanted to pull back and stop. But she'd come too far to quit now, and dropping to her knees, she reached for the other piece of rope and looped it around Maddie's ankles, pulling tightly.

Even as she did this, she struggled to find some balance between her guilt and her rage. Squeezing her eyes closed, she desperately tried to convince herself that none of this mattered. That this woman was just an object. Something to control and handle. She was nothing else.

"Why?" Maddie asked, in a near whisper. "I haven't done—"

"Shut up." She felt her hands shaking as she tied the knot around Maddie's ankles. Why did she want to just get up and run from here? Run from her?

"Why are you doing this to me? Please, Kali," she said, looking up at her with such innocence.

Kali didn't know if it was the look in her eyes or the use of her name that shattered the last vestige of her control, but possessed with a new fury, she lunged forward, grabbing for Maddie's hair. Her fingers racked across Maddie's scalp as she gathered as much hair as she could hold. When Maddie screamed, she pulled harder. The sound was like a siren, driving her onwards. Oh, how she wanted to hurt her!

Giving into her desire, she shifted her hand from Maddie's hair to her neck. It fit nicely in her palm, and under her fingers she could just feel the bones of her spine. It would be so easy to break it. The muscles weren't strong enough to protect the fragile vertebrae. One quick twist and it would be over.

Under her, Maddie had gone still. Did she sense her death? Was she afraid?

As she dragged out the agony of the wait, she slowly became aware of a familiar scent rising from Maddie's skin. She inhaled. Roses. Maddie smelled of roses. Her hand went slack.

"Where did you—"She stopped, remembering the bottle of lotion in her bathroom.

Even now, she couldn't explain why she'd bought the fragrance. It has been impulsive. A vain attempt to remind her of something good. Except, that memory had never been good, and the scent only reminded her of what she'd lost. She hated roses. More, she hated that this woman was now marked with that memory. Pulling back, she got to her feet. Her thoughts were disjointed and jumbled.

The woman was sobbing now, her body shaking with almost silent cries. Blinking at her, she tried to make herself feel nothing, but almost painfully, she acknowledged that she did care. She had caused this woman's pain, just as she'd caused the pain of so many others.

Turning, she fled into the bathroom and shut the door. In her head she tried to focus on simple tasks, and it was almost robotic the way she washed her face and brushed her teeth.

When she reached for her towel, the smell of roses came to her again and she dropped the towel as if burnt. Of all the things she had to use, why had the woman picked that one bottle? Reaching for the lotion, she tossed it in the trash. She had been weak when she bought it. There was no way Sarah was ever going to live again. Why couldn't she let her memory die, too?

It never took much for Kali to recall the events. It had been four days before her eighteenth birthday. Four days until she was emancipated from the Atlanta foster system.

Sarah had been exactly one month younger. It was for very different reason that they'd both ended up in the same foster home. When Sarah was delivered to the overcrowded home at the age of twelve, Kali was already a two year veteran of the system.

The girl was just a broken shell when Kali first met her. It wasn't until later that Kali learned that Sarah's father had been selling her to his friends for drugs, alcohol and sometimes money. For three years, he pimped his daughter until he overdosed on bad heroine, leaving Sarah an orphan.

Partly because of their age and partly because of their histories, Kali and Sarah had gravitated to each other. In time, they became like family.

Life in the foster home wasn't ideal. It didn't take Kali long to realize their foster mom only took in kids for the money, and if there was anything she or Sarah needed, it was up to her to get it.

Kali liked to pretend that it had been necessity that had driven her into crime, but the truth was she liked it. It was a lot easier to boost the things they needed instead of trying to earn the money or learning to do without.

She was just fourteen when she was arrested for the first time. During her time in juvenile hall, Sarah had been her only visitor. That was the first time they'd pledged to take care of each other forever. It was a bond that Kali clung to with all her strength.

Her third arrest at almost seventeen earned her a six month sentence in the adult lockup. Again, it was always Sarah who came to her. She was her foundation and the only thing Kali could believe in.

It was during her time in lockup that Kali began to formulate a plan to take Sarah away. In a matter of months, they would be free to go anywhere. All they needed was enough money to give them a fresh start. Kali knew that Sarah was smart. She could do anything, and Kali just wanted to be there to help.

She'd been so stupid. So naïve.

The irony was that prison, instead of rehabilitating Kali, had just introduced her to a whole new group of contacts. There was a job waiting for her right after her release. She never told Sarah that she was doing drug runs, but it wouldn't have mattered anyway. It was the fastest way to make the money they needed.

Four nights before her eighteenth birthday she was making her final run. She'd saved enough money to get them to California. It was the land of beauty and opportunity, and they had it all planned out. Kali would get a job and Sarah would take some acting classes. Kali had no doubt that Sarah would be discovered. The plan was so simple.

Her last run was like her others. All she had to do was drop off a package and collect the money. Since it was an apartment that Kali had visited before, she never considered it to be dangerous, so she took Sarah with her. They were going to celebrate afterwards.

It had all happened so quickly. Everything had been normal as they climbed the steps to the second floor. Standing on Sarah's right, she knocked on the door. To this day, Kali never knew why the man inside started shooting.

The first bullet hit Sarah in the middle of the chest, the second her neck. Kali dropped to the ground, bringing her face to face with Sarah's lifeless eyes. She was gone that fast.

As much as she wanted to stay with her, Kali's survival instinct kicked in and she ran. Without knowing how, she made her way home.

Sarah's blood was splattered all over her, and reluctantly, she washed and changed. Then, after packing a small backpack, she grabbed her money and went out the back door. The night air had been fragrant with the scent of roses, and for a moment, Kali just stood there. The backyard of their foster home was nothing but dirt and weeds, but Sarah had discovered a small rose bush near the water spigot. Over the years, she'd nursed the bush into full bloom. As she passed by, Kali broke off a single flower. The rose died and started falling apart before she reached the port of New Orleans, but the scent Kali carried with her always. It was Sarah. It was always Sarah.

Until now. Now, it would also remind her of Madeline Cross. In that moment, Kali knew why she'd never be able to kill her.

Chapter Eight

Pasqual smiled as Jack paced back and forth in the small galley. It had taken very little effort to incense him against Kali, almost as if he had just been waiting for a reason to turn. The man was an idiot, but worse he was disloyal. While it suited Pasqual's motives at the moment, he had no intention of letting Jack live long enough to find a reason to betray him.

"Where the hell is she?" Jack growled, stopping and staring down the stairs.

"She'll be up in a minute," Renny said, his voice growing weary.

It was the Frenchman who worried Pasqual the most. He was desperate to return to his family in Macapa, and that emotional response was blinding him to reason. However, he knew it was to that emotional side he needed to aim his appeal. That was where poor Amado came into play.

"Gentlemen," he said, twisting his coffee cup between his hands. "I thought you promised to take my nephew to a hospital this morning."

"We will," Renny answered. "As soon as Kali comes out."

Kali's absence intrigued him. Surely the woman sensed the precariousness of her position? "It's nearly seven," he said, stating the obvious. "What could she be doing for so long?"

Jack, as he expected, was the first to jump to conclusions. "It's that bitch, isn't it?" he demanded, pacing again. "Well, if she's that sweet a fuck, I want some, too."

"Shut up, Jack."

It was almost amusing to think of the innocent Dr. Cross being used in such a way. Regardless of whatever pity he may feel towards her, he had no use for weakness. People, like Dr. Cross, who were unable or unwilling to save themselves usually got what they deserved. But if what Jack assumed was true, then he applauded the woman. Even though he had no way of knowing if the enigmatic Kali would be open to such an advance, it was just such an angle that he'd suggested to Dr. Cross yesterday. Sex was a powerful weapon.

Even as he considered this, Pasqual wished that he'd been able to learn more of Kali before meeting her, but the woman's history was patchy at best. She existed at times and then just vanished, only to reappear with another criminal cartel in another part of the world. His clearest picture of the woman was from her childhood, when she'd called herself Dana Sanders. It was ordinary, even by American standards. She'd been wise to change it. No one would follow or fear a woman named Dana Sanders.

Her childhood was average. A broken home. A broken life. It was often these types of lost souls who found their way down the darker path. Pasqual knew a dozen more with just such common beginnings.

However, it was what Kali did after leaving the United States that made her so interesting to Pasqual. A woman with her looks might have ended up being trapped in a life of prostitution and drugs, but Pasqual couldn't find one time when Kali earned her living on her back or pushing product. He had, however, uncovered a few times when she'd used her body to gain advantages, but never for money.

Money, he'd been surprised to learn, was often not a primary motivator for Kali. That wasn't to say that she didn't command a hefty fee, but some of her jobs appeared to be almost for pleasure.

Yet, what pleased her, Pasqual had been unable to determine. There were no known relationships with anyone, and for all intents she appeared more asexual than anything. He admitted to hoping her heroic rescue of Dr. Cross was somehow sexually motivated. It would have made her so much easier to manipulate.

If only he'd had more time to dig into her past, he thought he might have been able to uncover exactly what drove someone like Kali. He suspected it might be as simple as the work. She was a professional with a reputation for efficiency and honesty, yet she was known to be ruthless and unyielding to any who crossed her. It all painted a picture of a woman who still valued honor despite the world she inhabited.

It was a simple deduction to realize that his brother would use Kali to assassinate him. Duarte rarely spoke of anyone with as much pride as he did Kali. But Pasqual also knew that Kali was doomed from the start. His brother, despite his love and admiration, would have killed Kali as soon as she returned to Macapa. That was just his way. Duarte never fully trusted anyone.

What he found disappointing was that Kali hadn't grasped that fact, of if she had, still proceeded with her attack. It made him wonder if Kali had planned on double-crossing Duarte all along. It might even explain why he was still alive.

Strangely, he'd felt the finger of Death upon him as soon as Kali began her attack. He'd never experienced such an emotion before. It was almost insignificant that Amado had gotten him off the barge. He had just known that Death had chosen him. Yet, for whatever reason, Kali hadn't killed him, and now his destiny was unwritten.

He supposed the same could be said for Dr. Cross. Her fate had been sealed, her life decided. Yet, it was once again Kali's hand that had altered her destiny.

Pasqual suspected that on some deeper level Kali might comprehend what she had done to change the fabric of fate. It may also explain why she was so hesitant to act against him or Dr. Cross now.

Kali's reluctance to act was completely uncharacteristic of what he knew of the woman, but Pasqual could only hope her uncertainty continued. It had opened the door to possibilities, and by God, he was going to seize that opportunity — even if Dr. Cross didn't.

"What are you smiling at?" the Frenchman said, eyeing him suspiciously.

He brought himself back to the conversation. "I was just thinking about what Kali might be doing to the woman."

Jack's eyes glazed over at his comment, and Pasqual didn't need to work hard to deduce what was going through his dimwitted mind. He despised that he was dependent on this cretin. Looking to Renny, he met his eyes as if to convey his disgust for Jack's sexual appetites. The Frenchman gave a quick, but telling, nod.

"Since your captain is otherwise occupied, would one of you be kind enough to start our journey to the hospital? I fear my nephew is getting worse."

Truth be told, he was worried for Amado. The boy was only a pawn, but he still didn't want to see him die. Over the years, he had invested in his relationship with Amado. As Duarte's second son, he was never shown the same attention or love from his father that his older brother had received. It was a gap that Pasqual was only too willing to fill. At the time, he hadn't realized that he would call on Amado's loyalty so soon in his young life, but it was a debt Pasqual would attempt to repay.

Although Duarte's decision to send his son on this job had ultimately saved Pasqual's life, he still thought it a fatal mistake. As usual, his brother had been overconfident in his plans, never stopping to think what Amado's presence would mean should the job fail.

It was that message Pasqual was anxious to have delivered. He smiled to himself as he tried to imagine Duarte's face when he learned of his precious Kali's catastrophe. It would be a triple strike. His life. Amado's life. And the cocaine.

The part he found most amusing was that he'd been carrying no cocaine on his barge. He'd known all along that he couldn't fool Duarte forever, and he had spent the past few months setting up things to his advantage.

As soon as he had learned that Duarte was onto him, he had attempted to barter a reconciliation – just as his brother would expect. Although he rarely traveled by river, he knew his presence on the barge would not only lend credibility to his request, but also give Duarte the perfect opportunity to strike.

Ever since childhood, Duarte had been untrustworthy. It was one of the reasons that Pasqual had pawned his younger brother off on associates in Brazil instead of taking him into his own organization. At the time, he had never expected Duarte to rise so high, but always the pragmatist, he had found his brother's position useful at times.

But of late, Duarte's greed and hunger for power had made him more of a liability. Even if Duarte hadn't forced his hand, Pasqual had been prepared to end his brother's reign. Business was about balance, not domination, and Duarte had never learned that lesson.

It made him sad that his ties to his brother had to end so badly. Perhaps it was his fault, and he imagined he would lament the loss for many year. However, life wasn't about regrets. It was about possibilities, and right now, all he had to do was manipulate these two buffoons to do as he wanted.

"Gentlemen, please help me. If Amado dies, so do your options. His only hope, and yours by extension, is to get him to the hospital at Porto Franco."

"Shut up, old man," Renny said, tossing his coffee into the sink. "We'll leave when Kali says we'll leave."

"I say we go now," Jack said, with more authority than Pasqual knew he felt.

"And I say we wait."

Getting out of his seat, Pasqual crossed to where Amado was lying on the couch. His burns seemed worse today. The skin had begun to blister and ooze, and there was a heavy sheen of perspiration on his forehead. Reaching out to touch him, Pasqual pulled his hand back in alarm. "He's burning up."

"Infection," Renny said, refilling his coffee.

Pasqual touched Amado's forehead again, feeling a sudden and unexpected sympathy. "Help me."

"How, old man? We don't have any antibiotics or whatever it is he needs."

"Then help me get him somewhere that does," he said, over his shoulder. "Do you know what your lives will be worth if this boy dies? There will be no homecoming."

The Frenchman's eyes jumped at that, but Jack only stared blankly. Unlike Renny, he had no desire to return to Macapa. Jack wanted something more intangible.

"Kali has the boat keys." Renny held his hand out. "There's nothing I can do."

"Get them," Jack said, turning on Renny. "If she won't come out of her fucking cabin, then I know where she stands. Against me."

Pasqual smiled. Jack wanted power.

"She agreed to everything," Renny countered, his voice rising. "She's going to take Amado to a hospital. She'll email the cartel. There's no need to get drastic."

Looking back at his nephew, Pasqual let them argue. He knew what to offer Jack, and he had no doubt that the little Frenchman would either follow or die.

"Give her a few more minutes," Renny was pleading. "I'm going to clean up. If she's not out by the time I'm done, I'll get her myself."

"Fifteen minutes."

"Jack," Pasqual said, softly. "Would you bring me some water?"

He listened as the Frenchman descended to the cabin level. It was exactly the opening he needed.

"Here." Jack held a glass of water.

"And a spoon. Please."

"He looks bad," Jack said, returning with the spoon.

Dipping the spoon in the water, he held it to Amado's lips. "Yes. If he dies, my brother will not rest until he has revenged himself on all involved." He tipped more water into Amado's mouth. "You're smarter than your friend, Jack. I know you understand what that means."

"He's not my friend."

Pasqual hid his smile. "Will you help me?"

"We said we'd take him to Porto Franco. What more do you want?"

He stopped with the spoon resting on Amado's lips. "My freedom, Jack. You can give that to me, and in return I can give you everything you ever wanted."

Jack laughed. "And what do I want?"

No, no, no. It wasn't that simple. Jack had to feel it. He had to be able to taste it. Then, Jack would belong to him. "Help me and name your price."

"Just like that?"

There was no need to answer him. He'd made his offer. All Jack had to do was accept it, so Pasqual kept tipping water into Amado's mouth, relieved when he finally swallowed.

"If you betray me, old man, I'll kill you."

"I'm a man of my word," Pasqual said, looking up at him. "I expect you to be the same."

"Do you have a plan?"

"Yes. Firstly, we need to get my nephew to that hospital."

"Why?"

Pasqual stared at him. Did he not understand? Not willing to spell it out, he turned back to Amado. "Make that happen, Jack. I'm counting on you."

"Renny!" Jack called out, turning for the stairs.

As Pasqual ladled more water into Amado's mouth, he smiled. It had begun.

Opening the bathroom door, Kali stood on the threshold, looking down at the woman. *Maddie*, she reminded herself. *Her name is Maddie.* Why it was suddenly important was beyond her comprehension. Her eyes shifted to her cabin door. She should be out with her crew. Every minute she spent away from them was putting her a minute closer to losing her ship. She knew it, and yet she couldn't leave things like they were.

Crossing the floor, she stopped near Maddie's feet, suddenly unsure of what to say. At the very least, she could undo some of what she'd done. So taking out her pocket knife, she leaned over to cut the ropes off Maddie's feet. Then, reaching up, she did the same to her hands.

Almost immediately, Maddie pulled herself into a fetal position with her knees tight to her chest and her arms protecting her head. At seeing the display of fear, Kali felt an unexpected and overwhelming sense of remorse over how vicious she had been to this woman.

With a sigh, she lowered herself onto the edge of the bed. She knew there was only one thing to say, but the words were almost foreign to her. Rolling them around in her mouth, she leaned forward and looked down at Maddie.

"I'm sorry," she said, in a rush. When Maddie didn't even move, Kali frowned. "Didn't you hear me? I said I'm sorry. I won't hurt you again."

A muted sob escaped Maddie, but Kali didn't know if it was from relief or fear. Reaching down, she laid a hand on Maddie's hip. "Look at me."

She was about to repeat herself when Maddie finally moved. As she lifted her head, Kali could see the red and swollen imprints of her knuckles and fingers on the side of her face, less than an inch from her eye.

Angry with herself, Kali looked away. She hadn't wanted to hit Maddie. All the woman had to do was follow a simple command. Dogs could do it, why couldn't this woman?

Before she could do something else she regretted, Kali stood and walked into the bathroom. Something needed to change. She needed to change.

Grabbing a washcloth, she ran it under the faucet and returned to the bedroom. At Maddie's side, she lowered herself to one knee and reached out to touch her shoulder.

Immediately, Maddie tightened her fetal position.

The gesture caused a mixture of emotions in Kali, but the one she understood was anger and she leaned back. "Goddam it," she said roughly. "I'm trying to help you."

Maddie only held her position.

Staring at her, Kali struggled for a different approach. Giving up, she shrugged. "I don't know what to do," she said, leaning forward and laying the washcloth near Maddie's arm. "I'm going to leave this for you. Put it on your face. It will help with the swelling and pain."

Slowly getting to her feet, she turned for the cabin door just as it began to shake with an angry pounding. "Kali!" It was Renny. "You need to get up here. Now!"

It wasn't an order he was shouting to her, it was a warning. She'd just run out of time.

For some reason, she felt the urge to look behind her, and doing so, she found Maddie staring at her from the floor. As soon as Kali turned towards her, Maddie dropped her eyes.

Renny pounded harder. "Kali!"

"Look at me," she said, trying to keep her voice gentle. "Please."

It took a second, but Maddie's eyes slowly turned up to her. They were so afraid that Kali almost gave up. How could she undo what she'd put there?

"I'm sorry for what I did to you." She gestured weakly at the door. "There are things I have to go do. I won't restrain you if you promise that you'll stay in here. Don't try to leave without me. Give me your promise."

"Kali! Answer me." Renny was sounding desperate, but Kali waited.

Nodding her head, Maddie averted her eyes. "I promise."

As she turned for the door, Kali wondered if Maddie had responded only out of fear. If so, that wasn't what she wanted. Or was it? Reaching for the door, she had half a mind to turn back and tell Maddie she was safe now, but was that really true? How could she make such a vow when her own life was in danger?

Putting Maddie out of her mind, as she knew she had to, Kali pulled open the door. She wasn't surprised to see Jack standing behind Renny. "What?" she demanded, using her body to block the door.

"It's time we started for Porto Franco. Amado is getting worse."

"I'll be out in a minute."

"You said that a half hour ago," Renny said, his eyes wide with warning.

"Unless you're having fun in here," Jack taunted, as he tried to see past her. "In that case, invite me in and I'll enjoy the bitch, too."

The comment made her body tense, but she relaxed it with effort. "I'll be out in a minute," she repeated, evenly. "Get the ship ready, and secure the old man."

"What about the cartel?" Jack demanded. "Renny said you agreed to email them. Is that right?"

"What the fuck do you care?"

"I want to go home," Jack said, with a devious smile. "Just like Renny."

"You did promise, Kali."

"Do you want me to do it now or after we take Amado to the hospital? I can't do both at the same times, so make up your mind."

"Oh, let's do it now."

"Is that what you want, Renny?" Kali asked.

He thought for a second. "Yes. It gives us time to decide."

She shrugged as if it meant nothing. "Whatever. Go get the ship ready and I'll be up as soon as I'm done with the email." She tried to close the door, but Jack threw his hand out to stop her.

"We want to watch you send it." His eyes glowed at what he thought was a cunning move.

She met and held his gaze without challenge. "Fine with me, but it will take ten minutes to boot everything up and connect to the satellites. That gives you plenty of time to secure the old man and prepare the ship."

"Renny can do that. I want to watch."

"Not a chance, Jack."

"That's fine. It's your thing and we understand," Renny said, quickly. He sounded so naïve. So harmless.

"Then go do what I told you." This time she managed to shut the door without interference.

Turning around, she exhaled a tense breath. Everything was crashing down around her. She felt it falling, piece by agonizing piece. Her hand tightened into a fist, and standing there, she let all the options run through her head.

Jack was growing bolder. He was no doubt being encouraged by Pasqual, but he was too stupid to realize the old man had his own agenda. Maybe she should just kill Pasqual and remove that temptation. Or kill Jack. Or kill them all.

Except to do that, she'd have to open her gun safe, and that wasn't something she wanted to risk right then. She'd already planned on dumping her guns into the river as soon as she could get Jack and Renny off the ship. What she didn't have couldn't be used against her; which meant she needed to cooperate with everyone until Porto Franco.

It was obvious that she wasn't the only one using the guise of getting poor suffering Amado to the hospital to buy time. She only wished she could figure out what the old man was planning.

As she stood there, she slowly became aware of eyes on her, and shifting her gaze, she found Maddie staring at her. *Blue*, she noticed almost randomly. *Her eyes are blue.* The detail distracted her, and she forced herself to look away. Needing to focus, she walked to her desk and opened her laptop, surprised when her login screen appeared. It only took her a second to connect the screen with the woman.

"Did you do this?" she demanded, her temper surfacing quicker than she could cool it. When Maddie didn't respond, Kali lunged forward and grabbed her arm. "Don't fucking ignore me! Tell me if you tried to guess my password?" She shook her.

There was no way for the woman to know, but her laptop was set to lock up after two incorrect password attempts. If a third attempt failed, the hard drive automatically began a deep level re-formatting, wiping out any stored information.

"Answer me!" she demanded tightening her grip.

"No," Maddie said, her face turned away. "I didn't type in anything."

"So you expect me to believe that you saw the login screen and just shut the lid?" She yanked on her arm. "And look at me when I'm speaking to you."

Maddie's head jerked up, and for the first time, her blue eyes were angry. "Believe whatever the hell you want," she said, pulling her arm away. "I answered your question. If you don't believe me, then that's your problem."

The sudden audacity stunned Kali, and staring blankly at the woman, she couldn't think of a single thing to say. It was obvious from the way Maddie backed away from her, that she expected the worse, but strangely, Kali didn't want to hurt her anymore.

"If you lied to me," she said, turning back to her computer, leaving the rest of her threat unspoken. She carefully typed in her password and hit enter. The screen went black and her desktop appeared.

"I don't lie," Maddie said, softly. "Even to someone like you."

The slight might have hurt, but Kali's concentration was too focused on the screen. "I'll remember that," she said, vaguely, as she typed in another password to access her satellite connection.

Her mind was turning over how to best phrase an email to Duarte. The wording had to be perfect. It had to satisfy her crew that she sincerely wanted to return to Macapa, but still be vague enough to keep her options open. Most of all, she had to conceal her location. She had no doubt that Duarte would come after her with everything he had, but to do that, he needed a place to start.

"May I use the bathroom?" Maddie asked.

Absorbed in her thoughts, she waved her hand in dismissal. As she accessed her email program, it occurred to her that sending an email might leave her open to a message trace. From what she knew of Duarte's organization, they weren't exactly on the cutting edge of technology, so it didn't seem likely that he would try to piggyback his email with a tracer, but she couldn't take that risk.

She heard the bathroom door close, but didn't think anything about it as she typed in another password to access an anonymous proxy server. Even with a satellite connection, it was possible to trace her IP Address to a general location using a WGS84 geodetic datum. The proxy server would bounce her email through several points, making it much harder to follow.

Once that was done, she accessed the mail scheduler. She knew that contacting Duarte at this point was a mistake that could come back to haunt her.

Yet, if she were to lose her ship to Pasqual and Jack, notifying Duarte would work to her benefit. It would give him a starting point in his search, and with luck, neither Jack nor Pasqual would survive Duarte's vengeance.

Since she had no idea what was going to happen over the next few hours, she decided that her best option was to delay the sending of her email. Two hours should be enough of a window for whatever was going to happen to happen. If she managed to keep control of her ship, she'd cancel the transmission. But, if, by chance, she failed, Duarte would be notified.

As she set the scheduler, there was an insistent knock on her door announcing Jack and Renny's return. Kali didn't bother responding.

"So?" she demanded, as they surged into her cabin. "Is everything done?"

"Yes, but we've secured the old man in the salon," Renny explained, stopping halfway between her and the door. "He wanted to stay with Amado."

"Of course he did."

"He's concerned about his nephew."

Kali just nodded. "How is the boy?"

"Feverish. His burns are worse than I thought, and he's probably got an infection."

"But we're taking him to the hospital," Jack said, snidely. "He'll be fine." He stepped up behind her and leaned in. "Where's the email?"

"Back up," Kali growled, barely resisting the urge to slam her elbow into his chest. "I'm writing it now."

He took a small step away from her, but like hot breath on the back of her neck, she still felt his presence. This may be a fight for her life, but that didn't stop her from being annoyed that he thought he could bully her so easily. Replacing her fingers on the keyboard, she began what turned out to be a very short email:

Papa,
My brother is badly injured. We are seeking treatment before returning. Since Uncle's boat was sunk in a collision with another, he is returning with us. Everything was lost. Advise on your wishes.
Tu Hija

"That's it?" Jack asked, in disbelief.

"What else do you want me to say?"

"I don't know."

Kali gritted her teeth. "It says everything we need."

"Did you ask if we can come back to Macapa?" Renny asked, moving closer.

"I said we were coming back."

"Are we?"

"If that's what you both want," she said, turning to look at Renny first. "I thought about it, and you're right. With the old man, Amado and the woman, we do stand a chance of convincing Duarte it wasn't our fault."

"That is good news, Kali!" Renny smiled. "So are we still taking Amado to the hospital in Porto Franco or starting for home immediately?"

"Yes, we're going to Porto Franco," Jack said, with an air of importance. "We'll get him fixed up before leaving for Macapa."

That was where he would make his move. Her eyes slipped to Renny, not sure where he would side. She hoped it would be with her, but she couldn't count on it. "That's right," Kali said, throwing her weight into the mix. "And when Duarte responds, we'll know where we stand."

"I've decided that the woman serves no purpose," Jack said, meeting her eyes. "I want her dead." He smiled. "To prove your loyalty to us."

"My *what*?"

"Kill her, Kali. Prove that you're still that cold bitch we know so well."

"I've got nothing to prove to you."

"Come on," he goaded her on. "You love killing. Think of how much you enjoyed killing Paco, and he was part of your crew. This cunt is nothing." He looked around the room in question. "Where is she anyway?"

Kali reached out and grabbed his shirt. "If you want her," she said, pulling him to within an inch of her face, "you'll have to get through me first. And we both know you're not man enough to do that."

"Wait," Renny said, trying to pull Jack back. "This is madness."

"Get off me," Jack said, struggling in Renny's hold.

"No. We don't have to do it this way, Jack. We're getting what we want. There is no reason to kill the woman now."

"There's no reason to keep her alive."

"I want her alive," Kali growled, taking a step towards him. "That's reason enough."

"What you want no longer matters."

"It's all that matters."

"You really have lost it, you dumb bitch."

"That's it," she said, lunging for him. "You're dead."

"Stop!" Renny yelled, pushing himself between them. "That's enough."

"Get out of my way, Renny!" she said, shoving him aside.

"No!" he yelled, deftly pulling a knife from his waist band. "We have an agreement, and if either of you fuck up my chances of going home, I'll kill you." The knife was turned on her. "You send that email." The blade shifted to Jack. "And you get out of here. We're leaving for Porto Franco immediately."

Both she and Jack were silent for a moment, but she was the first to nod her agreement. "Fine," she said, digging in her pocket for the boat keys and tossing them at Renny. "Go power up the engines. I'll get the coordinates for Porto Franco into the GPS and be up shortly. Until then, take us north off the Xingu and then east, north east." She looked to Jack. "Get the fuck out of my sight."

He glowered at her, but then pointed to the laptop. "Let us see you send the email first."

Shrugging, Kali turned and clicked the send button. A status bar appeared on the screen as the message was scanned. Neither of them even noticed that the email was now sitting in her outbox just waiting.

"Satisfied?" she asked, looking back at them. "Now get out of my cabin."

Jack slammed the door on his way out, and Kali leaned back against the desk. The exchange had left her feeling exhausted yet on edge. If she thought she could get them first, she'd open her gun safe and kill both Jack and Renny just to be done with it. How dare they put demands on her!

As all this was going through her head, the bathroom door opened and Maddie stepped cautiously into the room. "Why?" she asked.

Wearily, Kali dropped her head forward. "Why what?"

"I don't understand you."

"There's nothing to understand." Standing, she turned shut the cover on her laptop.

The floor under her feet rumbled with the ignition of the twin diesel engines. She stared down at it, dreading the next few hours. It was hell not knowing what to expect.

"I heard what you said to that man. You were going to protect me, and after all you've done to me, I don't understand why?"

"Just accept it. The why doesn't matter."

"It matters to me."

Not responding, Kali continued to stare at the floor. The idling engines were loud, but strangely, Kali thought she could hear the sound of Maddie's breathing over the noise. It was ridiculous, but she could. She also knew without looking that the woman had gotten closer. It was as if she could just feel it.

"I'm scared," Maddie said, her voice quivering slightly. "I've never been so afraid in my life. I'm afraid of you. Afraid of what's going to happen to me. And I'm terrified that I think dying might be better than living another hour like this. Better than living one more hour with you."

Looking up at her, Kali tried to feel nothing for her words. There was a pressing urge to apologize again, but she refused to do that. Staring into her blue eyes, Kali was surprised when they grew dark and angry.

"I hate you," Maddie continued, her voice deeper. "I hate what you've done to me. I hate that I'm so afraid of you that I actually considered killing you. Jesus Christ! I almost took that precious laptop of yours and bashed your head in!" She laughed shrilly. "What have you done to me?"

"You've survived."

"For how long?" Maddie demanded, with rising anger. "How much longer am I supposed to endure torture and beatings? How much longer will you protect me just to abuse me when I displease or challenge you? It would be better if you just killed me and got it over with!"

Shaking her head, Kali started to turn away. "I don't have time for—"

Before she could complete her sentence, she felt a blow on her chin. Her head snapped backwards and her jaw erupted in a pain that radiated up the side of her head. She thought she might have even cried out, but wasn't sure.

Realizing what had happened, she looked back at Maddie just as she was swinging again. Before she could connect, Kali's instincts took over, and she shifted away from the approaching fist, grabbing Maddie's wrist as it passed by her face.

"Stop," she yelled, making the mistake of looking into the woman's blazing eyes. Captured by what she saw, Kali was totally unaware of the fact that Maddie had swung her other arm up until she felt it slam into her ear "Fuck!"

The second blow sparked her anger, and she almost lashed back at Maddie. Instead of hitting her, Kali reached out and grabbed Maddie's other arm, holding them down and away from her. It should have been enough to let the woman know she was beat, but Maddie continued to thrash wildly.

The movements put Kali at risk of losing her hold, so she stepped closer, bringing her body in contact with Maddie's, and pinning the woman's arms behind her back. This still did not diminish Maddie's fight, and she used her body to push back against Kali, nearly toppling them to the floor. It was only Kali's height and strength that kept them both on their feet.

It was when Maddie tried to lift her knee into Kali's groin that Kali lost control of her temper. Spinning Maddie around so they were both facing the same direction, she yanked Maddie roughly back against her body and immoblized her with one arm. She wrapped her other arm around Maddie's neck.

"Stop it," she hissed in her ear as she applied pressure to her throat. "Stop it or you'll force me to kill you. I'm only warning you because a crushed windpipe is not a quick or painless way to die."

"Do it!" Maddie yelled. "Kill me! Get it over with!" She pushed her throat against Kali's arm.

Willing to comply, Kali closed her eyes and increased the pressure. It only took a moment to feel Maddie gagging against her arm. It would have been so easy, given her height and the angle of Maddie's body, to yank her backwards, crushing her trachea and fracturing her spine. Yet even as this thought ran through her mind, Kali felt her arm relaxing slightly, and she opened her eyes.

"I don't think you really want to die," she said, her lips nearly touching Maddie's ear. "I think you're scared and I've given you every reason to be. But death is not the way out. It's a coward's choice, Maddie, and I don't think you're a coward. Now, if you understand this, then stop fighting me."

In her arms, Maddie held her body rigid, but then relaxed with a sigh. Kali immediately removed her arm from around Maddie's throat, but didn't completely release her hold on her body. She couldn't until she was certain things were finished.

As the situation became calmer, Kali was once again awashed in the scent of roses. Rationally, she knew it wasn't Sarah, but she wanted it to be. For one short moment, she wished she could be the person Sarah had once believed her to be – instead of the person she'd become.

Outside, she heard the bow anchor churning its way up from the bottom of the river. Soon it would clunk into place.

"Please let me go," Maddie said, her voice invading Kali's head. "I'm done fighting."

Kali dropped her arms, and Maddie turned to face her, but neither of them raised their eyes to the other. Under her feet she felt the engines revving up too quickly, but before she could say anything the screws kicked into gear with a jerk. Used to such things, Kali shifted her footing to keep herself upright, but Maddie wasn't prepared for the motion and she fell forward.

Unconsciously she reached out to steady Maddie, her hands slipping around her waist. It was all accidental, but that didn't stop Kali from feeling a jolt as Maddie's eyes finally met her own. It was like nothing she'd ever felt before, and shocked, she dropped her hands and pulled away.

"I'm sorry," she said, as the ship picked up more speed.

"You say that a lot," Maddie commented, her tone flat.

"Only to you, it seems." Her mind turned to the GPS coordinates she needed to get up to Renny.

"And just what are you apologizing for exactly?"

There was no easy answer for that, so Kali lifted a hand to her throbbing ear. "You know, no one has hit me in a long time," she said, changing the subject. "The last person who did is dead."

"Then why didn't you kill me? I wanted you to kill me."

Kali gave her a sour smile. "Sorry, but suicide by proxy isn't my style."

"I just want this to all be over," Maddie said, looking up and holding Kali's eyes. It was like a vice, squeezing something from Kali she wasn't sure she wanted to give.

"I didn't mean for you to become a part of this."

"No," Maddie said, with a small shake of her head. "I was meant to die yesterday. On your order."

Kali shrugged. "You'd be wise to learn how to live in the moment."

"Why bother? All my moments belong to you now, don't they?" Maddie asked, her eyes becoming sad.

Again, Kali shrugged. There was no point in trying to deny it.

"How long will you keep me before you do get angry enough to kill me? I know you're capable of it. I even know you thought about breaking my neck. I could feel it."

While that part intrigued Kali, she didn't have time to ask for more. "Bringing you into this situation wasn't my plan," she said, staring at the door. "But I can't change it now."

"No, I supposed you can't."

"Then all I can tell you is that I won't hurt you again." She met Maddie's eyes. "You have my word that, if I can, I'll protect you."

Maddie's blue eyes narrowed suspiciously. "And why would I believe you?"

"Because I said so."

"And why would you do that?"

Kali shook her head. "I have no idea."

On her desk, the intercom shrilled and Kali moved towards it. Even before lifting it, she knew it would be Renny reminding her that he needed the GPS coordinates. It was his way of telling her that her continued absence had consequences. With a sigh, she replaced the phone. "I have to go."

She started for the door, hoping to get away from Maddie without saying anymore, but she was stopped by her touch on her arm. "Wait," Maddie said, softly, and despite her resolve, Kali looked up at her. "I do believe you."

Not sure why, Kali felt a sense of relief. It was as if one thing had finally gone right.

"What can I do to help?" Maddie asked, and Kali frowned, not sure what to say. "I know things aren't going well, so if I can help, ask me."

"There's nothing you can do but stay in this cabin. I'll either keep control or we'll both be in trouble."

"Meaning we could die?"

"It's a guarantee for me," Kali said, taking a breath. "But you should demand to see Pasqual. He'll be in charge, and I think he might be sympathetic to you."

"And what if you do succeed?"

"Porto Franco isn't a large village, but you'll be safe," Kali said, quickly. "There's a convent there. The nuns will help you contact the American consulate, and I'll give you enough money to get home."

"You're just going to leave me there?"

"What more can I do?"

Maddie looked like she was going to say something, but then she shook her head. Satisfied, Kali turned for the door.

"Wait," Maddie said, as she reached for the knob. "You just want me to stay in here?"

"It's the safest place for you," Kali said, over her shoulder. "Remember to demand to see Pasqual if I don't come back for you."

"But—"

Kali pulled open the door. "No buts. Just stay," she said, stepping into the hall and closing the door before she could change her mind.

Not stopping to think about what had happened in her cabin, Kali went immediately to the navigation room and set coordinates for Porto Franco. All Renny had to do now was follow the waypoint trail for the next thirty minutes.

Vaulting up the stairs to the main deck, Kali found Jack and the old man deep in conversation. As soon as they saw her, Jack stood and walked towards the galley. The old man smiled sweetly.

"Good morning, Kali," he said, tugging on his bound hands. "Am I really such a threat?"

"Is there any coffee?" she demanded, ignoring Pasqual and focusing only on Jack. He was like a coiled snake; forcing her to keep her eyes on him lest he strike before she could move.

Grabbing a cup, he poured the last of the coffee into it. "Where's the girl? She should be secured out here." He thrust the cup at her.

Kali accepted it, staring at the dark liquid as she tried to discern what purpose having Maddie out here might serve Pasqual. They had only spent a short time together, but had it been long enough for him to infect her with his venom? Had Maddie been working against her all along? Was Maddie really a threat after she'd just decided to release her?

Across the room, Pasqual laughed. "How serious you look, my dear. Don't hurt yourself trying to figure it all out."

"What's to figure out?" she asked, sipping her coffee. "We're just taking Amado to the hospital for treatment, right? Nothing more."

"Yes. Nothing more." He looked down at Amado. "The poor boy is quite ill."

"Well, we'll get him all fixed up." She felt Jack's eyes drilling into her.

"How far to Porto Franco?" Pasqual asked.

"You know the river better than I do."

He laughed again. "Is that what my brother told you? This was only the second trip I've made to Macapa via the Amazon. It's much more pleasant to fly from Colombia."

"Then why'd you do it?" Kali studied him over the rim of her cup.

He cocked his head to the side. "Why would you have done it?"

"You obviously knew I was coming, which means either you knew your time was up or you have an inside source. The latter is more likely." She took another sip. "Given the same circumstances, I would only make the river trip if I wanted to draw out my enemy."

He smiled almost benevolently. "Precisely."

"What was your plan?"

"Simple. Your failure. You would have failed regardless of whatever success you had with my barge."

Kali slowly lowered her cup to the counter. It was so clear now. "There was no cocaine on your boat."

"Duarte was always overconfident. He doesn't realize how close he is to losing it all to me." The old man smiled, his pale lips thin. "With the exception of my nephew's injuries, things have worked out rather well."

"I might still kill you."

"Yes, you might." He studied her intently. "But forgive me, I've been remiss in asking after Dr. Cross. How is she?"

"She's a doctor?" Kali asked, before she could stop herself.

"Why yes," he said, his eyes sparkling. "Apparently, she's a scientist of some renown in the climatology field. How amusing that she didn't tell you."

Kali made her face like stone. "It wasn't something I needed to know."

"No, I can tell by the mark on your face that she didn't like you enough to share."

"Oh shit! Did she hit you?" Jack laughed incredulously. "I'd have paid to see that."

"Jack," Pasqual said, his voice commanding. "Bring me some water."

Turning, Kali watched as Jack went to serve his new master. What amazed her most was how obvious they were being, as if the game had already been won.

"Do tell me if I get breakfast this morning?" Pasqual asked, almost sweetly. "I would dare to assume that our Dr. Cross must also be famished."

It was the *our* that made Kali clench her jaw. Was everyone against her? She should just kill them all now and work it out later.

"So what say you, Kali? Breakfast would be wonderful. Nothing fancy. I usually just have fruit and some fresh squeezed juice."

"Get him a pop tart," she said, looking at Jack with loathing.

"I'll make him some eggs."

She slammed her cup on the counter, and Jack jumped at the noise. "I'm going to check on Renny," she said, turning away.

As she moved past Pasqual, she met his eyes. She needed to let him know that she knew what was coming.

Letting the door close behind her, Kali stood in the muggy air. It was hotter today. Already she could feel the moisture collecting on her skin. That usually meant rain. It always meant rain.

The dark water of the Amazon churned up behind the *Avatara*, leaving a white trail of bubbles. She watched it for a second, collecting herself for the next round.

She didn't like leaving Jack and Pasqual alone, but their devil's bargain had already been struck. At Porto Franco, they would attack. She didn't know how or when, but she had to be ready.

From the flybridge, she heard music. Renny had switched on the stereo. Hearing it was somehow comforting and mundane.

"Did you get the coordinates?" she asked, as she came up the stairs.

"Yes." Renny turned down the music and pointed to the GPS screen that was tracking their progress east.

With nothing else to say, Kali slid into the co-pilot's seat and stared at the river ahead. The wind blew over the windshield, taking her hair back off her neck.

"What happened?" Renny asked, pointing at her head. "Did the woman hit you?"

Lifting her hand, she covered her ear, which still felt warm. "Nothing happened."

"Why are you dragging this out with her? Nothing good can come of it."

She turned on him. "And what good will come from returning to Macapa? Duarte will only draw us back like flies to his web."

He held up his hand. "Until we hear back from the cartel, I will not argue this with you."

Not ready to give up on a fight, Kali leaned forward. "Then tell me if you're going to help Jack take the ship from me?"

Renny didn't look at her. "No one's taking the *Avatara* from you," he said, but Kali already knew the real answer.

"You've always been honest, Renny. I'd appreciate knowing."

"Jack knows I want to wait to hear back from the cartel." He looked at her. "He's not asked for my help in moving against you, but I know he's planning something with the old man."

"Where do you stand?"

"You know where I stand. I stand with my family."

Kali blew out a disgusted laugh. "If I'd known how attached you were to them, I would have kicked you off my crew."

"You never bothered learning anything about us. You used us but you paid us well."

She accepted his comment with a shrug. "I can't return to Macapa, Renny. There is no room for failure in our world. I failed and I will be killed."

"It wasn't your fault."

"Stop being so naïve! If you'd failed me, I'd have killed you. That's how it works. You all know it." She sighed. "I can't go back to Macapa, but maybe we can come to another arrangement. All I want is to get out of this alive."

He frowned. "What are you suggesting?"

For a moment, she hesitated, but knew she had to take the risk. Betraying her plan to Jack at this point would do little to affect the outcome. "Take me to Santarem and I'll give you the *Avatara*. Go back to Macapa or go where you will."

"Just like that?" He studied her. "And what about everyone else?"

"I don't care about anyone else."

"You never have."

"That's not true," she said, feeling the need to defend herself. "I just learned that I can't afford to care about anyone. Maybe you're the lucky one with a home and a family. I don't know."

"Maybe you care for that woman in your cabin?"

"Stop," Kali said, forcibly. "That's none of your business." She looked out over the starboard side. "I'm leaving her in Porto Franco."

"You can't be serious. What if she—"

"She won't," she said, cutting him off. "And be realistic. What would really happen if she told anyone? She's not the threat Jack makes her out to be."

"The old man said you'd choose her over us." Renny looked sad. "He was right."

"What he says isn't important. If you agree to help me get to Santarem, he won't leave Porto Franco alive."

"And Jack?"

She knew her answer was critical. If she showed no mercy, Renny might turn her down. Yet, Jack deserved no mercy. He was going to betray her. He deserved to die. "You know what I would do," she said, looking directly into his dark eyes. "But I'll leave him to you. I just don't want him back on the *Avatara* when we leave."

On the dash, the GPS beeped, announcing that they were one waypoint nearer to Porto Franco. Every passing second was bringing this showdown closer, and she wasn't sure she was fully prepared for it. "What's your answer?"

"I'll take care of Jack."

She didn't try to keep the smile from her face. "Thank you."

"I never wanted to kill you," he said, with a shrug.

"This entire trip to Porto Franco is Pasqual's idea. Maybe he is concerned for his nephew or maybe there is something more going on. I know Jack is going to move against me shortly after we dock, but I'm anticipating the old man will play it safe. At least until Amado is at the hospital."

"I think he really cares for the boy."

"That's not my concern. He's just a pawn that we're all using to shift pieces on the board."

"What do you need me to do?"

"After we dock, you go to the hospital and return with a stretcher. That will keep Jack on the ship and in sight. I'll send you into the village to get supplies, giving you time to leave the ship first and get in position. If I can swing it, I'm going to send Jack to the hospital with Amado." She shrugged. "I don't know if he'll go or not, but I want him off the ship so I can get rid of the guns in the safe."

"Jack asked me if I knew the combination."

Kali ignored that. "Dumping the weapons might end up being futile, but right now, I don't want them around." She looked out at the vast forest clinging to the shore. "Can I count on you?"

"I'll be ready."

Her eyes turned to him. "Give nothing away about this. Jack may think he can sway you, but I'm fairly certain the old man isn't so sure."

"You have my word." He held out his hand. "Do I have yours?"

She took his hand. "Get me to Santarem and the ship is yours."

Chapter Nine

Pasqual was trying to loosen the ropes on his wrists when Kali entered the salon. He'd listened while she and the Frenchman had docked the ship. From the way her face glowed with perspiration, it must have been a difficult task.

Stopping just inside the door, she looked around the room. "Where's Jack?"

"You look quite the mess, my dear. Is it that hot out today?"

Her eyes blazed. "I asked you a question, old man."

By God, she was fierce looking. The devil himself couldn't have appeared any more menacing. If he wasn't so sure of his success, he might have felt afraid. It was, however, time to drop the pretense of politeness. "Do you really expect me to follow him?" he demanded, pulling at his bound wrists.

Kali lunged for him, raising her hand to strike, but stopping. He watched intently as uncertainty entered her eyes. It turned to panic as she pieced it all together. Pulling back, she turned for the stairs.

"Yes," he called after her. "That would be a good guess."

Dr. Cross was in no danger. He actually liked the young woman. Her purity and intelligence reminded him of his middle daughter, Francesca. For that reason alone, he would do what he could to protect her. It seemed, from what Jack had said of Kali's threats, he wasn't the only one with a soft spot for the dear doctor.

If given the bet, he never would have thought Kali would side with some woman over her crew. Perhaps she did feel something for Dr. Cross. He knew she was unsure why she'd saved the woman, but he'd never really believed she'd form any sort of emotional attachment.

Unfortunately, it was a weakness she couldn't afford. There was a good reason why people in their profession kept family connections so removed. He would sacrifice everything to save his family. Now the question was would Kali do the same for this woman?

Of course, if Kali was smart enough to take the woman off the ship, the question would be moot. Keeping her on board gave him an advantage over Kali. He suspected that as long as he had Dr. Cross, Kali would falter just long enough to subdue her.

In a way, he regretted the need to kill Kali. The woman was strong and courageous. In another time and place, he'd have welcomed her onto his payroll. But things had not worked out in that direction, and he'd been forced to pander to someone like Jack. Just how Kali had endured his stupidity was beyond his comprehension. He could only hope it was because he was a good fighter.

He leaned back in his chair as Jack came up the stairs. "Did she go to her cabin?"

"Just like you said she would," Jack replied, grinning.

"But she won't stay there long." He raised a brow. "Have you located any errant weapons?"

"Just my knife," he said, touching a commando knife hanging on his belt.

"Well, we knew your knife wasn't missing. I was asking about guns, Jack. Guns."

"I told you," he said, pointing to a spot on the floor where Pasqual could barely make out a break in the carpet. "They're in the safe."

"And neither you nor the Frenchman know the combination, correct?"

"No. But I was thinking we could cut the combo out of Kali. What do you think?"

"That you shouldn't," he said, his voice rising with anger.

"What's that supposed to mean?"

"It means that from what I know of Kali's skills, I imagine that she'd end up setting your toy knife into your heart."

"She's not that good."

"You pompous ass!" he yelled, pausing to bring himself back under control. "Just do what I tell you, Jack. Follow my orders and we'll win."

Footsteps sounded on the wooden planks outside, and Pasqual looked over his shoulder as three shadows passed by the drawn blinds. Jack leaned over and peered outside. "It's Renny with a stretcher."

"She'll be out in a minute," Pasqual said, glancing at the stairs. "Remember, I need you to do whatever she tells you. I'm certain she'll demand you go to the hospital with her. Raise no suspicion. Follow her and return back here as soon as she becomes distracted."

"And what of Renny?"

"Continue to reassure him that you plan on returning to Macapa. We'll get rid of him once Kali is out of the way."

The salon door slid open and Renny preceded two men carrying a stretcher. "He's there," he said, pointing at Amado. His eyes traveled the room. "Where's Kali?"

"Where do you think?" Jack asked, sarcastically.

Pasqual looked at him and sadly shook his head. There was no way he was going to take this buffoon back to Colombia. No, Jack's employment with him would be brief.

The two orderlies lifted Amado onto the stretcher, eliciting a small groan from the boy. Pasqual leaned forward in his chair. "Be careful with him!" He felt a genuine sympathy for his nephew.

Kali chose that moment to bound up the stairs. "Good. Everyone's here. I won't have to repeat myself."

"Where's your girlfriend?" Jack smirked at her, but Kali's face was deadly serious.

"Jack, you're to go with Amado to the hospital. I'll join you there."

"No, I don't think so," Jack said, before Pasqual could stop him. "I think you should come with me."

It was a slight deviation from what he'd expected of Kali, but now Jack had tipped his hand to that fact.

"Jack," he said, his voice like ice. "Please see to my nephew as Kali has asked."

Kali's eyes slipped to him and a ghost of a smile touched her face. It said enough, and she shifted to the Frenchman. "Renny," she said, holding out a thick pile of cash. "You get the supplies we need. Pay whatever is necessary, but not enough to be remembered."

There was something wrong with the way Kali was behaving. It was too relaxed. Too confident.

"Will do," Renny said, pocketing the cash and immediately leaving. At the door, he risked a glance back at Kali, and Pasqual closed his eyes in dismay.

No. No. No. He knew immediately that Kali had made a deal with him. But for what? As far as he knew the man only wanted to return to Macapa. What could Kali have offered him?

He looked up at Jack with a mixture of disgust and alarm. One glimpse at the man's blank face and he knew Jack had missed the subtle messages between Kali and the Frenchman, and there was no way he could warn him.

"We're ready," one of the hospital orderlies said as he secured the last cinch around Amado's body.

"Then get going, Jack," Kali said, smugly. "We're all counting on you to make sure Amado is taken care of."

Jack looked to him, but there was nothing Pasqual could say. He could only hope that Jack was quicker and stronger than his shipmate.

They were silent as the orderlies carried Amado out of the room, but once they were alone, Kali turned and smiled down at him. "You are every bit as clever as my brother boasted. I'm impressed, but curious as to how you secured the loyalty of the Frenchman?"

Kali dropped to her knee by the floor safe and peeled back the carpet. Quickly entering a combination, she opened the door to reveal a fine assortment of weapons. Glancing up at him, Kali began withdrawing guns and laying them on the carpet.

He looked on with admiration. Some of the weapons were not only expensive, but very difficult to acquire. Her contacts must be excellent. "I can't help thinking that with an arsenal like that and enough men, I could have taken Macapa from my brother by force."

"Only because your brother is too lazy to pick up a gun," she replied, getting to her feet with several weapons in her arms.

She carried them outside and Pasqual heard the telling splashes as the guns were dropped into the river. When she returned, he shook his head. "Such a waste when you've already won."

Not responding, Kali gathered another armful of guns and retraced her steps to the railing. It took four trips for her to empty the safe. After Kali had closed the door and replaced the carpet, Pasqual decided to try another approach. "I don't suppose you and I could some to an understanding?"

She looked at him with eyes as alert and dangerous as a jaguar. "What's your offer?"

"Leave the ship to me, and I'll guarantee the life of Dr. Cross."

Kali laughed. "I'm going to the hospital to make sure your nephew's identity is not known."

"Are you that confident of the Frenchman's abilities? He doesn't want it as much as Jack."

"You forget that I've seen Jack work. It's you who should be worried."

He answered her with a thin, humorless smile.

Bending over, Kali checked the ropes around his wrists and ankles. When she was satisfied, she stood up. "I'll see you in a bit," she said, turning for the door.

As she reached to pull it open, Pasqual saw the telltale bulge at her back. He'd wondered if she'd kept a gun.

Maddie was still sitting on the edge of the bed where Kali had left her. In her hands was a thick wad of hundred dollar bills. After accessing a small, hidden safe in the wall, Kali had handed her the money and told her to keep it secret. If she didn't return, Maddie was to try and talk her way off the ship and go to the convent. The money would help her get home safely.

The prospect of going home should have made her happy, but strangely it didn't. There was a new feeling of dread chilling her heart. Kali may have made a grand gesture with the money, but Maddie knew that her fate was still very much in Kali's hands. Should she not return, Maddie was no better off than before.

It was somehow incomprehensible how, despite all of Kali's cruelty, Maddie now realized that she had always been safe with her. It was an odd awareness that left her very confused.

As she sat on the bed, Maddie found herself thinking about all the things that had been her life. She thought about her parents, her brothers, her friends. The scenes of her life played through her head like an old black and white movie that left her feeling unexpectedly disconnected from it all.

She knew that if Kali hadn't saved her yesterday, her life would have been over. Her family would have grieved, but ultimately their lives would have gone on. She was sure she would be missed at holidays and parties, but in the end she would just be a memory.

The door rattled with a light knock, and Maddie felt her body tense. She said nothing. The knock came again.

"Dr. Cross?"

It was the old man, and subconsciously, Maddie stuffed the money under a nearby pillow.

"Dr. Cross, may I come in?"

Her heart beat faster in her chest. How had he gotten free? Did that mean Kali was dead? She swallowed hard.

The doorknob began to turn, and Maddie's eyes grew wide. Why hadn't she thought to lock it? Her hand dug into the comforter on the bed, balling it anxiously. The wood creaked ever so quietly as the door was opened, and soon she was staring at the weathered and wrinkled face of Pasqual de Tueste.

He stared at her, his eyes softening. "Did I frighten you, child?"

Maddie could only nod.

Pasqual walked into the room with that man, Jack, on his heels. When he reached the end of the bed, his bony hand stretched out and his cold fingers lifted her chin. She knew he was looking at her cheek, and Maddie pulled away, lifting her hand to cover the mark.

"I'm sorry she harmed you," he said, and Maddie almost believed him. "But you did well to survive." He smiled down on her like a proud grandfather.

Her eyes shifted to Jack, who wasn't smiling. In fact, he looked quite angry.

"Come," Pasqual said, offering her hand.

"Where?" Maddie asked, finally finding her voice.

"I would like your help." He stepped back, but when she didn't move, he sighed. "Don't make me force you, Dr. Cross. Please." The benevolence had disappeared from his voice.

"I'd rather stay here."

The old man's colorless eyes went winter cold and he shook his head almost sadly. "I would have protected you." He looked at Jack. "Get her."

"No!" Maddie screamed, as the man lunged forward.

She tried to get away, but couldn't move fast enough. Before she knew how it happened, she had been tossed over his big shoulder. Maddie tried to kick at him, but stopped when she felt Pasqual's cold hand grab her wrist. It was like the touch of death, and she went completely still.

"Dr. Cross," he said, looking forcefully into her eyes. "Do not make this harder on yourself."

It was then that Maddie understood just how different things had been with Kali. For all her uncertainty and violence, Maddie knew that her life had meant something to Kali. It meant nothing to the old man.

Kali ran at top speed down the rutted dirt road back towards the docks. She'd stayed at the hospital only long enough to give the Mother Superior a false name for Amado and a handful of money to cover his treatment. All in all, it couldn't have taken her more than fifteen minutes, but in her heart she knew it had been too long. She had expected to see Renny waiting for her outside the hospital, but when he wasn't there she feared the worse.

He'd known what to do with Jack, and she'd had little reason to doubt he'd fail. Not only did Renny have the element of surprise, she knew he was a better hand to hand fighter. Renny should have beaten him easily. Yet she knew he hadn't, and that was what spurred her on faster. If she didn't make it back to the ship before Jack, she would lose it all.

It was so hot. Her body was struggling just to keep going. Another drop of sweat dripped into her eye, but she blinked it away. Hitting the dock, her feet pounded the wood with rhythmic thumps. The *Avatara* was still there, and that, she supposed, was a good thing. As she came up on the bow line, she stopped running. All the blinds along the mid-level were closed. She couldn't see in, but that didn't mean she wasn't being watched.

Passing through the gate, she carefully stepped onto the aft deck. She reached behind her and withdrew the pistol, silently sliding the bolt back to chamber a bullet.

Her breathing was still shallow and labored from her run to the dock, but she didn't have time to rest. Approaching the sliding glass door, she tried to keep her body hidden as she pulled it quietly back and peered into the room.

It was dark inside. Too dark to see anything well. There was no other option but to go inside and face whatever might be waiting. If she died, she died. That was a risk she'd faced many times, but now, she absently wondered why dying suddenly mattered.

With a deep breath, she opened the door just wide enough to slip inside. The first thing she felt was the cool air hitting her face. Crouching slightly, she took a step deeper into the room, her eyes not yet accustomed to the light.

"Kali!"

Her name was shouted, and instinctively, Kali turned towards the noise with her gun held out in front of her. There was an outline. She focused on it, her finger tightening on the trigger just as she realized the voice had been Maddie. They had Maddie.

Before she could make a move towards her, something hard was cracked against her skull and her vision exploded with a burst of bright light. She felt her hand open and the gun falling. There was such pain. She managed one step before her knees buckled and things went black.

Pasqual sat on the flybridge. The air was stifling hot and still damp after a microburst of rain. He despised the rain forest, more so because he was now, apparently, stuck in it. Lifting his hand, he pinched the bridge of his nose where a headache was throbbing away. Things were not going as planned. With a sigh, he looked back at Jack. "What do you mean you don't know how to drive this thing?"

Nervously, Jack stared down at the console. "It wasn't my job," he explained, running his fingers over switches Pasqual knew were foreign to him. "I think this one means we need gas." He tapped a gauge.

"Well, that's hardly important when we can't go anywhere, is it?" Pasqual looked away. "The other one – the Frenchman – he knew how to pilot?"

"Yes."

"And you killed him?"

Jack looked shocked. "He was going to kill me!"

Fingering the pistol in his hand, Pasqual considered just shooting him. "I'm disappointed in you," he said, deciding to wait until he knew for sure if he still needed this jackass.

As if sensing how close he was to dying, Jack became anxious. "But I did everything you asked!" he cried. "You're free!"

"Yes I am. Should I now plan on swimming back to Colombia?" He gestured at the river. "You've done nothing but fail me, Jack. Thanks to your incompetence, I'm stuck here in this damnable village with no means of escape." He stared off at the horizon. "Well, since you have no skills at the helm, perhaps you know how to operate the ship's communications? At the very least I could contact my men and risk a dangerous river flight to get out of here before my brother arrives."

Jack didn't respond, and slowly, Pasqual nodded. He almost laughed. It was becoming that comical.

"Kali again?"

"It's her ship. She has the passwords for everything."

"And I'm beginning to see the wisdom in keeping such things from a dim-wit like you." He tapped the pistol against his leg when he saw Jack's eyes flash with rage. It was enough of a gesture to regain his dominance.

"I did what you wanted," he said, a touch more contritely. "And you never asked if I could drive the boat."

"No, I didn't." He got to his feet. "Well, I suppose, I shall have to make other arrangements."

"What does that mean?"

"It means that you better look around for some manual or something on how to operate this ship because I won't just sit here and wait for my brother to come kill me."

Shaking his head, he climbed down the stairs and entered the salon. The first thing he encountered was a very angry Dr. Cross. She yanked on the ropes that bound her to the same chair Kali had used for him.

"You bastard!" she fumed. "Did you kill her?"

He laughed softly, taking a seat on the edge of the coffee table. "Do you really care?"

"No." There was a momentary flinch in her blue eyes that betrayed her lie.

Interesting.

"But you didn't need to kill her."

"What do you think Kali was going to do to me, Dr. Cross?" He turned to glance at Kali. "But she's not dead. At least not yet."

"Prove that. Check on her. No one has checked on her since you left her tied up like that and that was almost a half hour ago." She didn't try to hide her concern this time. "Look at the blood. It hasn't stopped."

"Because her scalp has been cut. The head always bleeds the worse. It's very messy." He shrugged. "But see, she's still breathing."

"Then let me take care of her." She tugged on her bound wrists. "Surely I'm not such a threat to you that I have to be tied."

He smiled. "Excellent effort, but I'd prefer, for the moment, that you remained where you are." His eyes slipped back to Kali. "To be honest, Dr. Cross, I'm not sure if I should respect you or think you stupid. This woman was going to kill you, and yet you want to help her. Why?"

"I don't have to tell you anything."

"Then let me tell you about her. Dana Sanders is her real name."

"Stop. I don't need to know," she said, but Pasqual could see the interest in her eyes.

"She was born to a second rate prostitute in Atlanta, Georgia, and for reasons not germane to us, her mother was killed when Kali was but ten years old. It was Kali who found her mother's body."

Briefly, Maddie closed her eyes, but he continued.

"Since she had no other known family, she was placed in state care.

Maybe it was in her blood or maybe it was the environment, but it didn't take Kali long to find a passion for crime. Sadly, though, she was quite inept in the beginning. She was convicted three times for petty crimes before she was seventeen, but it was her last incarceration in an adult prison that introduced Kali to the lures of the drug trade."

"Please I don't want to hear anymore." Maddie shook her head.

He ignored her. "The police reports from the time are incomplete, but apparently Kali took her childhood friend — a sister one might even say — to a drug exchange. Her friend was killed, and Kali fled Atlanta shortly after that. Her life was forever changed."

"Why you are telling me all this?"

"So you know who it is you are so anxious to nurse."

"But I don't need to know her history to take care of her wound."

"No, but you need to know it all the same."

"I don't understand."

He nodded. "Answer me this, Dr. Cross. If I were to cut you loose and tell you to leave the ship this instant, would you do it?"

"And go where?"

"Away from here. Away from this ship." He gestured at Kali. "Away from her."

"So you can kill her?" Maddie shook her head. "If I'm all that's keeping you from doing that, I'll stay."

"Oh, you're not, Dr. Cross." He smiled. "Then you'd prefer to stay?"

"I want to talk to Kali."

"I thought you would have taken the first opportunity to leave. I misjudged you."

"I don't understand. What's going on?"

Kali groaned from the couch and he glanced at her. "You're about to find out."

Getting to his feet, he leaned over Kali. She was struggling to open her eyes, which were still dilated and unfocused. When she closed them again, Pasqual shook his head. He couldn't wait any longer. Reaching out, he slapped her face. "Wake up!" Her eyes opened, but then closed, and Pasqual repeated his slap, but harder.

"For God's sake," Maddie cried. "Stop it!"

Kali's eyes snapped open, but they were still unfocused. Reaching out, Pasqual grabbed her hair, his fingers becoming slick with her blood. "I said wake up!" He gave her hair a tug.

Kali yelled out, but to his relief, her eyes cleared.

"Stop hurting her!" Maddie screamed, the chair rocking as she pulled on her ropes.

"Oh, do be quiet," he said, glancing over his shoulder.

"What happened?" Kali asked, her voice hoarse.

His eyes returned to her. "Good, you're awake." He dragged his bloody fingers across Kali's shirt to clean them. "I'm sure your head hurts, so I'll make this brief."

Kali struggled to sit up on the couch, but fell back wincing in pain.

He watched her try two more times before reaching out to help her into a sitting position. "I say we call a truce," he said, sitting on the edge of the coffee table. "What do you say?"

Kali was quiet for a minute, but then she looked at him with the sharp eyes he remembered. "I'd say that's generous considering I'm the one tied up."

"Yes, well, Jack neglected to tell me that he can't pilot your ship." Pasqual sighed, wishing he didn't have to admit defeat.

"And what about Renny?"

He rolled his shoulders in a shrug. There was no need to say it.

With a nod, Kali sighed.

"Given the present situation, we can work together. We already know my brother wants me dead, but now he'll be looking for you, too."

"I can take care of myself."

"Oh, I've no doubt of that. Which is why I thought we could work together."

"You could have offered me this yesterday. It might have saved time."

"You wouldn't have listened."

She accepted that with a small smile. "What do you want from me?"

"Take me to Santarem."

Her eyebrow raised. "You really think you can escape Brazil from there? Duarte has contacts in Santarem. It would be easier to fly a float plane in here to save you."

"You really think that given my brother's communication network that's a risk I'd accept?" He shook his head. "No, you are my best bet."

"And why's that?"

"I know all about you, Kali. If anyone can turn this to an advantage, it will be you."

Kali was quiet a moment. "Well, in that case, I think you're trying to hire me." She smiled. "I don't work for free."

Pasqual relaxed slightly. It was progress. "What's my brother paying you?"

"Thirty million."

"Dollars?" Maddie gasped, but they both ignored her.

"But you failed."

"A point immaterial to us." Kali paused. "I've received fifteen up front."

"Very smart. You were covering your bases."

"With Duarte? Absolutely." She smiled. "You make up the difference in my contract."

He considered it. "So you want fifteen million dollars for a short boat ride to Santarem?"

"This pissing contest between you and Duarte has ruined my business in Brazil."

"Yes, but that's a lot a money for a fresh start."

"It's a drop in the bucket for you two. You've both pulled my strings like some puppet, and I realize now that no matter how things turned out, I was doomed to fail. Right?"

"I can't speak for Duarte, but yes, had you taken my barge, you would already be dead."

"Amado?"

Pasqual nodded. "But don't blame the boy. He never fully understood what was going on between Duarte and myself." He sighed and then gave Kali a shrug. "Well, it seems I have little choice but to agree to your terms. But I'll only pay ten million."

She considered this and smiled. "Then for only ten, I get to watch you kill Jack."

"He's part of your crew. Shouldn't you do it?"

"Has it been that long that you're squeamish?" Kali smiled thinly. "No, Jack is your mess. You clean it up."

"If that's what you want, I agree."

"Then untie me and let's get moving."

He leaned forward, but then stopped. "Before I do, give me your word."

"Why?"

"Because I know that your promise means something to you."

Kali didn't hesitate. "Very well. You have my word. For ten million dollars and Jack's life, I'll get you to Santarem alive."

Reaching out, he untied her hands. As soon as he set her free, he stood back and held out the pistol, but Kali's eyes were on the doctor. She frowned. "Why did you do this in front of her?"

"I gave her the option of leaving," Pasqual said, almost regretfully. "She was more concerned about you."

Kali glared up at him. "You didn't need to involve her."

"I was worried about you," Maddie said, and Pasqual watched as Kali's body got tense.

"Let's get this over with," she said, abruptly. "First, take care of Jack and then we'll transfer the money."

Pasqual gestured at the doctor. "You want me to do it here?"

"Do you really think it matters anymore?"

"Do what here?" Maddie asked, with a tremor of nervousness. "Oh God, you're going to kill him, aren't you? Here? In front of me?"

"Dr. Cross, please. You could have left. Remember that."

"Leave her alone," Kali said, her voice dangerously low.

"Then you keep her quiet while I call Jack."

"Oh God," Maddie said, again, as he slid open the door and called for Jack.

"Maddie," Kali said tonelessly. "It has to happen. Shut your eyes or look at me, but don't make a sound."

He glanced at the doctor, not surprised to see her turn her gaze to Kali. It was unfortunate that she would see this, but her fate was sealed.

Jack's footsteps sounded on the stairs overhead, and he turned his attention to the gun in his hand. Kali had been right. He hadn't personally killed anyone in a very long time, and the weapon felt strangely heavy in his old hand. Ordering an enemy killed was very anonymous. There was a distance, and the death was just a means to an end. A way to solve a problem. But this was far more personal. In a minute, he would take a life. True it wasn't a life worth much, but it was a life all the same. Oddly, he suddenly felt more alive than he had in years.

As the door of the salon opened and Jack entered the room, Pasqual took a step back. He knew Kali was watching. While he thought this should be her kill, he understood her reasons for forcing his hand. She was solidifying her position, and for that, he respected her.

"What's going on?" Jack asked, looking around the room.

"Bye, Jack," Kali said, triumphantly.

The poor dumb boy looked surprised as Pasqual raised the gun. "No, wait," he pleaded. "You can't do this. I did everything—"

Maddie screamed as the gunshot sounded.

The bullet hit Jack in the forehead, the force of the bullet's back blow catapulting blood and skull against the wall. His body just sort of melted to the floor in a puddle, blood continuing to pump from the exit wound.

"You were too close," Kali said, as the dark stain spread across the carpet.

"It's done. That's all that matters."

"Oh God. Oh God," Maddie kept repeating.

He glared at the doctor. "Do something with her."

"She shouldn't be here," Kali said, getting to her feet. The color drained from her face and she swayed dangerously, but managed to remain standing. "You know that."

"I didn't think you'd care one way or the other." He shrugged.

She glared at him before focusing on the doctor. "Look at me."

Maddie still stared at Jack. "I can't believe that just—"

"Quiet," Kali said, cutting her off. "It's over. That was it. Take a deep breath and get yourself under control."

"I never thought I'd have to see—"

To Pasqual's surprise, Kali reached out and pressed her hand to the side of Maddie's face. "Shhh," she said, almost tenderly. "I know you didn't want to see that, but you did and now it's over."

Strangely, Maddie seemed to respond to this tactic, and as she looked up at Kali, Pasqual watched as her body seemed to visibly relax.

"Okay," Kali said, softly. "Now if you promise to stay here and not run, I'll untie you."

Maddie hesitated, looking quickly at Jack's body, but then nodded. At that, Kali loosened the ropes holding Maddie's wrists. "Remember, no running."

"Are you just going to leave him there?" Maddie asked, watching her hands.

"For the time being. We'll get rid of him later."

"Well," Pasqual said, stepping closer and holding out the pistol. "I believe I can give this to you now."

Straightening up slowly, Kali's eyes were still angry as she looked down at the gun, and for a moment, he thought that she might just use it on him. Instead, she took the pistol and tucked it behind her back. "Do you want to do the transfer now or before we leave?"

"We'll do it before we leave for Manaus."

"You said Santarem."

"And just where do you think my brother will track us first?" He frowned. "No, it must be Manaus."

She stared at him for a second, her piercing green eyes sharp and dangerous. "Manaus will cost you another five," she said, raising a brow in challenge.

It was a bold move, and he smiled. "You agreed to ten."

"I agreed to Santarem."

The money meant little to him. "Well, I suppose my life is worth a bit more." He nodded his agreement. "I'll transfer half the money today and the rest at Manaus. Yes?"

"Fine," Kali said, cautiously probing her wound with her fingers, her face sharp with pain. "What the hell did Jack hit me with?" She stared down at her bloody fingers.

"A bat," Maddie said, as she got to her feet. "I'll get you a towel."

Kali's eyes followed her across the room before shifting back to Pasqual. "A bat?"

"It was more like a branch. Jack wanted to use his knife, if that helps."

She touched her head again. "Not really."

"Sit down so I can take a look at your head," Maddie said, returning with a paper towel and an ice pack from the freezer. She handed Kali the towel. "Wipe your fingers."

The quiet way in which the doctor ordered Kali into the chair amused Pasqual, but not nearly as much as the way Kali just submitted to the command.

"I think it needs stitches," she said, cleaning her fingers.

"Let me see," Maddie replied, gently parting her hair. "The bleeding's nearly stopped."

"Get it seen to at the hospital before we leave." He couldn't afford to have her injured.

"Speaking of the hospital," Kali said, looking up at him. "I'm going to bring Amado back on board."

"No," Pasqual said, firmly. "My nephew stays here."

"If you want me to get you to Manaus safely, I need to use Amado as a guarantee," she said, while Maddie took Kali's paper towel and pressed it into her wound.

"I won't let you use him as a pawn."

Kali winced in pain. "That's exactly what you've done," she said, her face going pale from Maddie's compress. "What's changed?"

"He's injured. I may have used him, but I certainly don't want him dead. He's burned, and staying here is his best chance of survival."

He watched as Maddie exchanged the compress for the ice pack. "This is going to be cold," she said, carefully touching it to Kali's head.

"Fuck," Kali said, pulling away.

"Hold still," Maddie replied, setting her hand on Kali's shoulder to keep her in place. "It will help with the swelling."

It took a minute for Kali to relax into the feeling, but her face was still quite pale. "Are you sure you're alright?" he asked her.

"I'm fine," she said, looking up at him. "And you know I'm right. Duarte will stop at nothing to find us. Amado can be our shield."

"Until he dies. Then what?"

"He won't die. We'll get enough medicine to get him to Manaus."

"You don't sound very confident," he said, hating that her plan had merit.

"You're paying me to keep you safe. If Amado can help, I'll use him. It's that simple."

With a sigh, he gave up. "Before I agree, I'd like to see him personally. If he's too unstable, I forbid taking him."

"If you like. Maybe I'll come along and get my head looked at."

"No, Kali. I think you have other things to do first." He glanced at Maddie. "But come after you're done. I'm anxious to leave as soon as possible."

Kali stared at the floor, but finally nodded.

"I'm sorry it worked out this way, but I needed to be assured of your cooperation one way or the other."

"Well it's done now, isn't it?"

He smiled, but felt no joy. "Yes. Perhaps we can work something out farther down the river, but I trust you understand the significance of covering our tracks here."

"I get it."

"Very good. I'll see you shortly," he said, before turning for the door.

As he stepped onto the dock, he wondered how Kali was going to handle that situation. There was no way they could to leave Dr. Cross in Porto Franco. Even if she hadn't heard their plans, once his brother learned of her involvement, he would torture her to death before he believed her innocent.

It was unfortunate that things turned out the way they did, but there had been few options for him to explore. Had he and Kali not been able to come to an agreement, he would have used Dr. Cross as leverage. Kali maybe angry with him, but the irony was that she would have done the same thing. The two of them were not so different. She may resent the fact that he'd brought Dr. Cross so deeply into their affairs, but he knew she also understood why.

Walking up the road to the hospital, Pasqual let himself speculate on how his brother was handling the news of Kali's failure. Strange that a short time before he'd been reveling in the news, but now he realized he'd only made things worse for them all. Without that email, Duarte would still be clueless, and their chances for survival much greater.

Now, Kali had to be every bit as good as Duarte believed her to be. Pasqual thought it might just be his brother's awe of the woman that would give them the edge.

Chapter Ten

Duarte de Tueste drummed his fingers against his solid mahogany desk in frustration. His bulging eyes followed the diminutive frame of his assistant, Luis Vega, as he paced back and forth across his office, his cell phone pressed to his ear.

The job had gone wrong. By now, that much was obvious. What he didn't know was how badly or if there was anything to be salvaged.

He needed this victory. His partners were closing in on him, and everyday brought new challenges to his position. He needed to prove his dominance by producing Pasqual's head.

Of all the people in his organization, Kali had been the perfect choice. Not only had she always performed well for him, but she was enough of a loner that no one in the cartel would miss her. Knowing he could easily eliminate her and recover that preposterous fee made her a simple choice. Fifteen million dollars! Kali must be insane if she thought he'd allow her to take so much from him.

His attention returned to his assistant as Luis disconnected his call. "Well?"

Luis smiled grimly. "No more than before, sir."

"What more have you learned of the missing science ship? It was in the same area as Kali, no?"

"There's been no more information, sir. The National Science Center is still searching for the *Luna Nueva*. Last active transmission is now approaching almost twenty hours ago from a location just west of Porto Franco. I did discover that the ship was scheduled to spend six months in the rainforest gathering—"

Duarte cut him off. "What the hell do I care what they were doing? I only want to know about my cocaine."

The laptop on his desk beeped and Luis went to it. "Kali's emailed you." He turned the computer around.

"I knew she wouldn't let me down." His thick lips compressed as he read her short description of the events. "The fucking bitch! She's failed at everything!" He nearly threw the laptop from the desk.

"What happened?"

"The cocaine is lost. My brother is alive. My son is hurt and in apparent need of medical attention and—"

"Amado?" Luis cut him off.

"Of course it's Amado."

"If he's hurt and they are taking him to a hospital, that can only be Porto Franco. There are few options on that part of the river."

"Porto Franco? How far is that from the place Kali was to attack?"

Luis considered the question, but finally shrugged. "I can't be sure. Perhaps an hour or two." He looked up. "I do know that all hospitals are required to report any serious injuries to the Health Service Bureau. So if Kali is taking him for treatment, all we have to do is listen for that communication."

"To prove what? That my son is dying?"

"To locate them, sir."

The obviousness of that irritated Duarte. He should have realized it before Luis. Looking up, he waved his hand dismissively. "Do what you have to do, but the second there is a report from Porto Franco, I want to know."

"We have men in Santarem. Why not send them to Porto Franco now?"

He shook his head. "Not yet. Let's see what Kali does next."

Luis pointed at the laptop. "She's waiting for you, sir."

"Then let her wait. If she knows what's good for her, she'll get Amado to that hospital. Once we know for sure that he's safe, we'll leave for Porto Franco immediately. Have my plane on standby."

"I understand your need to see your son," Luis said, slowly. "But have you forgotten the Japanese are here?"

"Who?"

"The men from Sumiyoshi-kai syndicate. You are scheduled to meet with them this evening."

"Change it."

"I can't! It took me almost six months to set this up!"

"I said change it. I will be there to watch Kali die."

"Screw Kali!" Luis cried. "The Japanese are moving into our business here. This visit has but one purpose, and that is to see if it's easier to work with us or just take us over."

"Then one day won't matter much. Explain to them I have a situation I need to contain. They will understand."

"I'll try," Luis said, his eyes still angry. "But I think you're making a fatal mistake."

"It's a good thing I don't care what you think. Now make the arrangements."

"And what if it's not Amado in that hospital? What if she's gone by the time you get to Porto Franco? Then it's all for naught."

"You're too dramatic, Luis. If Kali is gone, I'll just trap her on the river. She'll be mine."

"How?"

Duarte smiled. "That's for you to figure out. Bring me your plan before I leave for Porto Franco. I want her found immediately, Luis. Don't fail me."

"I understand," Luis said, dropping his eyes. "I'll have everything ready to go as soon as we know more."

"Then get out!" Duarte ordered, turning in his chair and presenting his back to Luis.

Left alone with Maddie, Kali knew she lacked the energy to face her. Her head was throbbing like nothing she'd every experienced before. The ice was helping to lessen the pain, but not enough for her to feel capable of telling Maddie her future was gone. She didn't even know how to begin.

"I thought he'd killed you," Maddie said, adjusting the ice pack. "I was so scared."

"Why?" Kali asked, but she wasn't sure she wanted to know.

"I don't know. I just wanted to help you, and I couldn't."

Her response caused a twinge of anger to surface. "And just why would you want to help me?"

Maddie paused, the question dragging out between them. Finally, she lifted the ice pack from her head. "Listen, I know you don't like questions, but I'd really appreciate knowing what just happened here?"

"Can't you figure it out?" she growled, getting abruptly to her feet. The movement sent new pains shooting through her head and she grabbed for the back of the chair to keep from falling. The room spun wildly, and she felt like throwing up.

"Well, it's obvious that you're working for him now. He's paying you an obscene amount of money to protect him and deliver him to Manaus. Is that right?" Maddie circled around to stand in front of her.

Kali forced a smile. "Give the girl a gold star," she said, lifting her hands to her head in the hopes of containing the pain. When she realized Maddie was staring at her with something different in her eyes, she lowered them. "What?"

"I'm sorry you're in pain," she said, with a new compassion in her voice.

"Don't be," Kali said, with irritation. "You didn't hit me."

"I know, but I can still feel sorry that you're hurting, can't I?"

"You could, but why would you?" Kali closed her eyes as the room twisted again.

"How about simple human compassion? Empathy? Maybe it's just a sense of friendship?"

"Friendship? Between us?" She laughed, regretting it when a spike of pain exploded in her head and her vision went out of focus. She staggered backwards, her feet heavy, not stopping until Maddie grabbed onto her arm to steady her.

"Are you okay?"

So violently nauseous, she couldn't answer. Instead, she just tried to breathe, taking in more and more air until the feeling passed. "I'm fine," she finally said, unconvincingly.

"I don't think you are," Maddie said, her fingers warm on Kali's arm. "I think you might have a concussion. We need to get you to the hospital."

Another bout of queasiness attacked her, and she felt Maddie's fingers on her face. "Jesus. You've gone totally white. Sit down."

"I'm fine," Kali repeated, with effort. "It will pass."

"You don't have to pretend with me. I'll help you."

"And why's that?"

"Because." Maddie looked away. "Because I don't want to stay behind."

"What?" Kali asked, not following.

"I know you were going to leave me here in this village, but I don't want that. And now that you're hurt, you could use my help. This is a big ship to drive alone."

"Pilot," Kali corrected, feeling ridiculous. "You don't drive a ship."

Maddie looked up at her with a hint of amusement in her eyes. "I know. I grew up on the Cape. My father taught us how to sail by the time we were ten."

Kali frowned. "What the fuck do I care about that?"

"It doesn't matter except that I can help you get to Manaus. If you let me stay."

She opened her mouth to respond, but no words would come out. It didn't seem possible that Maddie actually wanted to stay on the ship. It solved her problem. All she had to do was agree. It couldn't have been easier. Yet Kali felt unexpectedly guilty.

"I can't explain it," Maddie continued, oblivious to Kali's internal discord. "It doesn't even make sense to me. I know I should want to leave this ship, but I don't. I'd rather stay with you."

"And what happens when we reach Manaus? Do you expect me to take you with me again?" Kali asked, roughly, wishing her remorse away.

"No, I don't expect anything from you," Maddie said, timidly looking up at her. "Please don't leave me here alone. I'd rather come with you."

"Because I treat you so well?" Reaching out, she touched Maddie's face where she had hit her. The mark was starting to bruise. "Is it your thing? Do you like to be beat up or something?"

"Of course not," she said, pulling her face away.

Kali stared at her, not sure why she wanted to talk her out of staying. There was no other option but to take her along. She should just accept her offer and move on. "Fine," she said, with a wave of her hand. "Stay."

When Maddie smiled as if she'd just been given something precious, Kali felt ashamed. Angry with such an irrational emotion, she grabbed Maddie's chin forcefully. "This decision is yours alone," she said, tilting her face upwards so she could look into her blue eyes. "I take no responsibility for what may happen to you after we leave this dock. Do you understand that?" She dropped her hand.

"What's going to happen to me?" Maddie asked cautiously. "Am I in danger?"

"Not from me," Kali said, the confession unexpected. Blinking, she struggled to cover herself. "But I don't know what's going to happen. This isn't a pleasure cruise."

"I know that. I know what's at stake."

"No, you really don't." She closed her eyes as another wave of nausea gripped her.

"Well, I'm still staying," Maddie said, softly. "And I think we should get you to the hospital."

"It doesn't hurt as much," Kali lied.

Maddie nodded. "While I'm sure you're quite capable of taking care of yourself, after what I heard, I don't think you should show any vulnerabilities to Pasqual."

It was an astute observation, but not something Kali was truly concerned about. Pasqual needed her more than she needed him. But instead of telling

Maddie this, she gave her a small smile. "Maybe you're right. If you'll help me get supplies, then I should have time to go have someone look at my head."

"Whatever you need."

Kali looked at the stairs leading to her cabin, the distance seemed massive. Taking a deep breath, she hoped she could make it down the stairs without passing out. Cautiously, she took a step, stopping when the room began to spin.

"Here," Maddie said, slipping an arm around her waist. "Let me help."

She nearly refused, but then gave into her debility, leaning heavily on Maddie as they crossed the salon. By the time the reached the stairs, she felt a bit stronger and was able to navigate the steps by herself.

"Do you still have the money I gave you?" she asked, stepping into her cabin, but leaning back against the wall.

"It's here," Maddie said, going to the bed and digging under the covers. "I hid it when Pasqual came for me."

"Did you?" she asked, taking the cash from her. "That was smart."

Maddie looked up at her. "I tried to warn you about Jack."

She blinked, not recalling anything before being hit. "I don't remember," she said, meeting Maddie's gaze. "But thanks." There was an intensity in the way Maddie looked at her, that made Kali uncomfortable, so she looked down at the money. "I saw a market in town. Do you think you can get enough food and water to last at least two weeks?"

"Two weeks? But I thought Manaus wasn't that far."

"It's a precaution," Kali explained, counting out the money. "And a diversion. Two weeks of food will confuse the people following us." She handed Maddie a thick pile of hundred dollar bills. "This should be enough."

"But I don't speak Portuguese."

"You don't need to speak. Just point at what you want and be generous with the money. Have it carried back to the dock, but don't let anyone on the ship."

"And what about you?"

Kali took a bracing breath and walked across the room to her hidden wall safe. "I'm going to the hospital." She keyed in her code and held her eye to the biometric scanner.

After she did this, she looked down at her laptop in regret. Her two hour window hadn't accounted for her being knocked unconscious, and by now, her email had been delivered to Duarte. All she could do now was be prepared.

"Do you need my help getting there?" Maddie asked, as Kali opened the safe and withdrew another stack of money.

She paused in thought, wanting to refuse her offer, but knowing she was in no shape to try and make it to the hospital alone. "I think I might," she finally admitted, stuffing the money into her pocket and slamming the door to the safe.

"Kali," Maddie said timidly. "I know you wanted to leave me here, but thank you for letting me stay."

Turning towards her, Kali felt a surge of guilt that she buried under irritation. "Don't thank me. I'm not doing you any favors."

"No, I suppose you're not. But I wanted to thank you all the same."

"I'd save your thanks until you see how things turn out." She took a slow step towards the cabin door. "Let's go. The hospital is not far from the market. Help me get that far and I'll manage the rest."

"Or I could get you to the hospital and then find the market," Maddie said, her hand resting carefully on the small of her back.

"It doesn't matter," Kali said, ignoring her touch as she used the railing to climb the stairs.

Kali hated exposing any weakness, and she struggled to not lean too heavily on Maddie as they made their way to the hospital. The heat and humidity had made her head pound with each step, and she had to stop twice to overcome a bout of nausea.

Along the way, she regretted allowing Pasqual to kill Jack. *The bastard!* Killing him should have been her pleasure, although in her current state, she doubted if she would have enjoyed it much.

Maddie had seen her to the door of the hospital, but then she hesitated, as if she wanted to say something. Kali gave her no opportunity to speak. Too much had already been said, and without looking back, she entered the building.

The inside was just as she expected. There was a single ward, consisting of two rows of old metal beds with mosquito nets hanging down from the rafters. Ancient ceiling fans moved just fast enough to keep the air from getting stagnant, and the whole place had a dusty yet antiseptic smell to it. This hospital was run by a convent of nuns, and Kali stared at the large, yet crudely constructed wooden cross with a mixture of revulsion and fear. She looked away as an older nun came to greet her.

"It's my head, Sister," Kali said, gesturing at her bloody shirt.

"Come with me," the nun said speaking English.

Moving slowly behind her, Kali glanced around, easily spotting Pasqual sitting next to Amado's bed. His head was bowed, as if praying, but Kali didn't think it likely that God was listening.

The nun led her into what looked like a small triage room, and helped her to sit on a low chair. Kali gave her a brief explanation of what had happened while the nun snapped on a pair of latex gloves. Taking a stand behind her, the nun parted Kali's hair. Her touch was not as gentle as Maddie's had been, and Kali clenched her teeth to keep from crying out.

"You were unconscious for many minutes?" the nun asked, and Kali nodded. "And now you are dizzy and nauseous?"

"Yes. And the pain is terrible."

"I would think so." The nun chuckled. "The wound itself is not bad. It's already stopped bleeding, but the trauma area is swollen. I will clean it and give you some ointment to keep it from getting infected. If possible, ice it for the next twenty four hours."

"That's it?" Kali asked, relieved.

"No. I will also give you something for the pain and nausea. That may last for many days. If it's not better soon, you should try to get to a better equipped hospital for scans. The best you can do now is rest."

"I can't."

"You should try," the nun said, irrigating her wound with some solution that dribbled down Kali's neck and under her shirt. She patted at her head with some gauze before spreading something thick and oily feeling on the cut. "Now, wait here while I get what you need."

Sitting there, Kali felt very sleepy. Her eyes were heavy, and she jumped when the nun pushed open the door.

"Here," she said, holding out a tray with a paper cup with two pills. "Take these." She gestured to the small glass of water.

Suspicious, but in too much pain to care, Kali swallowed the pills. "Thank you."

"And this," she said, pushing a small tube of ointment towards her. "Needs to be put on your head at least once a day. It would be easier if you had someone else help you."

"Again, thank you," Kali said, hoping the pills started working soon.

"Our supplies are limited," the nun said, setting the tray down and withdrawing two small bottles of pills from her pocket. "But this should be enough for about a week. That should get you through the worst of it. Take one every twelve hours for pain and dizziness."

Struggling to her feet, Kali dug the money from her pocket. "Here," she said, pulling out three hundred dollar bills and holding them out. "Is this enough to replace your supplies?"

The nun stared at the money. "More than enough, but is the money clean? We do not accept drug money here."

"I don't run drugs, Sister," Kali said, pressing the bills into her hand. "But I thank you for helping me without asking first."

"We turn no one away."

Kali waited until the nun had left before finding her way to Amado's bed. The boy lay shrouded under a white mosquito net with a colorless IV dripping into his arm. As she got closer, she saw that a good portion of his face, chest and arms were now swathed in gauze. "How is he?" she asked, stopping at the foot of his bed.

Pasqual turned to look at her. "He has sepsis." His gaze returned to Amado. "The Sisters don't think he should be moved."

"And they think I should rest for a week." She gestured to the IV. "I assume that's antibiotics?"

"Yes." He dropped his head forward. "The hospital has already sent out a report about Amado. They are required to report any significant accidents to the Health Service Bureau."

Kali processed this information. "Then compounded with that goddamned email I was forced into sending, Duarte knows we're here. So, we don't have a choice anymore. We need Amado now more than ever."

"Maybe if we leave him here Duarte will give up. Maybe that will be enough."

"Do you believe that?"

Pasqual sighed. "No."

"Then let's get him ready to go." She looked around. "Who do we talk to?"

"I'll handle it." Pasqual rose from the chair and turned to face her. "You just do what you need to get us ready to go."

Kali conceded. "Get enough drugs to keep him alive until Manaus. Duarte can have him back then."

"If he survives that long." He looked down at Amado. "I never wanted him hurt."

Kali had no time for such sentimentality. "If possible," she said, tersely, "convince the nuns to transmit a follow up report that Amado has died. It may buy time."

"Yes, that would be wise." He gestured at her. "Go. I'll have Amado carried to the docks."

Kali started to leave, but then turned back. "Give this to the good Sisters," she said, taking the money from her pocket and splitting the pile in two. "Tell them that if anyone asks, they should say they heard us talking about heading for the Xingu."

He took the money. "Duarte won't believe them."

"I know." Kali smiled. "I want to leave in thirty minutes. Be back by then."

As she made her way back to the *Avatara*, it dawned on Kali that she was feeling better. Her head was still aching, but the pain was bearable. Even better, she noticed that the dizziness and nausea only seemed to come upon her if she shifted her eyes too quickly.

At the ship, she cast off the dock lines before climbing aboard. Taking the stairs to the flybridge, she started the engines and slowly inched the ship forward to Porto Franco's one diesel fuel pump.

The attendant hurried out of his small shack to grab the bow rope and pulled the *Avatara* snuggly against the dock. When the rear was also secure, Kali instructed him to fill the tanks before disappearing into the salon.

The first thing she saw was Jack's body. She had the urge to kick it, but instead crossed the room and descended to the ship's electronics room. Although not much bigger than a walk-in closet, it housed all of the *Avatara*'s high tech equipment. Besides basic communications and navigational aids, the ship was equipped with a sophisticated global positioning system, an ocean alert transponder and, of course, her satellite Internet link.

The first thing Kali did was manually deactivate the ship's transponder and ship to shore communications. She didn't think Duarte or anyone in his operation was sophisticated enough to track her through electronic signatures, but she wasn't going to risk it. Leaning forward, her finger hovered over the power switch for the GPS system. Her understanding of the technology was that the GPS was only capable of receiving signals, not sending them. She knew there were small tracking devices being used in conjunction with the positioning systems, but the *Avatara* didn't have one. It would be safer to just switch the system off, yet Kali knew it would be an invaluable tool to not only map her route to Manaus, but to help her find adequate inlets to hide them during the hours she needed to sleep. With no signal leaving the ship, Kali felt a bit more confident leaving the system up and running.

Which only left her Internet satellite connection to deactivate, but she'd do that as soon as Pasqual transferred her money. She also wanted to know if Duarte was going to respond to her email. She thought he might, if for no other reason than to keep her on the hook.

Sending that email had been a mistake. At the very least, she should have given herself more time to stop the transmission, but what was done was done. Duarte now had a general starting point, which meant her only edge was stealth and deception.

The Amazon River may look like it only went east or west, but in reality, there was a seemingly endless array of possible routes from Porto Franco. Not only would Duarte be unable to pinpoint her route, but it would be impossible for him to cover all possibilities. He would be forced to narrow his search down to the most logical routes. That would be Macapa, Santarem or Belem. If she knew anything of the man, he would employ planes as well as boats to cover these routes. It was the planes Kali feared the most.

All a plane had to do was spot her and radio her location. From there, it would be a futile race to try and escape whatever Duarte could throw at her. With no weapons on the ship but her pistol, Kali had no hope of fighting back. Surrender would be her only option.

Therefore, it was imperative for her to stay hidden from the planes. The only way she could do that was to travel by night. It was a dangerous decision, but one that Kali hoped would work.

Before leaving the electronics room, she grabbed two sets of night goggles from a shelf. She hadn't used them in months, but a quick test proved the batteries were still good. The goggles would give her the advantage of traveling at night without running lights. She would be a hole on the water. And best of all, she knew Duarte would never expect it from her. She doubted if he even knew she had the ability.

By traveling at night, Kali served two purposes. Firstly, she kept herself off the water during the daylight hours the planes would be flying, but more importantly, she would put some much needed distance between her and Duarte. The longer they escaped discovery, the more uncertain Duarte would become about their direction. It would keep his decisions off balance, and they just might make it to Manaus in one piece.

Of course, Duarte might already be a step ahead of them. She checked her watch. It had been almost an hour since that email had been automatically sent to Duarte and probably two since the hospital had reported Amado's arrival.

It was possible for Duarte to already be on a plane, but Kali doubted it. He was too cautious to just fly into danger. Duarte was the type of man who liked to have all his bases covered before acting. Yet, it was his son, so what Kali knew of him might not hold true this time.

If he hadn't left by now, it was probably too late for him to get a float plane from Macapa to Porto Franco. None of the float pilots Kali knew would risk a night landing on the rapid river. The current and floating debris made it just too treacherous.

Which left Duarte with the option of either waiting until tomorrow morning to make the four hour flight to Porto Franco from Macapa, or flying to Santarem tonight and catching a float plane at first light. The flight time from Santarem to Porto Franco was significantly shorter, and theoretically, Duarte could make it to the village quicker than flying from Macapa. If it had been her choice, she would opt to fly for Santarem today.

What Kali couldn't deduce was if Duarte would try and dispatch planes or boats today. She hoped the logistics of it would prove too difficult, even for someone like Duarte. Still, she knew that leaving Porto Franco in the daylight might be risky.

The time she gained leaving now, she felt, outweighed the risk. By leaving Porto Franco in the daylight and traveling throughout the night, she would put roughly sixteen hours between her and Duarte by first light tomorrow. Waiting for the sun to set cut that ratio almost in half.

"Kali?" she heard Maddie's voice echoing through the empty ship. "Are you here?"

Looping the goggles over her arm, she exited the electronics room and shut the door. "Yes," she called out, climbing the stairs.

"Hi," Maddie said, meeting her at the top. "How's your head?"

She brushed past her. "Better. Did you get the supplies?"

"Yes. It's all outside. I had it carried here, like you said. I hope it's enough."

"I'm sure it will be fine." Kali set the goggles on the counter.

"There's a man outside looking for you. Or at least I think he's looking for you."

Kali nodded. "Right. He probably wants money for the gas."

"I'll go start carrying in the food."

Reaching out, she stopped her. "Stay in here. I'll get them."

"But your head," Maddie began, but Kali silenced her with a glare.

"I said, I'll get them." She crossed the room and exited onto the aft deck.

As she expected, the gas attendant was waiting. She dug her money out of her pocket and counted off eight hundred dollars. It was double what the fuel cost, but Kali was buying more than just gas.

She stepped onto the dock, but kept the money held tightly in her hand. "*Se perguntado, você dirá fomos oriente*," she said, gesturing towards the east. "To anyone who asks. *Si*?"

The man looked briefly at the money. "*Sim. Eu serro seu barco vai por ali.*"

Kali handed him the cash. "*Bom.*" Looking down at the boxes of food Maddie had bought, she pointed to them. "*Ajude me com a caixas.*"

Picking one up, she carried it onto the *Avatara*. The man lifted the next one and passed it across to her.

"*Gratidão.*"

"I didn't know you spoke Portuguese," Pasqual said, coming up the dock. Behind him, Amado was being carried on a stretcher.

"Then your report on me wasn't very thorough." Kali took the next box and set it down. The effort was taxing her.

"I think I was lucky to learn what I did of you," Pasqual said, watching her closely.

Kali looked at the fuel attendant, waving him off. "*Vai. Havemos a daqui. Lembrar seu promessa.*"

The man nodded.

"What promise is he supposed to remember?" Pasqual asked, as the man passed him.

Looking at the two villagers carrying Amado, Kali gestured at the dock. "*Isto é bom aqui.*" After they set him down, she shooed them away. "*Vai. Vai.*"

"You speak like a native."

"Get that end," Kali said, waving at the stretcher. "Let's get him aboard."

"Very good." Pasqual went to one end of the stretcher. "But you didn't answer my question about the promise."

"I paid him to tell anyone who asked that we'd gone east."

"Back to Macapa?"

"Or Belem. Or wherever Duarte wants to assume. Are you ready?"

"Yes. Are you?"

Kali nodded for him to lift. They struggled, but finally managed to get Amado up. The exertion and the heat was making her head throb again, but she ignored it the best she could. Walking backwards, Kali navigated the step from the dock to the *Avatara*. Once Pasqual had crossed, she stopped. "Let's put him down here. Maddie and I can get him inside."

Pasqual looked up. "Then you talked to her?"

"You didn't give me much choice, did you?"

"Do not blame me. You know that even if I had excluded her from our talk, we couldn't leave her behind. My brother would not have fallen victim to your sense of conscience. She would be dead before he realized she knew nothing."

Kali shrugged.

"What did you tell her?"

"I didn't have to tell her anything. She wanted to stay."

"But you did explain what that would mean for her future?"

"It was her decision. Consequences and all." She bent and scooped up a box, grabbing for the rail as a wave of dizziness caught her.

Pasqual didn't seem to notice. "I see. It's not your problem, and you're not taking any responsibility for her. How convenient."

Recovering, Kali straightened up. "This situation is as much your making as mine, so if you don't like the way I handled it, then go tell her yourself." She thrust the box at him. "Now, take this in and send Maddie out."

"That would make it easier for you, wouldn't it?" Pasqual asked before disappearing inside.

Her head hurt too much to even try and figure out what he meant, so she just leaned against the railing until Maddie came outside. One look at her, and Kali was awash in remorse. Maybe she should tell her. It wouldn't change anything, but maybe Maddie deserved to have a choice.

"Are you alright?" Maddie asked, stepping up to her. "You look pale."

With effort, Kali smiled. She would tell her later. "I'm just tired," she said, dropping her eyes to Amado. "Will you help me get him inside?"

"Of course."

Taking the heavier end, Kali lifted Amado and then used her elbow to open the door. It was a wonder that neither of them dropped the boy. As it was, they managed to get him onto the sofa before Kali sat down heavily on the edge of the coffee table and closed her eyes.

She felt Maddie's fingers hesitantly touch the heated skin of her forehead. It was like a cool breeze, and Kali floated on the sensation.

"Are you sure you don't have a fever? You feel warm." She moved her hand to the back of Kali's neck.

"It's just the heat outside. It always drains me." She looked up at Maddie. "I'll be fine as soon as we get underway."

"Tell me what I can do to help," Maddie said, her hand still on Kali's neck.

For a moment, she felt caught in Maddie's eyes. It took effort to look away. "I need to get us out of here, so will you bring in the boxes and put the food away?"

"Sure," Maddie said, dropping her hand and moving away.

Kali felt the loss of contact, but shook the feeling off as she got slowly to her feet. "I'm going to cast us off. If you need anything, ask Pasqual or come find me above."

She didn't look back at Maddie before she left the room. Once outside, she began the process of untying the *Avatara*. It was an easier task with two people, but Kali sensed that she needed to be alone for awhile. For reasons she didn't want to examine, being near Maddie was messing with her already scrambled head, and that needed to stop.

Chapter Eleven

Duarte's steps were heavy and slow as he climbed aboard his private plane. It didn't seem possible that his only son was dead. Amado was dead. He lowered himself into the wide, leather seat and sighed sadly. *Damn Luis for telling him! Damn Kali for killing him!* Nothing seemed important now. If he reached deep inside he could feel his anger, but at the moment it was shrouded by a pressing grief. He hadn't even been able to tell his wife. At least not until he had seen his son's body.

This was all Kali's fault. And his brother's. He cursed them both to a burning hell. More than that, he hoped he would be the one to send them there.

"Let's go," he yelled, at the pilot.

"A few minutes, Señor de Tueste."

His head fell to his chest. What did a few more minutes matter now? His son was dead. The tarmac outside his small window danced with heat waves that he watched without feeling. Nothing was the same anymore.

He remembered the pain when his oldest son, Vincent, had died in a skiing accident. At the time, he thought the grief would never end. But like everything, it eventually faded, and Duarte focused all his energy on his remaining son.

Amado was brash and desperate to prove himself. They had never been close, but Duarte believed in his son. He believed that one day he would turn into something great, someone worthy of his empire. Looking out the window, he realized he had no one left to share his accomplishments. His life was suddenly without worth and purpose.

"We're ready now, sir," the pilot called back.

"Then get us in the air."

It was a two and half hour jet flight to Santarem, and during that time, he was impotent to do anything but grieve. Once he arrived, he would be better poised to strike at anyone who had a hand in his son's death.

Adjusting her heading, Kali slowly increased the speed of the *Avatara* to fifteen knots. She was pleased at how well the ship responded. It had been too long since she'd taken the helm, and as the warm wind blew across her face, she felt much better. Even the pounding in her head was, thankfully, improved.

Standing up, she guided the wheel with one hand while holding onto the windshield with the other. The air hit her full force, and she luxuriated in it. It felt as if all her heavy feelings of doubt and insecurity were being blown away. She felt in control.

"What are you doing?" Maddie asked, climbing the stairs with a bottle of water and an ice bag.

"Nothing," she said, sitting back down in her seat. "It just feels good to be at the helm of the *Avatara* again. Two hours ago, I'd thought I lost her."

Maddie handed her the bottle of water, and gestured to the ice pack.

"Since you're steering, do you want me to hold this on your head?" She didn't wait for a response, and carefully pressed the ice to the back of Kali's head.

Not sure how to respond, Kali opened her water and took a drink. "Thanks. I was thirsty."

As the ship plowed through the wake of a passing barge, the bow dipped in the water, and Maddie's footing was jostled, causing her to grab onto Kali's shoulder for balance. After the ship leveled out, her hand remained there.

"What does *Avatara* mean?" Maddie asked. "It's Hindu, like your name, right?"

Kali took a breath. It was a simple question, yet she knew it was the first step in letting Maddie closer. Already she had exposed her physical weakness to her. Did she want to open herself up any more?

"Listen," Maddie said, gently shifting the ice pack. "I'm just trying to make conversation."

"Well, I'm no good at conversations," she said, tightening her grip on the wheel. "But to answer your question, *Avatara* is the incarnation of a deity."

"Appropriate for a Hindu goddess. Will you tell me how you got the name Kali?"

"No."

Maddie was quiet. "Okay," she finally said, with disappointment.

Kali sighed. "Someone gave it to me."

"Really?" Maddie's voice brightened. "I can't imagine naming someone after a goddess of death and destruction."

"You don't want to know." Kali reached up and pushed her hand away from her head. "Enough with the ice."

Maddie did nothing for a moment, but then she lowered herself into the co-pilot's seat. "Here," she said, holding out the ice pack. "You need to keep it on your head."

Kali took it, but didn't use it.

"I only asked because I want to know you better."

"No, you really don't. And if I do tell you—" She stopped, unable to make herself go on. Telling Maddie about her name would be reliving a dark moment. Although it had been years, Kali could still picture it all in vivid detail. The images were washed in blood, and the screams still echoed in her head. They always would.

"Trust me," Maddie said softly. "I won't think any less of you."

"You mean less than you already do?" Kali looked at her.

Maddie dropped her eyes.

Turning away, Kali watched the river. Maybe telling her was best. If nothing else, it would cement in Maddie's mind an image of her as a barbaric murderer. The woman might even consider herself lucky compared to the others who had crossed her path.

"It happened almost ten years ago," she began slowly. "I was running guns out of Jakarta. I'd just earned enough to buy my own boat, but many in my circle resented my good fortune. In Indonesia, women have a place, and even foreign women are expected to conform on certain levels."

"And you didn't conform?"

"I knew what I wanted, and that wasn't working on my back. And fuck what the others thought, right? My employers liked my end results. Ironically it wasn't them I needed to worry about."

"It was your crew, wasn't it?"

Kali nodded. "I learned by chance that they were planning on killing me. Maybe they wanted to send a message. Maybe they just wanted my boat. But you can see why I couldn't allow that?"

"You killed them." It was a statement free of accusation or rancor, but it didn't begin to encompass what Kali had done to those men.

She hesitated, but needed to finish the story. "It happened on a moonless night. Like I said, we were bringing in a shipment of guns to Jakarta. I don't know if that was the night they were going to strike, but I wasn't going to wait to find out. Everyone was relaxed. The transfer had gone smoothly and we were heading back to port. I waited until we were about twenty minutes outside the city before I took a machete and began hunting the pigs down."

Maddie sucked in a quick breath, but said nothing.

"One by one, I hacked their heads from their bodies, carrying them all with me like gruesome trophies. I'd killed before, but never like that. There was so much blood. It covered me. It covered the deck." She stalled in the memory. "When I was finished, I docked us in Jakarta, and I displayed their heads along the gunwale." She smiled thinly. "I wanted everyone to know what happened to those who betrayed me."

"How many were there?"

"Five."

"And was that your whole crew?"

"No. Three weren't involved, so I spared them. Two fled as soon as we docked. I should have killed them for desertion, but I didn't care. I was beyond caring anymore that night."

"And the one who remained?"

"Wasseem." His name came out as a whisper. It had been so long since she'd said it. Taking a deep breath, she continued. "Wasseem fell to his knees before me, calling me Kali-ma. I didn't know what this meant, so with my blade against his neck I demanded an answer. He told me that I was Kali, the bringer of death and destruction. Kali, the dark goddess who stole souls at night. Kali who was bathed in blood."

"So this was the man who named you?"

"This man worshiped me." She lifted her chin. "As I stood there, literally covered in blood and surrounded by disembodied heads, Wasseem worshiped me." Kali looked at her. "You'll never understand that rush. That power. At that moment, I was a god. I was Kali."

Next to her, Maddie was silent and Kali didn't risk looking at her. Finally, she heard her take in a breath and exhale slowly. "Jesus," she said, shakily. "I'm...um...I'm not sure what to think about all of that."

"You wanted to know."

"I wasn't expecting all of that. Jesus."

"It's who I am."

"You almost sound proud of that." Her voice grew stronger. Confrontational.

"I'm not ashamed of my life."

"Aren't you?" Maddie looked at her. "I'm not so sure."

"What the fuck do you know about me?" Kali didn't like the edge in her voice.

"I know that you're not who you pretend to be. At least not from what I've observed."

"I'm a killer."

"Oh, I'm well aware of that fact. But I think you do it out of necessity. Or maybe fear. It's what you've learned to do, but I don't think it pleases you."

"Of course it does."

"Then why didn't you kill me? Or that man Jack? Or even Pasqual? And why did I see remorse and uncertainty in your eyes after what you did to me?" Maddie touched her cheek, which was an ugly purple.

Kali looked away from the mark. "What are you hoping I'll say?"

"What you feel."

"And what makes you entitled to know what I feel? If I feel anything, that is."

"You feel things. I know. I saw."

Kali clenched her jaw. "What do you want from me? Why are you even here?"

For a moment, Maddie was total still and Kali risked a glance at her. Her face was blank. "I don't know," she said, looking up at her. "Jesus, I really don't know."

"Well, when you find out, be sure to let me know. Until then, why don't you just leave me the fuck alone? I have work to do."

Maddie hesitated, but then got to her feet. "You should put that ice on your head," she said, looking down at her. "It's still very swollen."

"Get out of here. Go see if Pasqual needs help with Amado."

As Maddie turned and left, Kali stared straight ahead. Behind her, she heard Maddie's footsteps receding down the stairs, and then she was alone again. She felt angry and disappointed and didn't even know why.

Reaching for the GPS, she activated it and scanned the map west of Porto Franco. The next town would be Almeririm, and she judged that they should be there before dark. She set a waypoint and then checked her gages. Everything looked good. The job was before her and she was in control again. All she had to do was concentrate on the job. Nothing else mattered.

Maddie stopped on the aft deck and looked at the sliding door, unable to make herself go inside. What she really wanted to do was cry. The story Kali had told her had been far worse than anything she could have imagined.

Death dominated Kali in a way Maddie couldn't quite comprehend. She had read about people like her in novels, but she never thought they truly existed. Now she knew better.

Leaning on the railing, she stared out at the river. It had been so beautiful when she had first seen it a week ago. The thought stopped her. Dear God, had it only been a week since this had all started? A mere week in which she'd been forced to acknowledge so many personal mistakes and witness so much misery and pain? How naïve and innocent she had been standing on that dock in Macapa and arguing with Rob over something as trivial as her career. At the time, it was all she thought she had, but how little that mattered now.

Staring down at the dark water, Maddie remembered falling into it, her life over. It was from that water that Kali had saved her. It was by her hand that she had been thrust into a world so different from anything she'd ever known. It was a world of darkness, deception, betrayal and death.

Both Kali and Pasqual had given her the opportunity to escape, and looking back at the horizon behind her, Maddie wondered if not taking that chance was yet another mistake. True, staying in that village had been a more terrifying prospect than staying with Kali, but was that the only reason she'd chosen to stay on the boat?

It was obvious that Kali didn't really want her here. She never really had, and why Maddie had thought differently, she couldn't begin to understand.

An ache began in her chest, and Maddie covered it with her hand. It was beyond her comprehension why admitting the truth hurt so deeply, but it did. Maybe she just wanted Kali to like her. Or maybe she wanted Kali to need her. Maddie sighed. She didn't know what she wanted from Kali. Maybe it was nothing at all.

The one message that Kali kept repeating to her was that she was a killer. Her last story had driven that point home with a painful clarity. The woman was capable of profound brutality and violence.

Yet, Maddie had glimpsed something in her eyes that hinted at a humanity and sensitivity that put her at odds with everything else. Or she may just be seeing what she needed to see to justify the growing bond she felt for Kali.

She had, of course, considered the possibility that her attachment to Kali might just be a result of the situation and nothing more. The woman had held her life and her freedom in her hands, and that was a powerful thing. As Maddie felt her safety becoming more assured, her emotions had shifted from abject fear to morbid curiosity and finally to something Maddie could only describe as a need to be near Kali.

If she were to be totally honest with herself, she had stayed on this boat more because she was afraid of losing Kali than any irrational fear of remaining in that village. It made little sense, but there it was.

The irony was that Maddie remembered reading an article about kidnap victims suffering from something called Stockholm Syndrome. It happened when a captive became emotionally involved with their captors through a series of violent episodes coupled with unexpected acts of kindness. It twisted the minds of the victims so completely that many times these people not only defended their former captors, but often professed a love for them.

While Kali's actions towards her might be considered textbook to this syndrome, Maddie didn't think she fit the profile of a kidnap victim. If she did, then, by the same rule, she should feel some of the same emotions for Pasqual – which clearly, she didn't.

In fact, she knew that if she'd been given the opportunity to save Kali by hurting Pasqual, she would have done anything. She would have even killed him.

That realization was as sobering as it was terrifying, and Maddie took a deep breath. It was her first in a long time. As it filled her lungs, she felt some of the pressure she'd been holding there lessening.

From the flybridge above her, the sound of music drifted on the wind and she listened absently. When she heard Kali's voice rise with it, she turned, dumbfounded. Not only did she not expect Kali to ever sing, the pain and longing she heard in her song made Maddie's chest grow tight again. Why did this woman affect her so?

Turning her back on the stairs, she stared out at the water while listening to Kali's song. It was strangely surreal. When it became more than she could bear, she fled inside.

She was descending the steps to Kali's cabin when the door to a small room was opened and Pasqual backed out. He was sticking something in his pocket, but when he saw her, he quickly withdrew his hand.

"Excuse me," he said, with a short bow. "I'm confused. Do you know which door is the head?"

"No. Not really."

"Well, no bother. I'm sure I'll stumble on it." He pulled at his dirty, stained shirt. "I was thinking of taking a shower. Do you think Kali will mind?"

At the mere mention of her name, Maddie felt her throat seize up and she looked away. "You'll have to ask her." She gestured towards the cabin door. "I'm sorry. I have a headache. I'm going to lie down."

"Are you all right, child?"

Maddie nodded. "I'm fine. Probably just tired."

"Yes. It's been a long day already." He put a hand on her shoulder and gave it a gentle squeeze. "You rest and perhaps later you can help me move Amado to one of the empty beds."

"I can try."

"I'd ask Kali, but I don't think she's up for the effort. Her head is bothering her?"

Maddie shook her head. "I think she's doing fine."

He patted her arm. "You don't need to protect her from me any longer, Dr. Cross. We're all on the same side now."

And just like that, Maddie found herself lumped in with them. Except she wasn't like them. Or was she? She felt so confused. So alone.

"Go lay down, child," Pasqual said, with a fatherly tone. "I'll keep an eye on Kali for you."

All she could do was give him a weak smile as she turned for Kali's cabin and pushed open the door. It struck her that maybe Kali didn't want her in here anymore, but throwing herself on the bed, she decided she didn't care. It was the only place she felt safe, and she needed that right now.

It was almost five o'clock when they passed the village of Almeririm. The sun was beginning to set, and Kali watched as the light filtered its way through the trees in fractals of color that split and danced on the water. They were making good time. In about thirty minutes, they should pass the small village of Aquiqui. After that, she would start looking for a place to take a break.

Her head had been throbbing with an increasing intensity for the last hour, and she knew it was time to take some more pills. If possible, she also wanted to try and sleep for a couple of hours before continuing through the night.

From behind, she heard steps on the stairs. Without turning her head, she knew it was Maddie. As she got closer, Kali realized that, strangely, she'd been anticipating her.

"I've brought you some more ice for your head," Maddie said, stopping just behind her. "And another water." She held the cold bottle over her shoulder. "I'm sorry I didn't bring you something sooner."

"Thanks," Kali said, taking the water. "My head was starting to hurt again."

"Can you take a break? It would do you good to rest for awhile." She felt Maddie gingerly pressed the ice to the back of her head. "Do you mind if I do this?"

Kali briefly closed her eyes and leaned back into the cold. "No. It feels good."

"It's so hot up here," Maddie said, her hand falling casually on Kali's shoulder. "I saw another wheel below. Don't you use that?"

"I prefer this," Kali explained. "The view is better."

"Yes, it's beautiful with the sun setting."

Kali found it easier to talk when she didn't have to look her in the eye. It was almost like talking to herself, and she relaxed.

"Do you remember the bar in Macapa?" Maddie asked, surprising Kali. "Where we first met?"

Kali sucked in a quick breath. "Yes."

"Why did you come over to our table?"

She paused, not sure if she should answer. The air around her felt charged, like a storm was brewing. "I don't know why I came over," she answered, with a sigh. "I thought that man was hurting you. I didn't like it."

"Do you do that often?" Maddie asked, lifting away the ice. "Break into people's arguments because you don't like a certain behavior?"

"No."

"Have you ever done it before?"

"No."

"I didn't think so." Maddie replaced the ice pack. "Who did you notice first, me or Rob?"

Rob. Was that his name? She could hardly recall what he looked like, yet the picture of Maddie was emblazoned in her mind. She remembered the way her hair had looked and the innocence in her eyes. She had tried to thank her, and Kali remembered turning on her like some rabid dog. There had been fear in Maddie's eyes, and Kali had been proud of that. Proud that she'd terrified the very person she'd wanted to help.

"Answer me. Please."

Kali tried to shrug it off. "I don't remember."

"Try!"

The sharp shift in her tone made Kali jump slightly. "You," she admitted, softly. "I saw you."

"Then what does that mean? Because all I could see was you," she said, circling around to sit in the co-pilot's seat. Her eyes were intense but uncertain. "Tell me what it means?"

Looking back at the river, Kali tightened her hand on the wheel. "What do you think it means?"

"I don't know, but I need to understand it. After everything that's happened, it has to mean something."

"Sometimes things just happen."

"I don't believe that. Everything has an explanation. Everything happens because of something. Everything happens in pairs. You can't touch something without being touched. You can't push something without being pushed back. It's a simple goddamn law of physics!"

Kali turned in surprise. Everything Maddie just said, she had always accepted as true. Her own life had run on that principle of action and reaction, yet how could she let it be applied here? Doing so would force her to accept all the potential consequences.

"I should hate you," Maddie continued. "After what you did to me, I should want to be off this ship and as far away from you as possible. That's only logical, right?"

"Yes." Kali couldn't deny it.

"Then why do I want to be here? Why have I gone against logic and reason to stay here with you?" She took a breath. "I'm not a physicist, but I can still scientifically question why my behavior negates such a simple and factual physical law. As a scientist, I should be able to make sense of this. It should all distill down into a neat theory that can be justified with the application of reason and logic."

"This is making my head hurt," Kali said wearily. "What are you trying to say?"

"I'm trying to decide if my behavior is just a rogue result in an otherwise orderly universe, or is my decision to remain here the only rational conclusion I could have made in these circumstances?" Maddie shrugged. "To answer that, I have to go back to the beginning, to the moment when we first met, and I have to ask if this is where things started?

"Forces always come in pairs and those forces can be identified and quantified. Therefore, is my reaction to you now merely a force of that initial contact?

"Am I attracted to you beyond logic because of that brief moment in Macapa? Or are there other things about you that have led me to forsake my reason in order to remain here?

"And conversely, what has caused you to go against everything you are to save me not once, but twice, and then to put your own safety and life on the line to protect me? Do you follow what I'm saying?"

"Barely," Kali said, shaking her head. "You've really thought about this."

"It's what I do. It's who I am."

Kali's eyes flinched, not sure if Maddie was somehow mocking her earlier admission.

"Yes, I have thought about it. And you know what I decided?" Maddie held her hands up. "I can't solve it. I can't solve it because this has nothing to do with logic or science or any of the things I know. It has to do with how I feel and that is something I can't begin to quantify or explain."

Kali was unsure how to respond, so she concentrated on the river. It was wide here, and the surface was smooth. She only had to keep the heading straight.

"When you told Jack that he'd have to kill you to get me, did you mean it?"

"What?"

"Would you have protected me with your life?"

The urge to deny it rushed to her lips, but Kali found herself unable to do that. "Yes," she whispered.

"And would you give me your life?"

Kali was confused. "Do you want to know if I'd die for you?"

"Not exactly," Maddie said, leaning forward, the distance between them disappearing. "Do you want to know why I wanted to stay?"

Looking into her eyes, Kali nodded her answer.

"Because you wanted me to," she said almost triumphantly.

"Oh no!" Kali cried, looking away. "Don't bring me into this. It was your decision to make, not mine."

"Yes, but it related directly to you. And if you really wanted to protect me, wouldn't it have been safer to leave me in that village instead of dragging me on this race down the Amazon?"

"You don't know that."

"I guess I don't know that, but it makes sense. At least to me." Maddie leaned back. "I've tried to rationalize it, but in the end it came down to what I felt. I acted on what I felt from you and what it made me feel. It was action and reaction, so in that, I guess I have adhered to the laws of physics."

Kali's stomach tightened. "So this is my fault?" She felt her rage rising. "No! I won't take responsibility for that. For you."

"That's not what I'm saying."

"Then what are you saying? Because all I've heard is a bunch of scientific crap that doesn't mean a damn thing. You felt this. I felt that. I've got news for you. I don't feel anything for you. So you stayed for the wrong reason." She smiled pitilessly.

It was as if a light was flipped off in Maddie's eyes, and Kali looked away in shame. "I don't know why I'm surprised," she said, sadly.

"Yeah? I don't either. I don't know what you want from me, but forget it."

Maddie stood. "Then I'm sorry I wasted your time." She turned away, but Kali grabbed her arm.

"Hold on a second. Since we're discussing your monumental decision to stay here with me, tell me if you thought about what it would all mean in the long term? About what would happen to you when this is all over?"

Maddie's brow crinkled. "I guess I thought it meant I wasn't going home yet."

The innocence in her face doused Kali's anger, and she suddenly hated what she needed to say. "It meant that you are never going home," she said, looking back at the water. "By staying it means that Dr. Madeline Cross became the last official victim of the crash that claimed so many lives yesterday."

"What? I don't understand."

Kali couldn't look at her. "You're dead, Maddie. There's no going home."

It took a moment for the reality to set in. "Then take me back!" she cried frantically. "I didn't know. You should have told me!" A pitiful cry escaped from her. "My family."

Kali heard her whimper, her voice so small and weak that she turned towards her. Everything happened in slow motion. First Maddie's eyes closed followed by her head tilting back. She seemed to hover there for a moment before her legs buckled and she crumpled to the floor.

It was like watching a person die, but for the first time it provoked a response so strong that Kali actually felt pierced by the pain. Pulling the engines back to neutral, she climbed out of her seat and dropped to the ground next to Maddie, but hesitated to touch her. The boat was slowing, and Kali could feel the shift of the sun against her face as the river pulled them off course. She didn't care.

Carefully lifting Maddie's head, she laid it against her leg and smoothed back her hair. As she looked down at Maddie, her chest felt as if it would burst. "I'm so sorry," she whispered.

The apology didn't make her feel any better. If anything, it brought home the weight of her crimes and her shoulders sagged.

"Is everything all right?" Pasqual asked, coming up the stairs. "I felt us slowing down."

"Come help," Kali cried, relieved to see him. "I think she fainted."

"I can see that. What should I do?"

Looking around, Kali pointed to the bottle of water Maddie had brought up. "Hand me that. And the ice pack. It's there!"

"Was it the heat?" Pasqual asked, passing the water to her first.

She opened it and poured some into her palm. She carefully splashed the water on Maddie's face. "No. I told her."

"Oh. Well, then this is perhaps understandable. I'm sure it was quite a shock."

Kali applied more cold water to Maddie's face until her head jerked and her eyes fluttered open. Before she became aware of their positions, Kali extracted herself and laid Maddie's head gently on the floor. Getting to her feet, she looked to Pasqual. "I need to get us underway again. Help her."

It was an excuse. They both knew it, but as Kali powered up the engines, she told herself she didn't care.

"What happened?" Maddie asked slowly sitting up.

"You fainted," Pasqual said, his manner tender and conscientious. "It was probably just the heat."

"No," Maddie said. "It was something else."

There was a sorrow in her voice that Kali couldn't ignore. Turning, she looked at Pasqual. *Get her out of here*, she wanted to scream, but instead she returned her eyes to the horizon. "Take her below where it's cooler."

"Yes, child," Pasqual cooed. "Let's go below deck. You'll feel better when you cool down."

With her body held in a tight line, Kali gripped the wheel as the old man took Maddie down the stairs.

Pasqual held the door open as Maddie entered the salon. Her face was pale and drawn, and he felt deeply sorry for her loss. It must be quite a blow to be told that life as you knew it was over. And for what? The sad misfortune of being in the wrong place at the wrong time.

"Why don't you sit and I'll get you some juice." He pointed her towards the couch.

Maddie looked at him, and for the first time since he'd met her, he saw no life in her eyes.

Leading her to the couch, he waited until she sat before going to the galley and pouring a glass of juice. When he returned, he placed the glass in her hand and guided it to her lips.

"Drink. It will make you feel better."

She complied for a few sips, but then pushed his hand away. "No more."

Pasqual sighed sadly. "Your situation is most regrettable," he said, taking the glass and setting it on the table.

A long moment passed before Maddie looked at him. "You knew?" she asked, her voice rumbling with something deep and dark.

"It wasn't a secret, Dr. Cross. If you'd tried to think beyond your immediate needs, it was quite obvious."

"Maybe obvious to you, but there was no way I could have known this would happen."

"What did you think would happen?"

"Not this!"

He sat next to her. "Think it through, Dr. Cross. You're intelligent. There was no way that we could leave you in Porto Franco knowing my brother was coming. In a village that size, he would have found you almost immediately, and I hope I don't have to spell out what he would have done to you to gain information about us. My brother is not a kind man."

"Then this wasn't my decision at all. I had no choice. Either way, I was dead." She closed her eyes. "I'm not sure how I should feel."

"Kali did what was best for you. You just made it easier for her." He smiled sadly. "At least for a short while."

"She did what's best for me? She owed me the truth."

"You weren't looking for the truth. If you were, I imagine you would have seen the danger you were in at every turn. Kali offered you security, and you seized that."

"So now I'm opportunistic?"

Pasqual chuckled. "I think you're being dramatic."

"She's a killer! A murderer."

"As you've seen, so am I." He gestured to Jack's body. Maddie, he noticed, didn't glance at it.

"It's not fair," Maddie said, clenching her hand.

He chuckled again. "For someone so educated, you sound quite puerile. Didn't anyone ever tell you that life isn't fair? All you can do is deal with it and keep going forward. At least you have a choice."

"What choice?" Maddie yelled, pounding her fist against her leg. "I've never had a choice!"

When she hit her leg again, Pasqual reached out to still her hand. "Stop it." When she nodded, he removed his hand. "If you could, would you do things differently?"

For a long second, Maddie stared off into the distance again. Then she blinked and Pasqual watched a tear run down her face.

"My parents. My brothers. My nephews." Another tear fell. "It's not fair."

"I grieve for your loss, but it can't be changed now."

"Have you lost anything?"

The question surprised him. "I'm sorry, what?"

"From this whole messy ordeal, will your life change at all? Will Kali's? Or am I the only one here who is expected to give up everything?"

"I know what you're implying, but you must understand that this is our world, Dr. Cross."

"Stop calling me that! It's not my name anymore."

"Kali and I aren't like you. We are the shadows in your daylight world. It's our curse to know how to exist in many places and yet belong to none. You may think that what's happened to you is unfair, but it's not our doing."

"Then who do I blame? God? Me?"

He shrugged. "Blame whomever you want, but in the end, your situation remains the same. Perhaps Kali should have told you sooner, but again I ask you if you would have decided differently?"

"Would I give up my life for her?" Maddie frowned at him. "That's what you're asking, right?" She pointed at the ceiling. "And it's exactly what she let me do. No. I'm wrong. By not telling me, she took it from me."

"If that's how you chose to see it."

"I'll never know if I would have decided differently, will I?"

"Regardless, I think you know the truth." He smiled thinly when her eyes narrowed in anger. "You may dispute it if you like, but I've seen the way you look at her. I heard the way you pleaded for her life." He held up his hands in defeat. "But perhaps I'm in error."

When she didn't respond, Pasqual stood.

She had a right to be angry, but the longer she held onto it, the harder her transition would be. Reaching out, he placed his hand on the top of her head. "If you want an old man's advice, let it go, child," he said, smoothing her hair back. "Accept what has happened and search for something good in it."

"You don't understand at all."

He accepted her rejection with a slight bow. "Perhaps. Now, if you'll excuse me, I should go change Amado's dressing and give him his medication."

Maddie lifted her head. "I'm sorry I haven't asked about him sooner. Is he resting better in the cabin below?"

"Better than this hard couch, yes. He seems less restless. Thank you." He smiled sadly. "You know that in all likelihood, my nephew will die. My brother will lose his only son. And I will have to live with my decision to trade his life for my own." He sighed. "So you see, not everything is as black and white as you like to pretend. We all change. We all lose."

"Not Kali, or so it seems. But then again, I don't think she has anyone or anything she cares about losing."

He shook his head. "If that's what you want to believe."

"It's what I've seen. I've lost. You've lost and she just goes on."

"As you wish," he said, with a sigh. "Now, if you'll excuse me."

Leaving her, Pasqual felt frustrated. He'd done what he could to put her mind at ease, but if she chose to continue fighting her fate, there was little he could do for her. As he pushed open the door to the guest cabin, he wondered what Kali was planning on doing with Dr. Cross once they reached Manaus. He supposed she could just leave her there. It might be possible for her to contact the United States embassy. There might be some way she could reclaim her identity.

But really it wasn't his problem. His payment to Kali included not knowing all the details. He preferred things that way.

Stepping up to the edge of the bed, Pasqual looked down at Amado. He was still unconscious, and staring at him he felt all thoughts of the doctor slipping from his mind. Sitting on the edge of the bed, he cautiously began removing the bandages from his face. The sight of the burns turned his stomach. Amado would never be handsome again, and it was his fault.

Chapter Twelve

Duarte banged on the door of the plane. "Open this now!"

"It won't open until the plane is stopped," the pilot said.

"Then stop the plane."

"We're almost to the hanger."

Duarte waited, his breathing heavy, as the plane pulled into the hanger. "Open it. Now!"

The pilot nodded as he shut down the engines. Then squeezing himself between Duarte and the door, he unlocked it.

The second there was enough room, Duarte expelled himself from the plane like air from a balloon. "Where is my update?" he demanded, looking around the hanger.

"Here," a woman said, stepping forward with a sheet of paper. "Mr. Vega faxed this a half hour ago."

Duarte grabbed the paper, desperate for news on that bitch Kali, but only learning that Luis had postponed the meeting with the Japanese. As if that was nearly as important. He held out his hand. "Pen, please."

Luis, it's time to dispatch the boats. Send one from Macapa and one from Santarem towards Porto Franco. As soon as you can arrange it, get some planes in the air covering the same pattern. When she's located, eliminate everyone on board. And fuck the Japanese. Let them wait.

"Here." He passed it to the woman. "Code this and send it to Luis."

"Yes, sir," the woman said, giving him a quick curtsy.

"Now, where is the seaplane?"

A man dressed in a dark suit stepped forward. "I'm sorry, sir, but it's too dark to fly to Porto Franco."

"Who the hell are you to tell me what I can and can't do?" He looked at the late afternoon sky. "It won't be dark for an hour, at least."

"Sanchez, sir. And I'm not telling you what you can't do. It's too dangerous to risk a night landing at Porto Franco."

"Put lights on the plane."

"It's not that simple, sir." He dropped his eyes. "Mr. Vega was very insistent that I guarantee your safety. Flying to Porto Franco now would be an unnecessary risk."

"I'm the boss. You listen to me."

Sanchez took a step backwards. "As you wish, sir. But the pilot will not fly."

Frowning, Duarte turned away. Damn it all to hell. His safety was nothing when compared to getting to his son. He sighed. Amado was dead and could no longer be of use.

"Very well," he conceded. "A few more hours won't change Kali's fate."

Sanchez smiled. "I've arranged for a hotel. The plane will be ready in the morning."

"I want to leave at first light." He buttoned his suit jacket. "Now take me to the hotel."

"This way, sir," Sanchez said, leading him to a waiting car.

At six thirty, Kali pulled the *Avatara* around a small island and dropped anchor. It was almost dark. The horizon was a ribbon of deep reds and purples, but Kali didn't notice it as she turned off the engines and climbed down from the bridge.

"Where's Maddie?" Kali asked, crossing the salon.

The old man looked up from the galley. "I believe she's lying down."

She nodded, relieved that she didn't have to face her just yet.

"How's your head?"

"Better," Kali replied honestly.

"Still dizzy?"

"No." She looked around. "Is there anything to eat?"

"I opened some chili." He reached for a bowl. "I'll get you some."

"I can get it myself." Kali grabbed the bowl from him, but then stood there lost in thought. She didn't notice when Pasqual took the bowl back.

"She's very upset," he said, ladling chili into it. "You should talk to her. Explain things."

Kali shook her head. "Don't start."

"Very well. It's your business, but have you thought what you're going to do with her when this is all over?" He held out the bowl.

Kali grabbed it. "No."

"Interesting." He passed her a spoon. "I wonder why?"

Her reasons, as unfathomable as they were to her, were none of his business. She seized the spoon and turned away. "I think we should dump Jack's body here."

Pasqual was silent for a moment, but then he said, "If you think that's best. Do you have a plan to keep him from floating away though?"

"We'll weight him down." She dug into her food. "I just want him off the boat before he starts rotting."

"Charming." Pasqual sighed. "Then I suggest we try to get him on land. The jungle will eat him up quickly."

"No body, no trail." Kali smiled grimly. "We'll do it tonight. Before we get under way again."

"You're going to drive through the night?"

"I'm just stopping long enough to eat and take a quick nap. I want to be as far from Porto Franco as possible before morning." She took another mouthful of the canned chili. It was too salty yet totally tasteless.

"Do you think Duarte is in Santarem by now?"

"I suppose so, but he won't be able to fly until morning."

"I wonder if the hospital has notified him of Amado's sudden death."

"Did you pay them?"

"Yes, but the Mother Superior hesitated."

She took another bite. "It doesn't really matter. By tomorrow morning, he'll know Amado is alive and that we have him. All we can hope for today is that if he thinks his son is dead, he may make poor decisions. It's even possible that the news may prompt his partners to step in. That will give him pause in his hunt for us."

"We can hope, but I think Luis will just handle everything."

"That weasel can't wait to take over things," Kali said, dropping her spoon in the bowl. "I don't trust him."

"Yes, well he doesn't like you very much," he said, with a thin smile. "Or at least that was the impression I got when Duarte spoke of you."

There was something odd in the way he said that, but Kali shrugged it off. "Was that when you decided to investigate me?" She pushed her bowl away. "Just how much do you know about me anyway?"

The old man looked her in the eye. "Enough." He took her bowl and began washing it.

"Have you told Maddie any of it?"

He set her bowl in the drying rack. "You really should get some sleep. I'm going to heat some broth for Amado. He needs to eat."

"Did you tell her to protect her or manipulate her?"

"Does it matter?" he asked, taking a can of soup down from the cabinet.

Her head suddenly hurt again, making her exhaustion feel nearly overwhelming. With a sigh, she gestured at the couch. "I'm going to get some sleep. Will you wake me in two hours?"

"Not if you sleep there," Pasqual said, with a smile. "That couch is far too hard for a good rest. It will do neither of us any good if you become too tired to function, so please do us all a favor by sleeping in your bed."

"I'll sleep where I want to," Kali said defiantly.

The old man laughed at her. "Imagine what my brother would say if he saw his great Kali afraid of facing a small scientist." He laughed again.

"I'm not afraid of her."

"No? My mistake then." He chuckled as he opened the soup.

Frowning, Kali stalked past him. She wasn't afraid. It was just easier if she avoided Maddie.

Outside her cabin, she paused for a moment before pushing open the door. The room was nearly dark with only a sliver of light from the bathroom slicing across the floor. In its glow, she could make out Maddie's form lying on the bed with her face to the wall.

Relieved, she shut the door and went into the bathroom to wash up. It felt wonderful to get the sweat and grim off her face. Briefly, she thought about taking a shower, but decided not to waste the water or effort. Once she climbed back up to the flybridge, she'd only get dirty again.

After she dried her face, she shut off the light before opening the door. She stood on the threshold until her eyes adjusted to the darkness. Cautiously, she made her way to the bed. Maddie had been on the right side, so she moved to the left. It crossed her mind to sleep on the floor, but Pasqual had been right. She couldn't let herself get too tired.

Feeling the edge of the bed, she lay on top of the covers and pulled the pillow firmly under her head. *So far so good.* She closed her eyes and tried to sleep.

Slowly, she became aware that the room felt different. Cold. It felt cold. Reaching over, she switched on the bedside lamp and looked around. The cabin was empty. Maddie must have left when she was in the bathroom.

Kali rolled over and pressed her hand to the mattress. It was still warm, and inhaling she could still smell the faint scent of roses. Closing her eyes, Kali left her hand on the fading warmth of Maddie's spot. It had been selfish and shortsighted to not tell her about the consequences. It was a mistake she regretted.

But there was nothing she could do about it now, so rolling over she turned off the light and tried to relax. Sleep, she had learned, was paramount to survival. The decisions she needed to make over the next few days had to be quick and decisive. She couldn't do that if she let herself get exhausted or distracted. It took a few minutes, but she managed to finally drift off to sleep.

Kali's eyes snapped open at the second knock on her door. A quick glance at the clock confirmed the reason for the knock. "I'm up."

"Very good," Pasqual called back.

It was a little after nine. Late enough for any lingering boat traffic to have died down. She switched on the lamp, the sudden burst of light causing her head to explode in acute pain. Closing her eyes, she tried to sit up, the throbbing getting worse with her movement. Once again she cursed Jack, wishing she could kill him again.

Pressing her hands to either side of her head, in a vain attempt to contain the pain, she took in several deep, even breaths. The throbbing began to lessen and she cautiously opened her eyes. The light still stung, but was bearable.

She sat there until she felt capable of standing up. The room went in and out of focus and she felt slightly sick to her stomach. All she wanted to do was lay back down and sleep, but that was an impossibility. She knew that if she was going to get through the long night ahead, she had to take some more pills. At least they made things tolerable.

Moving slowly, she reached for the bottles and dumped two pills into her hand. Going into the bathroom, she swallowed them with water from the faucet before splashing some on her face. She stood there, praying the pills went to work fast.

When she felt stronger, she kicked on her shoes and exited her cabin. The door to the spare stateroom was open, its light spilling into the hallway. Kali stopped at the door, watching as Pasqual wrung out a wet cloth and laid it over Amado's forehead. Even from where she stood, Kali could see his chest rising with shallow breaths.

"Did you sleep?" he asked, glancing over his shoulder at her.

"Yes. How's he doing?"

Pasqual's bony shoulders fell. "He was awake briefly, but I don't think he looks good."

There wasn't anything she could say, so Kali stepped back. "We need to get rid of Jack. Can you help?"

Setting the bowl of water aside, the old man rose to his feet. "Of course."

She stopped in the main pilothouse to pull a flashlight off the wall. As she was turning back into the salon, she saw Maddie and nearly dropped the torch. She was reclining on the couch with a book in her lap, but from what Kali could see, she had turned very few pages. Slowly, she set the book down and climbed to her feet.

As their eyes met, Kali found herself wanting to say things that until that moment had been unknown to her. When Maddie looked away, she exhaled in relief.

"I found this book out here," Maddie said, gesturing at it. "I hope you don't mind."

Taking a step forward, Kali glanced at the title. "Why would I mind? It's not mine."

"Oh." Maddie almost sounded disappointed. "I thought it might be yours."

"Not my style" She shrugged as Pasqual came up the stairs. "And since there's no one left to claim it, I guess it's all yours now."

"Are we ready?" he asked, his old eyes jumping between them.

She passed him the flashlight. "Go look around, and I'll drag him out."

"Oh God," Maddie exclaimed. "You're going to dump the body here, aren't you?"

"It needs to be done." Kali refused to apologize.

"But just throwing him in the water?" Maddie shook her head. "It's...it's barbaric."

"Then maybe you should leave the room again." She hated the rancor in her voice.

"Again?" Maddie frowned. "But I thought you would want me to leave. It is *your* cabin."

"You didn't stay around long enough to ask, did you?"

"Ladies, please," Pasqual interrupted. "Let's focus on the task at hand."

"Oh, that's right," Maddie said flippantly. "We're tossing a human being into the river. As if he's garbage."

The arguing was making her head hurt, and she closed her eyes on the pain.

"Please, Dr. Cross," Pasqual said calmly. "There is no other option. In this heat, it's unsanitary, and, unfortunately, the river is all we have."

"It's all Jack would have done to you," Kali added.

Maddie's face darkened, but Pasqual jumped in again. "Kali is right."

"It's still savage."

"Well, that's what I am." Kali stalked past her. "Let's get this over with."

Pasqual held open the door as Kali grabbed Jack's ankle and dragged him out of the room. She did her best to not look down at him. Keeping him inside with the air-conditioning had likely slowed down the decomposition, but by now she knew the enzymes and bacteria were hard at work.

Pasqual was at the edge of the aft deck, shining the flashlight into the trees. "I think we can get him over there."

Dropping Jack's ankle, she joined him to look. "It's too far."

"Do we have anything to tether him to the shore? A rock or anything we can throw over that tree root? It will at least keep him from floating away."

"I think so." She opened the storage locker at her feet and extracted a dual pronged metal object. "Extra anchor."

"Perfect." Pasqual swatted at a swarm of mosquitoes that hovered around them.

Kali dropped a coil of rope near the anchor and stood up. "I'm going to try and get us closer to the shore. You tie this around his legs."

Sitting in the pilot's seat, she started the engines and lifted the anchors. She looked down at the depth finder by her knee.

The *Avatara* had an eight-foot draft. In the ocean, Kali never had to worry about bottoming out, but the river floor could jump and shift radically.

Adjusting the throttles, she spun them around until the stern was sitting perpendicular to the shoreline. Then nudging the engines into reverse, she backed the ship up slowly. With her eyes on the depth finder she watched the bottom of the river move closer and closer.

"That's good," Pasqual called up, before the river bottom became a problem.

Pulling the throttles back to neutral, she climbed out of her seat. "Let's do it," she said, dropping to the aft deck.

"We have to lower him," Pasqual said, looking down at the swim platform five feet below.

"Back up," Kali said, picking up the anchor which was now tied to Jack's legs. She passed it to Pasqual. Then using her foot, she nudged Jack's body towards the open gate before giving him a final push that sent him falling to the platform with a dull thud.

"Yes, well," he said, holding the anchor against his chest. "I suppose that works, too."

Kali climbed down to the swim platform. "Give me the anchor."

She pointed at the large tree root eight feet away. "Shine the flashlight there," she said, swinging the anchor. "Here goes." She let the anchor fly. The slack in the rope disappeared and Jack's body was yanked towards the edge of the platform.

"You got it," Pasqual said, shining the flashlight on the metal of the anchor.

"Then it's bye-bye Jack," she said, kicking him into the water. His body sank a little before rising to the surface.

"Nicely done," Pasqual said, stepping out of her way as she climbed back up.

"It's just done." She looked back. "With luck, he'll be eaten quickly."

"That's disgusting," Maddie said, standing by the door to the salon.

"That's life," Kali replied, heading for the flybridge.

"He was part of your crew. You knew him."

"And he betrayed me," Kali said, halfway up the stairs.

"Oh well, then it's a wonder you didn't behead him for another gruesome trophy."

Kali glared down at her. "Why don't you go read your book? You're good at that."

Continuing her climb to the flybridge, Kali dropped into the pilot's seat and reached for a pair of night goggles. They made a gentle whirring sound as they powered up, and pulling them on the night was transformed into eerie shades of green. She nodded with satisfaction as the water, shore and trees jumped out at her.

Engaging the engines, Kali sent the ship forward. Overhead, low hanging branches caught on the communication arch, squeaking and scratching their way across. Kali watched to make sure the boat cleared them completely before tapping the speed up a notch and pointing them west.

Through the green haze of the night goggles, Kali scanned the surface, pleased that it was calm and clear. It was lucky timing that they had missed the rainy season. During that time, the Amazon would be swollen and angry. The torrential rains could cause mud slides that would topple entire trees and other large debris into the water. But since that wasn't the case tonight, Kali only had to watch out for the occasionally obstacle.

"May I come up?" Maddie asked, from the stairs behind her.

Kali felt her chest clench, followed by a swell of anger. "Why?" she demanded, grabbing the throttles and pushing them forward. The ship responded with more speed.

"Because I want to."

"Who cares what you want?" she said under her breath, but shifted in her seat to motion Maddie up the stairs. "Fine. I could use your help anyway." Picking up the second pair of goggles, she powered them up and held them out. "Put these on."

"Night goggles? Why?"

Her anger crested and spilled out. "Don't be stupid. It doesn't become you," she said derisively.

"I wasn't trying to be stupid," Maddie said, pulling them onto her head. "Wow! Why is it green?"

She glared at her in annoyance, knowing her feelings were irrational and wrong, but still unable to let it go. "I don't know. You're the scientist, why don't you tell me?"

Maddie was quiet for a moment. "I didn't leave the room to hurt you," she said softly. "If that's why you're so upset with me."

Clenching her jaw, Kali didn't respond. The comment was too direct, and she didn't know what to say.

"I left because I thought you'd rather be alone. It is your room. Your space. And I knew you needed to rest without having to deal with me again."

Kali stared down the river.

"And just in case you might be remotely interested, I'm a global change biologist. I've doctorates in biology and biogeology. It was a private grant that brought me to Brazil where my colleague and I were to study the effects of carbon dioxide on the growth of sub-tropical trees." She paused. "But you know, in spite of all my years of education and study, I've no idea why night goggles are green."

At that, Kali smiled, the gesture evaporating all her resentment and anger. "Okay," she said, taking a breath. "I have been told that the vision processor is green because the human eye can see more shades of green than any other color." Turning her head, Kali looked at her. "And I am interested."

Maddie accepted her comment with a nod. "So what am I supposed to be watching for anyway?"

Kali waved her hand at the water. "You'll need to help me see turns, submerged objects, and such. The river can be dangerous in the dark."

"It's dangerous in the day, too. No telling who or what is waiting to end your life."

The comment brought her anger back, and she fought to keep it at bay. "I know that was meant for me. And while I'm sure you hate me, can you put it aside long enough to help me tonight?"

Maddie was quiet for a moment. "I don't hate you," she said, with a breath. "I'm still angry and upset, but I don't hate you."

Hearing that admission, Kali looked at her, distorted and unfamiliar in the green haze.

"You should have told me," Maddie said, shifting to meet her gaze.

Unnerved, she turned her eyes back to the river. "It wouldn't have mattered."

"I know you were going to take me regardless of what I decided. It was for my protection, and maybe I should feel grateful, but I can't get over the fact that not only did you take the choice from me, but that you didn't even respect me enough to tell me the truth."

"You told me what you wanted before I had the chance."

"I still deserved the truth."

Kali sighed. "Do you want an apology?"

"Do you feel like giving me one?"

Surprisingly, she did. "I'm sorry."

Reaching across the space, Maddie touched her arm. "Thank you."

The contact was brief, but intimate. To feel it again, Kali thought she would have apologized for anything.

"So how far are we going?" Maddie asked, the subject dropped.

Relieved to return to more stable ground, Kali gripped the wheel tighter. "I'm hoping to cover about a hundred miles tonight." She saw Maddie check the clock.

"But it's barely nine thirty. It's going to take us almost eight hours to go a hundred miles?"

"If we're lucky. I can only go so fast in the dark."

"Is it hard to drive a ship this big?"

"Pilot," Kali corrected again.

"Well, is it?"

"Not once you get the hang of it. It can be like driving a car in an empty parking lot."

"Unless you hit something."

"Yes, but we're not going to let that happen." She glanced at Maddie.

"Do you want to try?"

"Really?"

"Why not?" Kali slid closer to the wall. "Come here."

Maddie hesitated, but then rose to her feet. "Okay."

Pulling the throttles back to a slower speed, Kali took off her goggles. "I'm going to turn up the instrument lights, so take your goggles off."

As Maddie pulled them off, Kali flipped on the instrument panel. Next, she turned on a powerful spotlight attached to the side of the ship, and a swatch of white light cut through the darkness.

"Now sit here." Kali patted the seat next to her. "It's a little small, but—"

"It's fine," Maddie said, cutting her off and sitting down.

When Maddie's body pressed against her side, Kali felt her breath catch. It was closer than anyone had been to her in a long time, yet she felt no compulsion to move away.

"How's your head?" Maddie asked, lifting her hand to brush back her hair. "You looked pale earlier."

Kali closed her eyes as Maddie's fingers inched into her hair and moved ever so lightly across her wound. Despite the pain, Kali concentrate on nothing but Maddie's touch.

"It's still swollen." Her hand disappeared. "You should let me clean it later."

"I will," Kali said, trying to turn her focus back to the ship. "Alright, there are four things you need to know. Wheel, throttle, depth finder and speedometer." She touched each thing in turn. "Left side of the boat is the port side. Right is the starboard. Front is the bow. Rear is the stern. Feel free to use left and right. I'll understand."

Maddie had leaned forward to study the instruments, her hand sliding lightly across the skin of Kali's leg. "It says we're doing five miles an hour."

Holding very still, Kali struggled to find her voice. "It's knots. One knot is a little less than a mile per hour. So at five knots, we're going roughly four miles per hour. It can also measure nautical miles. One nautical mile is one minute of latitude or six thousand feet."

"Okay," Maddie said.

"Give me your hand," Kali said, lifting it off her leg and putting it on the throttles. "There are two throttles for the two engines. When going forward, you want to keep them equal. The only time to power one over the other is when turning. Now, push them forward a little and watch the speed pick up." She guided Maddie's hand before letting her have it all. "Take it to ten."

When the needle approached the mark, Maddie stopped. "Now what?" she asked, shifting against her.

"The wheel," Kali said, distracted. "Put your hand on the wheel and feel the motion of the water."

Maddie turned the wheel slightly and the ship responded. "I feel it."

"Hello up there," Pasqual called out. "I made some coffee." He climbed the stairs carrying a thermos and two cups. "A driving lesson? Pity you never taught Jack."

"Jack was too stupid to learn."

"Yes, obviously." Pasqual set the thermos down. "Shall I pour?"

"Not yet."

"Then do you need any help?"

Next to her, Maddie's body was rigid, but Kali had made no attempt to take over the wheel. "We're fine. Why don't you get some sleep?"

"Only if Dr. Cross promises to wake me should she need a break. I'm sorry, Kali, but I can't do your job."

"I wouldn't ask you."

"I'm fine," Maddie said, her hands tight on the wheel. "But thank you."

"Very well, I'll see you both tomorrow. Kali, *refletir em what você és fazendo."*

Turning her head, Kali glared at him. How dare he caution her to think about what she was doing. It was none of his goddamn business. She wasn't doing anything wrong. "Sure. I'll do that," she said, as he climbed down the stairs.

"What did he say?"

"To keep my eyes open." Grabbing the throttles, Kali slowed the engines. "We need to put on the goggles now."

"How many languages do you speak?"

"I don't know. A few."

"Such as?"

"Why do you want to know?"

"Because I just do. Because I..." Maddie started to move away. "Forget it."

"Wait." Kali stopped her with a touch. "I'm sorry. I forget that you like conversation." She smiled to herself. "Other than English, I speak Portuguese, Russian, Malay, French, Spanish, and a smattering of Mandarin and Japanese. But I don't really know how to read or write them. I just learned out of necessity."

As if satisfied with her response, Maddie returned to her earlier position, her body once again pressing against Kali. "I don't speak any language except English. I know some Latin and Spanish, but that's pretty worthless."

It was a truce, and without realizing it, she knew that she'd just silently agreed to Maddie's terms. For every piece of information she gave to Maddie, she would get one in return. On the surface it was harmless enough, but Kali knew that was probably deceptive. "Let's put the goggles on again," she said, bluntly. "We need to pick up speed."

She turned off the spotlight and lowered the lights on the instrument panel. Next to her, Maddie's goggles whirred to life and air seeped in between them as Maddie moved to pull them on. Kali did the same, and again, the night was bathed in green.

"Can I still steer?"

If she refused, Kali knew there would be no reason for Maddie to continue sitting next to her. "All right," she heard herself saying, as she dropped her hands from the wheel. "Go ahead."

Maddie seized it. "I like this. I feel in control of something again."

In response, Kali pushed the speed up. Quickly glancing to her left, she could see the smile on Maddie's face, and it made her feel curiously good to have put it there.

The warm night air rushed past them, and Kali found herself breathing in the scent of Maddie's hair. It was distracting. "Do you think you can handle it?"

"What? Are you leaving?"

Kali almost laughed. "No. I just want you to really feel it." Easing herself upwards, Kali climbed to the back of the seat.

"Where are you going?" Maddie cried, not taking her eyes off the river ahead.

She spread her legs. "Scoot over and take control."

"Are you sure?" Maddie asked, sliding between Kali's legs.

"Yes. The river is wide here and I'll be watching for anything. You just enjoy it." She placed her hands on Maddie's shoulders to steady her balance. "Do you mind this?"

"No. Not at all."

The wind whipped around her like a ghost. It lifted her hair and kissed her skin. Closing her eyes, she savored the feeling. It was almost easy to forget why she was there and what she was doing. Ever so briefly, she let herself contemplate what it would be like to really be as free as she felt in that moment.

Maddie laughed, and Kali smiled.

"You're doing great," she said, leaning forward. "But the river is turning, so let me take over."

Nodding, Maddie moved to the right, and Kali lowered herself back into the seat. When she put her hands on the wheel, Maddie stood up and moved back to the co-pilot's chair. The space between them seemed too wide.

"Thank you for letting me do that."

"Did you enjoy it?"

"Very much." Maddie pointed to the thermos. "Would you like coffee?"

"Sure," she said, slowing the boat to compensate for the shift in the river.

"Tell me something about you," Maddie said, passing her coffee. "Something I don't know."

Kali was silent for a moment. "And just how much do you already know?" she finally asked. "How much did Pasqual tell you?"

"He just told me, Kali. I didn't ask him anything." She paused. "I think he wanted me to hate you."

"No, he wanted you to be afraid of him. It's not really money that makes the world go round. It's knowledge. That's real power. Pasqual was using his knowledge to gain power over you." She shrugged. "And me, too."

Maddie shook her head. "I don't know how you live like this."

"It's no different in your world. It's just more subtle. If you looked, you'd see the same dynamics all around you."

"That's not what I'm asking. How do you work for people like Pasqual knowing that you may have to kill or steal or God knows what?"

"It's what I know. It's who—"

"It's not who you are!" Maddie cut her off. "I won't believe that."

"You should believe it."

"And what about me? How do I fit into all of this now? My life as I know it is over, so what do I do now?"

Kali sighed. "I don't know. This wasn't what I planned for you."

"No? You thought abandoning me in some shitty village was a better solution?" Maddie demanded, her voice becoming louder and more incensed.

"What else did you want me to do?" Kali responded, feeling her own anger surfacing again.

"I don't know. Do you ever think of anyone but yourself?"

"What's that supposed to mean?"

"Well, let me see if I have this right. Pasqual gets his life. You get fifteen million dollars. And I get left at the dock in Manaus with no name and no life."

"I'm sure you could go to the U.S. Consulate. Explain what happened."

"No. I've decided I want more than that." Maddie's voice held an edge that Kali hadn't heard before. It was ruthless and final.

"And what's that?"

"I'm in your world now, right? Everyone and everything in your world has a price. So I want to know if you'll pay mine?"

"Your price?" Kali didn't like this. "What's your price?"

"You."

Kali blinked. "What?"

"You, Kali. Your life. You've taken mine. I want you in exchange."

She turned towards Maddie, lifting off her goggles. She needed to see her. "That doesn't make sense." She slowed the *Avatara* to a modest seven knots.

"Nothing in your world makes sense to me. Why should this?" Maddie removed her goggles. "I'm acting on selfish impulse, just like the rest of you."

"Is this a game to you?"

"Absolutely not."

Kali waved her off. "Then drop this. Once we reach Manaus, I'll help you do whatever you want. I owe you that."

"The girl who was killed when you were younger, what was her name?"

She turned her head away to hide her reaction. "Pasqual knows about that?"

"He said your life changed after her death. Why?"

"That's none of your business."

"Did you love her?"

"Stop."

"Have you ever loved anyone?"

"I won't talk about this."

"That's my price, Kali."

"You want to know my fucking life story?" Kali felt her fury surging.

"You took my life, why shouldn't I get something in return?"

"Because it isn't yours to take!"

"Exactly," Maddie said softly. "All you have to do is ask me."

"What?"

"Ask me to stay with you."

"That's it? That's all you want?"

"No." She shook her head. "You have to mean it."

Options, moves, outcomes twisted in her head, but all eventually added up to anguish and unease. What was she supposed to do? Or say? Maddie didn't know what she was asking.

"I'll help you get back to Boston," she repeated. "Whatever you need."

"And what about what you need?"

Kali shook her head. "I don't need anything."

"What if you need me?"

"I don't."

"Do I remind you of her? The one you lost? Am I your second chance?"

That was it. Kali felt her anger break. "Shut the fuck up!" she said, her voice rising. "I won't talk about her, and I'm done talking about this. Now, if you can't help me watch the fucking river, then get the fuck off my bridge!"

Reaching for her goggles, she pulled them on and waited for her eyes to adjust before jamming the throttles forward. The bow of the *Avatara* rose out of the water as the speed increased.

Barely glancing at Maddie, she reached out and flipped on the stereo, cranking up the volume. There would be no more talk. It only made things worse. Talking with Maddie, she realized, was like dredging the bottom of a pond. Eventually, something long hidden was going to get snagged and dragged to the surface.

She cycled through her music until she found some mindless rock group. She didn't know their name, but the music was loud enough to drown out any unwanted thoughts or conversations.

Next to her, Maddie had pulled on her goggles and was staring ahead. Kali felt her gaze linger, but then she forced it away. She didn't need her. That was a weakness she couldn't afford.

It was around five o'clock when the GPS announced that they had reached the village of Nossa. The night goggles confirmed their position by showing a small grouping of buildings along the shoreline. Her night was almost over.

The sun would rise in about an hour, and Duarte would have planes in the air soon after. She couldn't let the *Avatara* be seen.

In the co-pilot's seat, Maddie was sleeping gently. They hadn't spoken since she'd turned on the stereo. The music had created a barrier between them, but as the music cycled from hyped up rock to a more calming jazz, Kali felt her anger dissipating.

By two o'clock, the music had begun to make her drowsy, and a quick look at Maddie confirmed that she'd already succumbed to sleep. Slowing the boat, Kali removed Maddie's goggles and placed a towel under her head.

Over the next three hours, she had found herself looking at Maddie more and more often. Since no one could see her or judge her actions, Kali didn't hide her interest. It actually relaxed her.

The GPS beeped as they approached her pre-set waypoint. The map had shown an inlet not far away that might be perfect to shelter in during the day.

Since the cove didn't appear to be very large, she knew she needed Maddie's help to locate it.

Slowing the engines to a crawl, she reached across to shake Maddie awake. "Hey, come on. I need your help." She shook a little harder.

Maddie inhaled deeply and lifted her head. In the green haze of the goggles, the whites of her eyes appeared huge as she blinked quickly. Rubbing at them, she yawned. "Did I fall asleep?"

"A little while ago."

"I'm sorry."

"Don't be. I just need you to help me find an inlet and then you can go to sleep again."

"What about you?"

"I'll sleep, too." She fought back the yawn that was hanging in her throat. "Put on your goggles."

Maddie powered them up.

"We're looking for a break in the tree line. It should be on this side of the river, but I'm not sure where."

They inched their way up the shore, both silent as they searched. The air was muggy and it clung to Kali's skin like mold. Thinking she had missed her target, she was about to turn around for a second try when Maddie pointed. "Is that it?"

Kali looked closer, smiling in the darkness. "Yes, I think it is." She turned the *Avatara* for the opening. "Now let's hope it's large enough to hide us." As they moved closer, Kali breathed a sigh of relief.

"Will we be safe in there?"

"I hope so. I'm going to sleep up here so I can hear anyone coming."

"No," she said fiercely. "You need real sleep. Pasqual can sit up here and watch."

She was too tired to argue, so she just ignored her. "I'm going to use the spotlight, so take off your goggles." Shedding her own, she flipped on the beam, casting the trees into eerie shadows.

"Things look weird in this light," Maddie commented as she glanced about.

"I'm going to turn the boat around so we can see what goes past us on the river." She alternated power to the engines, spinning them around, until the light shone on the opening of the Amazon.

Dropping the anchors, she waited for them to hit bottom before shifting the engines enough to set them. It took experience to feel the anchors, and Kali liked to think she had the touch. When it was done, she cut the engines and turned the light away from the opening.

"So what now?" Maddie said, turning to face her.

In the ambient glow of the spotlight, Maddie appeared a little out of focus. Maybe it was the light or her exhaustion, but she felt Maddie's eyes drawing her in, and without thinking, she kissed her.

The action seemed to stun them both, but then Kali felt Maddie's lips begin to move. It was slow at first, but then as the urgency between them increased, Kali was pulled deeper and deeper until the world around her evaporated, and Maddie became the only thing she could feel.

As she wove her fingers through the cool strands of Maddie's hair, she could feel hands moving up her body and settling on her shoulder. It took her a moment to realize Maddie was pushing her away.

"No."

Kali leaned back, the night air moving between them again.

"I can't," Maddie said, her voice hushed.

"Really? I think you can. I think you—" Kali stopped herself. Clenching her hand, she stared past Maddie.

"I'm sorry."

Turning away, Kali looked off the side. "I'm tired. Maybe I will just sleep up here."

"Because I stopped you?"

"Because I want to! Because I fucking can!"

A tense silence hung between them, and Kali found herself listening to Maddie's every breath.

Finally, Maddie sighed. "Why did you do that?"

There was no accusation or censure in her voice. It was a simple question. Almost childlike in its innocence.

"I don't want to talk about it. I'm too tired and my head is killing me again."

"Okay," Maddie said, softly. "Then come downstairs and sleep." Reaching out, she took her hand.

The gesture made Kali want to pull away and reject her. To get revenge. To hurt her. But before she could do this, she gave up in defeat. "You go ahead," she said, giving Maddie's hand a small squeeze and releasing it. "I have some things I need to finish here."

"Can I help?"

Still avoiding her eyes, Kali shook her head. "You go get some sleep. I'll be fine."

Maddie hesitated, but then in the haze of the spotlight, she nodded. "Don't you dare try to sleep up here. Understand?"

The sincerity of her tone made Kali smile sadly. "All right."

"I'll come back and find you."

Kali doubted that, but she didn't argue. With nothing left to say, Maddie turned for the stairs and Kali watched her go.

Once she heard the door close below, Kali flipped off the spotlight, returning the forest to darkness. Her body was heavy with exhaustion, and her mind was weighed down with regret. It would be a blessing to disappear into the nothingness of sleep. But what she wanted had never mattered much in the face of her obligations. Giving into that, she rose and descended the stairs to the aft deck. Opening the storage locker, she dug out an old machete before returning to the flybridge.

Once again turning on the spotlight, Kali shone it around the inlet. The jungle around her was overgrown and dense. Shining the light upwards confirmed that the canopy was thick with tightly compacted leaves. They should be hidden from the air, which left the opening as the only avenue for discovery.

She had anchored them as close to the shore as she could, but there wasn't enough low cover to blend them into the forest. If Duarte's boats passed from Santarem, it would be possible to see the *Avatara*.

"What's going on?" Pasqual asked, climbing to the flybridge. "Dr. Cross woke me and said you needed my help."

"She shouldn't have. I'm fine."

Pasqual looked around. "We're stopping for the day?"

"Yes. I think we're safe from the air, but I need to cut branches to cover us from the river."

"Can't you move us farther back?"

"Too shallow. And with the soft mud on the banks, I can't risk the anchors giving way and letting us drift."

"Branches it is, then." Pasqual held his hand out. "But let me. You look exhausted."

"I can sleep when I'm done." Reaching for the machete, she scampered up the communication arch where the low hanging trees were the most accessible. It took a second to get her balance, but then she began pulling at the branches and hacking them off. "Throw these on the bow," she said to Pasqual.

It took a few minutes to cut all the branches she could reach, but it didn't look like enough.

"We need more," she said, looking over the side. They were about five feet from shore, just far enough to put most of the foliage out of her reach. "I've got to go in."

"Absolutely not. We'll use what we have." He pointed at the opening to the Amazon. "I can barely see out from here, and I doubt any one will be able to see us."

"I can't risk that," she said, dropping to the deck.

"It will have to do. If you go ashore and get hurt, then we'll all be stranded here. Think about that."

It wasn't what Kali wanted to hear, but she couldn't dispute the logic. "All right, but we've got to make what we have work for us."

Looking around, she stopped on a large green tarp her crew had tied to the bow. It was supposed to make the *Avatara* look dingy, but it would be better used now as camouflage.

"That tarp," she said, pointing. "We'll use it to cover the windows. It will stop any glare."

"Good idea."

Even through the thick canopy, Kali could detect that the sky was lightening. Dawn was here. "We need to hurry."

"The boat is too white," Pasqual said.

"I know. But there's not much I can do about it."

He gestured towards the nearby bank. "Mud."

It took her a second to catch on, but then she smiled enthusiastically. "Of course." Turning, she dashed down the stairs.

Opening the storage locker again, she pulled out a nylon rope and a bucket. Tying the rope to the handle, she quickly moved to the bow of the boat.

"Here's the tarp," she said, handing it up. "Cover the bridge windows and then use whatever branches are still there to hang from the communication arc."

Kali picked up the bucket and tossed it towards the shore. After it sank, she pulled hard to raise it. She could feel Pasqual watching her as she poured the thick river silt over the bow of the boat, the bright white fiberglass turning to a dirty brown. Sticking her hands in the bucket, she extracted the mud from the bottom and began rubbing it over the shiny chrome that railed the bow.

"Excellent."

"It just might work," Kali yelled up, throwing the bucket overboard again.

An hour later, her arms were burning and her hands raw, but Kali was almost done. She had nearly covered the white fiberglass and caked enough mud on the chrome to make the *Avatara* look like it had been pulled from the depths of the river. It definitely did not look like something Duarte's men would be expecting.

She turned to study the flybridge and nodded with satisfaction. Pasqual had managed to cover the windshield and completely obscure the communication arc with strategically placed branches. "That looks good."

"What of those branches there?" Pasqual pointed to the heap lying near Kali's feet.

"I'll take care of it."

Picking up the branches, she began leaning them against the slant of the salon windows. She'd already dirtied the glass with mud to stop any glare, but the branches would help make the ship seem part of the surrounding forest.

"I think we're done," she said, making her way to the aft deck.

"You're a mess," Pasqual said, meeting her there.

Kali looked down at the mud caking her arms and legs. "I guess I'll get a shower."

"Do you mind if I take one, too? I know water is scarce on a boat, but," he scratched at his beard, "well, you know."

Kali didn't care one way or the other. "Sure. And rummage through the crew's clothes if you want. It's not like they need them anymore."

Sliding open the door to the salon, she stepped inside. The air-conditioned air hit her full force and she stopped for a second to enjoy it. The cooler she became, the more the mud began to itch and she headed for her shower.

Chapter Thirteen

Duarte climbed out of the car as the sun was cresting the horizon. The dock smelled of mold and rot, but he noticed none of it. His entire body was focused on the small single engine floatplane waiting for him at the dockside.

He glanced at his watch. "Six fifteen," he said to Sanchez, who walked by his side. "I want to know the minute the boat leaves Santarem for Porto Franco."

"I believe it was leaving at first light, sir."

"Then that's now," Duarte said, reaching for the handle to heft himself into the plane.

"Welcome aboard, Señor de Tueste," the pilot said, handing him a paper cup full of coffee. "I made this myself."

Duarte took the cup and dropped it outside the plane. "Fly low over the river," he said, shifting in the small seat. "I'm looking for a big, white ship."

"Well, if they're on the river, we shouldn't have a problem spotting them."

"Let's hope not," Duarte said, pulling a pair of sunglasses from his inside pocket.

He had studied several maps of the Amazon last night in his hotel room. If Kali was stupid enough to run towards Santarem, then he would find her. Between his planes and his boats, Kali was a dead woman.

"Why aren't we in the air?" he demanded, turning his mirrored eyes on the pilot.

The push for flight was one of the most fearsome moments Duarte had ever experienced. The little plane seemed to jerk and jolt its way across the water. Every ripple in the surface was like a speed bump that hit them hard. When, finally, the pilot pulled them into the air, Duarte let himself breathe again.

The Amazon stretched out before him, shimmering in the early light. He supposed it was beautiful, but beauty was something he would not recognize again for a very long time. This river only meant pain and grief to him.

"Sir," the pilot said, his voice exploding in the tight earphones. "I believe that's your search boat below."

"Where?" He leaned forward to see.

"There." The pilot pointed at a small craft zooming east. The thick, powerful white wake trailing behind told Duarte the boat was traveling very fast.

"Can you contact them?"

"No, but I can contact the dock."

"Fine. Tell them to have the boat slow down. At that speed they will miss her if she's trying to hide just off the river."

"Will do."

In his ear, Duarte heard the pilot contacting someone, but he didn't listen. His attention was riveted on the river below.

Two hours later, he leaned back and rubbed at his tired eyes. His head was beginning to throb from the never-ending hum of the propeller.

"How far is this forsaken village?" Duarte yelled over the noise.

The pilot didn't divert his gaze from the river. "We've had to fly slower to search, but," he pointed ahead, "Porto Franco should just be around that bend."

Another bend. The Amazon was endless with its twists and turns. It snaked on forever, and Duarte was growing weary of seeing nothing but trees and dirty water. He had thought that they would have spotted Kali's boat by now, but nothing they'd seen looked at all like the *Avatara*. Maybe Kali was truly returning to Macapa.

In spite of the time they had worked together, he knew very little of how Kali operated. As a business associate, she'd never given him a reason to distrust or question her. She was quick and meticulous, always coming through with a win. But most of all, Kali had no wish to supplant him, and for that, he had trusted her more than anyone.

Of course, none of this mattered any longer. In a small way, her decision to return to Macapa was appropriate. Her loyalty would bring her home. Bring her to her death.

"That's Porto Franco," the pilot said, interrupting his thoughts.

Looking out the window, Duarte could see the small village through the trees. He turned to the pilot. "Get through to Luis. I want an update on the search and other things." The pilot looked at him questioningly, but Duarte only shifted his eyes away. "He will understand."

By now, his absence in Macapa would be known. If Luis played things right, his partners would never know the full story. Although he was loathe to use it, he knew the death of his son would buy him sympathy and time.

He looked out the window at the small town that clung to the river like a child to a mother. In this dissolute place his son had died. He needed sympathy. He needed revenge.

Kali quietly entered her cabin, relieved to see that Maddie was already asleep. Stifling a yawn, she turned towards the bathroom. As the mud had dried, her skin began to feel as though it had shrunk around her bones, and she couldn't wait to wash it all off.

Turning on the shower, she let her mind turn to Duarte. He was probably in the air by now. Soon he would reach Porto Franco where all her deceptions would be uncovered. She wondered how he would he react as he slowly pieced things together.

From what she learned of him, Duarte liked to feel smarter and quicker than his opponents. He would, therefore, assume he knew her...or at the very least that he could anticipate her moves. She smiled. Soon he would learn that he knew nothing about her.

It was a race now. She only had to stay ahead of him. Santarem would be a test. If she could get past the city, she would have the upper hand.

When the shower was hot enough, she pulled off her muddy clothes and stepped into the warm jets. Leaning back into the water, she winced as the water hit her wound. She tenderly touched it, thinking that it felt less swollen today. The pain was definitely better.

With a sigh she leaned forward, the tight muscles in her back soaking up the heat. When this was over she was going to check into the most expensive hotel she could find. "The Hôtel de la Trémoille," she said, thoughts of the Seine rolling through her head in shades of gray. She reached for the shampoo. "Dinner at Senso and a massage. A nice long, deep massage." She leaned back to rinse her hair, lifting it and dropping it over and over.

"And just how did you get so dirty since I last saw you?" Maddie asked, her voice floating on the steam.

Opening her eyes, she found Maddie standing just outside the shower door. Her face must have betrayed her shock because Maddie began backing up. "I'm sorry. I'll go."

"No. Yes." Kali shook her head. "Wait. I wasn't expecting..." She lapsed into silence with a weak gesture that made Maddie smile.

"So, was that you making a ruckus over my head?"

"I didn't mean to disturb you." She forced herself to pick up the soap as if having someone standing outside her shower was totally normal.

"You were supposed to get some sleep, too."

"I'll sleep after this," she said, scrubbing at her legs but not looking at Maddie. "I had to make sure we were safe first."

"A plane just few over."

Her hands stopped. "Did you see it?"

"No, but it was low enough that I noticed it."

Kali nodded. If it had been anything important, Pasqual would have come to get her. "Thanks," she said, continuing to scrub at the mud.

Her eyes lifted as Maddie placed her palm against the wet glass. "Why did you kiss me last night?"

She avoided Maddie's eyes. "I'm sorry. I shouldn't have."

"That's not what I asked."

Dropping her hands by her side, Kali looked right at her. "I wanted to."

With a shaky nod, Maddie turned and left the bathroom. Kali stared after her, but then rolled the soap between her hands and resumed her task.

Fleeing the bathroom, Maddie forgot to close the door. She just had to get out of there. Kali's answer had left her feeling like all the air had been sucked from the room. She was suffocating and needed to escape. What she really needed to do was think. Surely this could all be put into some perspective she could comprehend.

Crossing the room, she sat on the edge of the bed and dropped her face into her hands. Was it her fault? Last night she had sounded so big making demands of Kali's life. It had sound so simple in her head, and it had given her a solid way to gain control of herself and everything that was happening to her. How foolish she had been to think she was in control of anything. With one shocking kiss, Kali had proved that she controlled everything.

Movement nearby made her lift her head, and she stared at Kali wrapped only in a towel. Her eyes ran down her body, surprised at the complexity of the feelings rising in her.

"Should I apologize again?" Kali asked, walking across the room and opening a drawer.

"Did it mean anything to you?"

"Did what mean anything?"

"Don't pretend you don't know. Don't belittle it like that."

Kali stood up, a t-shirt in her hand. "You liked it."

"And so what if I did? Did it mean anything to you?"

"Does it matter?"

"Just answer my goddamn question!" Maddie roared, slamming her fist into the mattress.

"Yes!" Kali responded, clenching the t-shirt tightly.

Sitting there in shock, Kali gave her a defiant look as she dropped her towel and pulled her clean t-shirt over her head. When Maddie didn't react, she turned away and dug in another drawer for a pair of underwear. After slipping these on, she stood up, her face suddenly pale and her eyes exhausted. "Was that all you wanted to hear?" she asked, wearily. "If so, I'm tired. I need to go to bed." Her eyes closed briefly and she seemed to sway in place.

There was nothing else Maddie could do but stand and move around the bed. Grabbing the covers, she pulled them down. "Get in," she said, pointing Kali into the bed.

"I can do it myself."

"I have no doubt. So what are you waiting for?"

Kali stared at her for a second, and then wordlessly climbed into the bed and pulled up the covers.

Not sure what else to do, Maddie looked at the door.

"Stay," Kali said, as if reading her thoughts.

"What?"

"I mean you didn't sleep very long. Stay and sleep."

"Do you want me to stay?"

Kali tensed, but then seemed to relax. "Yes," she said, with more vulnerability than Maddie thought possible. "I want you to stay."

Swallowing, Maddie looked at the other side of the bed, and then back at Kali. Was that fear she felt? Hoping to conceal it, she turned away and crossed to the other side of the bed. She hesitated only a second before crawling under the covers.

With her heart pounding, she lay there motionless. Overhead, the sunlight that pushed through the blinds was sliced in fractured lines. Light and dark. Black and white. It was so simple. There was no in between. No gray areas to trap or distort the truth.

She almost jumped when she felt Kali's fingers move across her arm. The touch was gentle and without demand, and with her heart pounding, Maddie waited for more. Her stomach swirled with anticipation, forcing her to acknowledge that she did want more.

It took her a few seconds to realize that nothing had changed. Turning her head, she found Kali already asleep. The contact had been seemingly unconscious.

Rolling carefully onto her side, she stared down at Kali. There was a peace in the way she slept. Gone were the rigid lines of tension and anger that so dominated her features when she was awake. In sleep, her skin was smooth.

Without even trying to stop herself, Maddie gave into the urge to touch her, and reaching out, she let the tips of her fingers lightly trace the lines of Kali's face. Strangely though, it felt as if she already knew every dip and plane. It was inconceivable how touching her could be so familiar, yet new.

As Kali's breathing evened out and became deeper, Maddie felt more and more conflicted over her feelings. When watching her shifted from being comforting to being tormenting, Maddie rolled out of bed.

She shouldn't be considering the things that were going through her head, and being close to her was only making things worse. At the door, she gave Kali one last look before shutting it behind her.

"Maddie, is that you?" Pasqual called as she reached the stairs. "Come here, please."

It was a surprise to enter the guest cabin and see Amado sitting up. She'd only seen him unconscious, and for some reason this let her put him completely out of her mind. One look at his dark eyes and Maddie disliked him.

"Maddie, Amado is awake."

"I can see that. How are you feeling, Amado?"

"Who the hell are you?"

"Amado, this is Dr. Madeline Cross. She's helped take care of you. We're going to get you well."

Maddie forced a smile. She didn't know much about health care, but from where she stood, she could see that Amado was far from well. His eyes were glossy and the skin that she could see was deathly pale. "I think you should rest," she said, formally.

"Is that your medical opinion, doctor?" Amado asked, licking his dry lips.

"Absolutely. And listen to your uncle. He has your best interest at heart."

"That I'm beginning to doubt," Amado said, shifting his dark eyes to Pasqual. "Again, Uncle, I will ask you to tell me what's going on?"

"You were hurt in the explosion," Pasqual explained, pouring a glass of water. "Dr. Cross was at the hospital in Porto Franco. She's come along to help you get back to Macapa."

"Macapa?" He laughed, his voice a rasp. "You expect me to believe you, Uncle, would go to Macapa? My father will kill you on sight."

"I'm going for you, Amado. I could not let you die. My life means nothing compared to you."

Maddie looked away. They were all alike. They lied with impunity and care nothing for anything but their own needs. "I'm going to go get something to eat," she said, taking a step backwards. "It was nice to meet you."

"Wait. Aren't you going to examine me or something?"

"I already have," Maddie said, realizing she, too, could lie with ease. "Your uncle has everything you need."

"That's right, Amado. And I say it's time for your medication." He reached for the pill bottles.

Backing away, Maddie turned for the stairs. Was there no where on this ship that she could escape this world of deception and lies? She was drowning in its darkness and rapidly realizing she didn't care.

In the galley, she stopped and leaned against a cabinet. With just the hum of the air conditioning, it reminded her of the quiet of her lab. If she closed her eyes, she could almost pretend she was there. Her computers churning through data and her mind afire with theories that would change the world. Maddie laughed to herself. What a waste her life had been.

But that was over now, and in some strange way, Maddie felt emancipated. As if the chains that had bound her to the conventions of her old life were now gone. Her slate had been wiped clean and she was free to remake herself into a new image.

But who should she be now that she was no one? The thought made her desperately sad.

"Take me to the hospital." Duarte demanded the second his Italian loafers touched the dock.

"Follow me," the pilot said, pointing him toward the road.

"It's so hot here."

"The rainforest is always hotter."

"I know that, you moron," Duarte boomed, shedding his jacket and continuing his plodding course up the dock.

The hospital was more disgusting than he anticipated. Besides being small, it reeked of antiseptic and sickness. Not a fitting place for a de Tueste to breathe his last. He shifted his jaw. Not a place his son should have been at all.

"Who is in charge?" Duarte said, his voice carrying over the old crank-style beds that cluttered the ward.

An elderly woman in a white smock came out from behind a beat up metal desk and walked toward him. "This is a hospital, Señor. Please respect that."

"Who are you?"

"Mother Superior. I run the hospital."

Duarte nodded. "Where is my son?"

"Check with Sister Evangeline there," she said, sweeping her arm towards a younger woman. "I'm sure she can help you."

"I want my son's body," Duarte said, his voice dropping to such a level that the nun stopped in her tracks.

"Señor, no one has died recently."

Duarte felt his eye twitch. "That's not what your radio message said yesterday."

The nun didn't respond, but Duarte saw the fear shadow her old, wrinkled face.

"Maybe this will help." He snapped his fingers and the pilot produced a photo of Kali. "My son was brought in by this woman."

The nun barely glanced at the photo. "She was here. But it was an older man who told me to report that the boy had died. He said men were coming to kill him and to harm us. Unless I reported him dead, the old man said that many would die." Her head dipped in respect. "Understand that I was only protecting my hospital and my patients."

"What are you saying?"

"If that boy is really your son, he is not dead."

"You said my son was dead!" His voice rose as he fought an overwhelming urge to strangle her with his bare hands.

"I only wanted to protect this hospital," the nun repeated. "Please understand."

Duarte turned his back on her. He didn't think it was possible to feel such relief and rage at the same time. "She took my son then?" he asked, over his shoulder.

"They left yesterday afternoon." He could hear the old nun's anxious breathing. She should be nervous. He could have her killed without a single regret.

It took a moment to release his rage and focus on what was important. "How is my son?

"His burns were not life threatening," the nun said, and Duarte breathed a sigh of relief. "But I believe he has sepsis."

"Which is?"

"A bacterial infection that can become very serious if not treated."

"And you treated it?"

"I did what I could before they took him. The older man requested enough supplies for two weeks. I gave him oral antibiotics, bandages and pain medicine. I believe he will take care of your son."

Duarte gave her a cold smile. "You are obviously a poor judge of character."

The nun shook her head. "But why bring him here?"

He knew why. Kali wanted to trick him and make him suffer. For that, she would pay.

"Let's go," he said, turning on his heel. It was obvious that Kali was now working for his brother. Just what he had promised her, he couldn't guess. She was a whore.

Once outside, he stopped and looked around. The place was a pit, but perhaps it could still be of some use to him.

"What would you like me to do?" the pilot asked, keeping a safe distance between them.

"Question the village," he said, looking at the market, the post office, the houses, everywhere. "They did more than come to this hospital. I want to know everything they did, said or bought. Everything!"

"And that's it? You want to know what they bought?"

Duarte turned and slapped the man hard across his face. "You stupid man. I want to know where they went. Find me someone who knows!" Leaning his head back, he stared up at the cloudless sky. "Find them. Find my son!"

"Yes, sir," the pilot said, hurrying off.

With heavy steps, Duarte walked over to the small store and took a seat at the table outside. He sat there for nearly an hour before the pilot dared come near him again.

"You better have news," he said, mopping his brow with a handkerchief. "And it better be the heading for that cursed ship."

"Everyone who saw them says the same thing, sir," the pilot said, making direct eye contact. "There were three of them. They got fuel, water and food. The stories change when asked what direction they were headed. Some say Macapa, others Belem and others Santarem. But no one remembers seeing them go east or west on the Amazon."

His hand stopped in mid-swipe. "And you've talked to everyone?"

"Everyone I could find."

"Then tell me about the search. Do we have any word yet?"

"Nothing has been spotted by either the boats or planes."

"Then they just disappeared?" Duarte glared at the man. "Do you expect me to believe that?"

The pilot dropped his eyes. "Sir, have you considered that they might not be heading for either Santarem or Macapa?"

"Those are the logical places."

"If this woman is as intelligent as you think, then wouldn't she know that, too?"

"What are you suggesting?"

"Here," he said, producing a map and opening it. "We're here in Porto Franco." He pointed. "You think Kali has two options: Santarem or Macapa. East or west. But look at the river." He ran his finger down the long blue line. "She could be anywhere by now. She could have gone west of Porto Franco, making us believe she intended to go to Santarem. Then she could have cut down this little river here and headed back towards Macapa. Or done the reverse here and headed west."

"I'm still only seeing two viable options."

"Look at the veins of rivers running into Macapa, sir. There is the Canel do Norte, which is the most direct, but if she wanted to avoid you, she'd come through the maze of rivers by the Ilha Vieira. Or she can avoid Macapa altogether. See where the river opens and spills into the Atlantic here."

"So I'll post a ship just outside the harbor. They'll catch her."

"Why would she go to Macapa knowing you'll be waiting for her?" He traced a route south. "I think she's going to head for Gurupa. From there she makes her way to Bala das Bocas and the port of Belem."

"She wouldn't do that."

"Why not? She has a full tank of gas, plenty of water and food. And if you don't mind me being blunt, she has your son as an insurance policy, Señor de Tueste." He stood up straight. "One last possibility is that Kali could hide out on the Amazon for a long time. Then, when the time is right, she could just slip away."

"You're giving her too much credit."

"I am only giving options. I'm ready to do whatever you ask me to do."

"You're telling me that I've lost her? That I've lost my son?"

"No, sir. But you might if you don't cover every possible point."

"What should I do then? I only have access to so much."

The pilot nodded seriously. “Divert some of your planes. And when the boat from Santarem arrives here, send it towards Gurupa.”

“And not back to Santarem? What if Kali is just waiting for me to pass her by?”

“Put a man on the bank near Santarem. If Kali passes, he’ll see her. It’s cheaper and more effective than moving up and down the same stretch of water.”

“You take liberties with me.”

“I’m only trying to help.”

“I know what you’re trying to do,” Duarte said, hefting his bulk up. “Contact Luis and make it all happen. Then get me out of this place.”

“Yes, sir.”

He moved towards the plane and then stopped. “One more thing. Tell Luis to email Kali in my name and seek terms for the return of my son. He is authorized to guarantee her safe passage out of Brazil as long as Amado is returned alive. The money is hers to keep, but she must still give me Pasqual’s head.”

“Aren’t you giving in?”

Duarte shook his head. “Why should I keep my word? She didn’t.”

Chapter Fourteen

The sound of a low flying plane woke Kali. Opening her eyes, she stared at the ceiling as the rumble of the engine disappeared into the distance. She had no doubt that it was another of Duarte's planes.

Rolling over, she checked the clock. It was nearly two in the afternoon. She should feel rested, but her body was still heavy with sleep. Kali yawned as she threw back the covers and sat up. Thankfully, her head didn't hurt nearly as bad, and she got to her feet with relative ease.

Looking around, the first thing she noticed was that Maddie was gone. While walking towards the bathroom, she realized this bothered her. Of all the people who had shared her bed, Kali had slept with none of them. It was too dangerous to sleep with someone you didn't know and couldn't trust.

Yet, she had wanted Maddie to stay. She had invited her to stay, and the fact that she hadn't, put Kali in a foul mood.

After pulling on some clothes, she left the cabin, and passing through the salon, she didn't acknowledge anyone there. It wasn't until she was on the aft deck that she remembered Maddie's face.

She'd been sitting at the dining table playing cards with Pasqual. The smile on her face had brightened as Kali entered the room, but then fallen as she stalked past her. Shaking the image out of her head, Kali climbed to the fly-bridge where the sour smell of dried mud and silt assaulted her. She looked up at the sky, relieved to see very little blue. This had been a good place, and she doubted that the planes ever suspected they were there.

The sun wouldn't set for at least four hours, but staring out at the river beyond the opening, she felt the urge to get them out of there. It was just a tickle on the back of her neck, but Kali knew better than to ignore her instincts.

Sitting in the pilot seat, Kali activated the GPS receiver, waiting for the system to locate the satellites. With the thick tree cover overhead, she knew her exact position would be off, but it didn't matter. She was only interested in the map.

Their position from last night blinked on the screen, but Kali only used it to jump the map westward towards Santarem. The distance was approximately fifty miles. It would be an easy push at night, but as Kali moved from screen to screen, she saw something that alarmed her.

She understood that Santarem would be a testing point for her plan. All she had to do was get by the city without being discovered. Her decision to travel at night had been good, but now, as she stared at the river just outside the city, she saw that her plan had been deeply flawed.

Although the Amazon looked like one big ribbon of water, in reality it was a complex system of waterways that cut through the rainforest. Some of these waterways were big enough to navigate and others were more like shallow creeks that fed the massive trees. What Kali saw on the map was that right before Santarem, all these tributaries merged into one big lane.

Here she had thought herself so smart by hiding from Duarte's planes and boats, and she'd completely failed to recognize that all Duarte had to do was place a single man on the bank of the river east of Santarem and she was caught. There was no where to hide.

Leaning back in her seat, Kali looked up at the sky. She saw now that the planes and boats were really only driving her towards Santarem. If they caught her, all the better for Duarte, but he only needed to wait and the river would lead her to him.

With a sigh, she looked at the map again, uncertain what to do next. If she pushed for Santarem and was discovered, Duarte would have her trapped. None of them would live to see Manaus. Rubbing at her face, she shook her head. She would not give up now. There had to be something she could use to avoid such an easy ambush.

Zooming out on the display, Kali moved from screen to screen looking for anything that might work. The name Ituqui Island jumped out at her, and she zoomed in closer. There couldn't be an island without a waterway around it. When she saw the narrow ribbon of blue water, she smiled. Tracing the river around the island, her smile grew bigger as it rejoined the Amazon only a mile or two east of Santarem. Now this was something.

Looking away, she weighed the benefits and risks. If this small river was wide enough and deep enough, it would keep them off the main branch of the Amazon longer. Yet, it would add time to their trip. Also, depending on the condition of the river, it might be too dangerous to travel at night.

Which meant she would have to leave now, using the remaining daylight to traverse the loop. That, of course, would expose her for the time it took to reach the turn off. That wasn't a risk she felt confident taking.

Zooming back to a bigger map, Kali calculated the distance between her location and Santarem. The longer she looked, the less confident she was of getting by the city without notice.

She just felt so trapped, and once again she hated being on the river and not on the open expanse of the ocean. But since turning back now wasn't an option, she knew she needed to do something to reduce the risk. There was nothing she could do if Duarte had placed a man outside Santarem. Even circling around Ituqui Island wouldn't prevent someone from seeing her pass by the city. All it would do was minimize the time she was exposed on the main river and possibly confuse Duarte's search a little more.

The only option she saw to combat the possibility of someone watching from the bank was to wait until very late to try her run past Santarem. After all, Duarte probably still wasn't expecting her to travel at night, so maybe his watchman wouldn't either. It was a risk, but there were no other moves she could see. She had to get past Santarem tonight.

Decided, she set a waypoint for Ituqui Island and calculated the distance back to her current location. It was perhaps fifteen to twenty minutes. It was a long time to be out there on the river with nothing to hide her and very limited options for escape. Did she dare risk it or would it be safer to wait for dark? If anything swayed her, it was the possible depth and width of the channel circling the island. The *Avatara* wasn't a small ship, and it would be safer to navigate the channel in the daylight. The question was if she could reach the turn off in time. To do so, she knew she needed to leave the cover on the heels of the next search plane.

As if on cure, the air overhead crackled with another engine. Kali stared at the sky as the plane grew closer.

"It's been flying by every forty five minutes to an hour," Pasqual said, climbing the stairs.

"Why didn't you wake me?"

"What could you do?"

Kali didn't bother answering. "Have you timed the planes or are you just guessing at the hour mark?"

"I timed it. Give or take five minutes, it has been flying by every hour since just past dawn." He pointed to the sky. "Up and down the river."

"The same plane?"

"It sounds the same, but I can't be sure."

"Have there been any breaks for fuel?"

"Twice it's been about a half hour late. I assume it was refueling."

Kali nodded, and looked down at the map. "It's on a one hour loop pattern. It flies halfway to Porto Franco and then back to Santarem." She glanced at the sky. "Since it just flew towards Santarem, we have less than fifty minutes to get out of here."

"I thought we were waiting until dark when the plane won't fly?"

"I've changed my mind," she said, pointing to the GPS. "Look at this." She began to explain what she wanted to do, and then looked at him for his opinion.

"You don't sound confident," he said, meeting her eyes.

"We don't have a lot of options, and we have to get past Santarem tonight. This," she said, tapping the screen, "is the best thing I can come up with. It keeps us hidden until the last possible second and then we just make a run for it."

"And what if this tributary is not navigable?"

Kali hesitated. "I don't know. I'd just feel better if I was on the offense instead of waiting for Duarte to find me."

Standing up straight, Pasqual stared out at the river. "I'm uneasy with this, but I trust your judgment." He looked back at her. "But I think we should wait until the plane passes us going east. That will give us the most time to reach this turn-off. Agreed?"

"Fine." She studied the map again, as Pasqual sat in the co-pilot's seat and sighed. "What?"

"Amado woke up and I'm afraid he's being difficult. He wants to know what's going on."

"And?"

"I fear that we won't be able to control him."

"Then kill him. We don't really need him anymore. Duarte will act as if Amado is alive, and that's what's important."

"No. I won't do that."

"Perhaps you'd rather he kill you first?" Kali demanded. "If he gets strong enough or suspicious enough, he might do just that."

"I won't have my nephew's blood on my hands." He shook his head. "And unless it's absolutely necessary, I won't allow you to do it, either."

"I think it is necessary, but," she thought for a moment. "If you won't kill him, then stop his medication."

Pasqual's eyes grew wide. "But his infection."

"Stop acting like a sentimental fool! If we stop his medication, he'll stay weak. If he's weak, we don't have to worry about him."

"It might kill him."

"It might."

"What if it was your Dr. Cross? Would you withhold her medication to save yourself?"

Kali narrowed her eyes. "Now you're just trying to piss me off." Turning her wrist to see her watch, she rose to her feet. "I'm going to get something to eat before taking us out of here. If that plane is on time, we'll leave in about forty minutes."

"Amado's not bad," Pasqual said, as she approached the stairs.

"I don't really care. You paid me to get you safely to Manaus, and I'll do that." She looked over her shoulder. "However I have to."

After grabbing a sandwich and a bottle of water, Kali climbed back up to the flybridge. She wanted to be there when the plane flew by again. By her watch, it was due soon. That was unless it stopped to refuel. Unless it landed for the day. Unless a lot of things.

She didn't like all the open-ended questions, but she didn't have a lot of choice. Although she did her best to guarantee the outcome of every job she took, there was always the chance that something would go wrong.

The difference between this and her other jobs was that she was not on the offensive. It wasn't her decision to attack or withdraw. This time she was the prey, and that held a certain and disturbing irony for her.

She lifted the bottle of water to her lips, and tipped the last of it into her mouth. The heat was beginning to get to her. Her skin was heavy with sweat, and it was almost too much of an effort to swat at the screen of mosquitoes buzzing around her.

Looking up at the sky, she strained to hear any engine noise, but heard nothing but the squawking of birds and the hum of insects. She checked her watch, counting the minutes since she'd last heard the plane. Ten more minutes at least. She hated waiting.

Her mouth was dry and she shook her empty bottle, wanting more but not sure she had time. Deciding to chance it, she got out of her seat and nearly ran into Maddie who was climbing the stairs to the flybridge. Before they could touch, Kali stopped and pulled back.

"I'm sorry," Maddie said, taking a step down. "I was bringing you more water." She hung on the stairs as if she were afraid of coming closer. "Is everything all right?"

Kali gestured at the bottle in her hand. "I was actually going to get something to drink."

"Oh. Well. Here." Maddie held out the water.

"Thanks." She stared down at the bottle, unable to come up with anything else to say. There had to be something...anything. "You don't have to stay up here," she finally said.

"Oh." Maddie took another step backwards. "Do you want me to go?"

Her tone forced Kali to look up, seeing the visible hurt in Maddie's eyes. "I didn't mean it like that. It's just hot up here. That's all."

"You're up here."

"That's my job."

Before Maddie could respond, Kali heard the low rumble of an approaching plane. Turning away, she stared up at the canopy. The plane passed less than fifty feet above the trees, its white body shimmering like a mirage and then disappearing.

A familiar rush of adrenalin surged through Kali's body and her heart began to pound with anticipation. This was it. Moving back to her seat, she started the engines and raised the anchors. As they clinked up, Kali reached for the green tarp covering the windshield.

"Let me help," Maddie said, grabbing the other side of the tarp and hefting it up.

"Thanks," Kali said, making the mistake of looking right into Maddie's eyes. It didn't seem possible that she could so abruptly stop caring about anything else. Duarte. The plane. Santarem. Pasqual. Their importance dimmed when compared to this moment.

"Kali?" Maddie asked. "Are you all right?"

Blinking, Kali looked away. "Can you finish with the tarp? I'm going to start moving us out of here." She sat behind the wheel and grabbed the throttles. Her mind kept turning back to Maddie, and she struggled to focus herself. *It was little slips like that which could get them all killed.*

As Maddie folded up the tarp, Kali pushed the throttles forward and took the *Avatara* out of the inlet. The river was clear in both directions.

Swinging the bow west, she gradually increased the speed. "Watch those loose branches," she called over to Maddie. "They're going to fly." Activating the GPS, she waited for their position to be displayed on the color screen. Now that she had a clear path to the satellites, she knew her estimated positioning error would drop significantly.

"What are you doing?" Maddie asked, holding back her hair in the wind.

"Setting a course. The GPS will let me know when to turn."

Leaning forward, Maddie peered at the screen. "We're going around an island?"

"Yes." Kali switched to the positioning screen, waiting for their speed, bearing and distance to destination to be displayed. At their current speed, it was twenty minutes to the turn off. Too long. She needed to be off the river and far enough in to not be seen by the plane pilot. Pushing the throttles forward, she watched as the time to target dropped. She smiled.

"You look devious when you grin like that," Maddie said, plainly. "Scheming and crafty. Just like Pasqual."

Her smile fell.

"It's not a bad thing. It's just not how I choose to see you."

"I'm just trying to keep us all alive."

"I understand, but when you smile like that, I think that you enjoy it."

Kali frowned.

"After you told me that story about your crew in Indonesia, I thought it might be the killing you liked, but I don't think so anymore."

"You don't?" Kali asked, irritated. "Well good for you."

"Don't mock me. I'm trying to understand you."

Kali wiped at the sweat she felt on the back of her neck and forehead. Her mouth was dry, but as she reached for the bottle of water Maddie had brought up, it was swiped away.

"Answer one question first," Maddie said, holding the bottle against her chest.

"No." She held her hand out. "Give it to me."

"It's just a question."

Kali shrugged. "Keep the water." She looked at the GPS, the dotted waypoint line pulling them closer to the turn.

Standing, Maddie set the water back in the holder. "I think that what you like most about your life is that no matter what you do or who you hurt, you just walk away pretending it never touches you. But you can't do that here, can you? You can't pretend with me."

"If you say so." Kali didn't take her eyes off the river.

"That's very mature," Maddie said sadly.

The GPS emitted a tiny beep to notify Kali that the turn was coming up. She slowed the *Avatara*, spotting the opening a few hundred feet ahead. It was smaller than she thought possible, and the trees hanging over the water made it look more like a tunnel than a tributary.

"Now," she said, looking at the depth finder. "Just be deep enough."

She beamed a smile when the *Avatara* passed the opening and the depth remained fine. It even grew a little wider, too.

"I think we'll make it," she said, turning to look at Maddie, but the flybridge was empty. With a sigh, she shifted her eyes back to the channel.

The narrowness of the channel had forced Kali to keep her speed slow, but she really didn't mind. She had never been this deep into the jungle before, and what she saw fascinated her. All around her, the forest was alive with animals and birds she'd rarely glimpsed. Colonies of monkeys chattered and shrieked as she slowly passed by, and more than a few crocodiles hurried out of her way. Every time she saw something new, she wished Maddie was there with her. Being a biologist, she thought Maddie would have appreciated it all on a much deeper level. But mostly, Kali had just wanted to see Maddie's excitement. Her face could be so expressive.

After an hour, Kali stopped wishing for her.

The GPS had diligently monitored their position, but still Kali was relieved when they started swinging back towards the Amazon. This far off the main branch of the river, she hadn't seen or heard any more planes. In a way that strengthened her decision to take this route instead of waiting until dark to head for Santarem.

She realized that she still had to get them past Santarem, but she would wait until it was very late to attempt her approach. The lateness combined with the bare sliver of a moon might just let them slip by without notice. She would also keep them to the far north side of the river, making it harder for anyone on the bank to notice or identify the ship.

Lifting her hand, she wiped at another layer of sticky sweat covering her neck. This deep into the jungle and there was very little air circulation, making the heat nearly unbearable. She wished the sun would set, taking some of the stifling heat with it.

It was already after five, so Kali knew it wouldn't be too much longer before she felt some relief. Already the sky was aflame with amazing shades of red and orange. Someone had told her it was the water molecules in the air reflecting the sun's rays that made the sunsets brilliant, but Kali didn't know if she believed that. She'd seen beautiful sunsets in the desert, and there was no water to reflect there.

As she stared at the colors, she realized that Maddie would know the answer. After all, she'd come down here to study the climate. She was trying to find something of value in the world. Maddie was important. Much more than Kali would ever be.

This made her eyes fall from the beautiful colors of the sky to the drabness of the water. It would be easy to start hating the choices she'd made in her life, but that would get her nowhere. This is who she was and where she had ended up. It wasn't right, but it wasn't wrong. It just was.

The GPS beeped as she approached a waypoint. A half mile ahead, she could just see the width of the Amazon coursing past. She'd gone as far as she could. Now she had to wait.

Stopping the *Avatara*, she cut the engines and dropped the anchor. Once finished, Kali let her head fall forward. She was tired and hot. The lack of movement brought in the mosquitoes, and she swatted at them.

Her body was tight and sore. Kali raised her head, looking at the communication arch. Jumping for it, she let her body hang loosely, the muscles in her shoulder pulling and releasing hours of built up tension.

"Very nice," Amado said, struggling up the stairs.

Kali dropped to the ground. "What are you doing out of bed?"

"I needed some air." He stopped, breathing heavily.

There was a thick sheen of sweat clinging to his skin which had more to do with a fever than the stifling heat. The side of his face that wasn't bandaged was blotchy and swollen, and what burned skin she could see turned her stomach.

"You should be in bed," she said, turning her eyes away. "Pushing it will only make you sicker."

"I'm sure you really care," he said, clinging to the rail to steady himself.

"I don't." She twisted her body from side to side, her lower back cracking back into place.

He looked around. "Where are we?"

Kali had no intention of answering, so she merely stared at him. "You don't look well. Shall I call your uncle to help you back to bed?"

He waved her question off. "What happened? I remember an explosion, but that's it."

"Ask your uncle." Kali walked to the stairs. "Now, if you don't need any help, I'm hot and want to go inside." Amado blocked her. "I'd move if I were you."

"I demand to know what's going on here!"

"You're in no position to demand anything. I suggest you just concentrate on getting better." Kali leaned closer. "Get out of my way."

His eyes narrowed in anger, but he turned. "Something is not right here, Kali. I'm going to find out."

Continuing down to the aft deck, she ignored him. She heard him struggling back down the stairs, but she offered no assistance as she entered the salon.

"Kali!" Maddie cried, her voice strained. "I was hoping you'd come down soon."

"Why? What's wrong?" she asked, as Amado pushed in behind her.

Maddie's eyes slipped to him and then back again. "Nothing."

Turning, she almost pinned him to the glass. "What did you do?" Amado stared at her with a vile look in his glassy eyes that made her want to kill him. "Stay away from her."

"Why?" he asked snidely. "Does she belong to you?"

"Yes."

For a brief second, Amado's eyes became as cruel as she remembered. "Your crew said you were a dyke, but from what I'd seen of your beauty, I'd, naturally, hoped otherwise."

"Kali," Maddie called out. "Will you help me, please?"

She didn't take her eyes off Amado. He was blinking rapidly as if everything was out of focus. Smiling, she just waited.

"Aren't you going to help your little bitch?" he asked, taking a step towards a chair, but then collapsing like a rag. She was close enough to catch him, but didn't.

"Jesus," Maddie cried, as he hit the floor hard. She ran over and dropped to the ground near him.

"Leave him alone," she commanded. "If we're lucky, he'll die."

"And if we're not?" Maddie asked, glaring up at her. "He's sick. Have some compassion."

"That's an emotion I can't afford." She looked around. "Where are his pills?"

"Why?" Maddie asked, sitting back on her heels. When Kali only stared at her, she shook her head and pointed. "Pasqual keeps them on the counter."

Grabbing the two bottles she stared down at the labels in frustration. "Do you know which one is the antibiotic?" she asked.

"Why? What are you planning?"

She glanced up at her. "Will you go to my cabin and get my pills? I left them on the nightstand."

"Oh no," Maddie said, getting to her feet. "I won't be a party to that."

Kali waved the bottles at her. "Then just tell me which one is the antibiotic and I'll go get them." Not waiting for a response, she hurried to her cabin and grabbed her bottle of pain pills.

Returning, she stood next to Maddie and didn't say a thing. This was her decision, and she would either help or not. If Maddie refused, Kali would just add her pain pills to the top of both bottles. It would, hopefully, be enough to keep Amado incapacitated until they reached Manaus.

Just when she thought Maddie wasn't going to help, she sighed loudly. "It's this one," she said, pointing at a bottle.

"You sure?" Kali raised a brow in question.

"Yes." She looked away. "I know what you're going to do. It's wrong."

Of course it was wrong, but Kali cared little for that as she opened the bottle and poured the antibiotics into her hand before stuffing them into her front pocket. Next, she dumped her pain pills into the now empty antibiotic bottle. All she could hope was that Pasqual hadn't looked too closely at the size or shape of the pills.

"Why are you doing this?" Maddie asked, watching her intently.

"You know the answer," she said, curtly. "I can't let him get in the way."

Maddie frowned at her. "And do you really think giving him a double dose of pain medication is safe? You could kill him."

"I'd rather kill him," Kali said honestly. "But Pasqual won't allow it. His sentimental attachment to Amado is putting us all at risk."

"You don't know that."

"Yes, I do," Kali said, reaching out and touching Maddie's shoulder. "You have to trust me. Now, will you promise that you won't tell Pasqual what I've done or try to help Amado?"

For a long moment, Maddie stared up at her. "I promise," she said, briefly closing her eyes.

"Thank you."

"I never thought I'd have to weigh a life against my own, but I've done it twice now."

"My life being the other time?" Kali asked, her voice tight. "Well, I'm sorry you've had to learn how to do it. But, if it helps, it never gets any easier."

"Except you do make it look easy," Maddie said, looking up at her. "I guess it comes with practice."

Kali just stared at her. There was nothing she could say to defend herself.

"Well, it's done, right?" Maddie said, looking down at Amado. "All that's left is to put him on the couch before Pasqual comes up from his nap. I think it will look less suspicious."

"Thank you," Kali said, pointing Maddie to Amado's feet while she took his heavier upper body. After depositing him on the couch, she followed Maddie into the galley. "You looked scared when I came in. What did he do to you?"

Turning, Maddie leaned against the counter. "He didn't really do anything to me. It was you I was scared for."

The admission stopped Kali's hand as she was reaching into the refrigerator for a beer. "I can handle him." She grabbed a bottle, and on second thought took one for Maddie. "Here."

"I know you can handle yourself," Maddie said, accepting it. "He just was so demanding. As if I knew anything."

Kali opened her beer, then reaching out, popped the top off Maddie's, her fingers brushing over the back of Maddie's hand.

"He wanted to know if you'd seduced me," Maddie said, staring intently at her beer. "Is that something you do?"

"Yes, but not often." She took a sip.

"You've really done it? Seduced women?"

"And men."

"Why?"

"I needed something they could give me, and," she shrugged, "sometimes it's just quicker to fuck someone than find another way."

Maddie shifted her beer between her hands. "So it meant nothing?"

"Nothing more than necessary to get what I wanted."

"I don't understand how you can do something like that. How can you kiss someone...touch someone...without it meaning anything." She looked up at her expectantly.

"I've enjoyed it at times. Is that what you want to know?"

"No."

Kali hadn't thought so, and she shrugged again. "I don't know what to say. Have you loved everyone you've ever slept with?"

Maddie's eyes fell. "I've only been with four men. And each time I thought it would mean something. I really wanted it to mean something, but it never did." She turned away. "I was beginning to think it never would."

Before Kali could ask her what she meant, she heard Pasqual coming up the stairs, his steps hurried. "Amado?" His face was haggard and creased with sleep.

"He's there," Kali said, pointing.

Turning, he stared at the boy, his face falling with relief. "I fell asleep..." he began explaining, but Kali shook her head.

"It's all right. He was feeling better, but then overdid it. He passed out and we put him on the couch."

"Thank you both."

"Isn't it time for his medication?" Maddie asked, and Kali dropped her eyes to hide her surprise.

"I'll let him rest a bit and then give it to him." He sniffed the air. "What have you been making, Dr. Cross? It smells excellent."

Maddie blushed. "Just spaghetti. I opened a jar and was adding to it." She looked up at Kali. "I don't even know if you like spaghetti."

"Doesn't everyone?" Pasqual asked, some spirit returning to his voice. "Do you mind if I have one of those beers?"

"I didn't figure you for a beer drinker," Kali said, not looking away from Maddie.

"If you prefer, I found a bottle of wine," Maddie said, her eyes pulling Kali closer. "I thought we'd have it with dinner."

"I see it," Pasqual said, stepping around them. "I'll open it and let it breathe. Excuse me." He reached between them to retrieve the wine opener hanging from the cabinet. "Kali, why don't you go clean up? Dr. Cross and I can finish up with dinner."

She nodded, stepping closer to Maddie. "I love spaghetti," she whispered in her ear as she passed. Her steps as she descended to her cabin were lighter. She didn't know why she'd told that to Maddie. Spaghetti had never been her favorite, but she suspected that it didn't really matter.

"Where are they, Luis? And for your sake, the answer better not be you do not know," Duarte said, staring down at his half finished dinner. He hated having his meals interrupted. Luis knew better.

"I'm doing everything I can," Luis replied, his voice strained across the phone line. "It isn't exactly easy to coordinate this search and keep things going here."

"Are you complaining?" Duarte reached for a soft roll and bit into it.

"I'm saying you should be here in Macapa. We have men to handle this matter."

"Men who have done nothing but fail. I want Kali found. Immediately."

"I'm doing everything I can," Luis repeated.

"Then do better." He paused. "How many planes are still in the air?"

"None. It's dark."

Duarte shifted in the antique Queen Anne chair. "So my whole operation comes to a halt because the sun goes down?"

"It is unlikely that Kali will try and travel the river at night. It's just too dangerous."

"You idiot. She lives for danger." He held up a finger. "And since there has been no sign of her in the daylight, when do you think she is traveling?"

"The river is different from the ocean, sir. She wouldn't risk her ship by traveling at night. It's more likely that she's simply hiding somewhere, waiting for us to give up."

"Do not treat me like a child! I know Kali, and she does not hide." He inhaled a labored breath. "What disturbs me, Luis, is how poorly prepared you are to track her."

"Tell me what else you'd like me to do? I've been a little busy here trying to find Kali, placate the Japanese, and quell the rumors your departure have started."

"What rumors?"

"That you're finished. Your partners smell blood."

"Deal with it. Tell them that nothing is wrong."

"My word means nothing anymore. I'm just as tainted as you." He laughed ruefully. "I'm surprised I'm even still alive."

"Yes," Duarte replied, his voice low. "That is a surprise."

He heard Luis swallow. "I'm doing what I can, but I can't do everything. If you don't return soon, it's all over."

"Then find Kali!"

"Tell me how, sir? I've tried tracking Kali's transponder signal, but it was deactivated yesterday."

"What about her GPS?"

"It is only a receiver. I've tried tracing her email back, but it was sent through numerous proxy servers. And as far as I can tell, her Internet link is also severed. She did not respond to that email I sent in your name."

"All I hear are excuses!" Duarte exhaled slowly. "Find someway to track her, Luis. Your life depends on it."

"I understand."

"And continue to stall my partners. Rumors will always exist. Let them waste their time confirming them. By the time they know one way or the other, I'll be back in Macapa and will deal with them personally."

"Of course."

"And tomorrow, keep the planes in the air and send out more boats. Cover Belem, too."

"I'll call you with updates."

"Yes," Duarte growled into the phone. "Do that."

Maddie was dumping a bag of pasta into a pot of boiling water when Kali quietly climbed back up the stairs. Strangely, she hadn't even needed to turn her head to know that Kali was there. She'd just felt her.

"You look more refreshed," Pasqual said, setting plates on the table.

Turning slightly, Maddie let her eyes run down Kali's body, but when Kali caught her, she shifted her gaze back to her pot. "How's your head?" she asked, stirring the pasta.

"It hasn't bothered me today," Kali said, leaning against the wall and watching her. "How's your arm?"

"Better," she said, smiling.

"That's good," Kali replied, looking away as Pasqual came into the galley to gather silverware.

"So where are we?" he asked.

"Close to rejoining the Amazon. We made it around the island."

"Your gamble worked," Pasqual said. "Very good. I'm proud of you."

At this, Maddie turned to see Kali's reaction to the compliment, expecting her to look indifferent. Curiously, Kali seemed to glow under the praise.

"So what's your plan from here?" Pasqual asked, placing the silverware around the dining table.

"The moon doesn't rise until after midnight, so I'm not going to leave here until after eleven. With luck, the darkness and hour will let us speed past Santarem."

"The port is usually busy. Do you think it's safe to go fast?"

"It's a Saturday night, so I don't expect much traffic. Besides, I'm going to be staying on the far north side of the river."

Pasqual nodded. "I trust you know what you're doing."

"It's a risk, but hopefully a calculated one."

"By now, I would assume that my brother has figured out that we're traveling by night. Will that affect our plans?"

Kali entered the galley, stopping to grab a bottle of beer from the refrigerator. This put her within a few feet of where Maddie stood at the stove, stirring the sauce. Being this close made Maddie's body vibrate, although Kali, seemed to remain, thankfully, unaware.

"I'm not changing my plans," Kali said, popping the top on her beer. "Duarte is not equipped to deal with a night search." She stepped closer to the stove, bringing herself to within inches of Maddie. "That smells great. Can I help with anything?"

She opened her mouth to speak, but found that words failed her. All she wanted to do was lean back, just enough to feel Kali. That would say more than she ever could.

Before she could do anything, Pasqual walked into the galley and Kali shifted away. "I agree. From what I saw of my brother's operation, he's lagging in technology."

"He has what he needs to succeed in Macapa, but that's a long way from here."

A thought occurred to Maddie, and she turned. "What if he puts someone on the shore with night goggles? Like the ones you have."

Kali looked at her with the most enigmatic expression. Her green eyes were vibrant, and a small, amused smile tugged on her lips. "That's a good question. What would you do?"

"Me?" Maddie frowned. "I don't know."

"You're intelligent. Think it through."

"Kali, stop. She's not like us," Pasqual said reprovingly. "Don't sully her innocence with such matters."

The smile fell from Kali's face. "Sorry," she said, looking away.

"Wait," Maddie said, grabbing her arm. "I'd like to answer."

"Please, Dr. Cross. I insist. Let Kali handle it." Pasqual took a seat at the table. "So how long before we reach Manaus?"

Kali gestured at the stove. "Maddie, your water is about to boil over."

"What?" She turned back to her pot and lifted it from the heat. A sudden and inexplicable anger seemed to fill her chest. Why did there have to be a line between them? She'd been told by everyone that her life as she knew it was over. Was she also not allowed to join this life now surrounding her?

"Here," Kali said, coming up behind her and taking the pot. "Let me." Turning, she dumped the pasta into the strainer in the sink. Steam rose around her face, momentarily obscuring her.

Maddie switched off the burner and picked up a plate. "Why don't you go sit?" she asked, reaching into the sink for the pasta. "I'll serve."

"I can help," Kali said, trying to take the plate.

"No. Go and sit. Continue your plans. Don't let my innocence get in the way."

Kali held herself still for a moment, but Maddie couldn't bring herself to look up. "That's not what I think," she said, backing away.

"Grab the wine," Pasqual called out, as Kali left the galley. "Then tell me how long to Manaus."

The area felt empty without Kali, but as she ladled sauce onto the noodles, she tried to let it go. The truth was she knew Kali didn't think of her in the same terms as Pasqual, but she treated her differently all the same. To Kali, she was an unavoidable mistake. Regardless of whatever Maddie wanted, it would never be enough to outweigh Kali's conscience. She would never be more than Kali's regret, and it was that which hurt the most.

"I figure, if everything goes well," Kali said, taking a seat at the table. "We'll make Manaus in a day or two."

Maddie took the first plate and laid it in front of Kali. She didn't even try to look her in the eye. Returning to the galley, she prepared Pasqual's plate.

"I don't think Duarte will expect us to go past Santarem," Kali continued. "At least not for another day or two."

"And will he then look for us in Manaus?"

"As long as he can't locate us, he'll have no idea where we are. Given your resources, he might expect you to charter a plane out of Santarem. Given his knowledge of me, he might expect me to make for open water as soon as possible. He just has so many choices, doesn't he?"

Maddie caught sight of Kali's grin as she set Pasqual's plate in front of him.

"Thank you," Pasqual said gently.

Not responding, she returned to the stove to make up her own, smaller plate. In the last few minutes, she found her appetite had gone.

"After we pass Santarem," Kali said as Maddie took her seat, "and if everything looks safe, I'm only planning on stopping long enough to rest for a few hours and eat."

"Does that mean we'll be traveling in the day?"

"I don't see why not." Kali picked up her fork and contemplated the spaghetti. "This looks really good," she said to Maddie.

"Yes," Pasqual said, reaching for the bottle of wine and pouring some into each of their glasses. "A toast for Dr. Cross."

Maddie lifted her glass. "As long as I can serve some purpose on this trip," she said sarcastically before draining her wine.

After dinner, Kali excused herself to rest. With her stomach full, it was easy to slip into a deep, restful sleep. The knock on her door jolted her out of a wonderful dream.

"Kali, it's after ten," Pasqual said, knocking again.

"I'm up," she yelled, still lingering in the warmth of her dream.

"Very good," Pasqual responded, and she listened to him move away from her door.

Laying there, Kali fought the urge to go back to sleep. If for no other reason than to return to her dream. There wasn't anything specific she could recall, no place or face, but she'd felt happy. The feeling still clung to her like something long forgotten.

But it was over, and with a sigh, she rolled out of bed and began dressing. As she was pulling on her shorts she heard the sound of Maddie's laughter pushing under the door. Stopping, she stared at the wood, not sure if she liked it or not.

Not deciding one way or the other, she turned her thoughts to the dilemma of what to do with Maddie once they reached Manaus. With Duarte hard on her heels, she knew getting out of Brazil was her top priority. The short-term answer would be to just take Maddie with her. It would be a simple matter to make a few calls and a fake passport would be waiting for them at the airport.

It was an effortless solution to the problem, but not the wisest. She could see that Maddie was changing. It was becoming easier for her to understand the decisions Kali needed to make, and for that, she blamed herself. Pasqual was right. Maddie didn't belong in their world.

No matter how difficult it was for her to admit, sending Maddie home was the only decision she could make. Maddie had a home and people who would miss her, and that meant more than anything Kali could offer her. It wouldn't be easy, but this was a rare chance to do something right in her life.

Kicking her feet into her shoes, she decided to put things in motion tonight by not asking Maddie to sit with her. She would use music to keep her awake and alert.

As she climbed the steps to the salon, both Maddie and Pasqual looked up from where they were playing cards. She could feel Maddie's eyes burning into her, but Kali kept her face as cold as stone. Muttering a good night, she passed through the salon and out onto the aft deck.

Climbing to the flybridge, she flipped on the spotlight and checked around the boat. Turning it off, she reached for a pair of night goggles and quickly got the *Avatara* underway.

Chapter Fifteen

With a grin, Pasqual laid his cards down on the table. "Gin."

"Again?" Maddie asked, closing her pile up and reaching for more wine.

"You don't play much, do you?"

"The wine's gone," she announced, shaking the bottle.

"I think I saw another bottle in the cabinet."

"I shouldn't." Maddie gave a sly smile.

"Probably not," Pasqual said, gathering the cards. "But at least you're in high spirits."

"Only because I'm very close to being totally drunk," Maddie said, getting up and searching through the cabinet for the other bottle of wine. She pulled it out and turned around with a smile. "Success!"

"Aren't you going to sit with Kali tonight?" he asked, as Maddie opened the bottle.

"You saw her face," she said, pulling the cork from the bottle. "Besides, she didn't ask me, did she?"

Bringing the wine back to the table, she offered some to Pasqual, but he shook his head. "Are you sure you still want to play?" he asked, as he began dealing the cards.

"Why not?" Maddie filled her glass. "It's not like I was a challenge to you sober."

"So you will be getting off in Manaus with me?" he asked cautiously.

It took all of her strength to sit there. "How would I know?" She pointed towards the ceiling. "Do you think she tells me anything?"

"Well, in case she does not, I would like to offer you the hospitality of my home." He reached over and patted her arm. "Have you ever seen Bogotá?"

"No."

"You will hate it. A filthy place." He raised a finger. "But Barranquilla, where I live, is beautiful. My house sits on a cliff overlooking the sea where cool breezes greet you every day. There are trees around the house that drip with exquisite fruits and my cellars are stocked with my private label. Much better than that trash." He pointed at the wine in her hand.

"I'm..." Maddie searched for the words. "I'm overwhelmed."

"Think nothing of it. You may stay as long as you like. My wife will make you feel welcome, and if we're too old for you, one of my daughters is usually visiting, or my young grandchildren if on holiday. You will not just be my guest, Dr. Cross. You will be like family."

"Thank you. I appreciate the offer."

He patted her arm. "It's the least I can do. Should things change, then Kali is most welcome, too."

The mere mention of her name sent her hand reaching for more wine. As she poured it, the boat engines sped up.

"We must be back to the Amazon," Pasqual said, collecting all the cards. "Check the blinds and turn off all the lights but this one."

"Why?" Maddie asked, reaching for the blind handle.

"So no one can see us. Even a little light from in here could give us away."

"You're right. I'm not very good at thinking of these things."

"Let's keep it that way," Pasqual said, standing. "I think I'm going to bid you good night. Amado needs his medication, and I'm actually very tired."

Maddie looked up at him. "Sleep well."

Pasqual gave her a slight bow. "It was nice playing cards with you. Thank you for a simple pleasure."

"Yes, it was nice."

After he was gone, Maddie switched off the table light, and in the haze of the green microwave display, she poured more wine. She'd never felt more alone in her life.

The nearer she got to Santarem, the wider the Amazon became. It was at least a mile across from bank to bank, leaving lots of dark, shifting water for someone to stare at all night.

Since it seemed most logical for Duarte to place someone on the more populated southern bank, Kali kept the *Avatara* to the north. With no lights and most of the ship still dark with river mud, she hoped it was enough to slip by.

Traffic on the river was light, just as she expected. That worked both for and against her. No traffic meant she could travel faster, but then again, it would have been just as nice to use a long barge going west to camouflage her.

The air coming off Santarem stank. Exhaust fumes. Garbage. Pollution. Human habitation. They all floated on the breeze until Kali wanted to gag on it.

It was the ramshackle shanties and open fires that first let Kali know she was approaching the outskirts of the city. The poor lived here, using the river for everything from food to sanitation. The green fires glowed brightly in her night goggles, and she forced her eyes away.

The shacks slowly gave way to rambling and haphazard docks. Local and indigenous people would use these jetties to deliver fresh fish and jungle wares. These shabby docks rattled on until Kali saw the first traces of tin warehouses lining the more sturdy concrete commercial docks.

This was where the big barges would load Brazil nuts, timber and other raw materials destined for ports around the world. During the day, the activity on the river would be frantic. Since there were no roads or highways into Santarem, everything was either floated in by the river or flown in by plane.

Away from the river, Santarem was like any other city. It had its luxurious hotels and high-rise apartments as well as its middle income tract housing. The only difference was the vast rainforest surrounding it.

Once she cleared the commercial docks, she pushed the speed up. In a few minutes, the lights would begin to fade until she only had the darkness again.

Although she hadn't expected anything to jump out, she was still relieved that there had been nothing alarming. She still knew it was quite possible that someone was, at that very moment, reporting to Duarte that they had been discovered. If that happened, tomorrow Duarte would broaden his search to west of Santarem. Not knowing was the most frustrating part for Kali, and she once again considered hiding the *Avatara* during the day until she was sure.

As the smells of Santarem gave way to the wet, musty scents of the jungle, a heavy feeling of isolation and loneliness descended upon her. It was as if she were yearning for something she couldn't name. To distract herself, she reached over and turned on the stereo.

Music had always been a release for Kali. It was the one enjoyment in her life that she didn't have to second guess or manage, and through music she was able to experience the emotions she otherwise denied herself. It made her feel happiness and it let her release pain. It was everything she would never allow herself to be.

Tonight, she felt like the Blues. There was something deep and primal in the genre that, in a few simple chords, stripped her heart bare. It was painful and poignant and it always left her aching.

For reasons Kali couldn't quite admit, the music that evening seemed to affect her more than normal, leaving her with a strong urge to just give into the pain. Just as she was about to raise her voice with it, she heard movement behind her and she reached out to turn down the stereo.

"Please don't," Maddie said, softly. "I like Nina Simone. Her voice is just so – I don't know." Her voice trailed off into a swish of liquid.

Kali's hand tightened on the wheel. "How long have you been back there?"

"A while."

"You should have said something."

"Why? You don't need me, right?" The liquid swished again. "And I really just wanted to be—" She paused. "I wanted to be here with you."

Staring ahead, Kali kept silent.

"Was that Santarem we just passed?"

The simplicity of the question relieved her. "Yes."

"Nothing happened, did it?"

"I think we got through," she said, as Maddie got to her feet.

"May I stay up here?" She dropped into the seat next to her, sticking a bottle between her legs.

"You're still drinking."

"Can't sneak anything by you," Maddie replied, leaning forward and turning up the stereo. "I love this song." She settled back against the seat. "But I can never remember the name."

Kali listened for a second. "'Since I Fell for You'."

"Yes, that's it. The words are so simple, but the meaning is so deep. It's about how she can't control her love. He makes her leave her home and all she's known. He loves her then he snubs her. But she's still in love." Maddie took another drink of wine. "It's so tortured. So anguished."

"It's the Blues," Kali said, clenching her jaw.

"But the harmonica and the piano. It just makes you ache." She touched her chest. "Here."

Kali didn't bother looking. She knew the pain. The song ended and was followed by something by Etta James. It wasn't nearly as personal, and Kali relaxed.

"I wouldn't have thought you liked this kind of music," Maddie said, reaching out to turn the music down a notch. "But you're full of surprises."

Kali shrugged. "Am I?"

"Your singing the other day surprised me." She paused to take a drink of wine. "Your voice was beautiful. You're beautiful. More beautiful than anyone I've ever seen."

"You're drunk."

"Not that drunk. I know what I'm saying. And I now realize that I've wanted to say it since the first time I saw you. In that bar. You were—"

"What's your point?" Kali cut her off.

Shifting in the seat, Maddie leaned closer. "Most people think I'm a bitch. Cold and unfeeling. They think I live for my work, and," she took another swig of wine, "they'd be right. My work has been my life."

"So?"

"So we're not that different. I know people think you're a cold bitch, too."

"Assuming this isn't just a drunk rambling, what are you trying to say?"

"I've been trying to figure out why we're both so isolated and alone. And why we hide all our emotions in our jobs. Do you want to know what I discovered?"

"Does it matter what I want?" Kali tried to laugh, but it came out more like a mean rumble. "You obviously want to tell me. So go on. Tell me."

"Stop it!" Maddie said sharply. "Don't discount and dismiss me like that. Like you and Pasqual did earlier. I deserve better."

Kali opened her mouth to object, but then closed it. "Fine. Go on."

"We're afraid," she said, taking another sip of wine. "We're so terrified of making an emotional connection with anyone that we push them away before we can be rejected."

Kali shook her head in annoyance. "That's bullshit."

"Come on, Kali. You can do better than that." The wine swirled again. "Why not try telling me I'm stupid or that I don't know what I'm talking about? Go on and prove my point. Try to push me away, but I've got news for you. I'm not going anywhere. I'm not afraid of you."

Her hand tightened on the wheel. "You should be."

"See what I mean? You fear me and that was meant to push me away." She gestured towards the stereo. "But just like that song, I'm ready to do it. I'm ready to give up everything – my home, my family, my career, my life – all for you. I'll leave it all for you."

"Then you didn't listen to the song. She regretted giving it all up. And so will you."

"No! You don't get it. I'll regret it more if I don't," Maddie cried, her voice loud and emotional. "Don't you see that I can't help it? I can't stop it. I love you."

"You what?" Kali stared at her for a long second before shaking her head. "No. I won't allow it."

Maddie actually laughed. "You can't control it. In spite of everything that's happened and everything we are...I think I'm in love with you."

The words were painful, and Kali wished she'd never heard them. "You don't know what you're talking about. You don't know me."

"But I accept you."

"This is insane."

"Sleep with me."

Kali's mouth went dry. "What?" she managed to utter.

"You told me you've fucked women. You don't have to love me to have sex with me."

"I said I've used sex to get what I want."

"Then want me." Maddie drank quickly from the bottle again. "If you can sleep with me without loving me, then I'll never bother you again."

"This is ridiculous. And you're drunk."

"Are you saying you can't do it because you do love me?"

"I didn't say anything."

"Your words aren't required." She stood, grabbing onto the windshield to steady herself. "Take me to bed, Kali. Give me something to remember you by. Something besides your abuse."

Kali clenched her jaw.

"That was wrong. I'm sorry." Maddie sank back into her chair and held her head. "I don't feel so well."

"Then go to bed." She would be glad to be rid of her and this ridiculous topic.

"I think I'm going to throw up."

One look at her, and Kali knew it was true, so she gave the river a quick scan before pulling back on the throttles and slowing the ship to a crawl. Then jumping out of her seat, she grabbed Maddie around the waist. "Come on," she said, helping her to her feet and leading her to the side of the ship.

Almost immediately, Maddie's body began to convulse, and Kali gathered back her hair, holding it as she gently rubbed her back. "It's okay. Just let it out."

She looked down the river for any sign of danger. It would be safer to leave Maddie, even for a second, to flip on their running lights, but she didn't dare.

"I'm so sorry," Maddie said, before another spasm gripped her and she leaned out over the edge again.

Kali continued to rub her back in circles. "It's okay."

It didn't take long for Maddie's legs to buckle from weakness. When they did, Kali wrapped an arm around her and lead her back to the co-pilot's seat. "Here you go. Sit."

"Oh God," Maddie groaned, laying her head against the seat.

"Wine will do that to you." Kali pressed a bottle of water into her hand. "Drink this and I'll be right back."

She climbed down from the flybridge and hurried through the salon. Once in her cabin, she retrieved a clean shirt, a bottle of aspirin and a wet washcloth.

Almost as an afterthought she grabbed a pillow off the bed and stuck it under her arm. In the galley she added three bottles of water to her load and quickly made her way back to the flybridge.

Maddie hadn't moved, and, as Kali looked down the river, it seemed neither had anything else. She put everything in her chair and picked up the washcloth. Dropping to her knee, she began cleaning Maddie's face.

"I don't feel so good," Maddie croaked.

"I imagine you don't."

Pulling away, Maddie looked at her. "After what I said, why are you being nice to me?"

"Just be quiet and let me do my job."

"Always your damn job," Maddie moaned, leaning her head back against the seat. "I want you to make me your job."

Kali smiled a little. "Right now, you are my job." She poured a little more water on the cloth and finished. "All right, I need you to sit up straight."

"Impossible. Not with this spinning."

Not willing to argue, she pulled Maddie upright. "Now stay up."

Maddie gave her a crusty look, but complied. Unbuttoning the shirt, Kali almost gagged at the smell as she carefully slid it off Maddie's body. She wadded it into a ball and threw it over the side.

"You shouldn't litter," Maddie said absently. "It's bad for the environment."

"I could have let you sleep in it."

"Good point." She wrapped her arms around her body. "I'm cold."

"Here," Kali said, holding out another shirt. "Let's get you in this." She waited for Maddie to stick her hands through the arm holes and then carefully moved it past her wound, watching for any reaction. When it reached her shoulders, she helped Maddie pull it over her head and then down around her waist.

Reaching for the aspirin bottle, she shook a few tablets into her hand. "Okay, now something for your head." She waited until Maddie opened her mouth. "Now water." She held the bottle, trying to force more water than was needed to take the pills. "Come on, drink some more." Reluctantly, Maddie lowered the half-finished bottle.

"I'm tired." Maddie started to close her eyes.

"Can you stand for just a second?" She helped Maddie to her feet before quickly lifting the seat and unfolding it into a skinny bed. "Okay, now lay down."

"Kali?" Maddie asked, as Kali put the pillow down and helped her onto the bed.

"Yes?"

"I love you. I think I really do."

Kali felt her heart clench, but she forced a smile. "Okay."

"I don't want to lose you." Her eyes closed. "Don't let me lose you."

Kali smoothed her hair and then turned back to her seat. In a few seconds, the boat was again racing down the river. In the darkness, Kali tried to ignore it all. A drunken announcement wasn't going to change anything.

As the sun was beginning to lighten the sky, Kali stopped the *Avatara* and reached for the GPS. Since she hadn't paid attention to anything during the night except the immediate need to keep the boat moving, she had no idea how far she had traveled or exactly where they were.

She activated the GPS and waited for the signal to return. It didn't look right, so she checked it again. Saracura. They had passed the small town of Saracura. It was much further than she'd expected.

Shifting through the screens, she found a split in the river ahead. It circled around Ilha do Arco, and Kali thought it would be a good point to stop for a few hours. With luck, it would also offer a dense enough canopy to protect them from any aircraft Duarte might send westward.

She navigated the *Avatara* up the channel, pleased that it was isolated enough to protect them from any passing river traffic. The tree canopy could have been denser, but she was too tired to try and find a better spot.

As she was setting the anchors, Maddie made a small sound, and Kali turned. With the engines idling, she sat staring at her, never wanting to move. When a parrot screeched overhead, the spell was broken and Kali looked up.

Getting to her feet, she stuck the boat keys into her pocket and approached Maddie. "Come on," she said, rolling Maddie into her arms.

With Maddie's weight spread across her body, Kali picked her way down from the flybridge and through the salon. Struggling down the stairs, she kicked open the door of her room and hurried inside. After laying Maddie on the bed, she stood up and rubbed at her arms.

Bending over, she gently removed Maddie's shoes before slipping her under the covers. Looking down at her, Kali felt a swell of contentment. Was this what happiness felt like? She'd almost forgotten.

Grabbing a pillow, she dropped it on top of the covers and lowered herself down. All she needed was a few hours of sleep, and if the sky remained clear of planes, she would get them under way again. Manaus was now closer than she expected.

Holding a linen handkerchief to his nose, Luis Vega pounded on the metal door. The hallway of the nearly abandoned commercial building stank of urine and stale alcohol. A single, exposed bulb swung over his head, distorting his shadow against the wall.

He banged on the door again, knowing Roman Reyes was inside. With all the money he owed the cartel, he didn't dare leave his little metal fortress.

"Open up, Roman. I'm not here to kill you." He pounded again. "Although you deserve it," he added under his breath.

"I'll get your money. I just need another week."

It was always another week. Another game. Another wager. Another debt.

"Open the door." He banged again. "Are you hoping to irritate me?"

The bolt slid back and the door cracked open. A single, blood shot eye peered out. "I've almost got your money. I swear."

"Relax. Do you really think I'd personally come to collect? Now open up. I need your services."

"Is anyone else with you?"

As if he'd be stupid enough to bring someone here. "Open the fucking door or I will kill you!" He palmed the door, the sound reverberating down the hall.

Roman appeared to be weighing his options, but then he nodded and the door opened. "What could Luis Vega need from me?"

"Your computer skills." Luis pushed his way into the loft. "I need to locate a boat."

He looked around at the sty with a sense of disgust and satisfaction. It was exactly as he'd imagined someone like Roman living. The only thing of value in the entire place was a bank of computers lining one dirty brick wall. It was to these he walked.

"Hold on," Roman said, following him. "You don't need me to find a boat. Most ships have locational transponders. Log onto the Internet and check ShipLoc."

"How informative." Luis smiled coldly. "But the ship I'm looking for won't have any such tracking device enabled."

"Then how do you think I'm going to track it?"

"If I'm correct, a rogue signal will have been activated by now."

"A rogue signal?" Roman laughed. "And just what is that supposed to be?"

Reaching out, Luis patted the side of Roman's cheek. "That's what you've got to find out."

"Do you have any idea how hard that's going to be? And just where am I looking?"

"That's easy. The Amazon River."

"The whole river?"

"I'll narrow it down slightly, but in effect, you'll have to track and verify every transmission." Luis gave him a hard stare. "Can you do it?"

"I don't know." Roman stared at his computers. "Let's say I can. What do I get in return?"

Luis almost laughed. He already knew Roman could do it. Why else would he be here? "I'll consider it a personal favor," he said, kindly.

"That's great, but I'll need something more concrete." Roman met his eyes. "If I deliver this boat, I want my debts to the cartel erased."

"Really?" Luis chuckled. "And do you think I have the power to just wipe out a hundred thousand dollars?"

"Everyone knows Duarte de Tueste counts on you. If you're here, it must be for him. And if anyone has the power to erase all that I owe, it's Duarte."

"That's true." Luis smiled thinly. "But don't weaken your position by thinking you can negotiate with me." He pointed to the computers. "If you find what I want, I'll speak to Duarte about your debts. That's all I can promise."

He watched as Roman considered his choices. In the end, he knew what Roman would do. It was his only option. The man was living on borrowed time as much as borrowed money, and sooner rather than later his time was going to run out. "Shall we get started?" Luis asked when he saw resignation in Roman's eyes.

The sound of a groan broke through Kali's sleep. It was close enough to bring her slowly back to consciousness, but not urgent enough to make her want to move. She began to drift back to sleep when the bed shifted and Maddie's body pressed against her side.

"God my head hurts," Maddie croaked, her breath warming the skin of Kali's neck.

Kali felt herself smile briefly before realizing the situation and snapping her eyes open. Throwing the blanket back, she sat up. "I'm sorry," she muttered, climbing out of bed.

"Wait," Maddie said, as she headed for the bathroom. "You don't have to leave."

But she did. She knew it like she knew nothing else.

Closing the bathroom door, she turned on the water and quickly washed up. She picked up her brush, running it through her tangled hair and then pulling it back in a tight ponytail. Although the routine was familiar to her, Kali had the strangest feeling that someone else was doing it. Almost like she wasn't in her body, but watching it from some other place.

Trying to shake the feeling, she grabbed a small bottle of aspirin and dumped some tablets into her hand. Maddie would need them for her headache. As she stared at them, she had the strongest urge to withhold them from her. If she didn't give them to Maddie, she might stay in bed for most of the day, allowing Kali to keep some much needed space between them.

She clenched the tablets in her hand. Maddie was not Amado. She wasn't some problem to be handled. Kali owed her more.

"Your hair looks nice like that," Maddie said, sitting up as she exited the bathroom.

Avoiding her eyes, Kali held the aspirin out. "Here. For your head." When Maddie took them, she frowned. "I forgot the water. I'll get some."

"Behind you," Maddie said, pointing. "There's a bottle on the desk."

Kali grabbed the water and passed it to Maddie.

"Tell me," Maddie said, after swallowing the aspirin. "What happened last night? I don't remember much after coming up to see you." Her eyes were bleary and bloodshot. "I finished off the wine, didn't I?"

"And then passed out."

"What an impression I must have made." She gave her a sour smile.

"It was no big deal." Kali shook her head. "You slept upstairs with me."

"You drove through the night alone again?"

"No. You were there." She looked at the cabin door and then back at Maddie. "You should drink a lot of water today."

Maddie tugged at her t-shirt. "Where did I get this shirt?"

"You were sick." Kali tried to shrug it off.

"And you took care of me?"

There was enough hope in Maddie's tone that Kali panicked. She gestured towards the door. "I have to go," she said, hurrying across the room.

"Kali!" Maddie cried, stopping her. "Tell me. Did I say something wrong last night?"

Staring at the door, Kali shook her head. "You were drunk. You said drunk things. Don't worry. I didn't take any of them seriously."

"Oh. I see."

Kali opened the cabin door. "You should rest some more," she said, before stepping into the hall and closing it.

The boat was quiet as she crossed through it. Stopping in the galley, she grabbed some fruit and a bottle of water before heading for the flybridge. She didn't expect to find Pasqual sitting there, and she scowled in annoyance.

"What are you doing up here?" she asked, dropping into the pilot's seat.

"Just getting some air and keeping an eye on things." He looked slightly amused, and Kali shook her head as she opened her water. "Did you sleep well?"

The memory of waking up next to Maddie rushed at her, and Kali barely had time to side step it. "Well enough."

"And Dr. Cross? How is she this morning?"

Kali checked the gages. "Hung over," she said, sticking the key in the ignition and starting the engines.

"I was hoping she would quit drinking, but she was determined."

Kali grunted while calculating their fuel levels. "I'm not familiar with the area. Do you know where we can stop for fuel?"

"Where are we?"

"Near Saracura."

"Really?" The old man's eyebrows raised. "Quite admirable, Kali."

"So, do you?"

"I believe my barge stopped at Itaquatiara."

Kali powered up the GPS and scanned forward to locate the town. "That will work." She raised the anchors. "Have you seen any planes or other signs that a search is going on?"

"No. Nothing. It's been pleasantly quiet."

The news was good, but Kali didn't dwell on it. "And Amado?" she asked guardedly. "How is he?"

"Getting worse. Which is why I'm relieved that we're so close to Manaus. Another day and we'll be done with this business. Amado needs proper treatment."

"Yes, that's probably best." She pushed the throttles forward, and steered the ship more to the center of the channel.

"And what of Dr. Cross?" Pasqual asked, simply. "Have you decided what to do with her?"

She really didn't want to answer, but knew the time had come to face it. "When we arrive in Manaus," she said, looking at him, "will you take her with you? Keep her safe. Keep her away from me."

Pasqual was quiet for a moment. "Is that what you really want?"

"It doesn't matter what I want. It's the right thing to do."

"How selfless." He smiled almost sadly. "And what does Maddie think of this?"

"I'm not going to tell her. She'll only fight me."

"Maybe that's because it's not your decision to make."

"I'm the only one who can make it!" Kali clenched her fist. "She doesn't know what she wants, and I can't explain it all to her."

"She thinks she's in love with you. Did you know that?"

"That just makes me more resolved." She sighed. "Promise me you'll take care of her? Promise me you'll keep her safe?"

"Forgive me for saying this, but I think you do care about her. Deeply."

"I don't love her. I hardly know her." Kali shook her head. "I'm only sorry that I got her involved." She looked to him in appeal. "She has something to offer the world. And...and I can't take that."

"And that's not love?"

"Goddamn it!" Kali cried. "If you won't help me, I need to know now."

"If I don't, you know you will have to face her. You'll have to be honest."

"Is that a no?"

He smiled cunningly. "I'll let you know my decision before we reach Manaus." He pointed at her with reproach. "But I would prefer if you were truthful with Dr. Cross. She deserves that much."

Kali didn't need to reply. There wasn't anything more to say. Pasqual would either help or he wouldn't. It was that black and white.

If he didn't, Kali figured she would just hire someone from the docks to get Maddie to the airport. At that point, Maddie would have no choice but to contact the American consulate. She would hate her, but just until she got home. Of that, Kali was certain.

"Well, since we appear to be done talking, I'll leave you to concentrate on the river." He rose to his feet.

"I'll ask you to not say anything to Maddie."

"And ruin the surprise of your betrayal?" He gave her a gloomy smile. "Of course not."

"I'm not betraying her."

"No? What do you think she will call it?"

"Once she's back in Boston and has her life back, I'm sure she'll be glad that I did what I did."

"Perhaps. Or perhaps that's only what you hope happens? What if her life is never the same? What if in the great scheme of life you were meant to meet her? It does seem very coincidental, you interfering in her life twice."

Kali felt herself growing angry. "That's enough. I've heard you."

"Then think about what I've said." Pasqual briefly touched her shoulder.

She shook his touch off. "I only need to know if you're going to help me. If not, I'll turn Maddie over to a stranger. Is that what you want?"

"You're that determined?"

"Yes."

He sighed in defeat. "Very well. You have my word. I'll look after Dr. Cross."

"And make sure she gets home safely?"

"If that's what she wants."

"It's what I want."

At this, Pasqual's old eyes became hard and cold. "Don't lie, Kali. Especially to yourself. You're afraid of what you feel for her. Don't hide behind doing what's right. Be honest and admit that much."

"If that's what you need to hear to help me, then yes, I'm afraid. Satisfied now?"

Reaching out, he once again patted her shoulder. "I didn't need to hear it. You did." He stepped away. "Please call me if you need any assistance today. Otherwise, I'll be below deck. The sun's too bright for my frail skin."

Kali didn't bother commenting, and she was relieved when she heard his steps descending the stairs. It was enough that he had agreed to take care of Maddie. That was all she needed from him.

Pushing the throttles forward, she increased the *Avatara*'s speed. Each mile that passed would take her closer to the end. She only had to get past that and her life would return to normal.

Chapter Sixteen

The phone in the hotel suite shrilled and Duarte waved Sanchez to it. "Tell Luis to wait," he said, leaning back so the hotel barber could finish shaving him.

"He thinks he's found a way to track the *Avatara.*"

Sitting up so fast the razor nicked his skin. Duarte grimaced, but held out his hand for the phone. "*Diga-me,*" he demanded, pushing the phone to his ear.

"It's not technically legal," Luis began his voice hesitant. "It could bring us to the attention of certain international governments."

Duarte laughed mirthlessly. "Just tell me what you've found."

"I've found a man who can hack ship signals."

"Really?" Duarte sighed. "Is it expensive?"

"It is, but we have some leverage." Luis paused. "I'm going to see him, and I've already authorized the money to pay him."

Duarte ground his teeth together. Authorized? Luis didn't have the power to authorize anything! "You've overstepped your bounds. If my partners were to know—"

"I can stop the search."

"No!" Duarte boomed. "Just tell me how long before we know Kali's location?"

"The Amazon is massive, sir. It's going to take time to locate and verify each and every signal. Then our time is limited by the satellite orbiting patterns."

"Yes, yes." Duarte waved his hand. "Just get it done!"

"I'm doing my best."

"Do better!" His heart clenched dangerously in his chest and Duarte stopped to let it settle. Taking a deep breath, he tried to calm himself. "Keep me informed," he said evenly. "Now what else is happening in Macapa?"

"I postponed the meeting with the Japanese."

"Very good."

"And your partners are becoming more vocal about your secret deals."

"What exactly are they saying?"

"It's what they are suggesting that alarms me. If possible, you should conclude this situation very soon and return home. Otherwise, there may be nothing left for you here."

His heart thumped wildly and his breathing became shallow. "Your tone sounded very superior, Luis. Remember who found you starving on the streets!" He pressed a hand to his chest and sucked in as much air as he could get.

"As always, I'm aware of the debt I owe you."

"Then do what I command! Find Kali! Or else." Sanchez held out a glass of water, but he waved it off. "Today, Luis! Today!"

"I'll do what I can."

Disgusted, Duarte threw the phone to the floor. The barber was standing nearby, carefully averting his eyes. "Finish me," he said, leaning back in the chair.

"Sir, are you all right?" Sanchez asked, retrieving the phone and hanging it up.

"Get me one of those little blue pills," he ordered, closing his eyes. "And then get the plane ready. I'm going up to search again."

It was all coming down around him. He could feel it. Luis. The Japanese syndicate. His partners. Amado. His damn brother. All his cards were about to topple. His heart pounded in his throat. He had to find Kali today. That was the only way to stop his fall. The only way.

Sitting outside the small village of Itaquatiara, Kali waited for the dockhand to finish refueling the *Avatara*. The village was larger than most, but still a mud hole in Kali's opinion. She hadn't even bothered getting off the ship.

It was Pasqual who had hurried ashore as soon as the lines were tied. He said he wanted to buy something special for their last dinner together, but Kali knew he was making arrangements for their arrival in Manaus.

Every time she thought about tomorrow, Kali was stunned by how little time was left. It was as if everything she did was a final act. Even refueling her ship had taken on a finality that saddened her.

The *Avatara* had been the first thing in many years to which she felt an attachment. It had become an extension of the image she had of herself. Sleek. Powerful. Intimidating. But most of all, free. The *Avatara* was freedom to her, and no matter what happened, she always had her ship.

Tomorrow that would end. Like a tool she no longer needed, the *Avatara* would be abandoned and forgotten. She wondered if along with her ship she would also be losing her sense of self?

The question loomed before her. If she wanted, she knew her life could continue just as before. There were always people in need of her special skill set, and Duarte for all his power in Brazil, would have little impact on her job prospects.

It could all be so simple, but even as she considered finding a new employer, Kali was sickened with the prospect. Her whole life had been dominated by money, blood and deception, and she wasn't sure she wanted that any more. Maybe it was time for a change.

"You look quite serious," Maddie said, coming up behind her. She slid a hand across her shoulders. "I argue with myself, too."

"I wasn't arguing with myself. I was only..." Her voice trailed off. What was the point in denying it? "How are you feeling?"

"Better," Maddie said, sitting in the co-pilot's seat and pulling her knees to her chest. "I'm sorry if I said or did anything inappropriate last night."

She didn't want to get into that again. "I told you not to worry about it."

"Did I tell you that I think I'm in love with you?"

She turned her head away and stared down at the dock. Where was Pasqual? They should be underway by now. Sitting here was dangerous. It was giving Duarte a chance to catch up with them. She had to—

"Kali," Maddie said softly. "Look at me."

"No." The word almost caught in her throat.

"Is it that hard for you to hear?"

"You were drunk. You didn't know what you were saying."

"I'm not drunk now. And I think I love you. Or at least I'm starting to."

"No," Kali repeated. "You don't."

"You can't decide for me."

Finally turning, Kali looked at her. "You don't even know me. And I—" She shook her head. "I don't know you."

"Since when has that ever mattered? Most people I know don't fall in love with someone they know."

"Most people you know aren't like me. You've seen what I can do. Even to you."

"I know, and it doesn't scare me."

"It should."

"Why are you so determined to see the worse in yourself?" Maddie asked, dropping her legs to the floor and leaning forward.

"I don't know. Why are you trying so hard to see something that isn't there? I'll never be what you want me to be."

"You don't understand, do you? You already are."

Kali met Maddie's eyes. They were so familiar now, but she forced her gaze away. "I'm sorry that you feel that way," she said without feeling. "But it's really your problem."

On the shore, she saw Pasqual hurrying towards the docks with two delivery boys in tow. Both were laden down with boxes brimming with fruit and other items.

"I know you don't mean that. The way you kissed me the other night. It was—"

"It was what?" Kali cut her off. "It was nothing. A kiss. A mistake. Nothing more."

"No, it wasn't! It meant something. It meant something to me."

She looked down at the docks and frowned. "Let's go!" she yelled, at Pasqual, before turning her attention to the men standing nearby. "*As linhas, menionos. Agora*!" She started the engines and waited for the men to untie the lines.

Kali didn't know if Maddie was still there or not; she didn't trust herself to look. As soon as the lines were off the ship and Pasqual was on board, she backed the *Avatara* away from the dock and pointed the bow towards Manaus.

Her heart ached, but she ignored it. She had to ignore it. Maddie had no idea what she was saying. Love her? Besides being impossible, it was laughable. She deserved no love, and pretending otherwise would only make things more painful for them both.

Keeping herself focused only on the river, she barely glanced at a long barge heading east. Twenty more hours and this would all be over. Then she could put real space between her and Maddie. Hopefully, it wouldn't take Maddie long to realize that whatever feelings she had were situational and nothing more. It could never be anything more.

On the dash, the GPS beeped as she passed a preset waypoint. There were only eight more set points left before reaching Manaus. Eight more beeps and it would all be over.

Then what? The question seemed to circle in her head.

Her favorite distraction came to mind. Paris. Yes. Tomorrow, she would catch a plane to Paris and lose herself in her fantasies. If there was one place in the world where she felt free enough to imagine a different life for herself, it was Paris.

It didn't matter if she was wandering the streets of the St. Germain or sitting in *Les Duex Maggots*, Kali always pretended that there was someone just waiting for her around the corner. Someone beautiful and alive and so different from the world she'd always known. Someone who loved her.

Even as she let herself get lost in her fantasy, she realized it was very hollow. The dream would never be the same now. There was now a face to put to her lover, and Paris would never be the same without her.

Ignoring the ball of sweat he could feel rolling down his forehead, Roman Reyes concentrated only on the bank of monitors before him. Luis Vega was not a technically proficient person, so getting the right information out of him had proven difficult, but from what he could deduce, he was looking for a needle in a haystack. For his sake, he could only hope he stumbled across it. After Luis hung up on another of his endless cell phones, Roman cringed when he pulled a chair up next to him.

"What is all that?" Luis asked, pointing to the largest monitor where the Amazon River snaked across the screen. Hundreds of dots blinked along it.

"GPS locational transponder signals. Each dot is a ship that is transmitting a signal."

"I told you this ship won't have a signal like that."

"I have to start somewhere," Roman responded, typing in a long command string. On the screen, a large portion of the dots disappeared.

"Jesus! What'd you do?"

"Set a parameter search excluding ships over two gross tonnes. That wiped out most of the commercial vessels and barges."

"I don't know what you hope to gain by this. There won't be any transponder activity."

Roman looked at the small man next to him. "But you said the ship has a GPS system, right?"

"One of the best."

"Then it will be tied into the main power center and not some shitty handheld or dash mounted unit."

"Probably."

"And by rogue signal, I'm assuming you're saying that someone has a small transmitter on board."

Luis nodded. "I told you that."

"Well, since there aren't any cell or radio towers along the Amazon, that little transmitter is going to need amplification if it's going to get picked up. The logical source for that power is the main GPS system."

"But you said a GPS only receives signals." His dark eyes narrowed suspiciously.

Roman didn't have time to explain the whole system to him. "The antenna that a sophisticated GPS system uses is tied into the ship's main power. If your rogue unit is plugged into the GPS, it can use the antenna as an amplified transmitter. But, the signal will only get stronger when the GPS system processes a locational request."

"So it makes the GPS a transmitter?"

"Sort of." Roman took a deep breath, not sure how else to explain it. "In a way, the signal can be tracked the same way as a nautical transponder, but only when the GPS system is processing a request. At that moment, I'm guessing your little rogue unit draws enough power to amplify its signal. Got it?"

Luis waved at the monitors. "I don't need to get it. You just need to find it and soon." A cold, sardonic smile lifted his full lips. "You have two hours."

Two hours! It was impossible. Yet, Roman knew that this was perhaps his only chance. There was no way he could pay off his gambling debts to the cartel. That Luis needed him now was perhaps the best thing that had happened to him in a long time. Not sure if he was being suicidal or smart, he turned to Luis.

"I can do it," he said, forcing a sense of bravado into his voice. "But in return, not only do I want my debts cancelled, but I also want out of Brazil with enough money to start somewhere else."

"And why would I do that?"

"You need me."

Luis laughed. "Do I?" He looked at the screens. "It appears I have everything I need right here. I know several hackers who can run queries."

"You don't know half of what I can do." Roman licked his suddenly dry lips. "This," he pointed at the monitors, "is only part of it. When I find your signal, how are you going to know it's the right one?"

"You really believe there are lots of rogue signals out there? I'll have someone fly over the area."

Roman smiled. "Besides taking time and money, you're going to be running down hundreds of signals. The signal is going to be intermittent, but that won't give it away. You're going to discover that it's probably a ship with power problems or maybe just cloud or tree cover interference. It could be anything, Luis." He pointed at his chest. "I'm the only one who knows how to give you a one hundred percent confirmation."

"And just how do you do that?"

"No. First, I want your promise that you'll get me out of Brazil."

"Don't be stupid, Roman. Telling me only helps me know I'm receiving something of value in return."

"Spy satellites. I can get into and control U.S. military birds."

"You're lying. You expect me to believe you can hack the U.S. government military system?"

"I never lie about computers. It's the one thing I know." Roman folded his arms across his chest. "And I can gain access to the OS/Comet program and the NAVSTAR system. Now, do I have your word?"

Luis studied him for a moment before dismissing him with a wave of his hand. "Fine. What do I have to lose? If you can do what you promised, you have my word." Luis pushed his chair back and stood. "You still only have two hours."

"That's almost impossible. The signal is going to be intermittent. Who knows when it will be used again?"

"I'm on a time schedule here, Roman. I can't give you days to hunt for this ship."

"I don't need days, but two hours is not enough."

"How long do you need?"

Roman shrugged. "Four, maybe six hours. It depends on how often your ship uses its GPS. The more they do, the faster I lock onto them."

With a nod, Luis picked up a pad of paper and wrote on it. "Then I suggest you look west of Santarem. That should help," he handed the pad back. "That's my personal cell. Call the second you find something."

Roman smiled his agreement, although he wasn't looking forward to seeing the little worm again.

"Call me," Luis repeated, on his way to the door.

After he left, Roman bent over his keyboard and began typing in command lines based on all the data Luis had given him. More and more dots disappeared until there were only about a hundred. That was manageable.

Now, he had to wait for any new dots to start blinking. Since he was concentrating west of Santarem, his job was easier. All that ship had to do was activate the GPS system a few times in the next two hours, and Roman would be a free man again.

Standing in front of the floor to ceiling windows of his hotel suite, it appeared as if the world was at his feet, but Duarte knew that was an illusion. For all his money, power and position, at that moment, he felt no better than some filthy beggar on the street twenty floors below. And it was a mere woman had reduced him to such a feeling.

His brother had clearly bought Kali's services, which meant she truly was no better than a whore. Strangely, he'd never thought of Kali as a sexual creature, but doing so now made it easier to understand her treachery. Many a man had been ruined by the deceitfulness of a woman.

There could never be trust with a woman, and he'd been wrong to overlook Kali's obvious physical flaw. She was destined to fail him eventually. He saw that now.

The only upside was that he knew Kali would fail his brother, too. Pasqual was making the same mistake, and he could only hope that he'd be there to see Kali ruin his brother.

He turned at a knock on his suite door. "I said I didn't want to be disturbed."

"I have a fax from Luis, sir."

"Bring it."

Sanchez handed him the paper and then stepped back. Duarte let his eyes run down the fax, a frown crumpling his face. "Failure is all he gives me." The paper fell to the floor.

"What shall I do?" Sanchez asked.

"Get Luis on the phone." He looked back out the window. From here, he could see the dark ribbon of the river. Turning, he pulled himself taller. "And then, Sanchez, I want you and every available man to go down to the river and find out if anyone has seen the *Avatara*. If she's passed Santarem I'm wasting time looking elsewhere."

"But wouldn't our man have seen her?"

"How the hell should I know? Maybe he fell asleep or sneezed, which is why we have to question the people who live there. Someone may have seen her."

"Where should we start?"

"The shacks east of the town. Start there and work your way west."

"You want us to go to every house?" Sanchez asked, stepping back. "I don't know how long that will take."

Duarte's eyes burned into the man. Did he have to solve every problem? "I don't care how you do it, but I want every vile creature who lives on those banks questioned." He looked back at the darkening skyline of Santarem. "Luis is wasting my time with his foolish technology. Get out there and find me someone who has seen that goddamn boat!"

As the sun was starting to set, the GPS announced the arrival at another waypoint. On the digital map, Kali could see the outline of a small cove, and she began looking for it. Now that the danger wasn't imminent, the need to camouflage wasn't so important.

Their escape seemed too simple. Too clean. In a way, she had expected more from Duarte. He'd always seemed to be in control of everything. Maybe she had just outsmarted him, or maybe he'd made too many mistakes. None of it mattered though. What was done was done, and now all she had to do was complete her job.

Dropping the anchor, she killed the engines and then sat in the silence. It took a moment for the jungle around her to come to life. Like a rusty music box, the noises began softly and then built as insects, birds, and God knew what else began moving again.

In the waning light, she looked up at the trees and the blood red sky overhead. Taking a deep breath, she inhaled the scents. She felt like a dying man who suddenly found beauty in everything. Burdened by this sorrow, she slowly climbed to her feet and made her way down to the salon. The smell of food greeted her before she pulled open the door.

"Is that *feijoada*?" she asked, surprised to see Pasqual in the galley.

Pasqual turned and smiled. "I couldn't let us part company without sharing a traditional Brazilian dish." He turned back to his pots. "My mother used to make black beans, rice and pork once a week," he said, stirring. "I've never been able to duplicate her spice." He shrugged with a tilt of his head. "But then again sometimes a memory is more precious than reality."

"My mother never cooked anything."

"We all have our pasts," he said, pointing at the fridge. "There's Brahma beer in there."

Kali licked her lips. "A very Brazilian night," she said, crossing to the galley.

"I thought Dr. Cross would appreciate a good memory of her journey with us."

She knew exactly what he meant, but she chose to ignore his implications. Grabbing a cold bottle of beer, she reached for the opener and popped the top. Tipping it into her mouth, Kali let the tart flavor spread before swallowing it slowly.

"I understand that you sing Choro."

"Your brother liked it."

"To sing is a great gift to all."

"So is silence." She took another drink, reveling in the taste. It was new and old and wonderful.

"You have about twenty minutes until dinner. Perhaps you'd like to refresh yourself."

"Do I smell or something?"

Pasqual smiled at her. "In my family, everyone comes to the table at their best. I would hope you would honor that tradition."

"Sure. Whatever you want."

As she pushed open the door to the cabin, Kali heard the sound of the shower. Stepping into the room and closing the cabin door, she inadvertently caught sight of Maddie. She knew she should turn away, but instead she moved closer, running her hand along the wood of the bathroom door to open it more.

Her eyes were caught by a stream of soap running down Maddie's neck. It gathered in the hollow point at the base of her neck. For a moment, Kali thought it might be content to stay there when a spray of water sent it plunging down, her eyes rapt on its descent.

"Don't you knock?" Maddie asked, and Kali lifted her eyes.

"The door was open," she stammered, surprised at how dry her mouth felt.

"It doesn't matter anyway," Maddie said, shutting off the water. "I'm done." Reaching up, she wrung out her hair before reaching for a towel.

Before Maddie wrapped herself in it, Kali blurted out, "You really are beautiful."

Crossing her arms, Maddie stared at her. "And is that my problem, too?" She was defensive. Guarded. Angry.

"I'm sorry."

"You always are."

Dropping her head, Kali backed away from the door. "I'll let you finish."

Why had she said that? What did she hope to gain from it? The potential fallout from her lack of judgment made her head spin.

Inside the bathroom, she could hear Maddie moving around. When the door opened, Kali looked discreetly at the ground.

"Why isn't there a mirror in there?"

"What?" Kali asked, although she'd heard her clearly.

"Are you that afraid of what you'll see? Or of what you won't?"

She didn't like the smugness of Maddie's tone, so she sneered at her. "Maybe I just don't like mirrors."

"Yeah. That's real believable." Her blue eyes became intense. "How old were you when you started hating and blaming yourself for everything? Was it your mother or that girl?"

"Don't go there," she said softly.

"Alright, I won't. But one day, Kali, you're going to have to look at yourself and see that you're not the monster you think you are." Maddie tilted her head sideways. "Or maybe you already know that, and that's why you have no mirrors. Maybe the only way you can do the things you do is by not looking at yourself."

Kali tried to shrug her comments off, but she ended up dropping her shoulders in defeat. She felt so overwhelmed that she didn't even flinch when Maddie stepped closer. All she could do was close her eyes and wait.

The touch of Maddie's hand against her chest caused her breath to catch, but it was the feel of her lips gently pressing into her own that almost made Kali's legs give out. Grabbing for Maddie, she pulled her closer. It might have been instinct or lustful desire, but she didn't want to let go.

But she had to. Though her chest pounded and her head spun wildly, she had to let go. Above her own wants and needs, she had to let go. Holding on was the worst thing she could do. To herself. To Maddie. Especially to Maddie.

It took all her will, but Kali forced herself to drop her arms and step away. Unable to look at Maddie, she hung her head as she walked around her and into the bathroom.

Closing the door, she leaned back against it. The pressure in her chest was heavy. It made her throat ache, as if she had something caught in it. Remarkably, Kali realized she felt like crying again, and this time, she almost did.

It took a moment to compose herself and then she went about cleaning up. Her movements were automatic. Wash her face. Brush her teeth. Comb her hair. It all meant nothing.

Lifting her eyes, she stared at the empty spot above the sink. What was she afraid of seeing in a mirror? Would her whole existence collapse if she were to look into her own eyes? Right now, she imagined that she must appear rather pathetic.

"You look refreshed," Pasqual said, as Maddie climbed the stairs to the salon. "I've always found a shower to be the best way to relax."

"Sure," Maddie said, leaning against a wall.

"Would you mind setting the table for tonight?"

She was grabbing the plates off the counter when she saw Amado sitting at the table with a dazed look on his face. It was the first time she'd seen him awake in a day.

"I thought Amado could join us," Pasqual said, waving his wooden spoon at him. "It might do him good, don't you think?"

Forcing a smile, Maddie nodded her head. "Yes. It might."

Taking the plates, she moved to the table. Amado barely looked up at her as she set the plates out. There was no color in his face, but the area around his ugly burns had turned a dark black. It looked like necrosis.

That disgusted Maddie, but it was what she saw on Amado's arms that concerned her the most. Two red streaks were running up his arms and towards his heart. She didn't have to be a medical doctor to recognize the signs of a blood infection. It was obviously moving. Fast.

She glanced back at Pasqual with guilt. He had no idea that Kali had switched the boy's medications. With no antibiotics, there was no stopping this infection now. In a way, Maddie felt sorry for him. He was so young.

When she set a plate in front of him, Amado finally looked up. It took a moment, but he eventually seemed to recognize her. A dark coldness entered his eyes, surprising Maddie. "I know you," he said in a raspy voice. "You're the bitch Kali's fucking."

"Amado!" Pasqual said, slapping the counter. "Apologize to Dr. Cross."

His gaze slipped to his uncle and then back again. "Never."

"Then you'll have to miss dinner."

Maddie stood there feeling as if she were caught in some bizarre family drama. With everything going on, Amado's lack of manners seemed almost innocuous.

"Dr. Cross," Pasqual said, his voice commanding. "Would you please watch the stove while I tend to my nephew?"

Relieved by the distraction, Maddie switched places with Pasqual in the galley. She didn't watch as he tried pulling Amado from the chair. Even in his weakened condition, he was still stronger than his old uncle.

It was then that she heard Kali enter the room, or more precisely, Maddie felt her. Kali had a presence that normally filled a room, but this time it was different. Something vibrated deep inside Maddie, the pitch low but strong. It pulled at her, and it took all of Maddie's fortitude not to turn to her.

"What's going on?" Kali asked, her voice sending a rush through Maddie.

"It's nothing," Pasqual explained. "Amado was going to have dinner with us, but now I think he should go below."

"Let him stay," Kali said, coming up behind Maddie and opening the refrigerator. "He doesn't bother me." The clink of bottles told Maddie she'd grabbed a beer.

"Very well." Pasqual stepped away. "But only if Amado minds his manners."

"You're a dog," Amado said, weakly. "I know what you've done, Uncle. If I'd known before, I would have killed you myself."

Behind her, Kali chuckled softly as she popped the tops on two beers. "Here," she said, setting the bottle near Maddie's hands, but not touching her. "Try this."

It was surreal that all this was going on around her — anger, deception, treachery — and yet everything appeared quite mundane. Kali was giving her a beer as if they were at a party. Pasqual was cooking a Brazilian dinner. Amado was here. It was normal, but there was a dark swirling undercurrent pulling her into it all.

"Are you all right?" Kali's concerned voice was simply another illusion.

"I'm fine," Maddie said, unable to explain it. "I just don't think I should drink tonight."

"It's your last night here. You should celebrate."

Celebrate? Another illusion. Did Kali honestly expect her to celebrate as if their cruise ship was docking tomorrow? The artifice had to stop. "I don't want it to end," she said, turning to see Kali.

For a moment, Kali looked as if she were almost ready to agree with her, but then she stepped away. "Maybe it would be better if Amado went back to bed, Pasqual. He doesn't look up to the challenge."

"Yes, I agree." He reached for Amado. "Come, boy. Let's get you back into bed."

"No!" Amado spat, struggling to his feet. "I want to contact my father."

Kali laughed with an indifference that tore at Maddie. "That's not going to happen."

"You've all betrayed me!" he cried, looking at everyone in the room.

Setting her beer on the counter, Kali held out her hand to Amado. "C'mon. I'll help you back to your bed." She glanced at Pasqual. "Isn't it time for his medication?"

"Yes," Pasqual said, and to Maddie he suddenly looked very old.

"Well get it. We don't want Amado to get any weaker." The smile on her face was like the very devil. "You want to get better, don't you?"

"No! I'm not going back to bed until I've spoken to my father. He needs to know that everyone he trusted has—"

Quicker than Maddie could blink, Kali's hand shot out and grabbed Amado by the throat. He howled out in pain as her fingers tightened over his burns. There was a certain glint of pleasure in Kali's eyes as she did this, and though she wanted to look away, Maddie found that she couldn't.

"Kali!" Pasqual yelled. "Stop. Please."

After driving Amado to his knees, Kali let go.

From where Maddie stood in the galley, he appeared more a boy than a man as he cried on the floor, holding a hand to his neck. Kali reached for her beer and looked down at him as she drank it. Dropping the spoon, Maddie went to help Pasqual get Amado to his feet.

"Thank you, Dr. Cross. Very kind of you."

Amado was placid as they lead him towards the stairs. Maddie tried to look at Kali, but Kali didn't meet her glance. Instead, she drank her beer, the pleasure of the act still clinging to her face.

The private lounge in the airport wasn't crowded, which Luis Vega appreciated. It gave him the luxury of watching the two men across from him without interruption. The Japanese seemed to think they were stoic and unreadable, but not to Luis. Lifting his glass of red wine, he swirled it and waited for them to finish whispering into each other's ears.

It had been surprisingly easy to set up this meeting without Duarte. In fact, the two representatives from the *Sumiyoshi-kai* hadn't even mentioned his name. They either didn't care who they dealt with in the cartel, or more likely, they already knew Duarte was finished.

The hushed Japanese tones slowed, ending with the younger of the two men bowing slightly. His bearing was subservient and Luis easily dismissed him.

"Do we have an agreement?" Luis asked, in English, which was the only language they had in common.

"Yes, I believe your terms are workable," the older of the two men said, his English halting but grammatically perfect. Hiroshi Matsui was his name. Luis hadn't bothered remembering the other one's name.

"Then it's agreed that I will head the new cartel in Macapa and *Sumiyoshi-kai* will back me?"

Hiroshi bowed his head slightly while he spoke. "The preliminary terms are an acceptable place to begin, Mr. Vega. If you can deliver the quantities of the Columbian product you have indicated, then I believe my superiors will find your offer very pleasing."

"So all I have to do is bring it to Macapa to be loaded into your ships and we split the profits?"

"Of course I cannot speak of such things currently," Hiroshi said, reaching for the last of his drink. "But my superiors will not be insatiable, if you are not so."

Luis was about to add another point when his cell phone chirped. Checking the number, he dipped his head in apology. "Forgive the interruption, but I must answer." He lifted the phone to his ear, smiling. "Go ahead, Roman. ... You have? Where? ... How would I know where Mura is? ... Near Manaus. Well goddamn." He glanced nervously at the Japanese. "Keep them in sight, and email the satellite pictures to my phone." He hung up and once again dipped his head slightly. "My sincere apologies."

"As I was saying, Mr. Vega, the *Sumiyoshi-kai* is anxious to become involved in the economy of South America. We hope to do much business here."

Luis smiled, although he had no illusions. The Japanese crime syndicate was ruthless in ways he couldn't imagine. His only hope was to ride this windfall into a nice fortune with which to escape Macapa for good. "Then I am honored to be able to assist."

"Thank you for meeting with us," Hiroshi said, standing up. "My associate and I have a plane to catch, but we will be in touch with you very soon."

Luis stood and returned their bow. He was watching them walk out when his cell phone rang again. "What now?" he demanded roughly.

"Am I disturbing you?" Duarte asked, his voice poison in Luis' ear.

"No, sir. I'm just," he paused, searching for words, "frustrated by failures. I thought we would have located them by now." He sunk back into his chair.

"Perhaps this is because you're not looking in the right places. We've been foolish to restrict our search."

"We've searched the most logical routes, and I believe we are making progress with our hacker."

"Your hacker is wasting time, and you have always been too quick to underestimate Kali." Duarte paused. "So I'm done listening to your advice. I want the search broadened to west of Santarem."

Luis felt his heart skip a beat. "But why?" he managed to ask.

"Because you've not been doing your job!" Duarte breathed heavily into the phone. "I'm not sure what idiot you got to sit on the bank of the river, but he completely failed. I've made my own inquiries and a boat matching the *Avatara*'s description passed by Santarem last night."

"Really?" Luis asked, clenching his teeth. "Are you sure?"

"You idiot!" Duarte boomed, his voice so loud that Luis had to pull the phone away. "If that drunk you hired had done his job, I would have known this yesterday. I'd have Kali and my son by now."

Luis suffered his insult, reminding himself that he wouldn't have to do so for much longer. "Sir, I've only done what I thought was right."

"You failed, Luis, but there is still a chance to redeem yourself. Although I have little faith in that computer person you hired, tell him to look between Santarem and Manaus."

He closed his eyes. "Yes, sir."

"I'm moving to Manaus tonight."

"What?" Luis cried. "But why?"

"Because that is where they are going. Haven't you been listening at all?"

"Sir, I think you should stay in Santarem. I haven't arranged for you to go to Manaus."

"All you have to do is have a boat ready for me tomorrow morning. Sanchez has booked me into the Hotel del Grande. Just get me the name of the boat and the location to meet it. Also, send any data you find west of Santarem. If we hurry, we'll be able to catch them unaware. Kali won't expect me to be ahead of her now."

Luis swallowed despite his parched throat. "Yes, sir," he managed to say, scribbling the name of the hotel on a napkin.

"I'm disappointed in you, Luis." He could almost see Duarte shake his head slowly and the thought agitated him. "Call me at the hotel tonight with updates."

Luis dropped the phone to his lap. How easily things could fall apart, he mused, staring into space. Duarte should be wasting his time in Santarem as Luis had planned, but now he was going to have to scramble to pull everything out.

Checking his watch, he realized he had about ten minutes to set things in motion before catching his plane. With an irritated sigh he dialed Roman's number, not exactly sure what he was going to say.

Chapter Seventeen

Dinner that night did not turn out to be the festive farewell that Pasqual had planned. After what had happened with Amado, the three of them ate in relative silence.

Kali couldn't help thinking that it was better. Throughout dinner, she tried to avoid looking at Maddie, but failed every time. With each glance, Kali felt more and more conflicted about her decision. It was absolutely the right thing to do, but when had she ever cared about doing what was right? In the end, Kali pushed her food away half eaten and excused herself.

Fleeing to her cabin, she pressed her head between two pillows, desperate to silence the contradictions warring in her head. There was no simple answer and, as she fell into a fitful sleep, Kali decided to ignore the question all together. It was easier to let things happen with Maddie than to take any personal responsibility.

She awoke at ten, but lay there for another thirty minutes. It was, she realized, her way of delaying this final act, as if she could remain in this place forever.

When she finally sat up, the room was dark, with not even a sliver of light spilling under her door. The darkness made her feel more alone, and she recognized, almost painfully, that she didn't like it.

Getting to her feet, she switched on the light and grabbed for her discarded shorts. As she pulled them on, she was struck again by the finality of her movements. This would be the last time she slept in her cabin.

She looked around, the teak wood gleaming in the light. Her cabin had been the closest thing she had to a home. It was the only place she'd ever felt safe. But it was only a place. Better things waited for her. After tomorrow, she would be richer than she ever dreamed, and free to be anything.

Even as she thought it, Kali knew she was deceiving herself. The money...the freedom...the wealth...it wasn't going to mean anything. Wherever she ended up would be, like this cabin, nothing more than a place.

Ignoring the sense of discontent building in her chest, she reached for her shoes and quickly left the cabin. There was a light coming from under the door of Pasqual's cabin, but Kali only glanced at it. Let the old man be.

Climbing the stairs, she saw Maddie asleep on the sofa. The book she had been reading lay open across her chest, rising and falling evenly with her every breath.

The sight made Kali stop. There was something so peaceful about the scene that she couldn't imagine ever leaving. In this one brief moment, she didn't try to pretend she wasn't happy. But it couldn't last. It never did.

Pushing herself forward, Kali walked across the salon and out of the door. The night air was thick and wet. It had rained recently. Leaning over the stern railing, she looked up at the sky. There was no moon yet, and the river appeared as dark as ink.

As she stood there, she felt herself slipping into her role, and her shoulders became heavy with the responsibility. Turning from the rail, she climbed to the flybridge and took her seat. She flipped on the dash lights to check the gauges and her GPS location before starting the engines.

She didn't know why she bothered with the GPS anymore. She didn't really need to know her position now. All she had to do was head west, and she would find Manaus sooner than she wanted.

"Stay focused," she said to herself.

Raising the anchors, she reached for her night goggles. After activating them, the world exploded into shades of green. It was unreal to see everything and nothing. Trees became outlines. The water morphed into a dark shifting road. Even her hands looked foreign as they gripped the wheel.

Briefly, she imagined that they weren't her hands. That it wasn't her speeding up the engines. That in some blissful way, this was all a strange dream. But dreaming was unrealistic. It was irresponsible. It was disappointing.

"Why didn't you wake me?" Maddie asked, as she slipped quietly into the co-pilot's seat.

The sound of Maddie's voice made Kali's chest constrict uncomfortably. Not able to look at her, she stared straight ahead.

"Don't ignore me, Kali. Please. Not tonight."

"I'm not ignoring you," she replied tightly. "I didn't wake you because there wasn't any need to wake you. I don't anticipate any problems between here and Manaus."

Maddie was silent for a moment, and then Kali heard her sigh. "Did you think I might just want to be here with you?"

"No." Kali shook her head. "I won't be drawn into another argument."

"I've never wanted that."

"It's all we seem to do."

"Then how do we change it?" Maddie asked, leaning towards her. "Because I really want to try. I don't want to leave you."

You don't have a choice, Kali almost said, but bit her tongue. Telling her now would only make it harder tomorrow morning.

"I won't tell you again how I feel," Maddie continued. "I promise. Just let me stay."

Turning a deaf ear on the plea, Kali adjusted the speed of the engines. With the width of the river and the calm surface, she knew she could hit twenty to thirty knots tonight, but instead, she kept it more near fifteen. She told herself that she was only being cautious.

"Tell me something about you that no one knows," Maddie asked softly. "Please."

It was the please that got her, and Kali sighed. "You already know more than anyone."

"Then tell me about the woman you loved. What was her name?"

"Sarah. And she was just a girl."

"You loved her?"

Kali glanced quickly at Maddie, not sure if she should answer or not. "Yes," she said warily.

"How did you know you loved her?"

"Why do you want to know?"

"Just tell me. Please."

There was a hint of desperation in Maddie's voice, and slowly, Kali nodded. "I loved Sarah, but I wasn't *in* love with her. She was my family. She was the only one who ever cared about me."

"I care about you."

"Not like her."

"Is that why you keep rejecting me? Because I'm not some dead girl who once loved you?"

Making a fist, Kali almost slammed it against the wheel. "No," she said, harshly.

Maddie held up her hands. "I'm sorry. But I just don't understand."

"I won't explain."

"Have you ever been in love with anyone? Or are you incapable of it?"

"Is this how you want our time to be spent? Arguing again?"

Maddie sighed. "I just don't get it. I know you feel something for me. You've almost admitted as much. But," she shook her head, "you're determined to ignore it. Ignore me."

"It's just the way it is. The way it has to be."

"Listen to yourself!" Maddie cried. "Do you think you're protecting me from something? If so, stop. I don't want that from you."

"You don't know what you want!"

"And do you? Do you know what you want?"

Kali waved her off. "Go to bed. I'm sick of talking about this. Nothing is going to change."

"No. I said I wasn't leaving. I meant it."

"Just don't expect me to respond anymore. It's done, Maddie. Accept it."

"All I want is a chance, Kali. Give me a few days. That's all."

"What is this, a fucking job interview?"

"Tell me you don't want it. Tell me you don't want me."

Pushing her goggles up slightly, Kali looked Maddie in the eye. "I take what I want. And if I wanted you, you'd know it." She pulled her goggles down and returned to the river.

"You lie so well," Maddie said with disgust. "But you forget that I've felt your desire."

"So what? It changes nothing."

"I'm not going to win, am I?" Maddie asked, with a sudden weariness. "No matter what either of us really wants, you've made up your mind."

"Yes."

"Then tomorrow you're going to do what with me? Drop me off at the U.S. consulate?"

"Yes." It was the only answer Kali could give. Pasqual would handle everything.

"And then what happens to you? Where do you go?"

"I don't know."

"You're a very rich woman now. Or were you rich before all this?"

"I rarely counted."

"No. You enjoyed your job too much to care about the money." Maddie shook her head sadly. "But what about now? I gather your job here in Brazil is over. Are you going to work for Pasqual?"

"Why do you want to know?"

"Because I'd like to know that I lost you to something important. Something bigger than me."

"You did," Kali whispered.

"What was that?"

"I'm not sure what I'm going to do next. Maybe I'll go to China. Or the Ukraine. Or God knows where."

"So you have no plan?" She blew out a laugh. "That's almost as degrading as having to take my cousin to the senior prom. Or having my date ditch me at a frat party. All the while I was left wondering what was wrong with me." Maddie stopped for a moment. "Do you have any idea what you're sending me back to?"

"Your life," Kali answered plainly. "I had no right to take you from it."

"I'd be dead if you hadn't. But before you go and play the saintly martyr for my cause, I'd like you to know about my life."

"Maddie—" she began, but Maddie cut her off.

"No! I need you to just listen to me. I'm not happy, Kali. I love my family. Probably more because I have to love them than because I want to, but that's how it is in my family. We're obligated to each other, but know very little of what we all think or feel. My father is never satisfied. I think I could be awarded a Nobel Prize and he'd ask me what I've done recently. My mother is like a mirage. Just when I think I might glimpse something real in her, its gone and she's all smiles and forced joy."

"It's something, Maddie," Kali interrupted. "It's more than most people have. More than I have."

"I'm not finished. I have two brothers who couldn't wait to leave home. They're both married with kids now, and every time I see them, they remind me more and more of our father. They are both harsh and unyielding, but convinced that they are just being encouraging. What's more, their wives have begun to take on the same vacant look my mother wears. I wonder when they'll wake up and leave, or if the change has been so gradual that they don't even know what they've given up. All I can think when I see them is dear God, don't let me end up like that.

"And yet, I've been so lonely. Do you know what it's like to have only your job? To only know responsibility and never love?" Maddie laughed bitterly. "Sorry. I forgot who I was talking to."

Kali let the slight go. "Don't you think you'd miss them? Miss the life you knew?"

"Probably. But if circumstances had been different, I would be dead.

Would they really miss me? Or would their lives go on as before?"

"What about your career? That means something to you."

"Yes. It does." Maddie paused. "But so do you. Does one have to outweigh the other?"

"It always does."

"Tell me you love me. At least let me hear it."

In response, Kali shook her head. It was all she could do.

"I don't know why I expected you to say it." Maddie looked away. "It's funny what we wish for, knowing all along we'll never get it."

On the console, the GPS beeped as the *Avatara* passed the next waypoint. Only a few were left. Already she could see Manaus displayed on the screen as it rolled west with their progress. Four hours. Five maybe.

She glanced at Maddie, who was staring blankly out at nothing. Her features were drawn, and her shoulders sagged.

"You look tired," Kali said softly. "Why don't you go below and rest?"

"Only if you'll come with me. I want you to hold me, Kali. I need your body to say what you won't."

"That's not possible."

Maddie sighed. "Of course it's not." She stood and crossed the narrow aisle between the seats. "Then, at least, let me sit here next to you."

Before Kali could refuse, Maddie had lowered herself down on the edge of the seat, pressing her body into Kali's side. The immediate warmth that sparked between them made Kali jump.

"Maddie," she said, trying to pull away but only succeeding in giving up more of her seat. "There's not enough—"

"Quiet," Maddie cut her off. "Please. This is all I want." She laid her head against Kali's shoulder. "Let me have this."

Suddenly exhausted, Kali was unable to fight anymore. She didn't know why she was still trying. Without realizing it, she lifted her arm and laid it across Maddie's shoulders, pulling her closer. It felt good. It felt right. As Maddie's head settled against her chest, she exhaled slowly, her whole body relaxing.

"I can hear your heart beating," Maddie said gently.

A lump lodged in her throat, preventing Kali from responding. She didn't know what she'd say anyway. Words would ruin it. The silence seemed to say it all. The night was rushing past her. Time was slipping through her fingers. She'd wasted so much of it because of her stubbornness.

Would it be so wrong to take what was being offered? Her whole life had been about taking things, and she'd never once considered anyone else. If Maddie was willing to give up everything she knew, why shouldn't she take it? The questions haunted her as time stole by.

Without any words putting them at odds, Kali felt a deep tranquility engulf them. It was like nothing she'd ever experienced before, and she never wanted to crawl out of the warmth.

Maddie's body became heavy against her side, and as she fell deeper asleep, her hand curled around Kali's waist. It was intimate. It was familiar. It made Kali's heart ache.

Around four thirty the GPS beeped as they passed another waypoint. That left only one. The glow of Manaus would soon be visible over the tree line.

Next to her, Maddie stirred and pulled herself upright. "I fell asleep."

Kali smiled. "You were tired."

"Aren't you exhausted?" Maddie covered a yawn.

"Mostly sore from sitting so much." She twisted her neck. "And my shoulders are killing me."

"Here," Maddie said, getting to her feet and moving behind Kali and settling her hands on Kali's shoulders.

"Maddie, you don't have to. Really, I'm okay."

"Quiet," Maddie said, leaning forward, her lips brushing Kali's ear. "Let me do this."

"All right," Kali said, trying to relax as Maddie began to rub her neck.

On the horizon, the goggles were already picking up the tell tale glow of many lights. It was too soon. She didn't want it all to end. Not so quickly. Not before she could come to terms with it all.

She didn't remember thinking it, but she felt her hand pulling back on the throttle. The *Avatara* began to slow. She steered to the right of the river, silencing the little voice that demanded she speed up again.

"Why are we stopping?"

"That feels good," Kali said, lifting her shoulders to encourage Maddie to continue.

Pulling off her goggles, she laid them on the dash. In the darkness, the world suddenly made sense. She killed the engine and dropped the anchors.

In her head all she could hear was her heart beat. Faster and faster. Could Maddie hear her heart pounding? Or could she feel the way the air crackled around them?

"Kali?"

Her voice sounded far away and Kali needed to get to her. If she didn't, Maddie would be gone. It was wrong. She should let her go. This would only hurt them both. Not speaking, she stood and held her hand out to Maddie.

The smaller hand trembled slightly in her grasp, but Maddie's steps did not falter as Kali lead her through the dark boat. Pushing open the door to her cabin, Kali hesitated, her conscience once again at war with her desire.

Paralyzed, she allowed Maddie to move past her and pull her into the room. The door clicked closed behind them, the sound so loud that Kali's head turned towards the noise.

Then all she could hear was Maddie's breathing. Or was it her own? Kali wasn't sure.

There was a silver ray of moonlight filtering through the blinds. Had there been a moon? She couldn't remember, but now, standing there in the dim light, she was fascinated with the way it played off the dips and planes of Maddie's face. She looked so serene. So controlled.

Staring at her, Kali realized that this was the last line. If she crossed it, she might not be able to go back. Before her, the line shimmered as invisible as it was tangible. She couldn't stop herself if she wanted, and closing her eyes she stepped forward and gathered Maddie in her arms. There was no resistance, only yielding compliance.

Laying her back against the bed, Kali realized this wasn't going to be tender or passionate. It was going to be ritualistic.

Removing Maddie's clothes revealed her beauty and Kali wanted to explore it all. With the tips of her fingers barely touching, she grazed the trembling flesh. It taunted her, drawing her closer until her warm breath danced over the skin. When she replaced her fingers with her lips, Maddie moaned.

The noise beguiled her, and she pulled herself up until she could look into Maddie's eyes. "Kiss me," Maddie breathed. "Please kiss me."

And she did. Slowly. Deeply. Completely.

They merged into each other, transcending the boundaries of reality and reason. In that moment, Kali felt everything. A world of emotions passed through her like water. Sadness. Joy. Elation. Anger. Pain. Pleasure.

She cried out and pulled back. It was too much. It meant too much. It was everything she'd never known. "I can't," she whispered, turning away.

"No." Maddie seized her hand and pressed it tightly to her chest. Under her fingers, she felt Maddie's heart jump erratically. "See. I feel it too."

She lifted her eyes to Maddie, and without blinking, she let Maddie guide her hand. It skimmed over a full breast. It felt a quivering stomach, and everything in between. Kali was powerless to stop Maddie's descent, and she didn't want to.

Looking into Maddie's eyes was like staring at a cobra. Hypnotic and absorbing, they lulled her into a state of bliss until Maddie struck by plunging her hand into her heat. Only when Kali moaned did Maddie's eyes flutter and close. Maddie sighed and moved against her.

Her body was unbelievable. Closing her eyes Kali fell into Maddie, wanting to give her everything she could. Touching her was like soaring. There was no ground. No earth. No heaven. Just an amazing warmth that embraced her completely.

She opened her eyes when she felt Maddie's touch on her. "I have to see you," Maddie said, gathering Kali's shirt. "I have to feel you."

Kali lifted her arms and let Maddie pull her clothes from her. The cool air kissed her body, but it felt like nothing compared to the heat of Maddie's hands on her skin.

"Lie back," Maddie commanded, her eyes pushing Kali down as easily as if she had used her hands.

Starting at her shoulders, Maddie's touch moved down her body. Like ice in fire, she melted herself into every fissure of Kali's body until she was drenched. Her hands gripped the sheets, and her body strained to be touched everywhere.

When she thought she could take no more, Maddie covered her with her whole body. She floated along Kali, skin moving against skin, heat matching heat. "Close your eyes," Maddie whispered.

With her eyes shut Kali found she didn't need them to see anymore. Her darkness was awash in colors she'd never seen. And blinded by the light, Kali walked into it. Shedding herself of the veil of shadows that clothed her, she stood naked and exposed before Maddie. She felt desperation in their movements, an almost crushing need to burn into each other.

She never wanted Maddie to forget. Never doubt her love. She heard Maddie cry out, and only then did she let herself go.

After, Maddie's body lay against her as light as it was heavy. With Maddie's head pressed against her shoulder, and her arm stretched across her stomach, Kali felt the first touch of wet tears hit her skin and roll away. Maddie cried quietly, and Kali wished she could cry, too.

There was nothing either of them could say. Good-bye wasn't enough now.

Clenching her jaw, she stared at the ceiling and waited.

Luis Vega stepped off the plane at Eduardo Gomes International Airport and yawned. The unexpected layover in Sao Paulo had set his schedule back. Checking his watch, he knew it would be a race to the docks. He hurried through the airport, looking for the men who were to meet him.

By now, Duarte, the great sloth that he was, would be rolling out of bed and searching for food. Luis had never seen a man so consumed with hunger as Duarte. *He is a pig*, Luis thought, spotting two men waiting expectantly by the entrance.

"You here for me?" he said, rubbing his eyes.

"You Luis?"

"Of course, I am." Luis sighed with exasperation. "Where is the car?"

The man blinked as if Luis had asked a riddle. "Outside," he finally said, hiking a thumb over his shoulder.

Stepping back, he waited for the men to precede him to the car. He lifted the cell phone from his belt and dialed a familiar number. It took Roman five rings before he answered. "You were sleeping?"

"Getting air," Roman shot back, but Luis heard the sleep in his voice.

"Status?"

"I got a visual before dark. The ship was heading west."

"I know that," Luis growled. "Where are they now?"

"I'm looking. The last GPS signal came about twenty miles east of Manaus."

"When?"

"An hour ago."

"They could be here by now!" He waved the thick, dense looking man off as he held open the back door of an older sedan.

"I'll find them."

"You'd better," Luis huffed, as he slid into the back of the car. "Tell me you remembered to fax the Hotel del Grande?"

"Yes."

"So there will be a boat waiting on the west side of the Manaus docks?"

"I guess," Roman said, his tone slightly insolent. "I only passed on the information you sent me."

"Fine," Luis said, looking out the rear window at the rising sun. "Find that ship, Roman. You have twenty minutes. If you call me within ten, I'll pay you an extra twenty five thousand dollars."

"Fifty."

The impertinence! "Thirty."

"Fifty. You want it bad enough to pay."

"Yes I do," Luis admitted, clenching his fist. "I'll pay and you never return to Brazil. Agreed?"

"Absolutely."

"Ten minutes then."

Luis hung up the phone, and looked at the two men in the front seats. "Did you prepare everything as I asked?"

"Give it to him, Julio," the man driving said, poking his companion.

"It's on the seat," Julio said, pointing at a manila envelope. "Two passports. One Columbian and the other American."

"Camera and clothes?"

"In the trunk."

"And the other matter?"

The man driving turned around and smiled. "Julio and I could make the Pope disappear."

Luis looked out the window. "Just drive us to the east docks." He checked his watch.

Duarte stuffed a croissant into his mouth. He nodded to Sanchez who was waiting by the door with a cup of coffee, its strong smell filling the room. He swallowed the last of the bread and held his hand out for the coffee. "Do you have the fax?"

"Yes, we're to go to the west docks and look for a fishing shack called Mamacita. We'll be met there by a man who will take us to find the *Avatara*."

"How far are the docks?"

"Twenty minutes."

"Then, let's go," Duarte said, pushing himself out of the room and striding towards the elevator like a charging rhino. "I want to be on the river as soon as possible."

"Of course." Sanchez pushed the elevator button.

"I have a good feeling about today," Duarte said, stepping into the lift. "If you serve me well, I will reward you, Sanchez."

"Of course," Sanchez repeated, looking straight ahead as the elevator doors closed.

Chapter Eighteen

Kali waited until she heard Maddie's breath even out in sleep before carefully sliding away from her. In the last half-hour she had hardened herself against everything she felt. Gathering her clothes, she dressed in the bathroom, careful to make as little noise as possible. Despite her resolve, she knew she would break down if Maddie confronted her.

No matter what Maddie said, Kali wouldn't take her life from her. Even if she didn't want it right now, eventually she would. As far as Kali was concerned, Maddie had people who loved her and were waiting for her return. They could give Maddie so much more than she ever could.

Opening the bathroom door, she didn't look at Maddie as she sat quietly at her desk and pulled out a pen and paper. It only took a second to write what she wanted Maddie to know, and folding the note, she wrote Maddie's full name across the front before placing it on the pillow next to her. Then collecting her laptop, she silently left the room.

Turning on the light in the electronics room, Kali plugged her laptop into a network connection. While the systems booted up, she went to get Pasqual. It was time to finish their business.

She quietly pushed open the door to the crew cabin to find Pasqual kneeling next to Amado. The boy was white. He looked closer to death than Kali had thought possible. It disturbed her, but not enough to waste time dwelling on it. "Pasqual," she whispered. "We're almost to Manaus."

"Of course," Pasqual said, weakly getting to his feet. "You want your money."

Kali waited in the hall, and then led the way into the small electronics room. "I'm sorry about Amado."

The old man sank into the chair. "So many mistakes. So many regrets."

There was nothing to say, so Kali remained silent as the laptop connected to the Internet. Using the browser's stored history, she navigated to Pasqual's bank. Turning the laptop, she leaned back as Pasqual entered his information.

"Are you still going to leave Dr. Cross with me?" he asked, not looking up from the screen.

Kali felt her heart clench. "You will see after her, right?"

"Of course. I will treat her like one of my own daughters." He glanced at her. "It was seven and a half million, correct?"

She dropped her eyes. "*Señor* de Tueste," she said, using his full title with respect. He had to understand how important this was to her. "May I ask you to do two more things for me?"

He lifted his hands from the keyboard. "If I'm able."

"First," Kali said, pointing at the web page. "Please open an account at your bank and give her five million from the last half of my fee."

The old man's eyes constricted slightly before he nodded. "That's very generous. Consider it done. And your second request?"

Kali had to force it out. "Don't let her look for me."

He smiled sadly. "I will do my best. And although you may not want an old man's opinion, I think you are doing the right thing."

"Do you?" For the first time in her life, Kali realized she was desperate for affirmation.

"You are far more honorable than I believed." He held his hand out. "It has been a pleasure knowing you."

Kali took his hand. "Thank you, Señor de Tueste." She pointed at the laptop. "I'll trust you to finish things with your bank while I take us into Manaus." She moved past him.

"Kali?" Pasqual called after her. "If you ever need a place to go, I will always welcome you. For business if you're interested, or pleasure if you're not. My home and my hospitality will always be open to you."

She paused, aware of the honor he had given her. "Thank you," she said quietly. "For taking care of Maddie, you have my gratitude. But more than that, you will always have my respect and my loyalty."

Pasqual dipped his head. "Then our business is done."

"Almost." Kali turned and headed for the flybridge.

Luis lifted the phone before the first ring faded. "You better have what I want."

"Ten minutes ago, an Internet request was sent via SAT/COM satellites from just outside Manaus," Roman said, his voice excited.

"And? What does that have to do with GPS?" He held up his hand. "No, don't explain it to me. Just tell me what that has to do with the *Avatara*?"

"It came from the *Avatara*."

"Did you confirm that?"

"I didn't have to. Her transponders came on line at the same time."

"Then it's her?"

"That's what I said."

"Where?"

"Now? Probably less than three miles outside Manaus."

Luis looked up to find Julio watching him from the front seat. "What are you staring at?" He glared at him.

"We're here," he said, pointing to the row of docks that were just outside the car.

Luis looked, taking in the offensive the stench of rotting fish, oil, and gas. "And did we have to park near a garbage can?" He reached inside his pocket for a handkerchief and pressed to his nose. "Roman!" he yelled into the phone.

"I've got a satellite view now. It's your boat and it's moving fast."

Luis checked his watch. "How long before they get here?"

"I can't tell from this view."

"Give me a guess."

"Ten minutes. Twenty. I don't know, but they aren't far."

"Fine." He disconnected the call. "You," he said, pointing at the driver. "I want that berth there." He pointed to the open docking point. "Put the signal out."

"Go," the man said to Julio, who climbed out of the car and circled to the trunk.

The outskirts of Manaus appeared as the *Avatara* rounded a bend in the river. The buildings on the shore and beyond multiplied with each passing minute, and after the solitude of the river, Kali found herself unable to stomach the stench and sounds of the city.

She heard footsteps on the stairs behind her, and she held her breath. There was no way she could face Maddie. Keeping her eyes straight ahead, she waited.

"Look for a yellow flag," Pasqual said, his hand resting on the back of her seat. "They will be waiting for me."

Kali didn't ask who. "I'll be leaving the boat as soon as we're docked," Kali said, looking for anything yellow as the first sign of the east docks appeared.

"I presumed as much."

"Is Maddie still asleep?"

"I suppose so."

"There," Kali said, pointing at a splash of yellow near an open berth.

"Yes," Pasqual said, peering forward. "That could be it."

Kali swung the *Avatara* wide enough to turn into the berth. Tapping at the throttles, she gave the boat a push of power before returning to neutral. The momentum of the water would slide her into the mooring.

"I have to get the ropes." She cut the engines and moved down the stairs. Grabbing the aft rope, she jumped onto the dock and quickly looped the rope around a tie. Running towards the bow, she stopped when a shiny pair of loafers stepped in her way.

"Hello, Kali," the voice said and Kali looked up.

"Luis?" she asked, looking up at the two large men that flanked him.

"A very nice run, by the way. Gave us all the slip for quite awhile." His smile was cold and unyielding. "Thank you for using the GPS. It helped boost our transmitter."

"Where's Duarte?" Kali demanded, looking around. If she was going to die, it wasn't going to be at the hand of this little punk.

"I'm sure he'll be along shortly." His eyes shifted to the *Avatara*. "Your boat doesn't look as pretty as I remember." He sniffed the air. "It smells, too."

"Luis," Pasqual called down from the flybridge. "Get out of her way. She has to leave." Kali looked up in surprise, but Pasqual just waved them on. "Come onboard, boy, we have things to do."

It suddenly made sense. "You're the reason Pasqual was able to run his cocaine under Duarte's nose for so long."

The small man pulled himself taller. "Duarte is finished."

"Well, so am I," Kali said, reaching for the bow rope. "If you'll excuse me."

Luis gestured to one of the men standing about. "Tie the boat for her," he commanded, giving her a smile. "If Pasqual says you have to go, then you should go."

Kali felt her eyes narrow. Lifting a finger she jabbed it in his smug face.

"If you betray him like you did Duarte, I'll come back for you."

"Loyalty in you," Luis said, turning his back on her. "How amusing."

Kali stood on the dock and watched as Luis boarded her ship. It was a defilement to let him on the *Avatara*, but she knew she couldn't stay any longer.

In a moment, Pasqual would come out with Maddie, and there was no way she could let Maddie see her. She had to let go. Walk away. Forget.

Turning, she began to walk up the dock, her steps slow but strong. When she reached the end of the wood, she stopped and looked around. Across the street, a small café had turned on its lights, and Kali headed for it. From there she could see Maddie for the last time.

"*Café, por favor,*" she said, entering the shop and sitting down by the window.

"Dr. Cross. Wake up."

The voice calling to her was familiar, but not, Maddie decided, slowly opening her eyes. She smiled, expecting to see Kali's face, but was shocked to find Pasqual.

"I'm sorry," he said, his voice calm. "I didn't mean to startle you."

"Where's Kali?" she demanded, clutching at the sheet and looking around the room.

"There's no time, Dr. Cross. Please hurry and get up."

"Why? What's happened? Where are we?"

"Manaus. You need to get dressed now or you'll force me to have you carried out in that sheet."

"Tell me where Kali is?"

"She asked me to get you off the boat before the cartel gets here."

"But they don't know where we are."

"Yes, they do." There was a tone of finality in his voice. "Now, dress. Quickly."

Maddie felt confused, but she nodded. Before climbing out of bed, she waited for him to turn his back, and grabbing her clothes, she hurried into the bathroom.

When she was finished, she returned to the cabin and looked around. Something didn't feel right.

"Dr. Cross. Please hurry."

She followed his voice into the salon where Amado was lying on the floor. Standing there, Maddie watched his chest rise in shallow, raspy breaths before looking up at Pasqual. The old man met her eyes, and she felt such sadness from him.

"Come, Maddie," he said, holding his hand out for her to step over Amado. "We must go." He looked at a short man standing by the door. "Luis will take us to the car."

"But what about Amado?"

"His father will find him. If it is in time, one cannot know."

"And Kali?"

"Come, we have to leave now."

Maddie let herself be lead from the boat and down the dock. It wasn't until she saw the black sedan that she understood that Kali had gone. Turning, she tried to go back to the ship, but a large man stood in her way. Beating on him, she tried to get past.

"Pick her up," Pasqual ordered, and Maddie turned to see him drop his eyes. "I'm sorry, Dr. Cross. I gave her my word."

"No!" Maddie yelled, her eyes whipping up and down the docks. "She wouldn't do this to me."

"Put her in the car," Pasqual said, opening the door.

Maddie was no match for the man's strength as he lowered her to the ground, and blocked her escape. With no choice, she climbed into the car only to find the other hulk of a man already sitting in the back seat.

The fight lost, Maddie composed herself enough to sit as Pasqual slid in next to her. "Why?" she asked, looking back at the *Avatara*.

"I'm sorry, my dear. Truly, I am." He handed her a folded piece of paper. "She left you this."

Maddie took it, looking down at her full name and title written across the front with a bold hand. That said it all. Kali was gone. Last night had been the good-bye she had felt. Maddie opened the paper. *Wherever I go, you'll be with me,* she read before dropping the note to her lap.

"I have a passport for you," Pasqual said, as the car started up and they drove off. "You'll come to my house first." He patted her hand. "It will be all right, Maddie. I promise."

Maddie looked out the window and said nothing.

Dropping a bill on the table, Kali left her coffee untouched and exited the cafe. It had been incredibly difficult to sit and watch as Maddie was manhandled into the car. She knew from the way Pasqual had glanced at the café window that he had known she was there, but luckily Maddie hadn't.

She didn't want to try and imagine how Maddie felt right now. For better or worse, it was done. Now all that was left was to get her things and disappear into the city.

Climbing back on board her ship, she found Amado barely breathing in the salon. As she looked down into his feverish face and vacant eyes, she almost felt sorry for him.

"You're just one more casualty," she said, stepping over him and hurrying down her cabin. She needed to get her money, various passports and her laptop. Everything else could be replaced.

It took her a few minutes to pull everything together. In the electronics room, she didn't bother powering her laptop down. She just closed the case, disconnected the cables and headed for the dock.

Stepping over Amado again, Kali looked around. The *Avatara* had been hers. She had loved this boat, and now to be leaving it behind was almost bittersweet. Turning slowly around the room, Kali realized that today was a day of good-byes. Not just Maddie and the *Avatara*, but of the person she was.

Stepping onto the dock, she paused. A motor boat was coming up fast from the east. Instinctively, she knew it was Duarte, and standing on the edge of the dock, she waited. She needed to see him. Needed to say good-bye to him, too.

As the small boat came into view, Kali easily spotted Duarte's bloated body. From this distance he looked more grotesque than she remembered. When he saw her, he quickly pointed and yelled something she couldn't make out.

She lifted her arm in a farewell before turning for the city. Breaking into a run, she reached the street quickly. Whistling, she hailed a passing taxi and slipped into the back seat. As the taxi drove off, Kali didn't look back. There was nothing but regret behind her.

Printed in the United States
98655LV00002B/75/A